T

LONG-

JULES

THE LONG-LOST JULES

A NOVEL

JANE ELIZABETH HUGHES

SparkPress, a BookSparks imprint
A Division of SparkPoint Studio, LLC

Published by SparkPress, a BookSparks imprint,
A division of SparkPoint Studio, LLC
Phoenix, Arizona, USA, 85007
www.gosparkpress.com

Published 2021
Printed in the United States of America

Print ISBN: 978-1-68463-089-9
E-ISBN: 978-1-68463-090-5
Library of Congress Control Number: 2021903615

Formatting by Katherine Lloyd, The DESK

For Jerry,
my best friend and husband of over four decades—
and it's getting better all the time. I could never have done
this without your patience, love, and support.

Chapter 1

A shadow fell across the table where I sat, devouring a scone and a novel with equal satisfaction. Frowning and shading my eyes against the watery London sun, I looked up to see a tall, dark stranger gazing down at me.

"Hey, Jules!" the stranger said. "I've been looking all over for you!"

Jules! What on earth?

With some regret—this was an interesting distraction—I shrugged my shoulders and turned back to my book. "Sorry," I said. "You have the wrong person."

He gestured to the empty chair across the table from me. "May I?"

"Sorry," I repeated, falling back on all-purpose Brit-speak for *I don't know what you're talking about, and I don't want to talk to you.* "You must have mistaken me for someone else."

He hovered uncomfortably between a standing position and a ready-to-sit position, and I eyed him with a mixture of amusement and curiosity.

"Um . . . I can't believe I finally tracked you down," he said, shifting from foot to foot and trying, unsuccessfully, to look as if he had never expected an invitation to sit. "It's such a pleasure to actually meet you."

"Sorry, but you have the wrong person." I tried again. "I'm not Jules."

He shook his head. "Sorry," he said, now lapsing into Brit-speak for *You are totally wrong, but I'm too polite to say it.* "But . . . well, the thing is . . . well, I believe you are Juliette Mary Seymour, and I've been searching for you for months. You covered your tracks very well, Jules!"

I sighed. "My name is Amy, actually, and I've never heard of Juliette whoever. I don't mean to be rude, but I have to be back in my office in fifteen minutes, and I'd like to finish reading this chapter."

He glanced at my book, a John le Carré classic, and raised his eyebrows.

I held my patience. "Look, whatever your name is, you have distracted me from my problems at work for a few minutes, and I appreciate that. But I'm not the person you're looking for, and I'd like to finish my coffee in peace."

"Oh? What are—sorry, I don't mean to pry—but what are your problems at work?"

"I work with a lot of sorority-ish mean girls, and they . . ." I stopped short; why on earth was I unburdening myself to this stranger?

"And are they mean to you, Jules?" He seemed genuinely interested, but I steeled myself against it.

"Sorry, I'm trying not to be rude," I said. "But I really have to go."

"The thing is . . . um . . . I do apologize for bothering you . . ." Now I saw that his body was tense and coiled, like a panther that has finally cornered its prey and is determined not to let it escape. It was body language that was strangely at odds with his hesitant speech. "You see, I'm Leo Schlumberger, and I'm a historian at Oxford."

A historian! That was the last thing I had expected. He looked more like a Mafia boss than an academic. He was tall and strongly built, with snapping black eyes and a dark five-o'clock shadow that probably appeared fifteen minutes after he shaved. His hair too was black, cut carelessly and curling against the back of his tanned neck. He wasn't quite handsome—his features were too strong for that—but his looks were compelling. I tended to like easygoing, laid-back men—definitely not stammering Brits who apologized every other sentence.

"A historian? And why are you looking for this Jules?"

"Sorry," he said. "That story is much too long for the remainder of your coffee break. Um . . . may I buy you dinner tonight?"

Despite my curiosity, I reminded myself that I was not the girl he was looking for. "No," I said. "I'm sorry."

"Perhaps we should stop apologizing to each other," he suggested, and, despite myself, I smiled. "Tomorrow night, then?"

"Sss . . . no. Thank you."

He muttered something under his breath, but it was too low for me to decipher. The language wasn't English, though, and my curiosity sharpened.

"Really, Jules," he said.

"Stop calling me that!"

"Sorry—Amy. The truth is, I've gone to a lot of trouble to find you, and it's quite important that we—"

As his tone became more urgent, the Britishness slipped, and I heard traces of a more exotic accent in his voice.

Time to end this, I thought. I pushed my chair back from the table and stood up. "Goodbye, then," I tossed over my shoulder as I turned to flee. "Sorry I couldn't help you."

"Hey, Jules!" he called after me, and I paused to look back. "It was great to finally meet you!"

Without another backward glance, I hurried away.

I was slightly out of breath when I got back to my office, having half jogged the ten blocks from the café. There were many cafés much closer to my building, but then I would run the risk of seeing one of the PYTs (my pretty-young-thing coworkers)—and having them see me eat. Frantically brushing off the telltale crumbs from my scone, I scurried back to my desk and turned on my computer.

"Amy! You missed a call from Sheikh Abdullah," said Kristen R., queen bee of the PYTs. "He wants you to arrange a trip for his granddaughters to the Dubai Atlantis."

I grimaced. As a private banker at Atlantic Bank in London, I was supposed to be managing the wealth of one, fairly minor, branch of the al-Saud family from Saudi Arabia. On paper, my job was to place their billions of dollars in conservative investments to preserve those billions for the generations to come, so that no grandson or great-grandson ever had to lift a finger in honest labor. In reality, the family treated me more like a combination of butler and poodle walker, calling on me to handle everything from buying them a new private jet to finding a masseuse for their horses.

Now, apparently, I was a travel agent.

"Which granddaughters?" I asked resignedly.

Kristen R. shrugged.

Kristen P. looked at me. "Amy, is that *jam* on your collar?"

I knew that the idea of eating anything sugary was horrifying in the PYTs' eyes; it was akin to drinking Diet Coke (only for fat people, they agreed) or eating white bread (only for the unwashed masses). I brushed at the spot, but it stuck to my fingers and settled more deeply into my silk blouse. Damn!

The Kristens exchanged arch glances while I thought of all the clever quips I could have made if I hadn't sworn to play nicely and keep this job. At all costs.

Kristen R. opened the Tupperware container on her desk and pulled it toward her. "Want some of my broccoli sprigs?" she offered. "I'm so full from that quinoa yesterday that I can't eat a thing."

I shook my head. *I would rather eat the bark off a tree*, I thought.

Kristen P. said, "No, thanks. I had a couple of bean sprouts earlier, and I have a hot-yoga session after work today."

The two Matts joined in the conversation, discussing the merits of hot yoga versus spin yoga versus vinyasa yoga, and I tuned out. My coworkers were all in their mid- to late twenties, thin as rails, appalled by any foods other than tofu and sprouts, and obsessed with extreme exercise. The head of our office, Audrey Chiu, was a size negative zero, with tiny wrists and a child's hips. She never ate lunch (or breakfast, or dinner, as far as I could tell), so no one else in the office ate either.

At thirty-four, I was the granny of the group, obsessed with scones and clotted cream. I exercised only because I absolutely had to if I wanted to keep eating. Since lunch was frowned upon and snacks were unthinkable at my office, I was usually hungry enough to gnaw off my arm by the time I got home at night—hence the hike to a café distant enough that I wouldn't be caught eating by one of my colleagues who had stopped in for a chai tea.

In fact, I could tell that my teammates often wondered why Audrey had hired me. Not only was I older than the other vice presidents; I was also cut from a very different mold. To a man (or woman), they had all attended American or British prep schools, Ivy League or Oxbridge colleges, and Harvard Business

School (or "the B-school," as they called it, as if it were the only one). All were tall, blond, and genetically thin. I was small, with auburn hair, and slim only because of my grim hour on the treadmill every morning. Even more appalling, I had attended a huge public university, mainly so I could sit in the back of the massive amphitheater and doze while my hand, on autopilot, scribbled notes. Lecturing, someone had once said, was when information passed from the notes of the lecturer to the notes of the student, without passing through the mind of either one in between.

That was my education.

And, this being an American bank, many of my colleagues were from the wealthiest enclaves of New York and New England, while I had grown up all over the world. My playgrounds were Moscow and Amman, Riyadh and Kiev; my schools were whatever American school happened to be convenient to my father's current dwelling.

I turned back to my computer, my stomach already growling. Damn that man for interrupting me before I finished my scone! I emailed our in-house travel expert and asked for assistance on the sheikh's request; then, putting on my meek, demure mask, I called the sheikh to tell him that I was on the job (one of the many frustrations of living to serve the man was his dislike of email).

Then I drew a deep breath. Glancing around cautiously, I pulled up Google and typed in *Leo Schlumberger.*

Chapter 2

Surprisingly, there *was* a historian named Leo Schlumberger at Oxford, and his picture *did* resemble the man who had accosted me at the café. But all I could find were quite impressive academic credentials and a list of publications. Good grief! That tough-looking man specialized in the queens of Tudor England! How very unexpected. His last published work was an article on the near hagiography of Queen Katherine Parr. I pressed my lips together, trying to remember what "hagiography" meant (practically conferring sainthood on the subject, Google explained helpfully) and which one Katherine Parr was.

I couldn't find any information about his personal life, though (why was he looking for a woman named Jules?), so I closed down Google and composed an email to my friend Rosie for help. Rosie was a computer search genius who probably could have made billions hacking into banks like mine but instead chose to use her talents at a gray metal government desk in Washington, DC. Go figure.

Hey, Rosalie,
    Just met a very interesting man called Leo Schlumberger (I think). Says he's a historian at Oxford, though he's clearly

*a lunatic because he kept insisting I was Jules somebody, but
still . . . Check it out for me?*

*Nothing else happening here. The Kristens caught me
with jam on my collar and shared a broccoli sprig for lunch. I
miss the Corner Bakery's almond croissants so much!*

*Love ya,
Ames*

Decisively, I clicked "shut down" and closed the lid of my
computer. The Kristens and the Matts were organizing a trivia
night at the pub after their yoga and spin classes. Matt S. sent
me a dubious glance. "Amy, would you like to join us at spin?"

"Thanks, but no. I have plans," I lied.

A palpable sigh of relief ran through the group. Aside
from being uncool, I was known to be pathetically unathletic,
incapable of keeping up with the PYTs at their various gym
pursuits.

It was Friday, which meant Friday Fun Facts at the weekly
meeting. Audrey announced, "Today's fun fact question is, if you
could be any TV or movie character you wanted, who would
you be?"

"Cinderella!" cried Kristen P., dimpling.

"Ariel!" said Kristen R., whose blond hair had a slightly reddish tinge.

"Jake the Pirate!" One of the Jakes.

"Elsa!"

Dear God, I thought.

"Rapunzel!" The Kristen with hair down to her waist.

"Prince Eric!" The Jake who had a crush on Kristen R.

I shrank back into my seat, hoping no one would realize I
hadn't participated. I tried never to participate in the Friday Fun
Facts, and usually no one cared enough to call me out.

But . . . "How about you, Amy?" asked one of the Matts, who had wanted to be Scrooge McDuck.

"Uh . . . Dora," I said, without thinking.

Blank stares all around. "Dora?" Audrey asked. "Dora who?"

"Dora the Explorer. You know, with Backpack and Map?" My voice sounded thin and scared, like a little girl's. I bit my lip, hating the whole stupid business.

"Ohhhhh," Kristen P. said. "Dora the Explorer! I have a niece," she explained to the table, then turned to eye me dubiously. "I thought you don't like to travel, Amy."

I thought of the years with my father. "Uh, no," I stammered. "I don't speak any foreign languages, and it's so hard . . ." I let my voice trail away.

"Ohh-kaay, then," Audrey said. "Let's move on."

So it was with a huge sigh of relief that I gathered up my things and left at the end of the day.

It was unusually warm for September in London, so I opted to walk home. My banker's salary was just high enough to finance a tiny little flat in Knightsbridge, a few blocks from Harrods. The single room was barely large enough for a pullout sofa, dresser, and doll-size kitchen, but the location was fabulous. As I strolled along the busy streets, dodging chic foreigners and the occasional English matron (identified by her sturdy shoes), I mused on my strange encounter.

Where was he from? His accent was intriguing but impossible to place; at first I had thought mid-Atlantic, with traces of American in his British, but then, at the end, I suspected something more Mediterranean, or even Middle Eastern. Perhaps he was Mossad, chasing after my chubby little sheikh? No, that was too obvious. Turkish? Ooh, maybe French Foreign Legion? Did that even exist anymore?

And what about Jules? How on earth had he connected

me to this mystery woman? I recalled how his eyes had flicked dismissively over my uncurvy body in its gray banker's pantsuit when I stood up to leave. He wasn't interested in *me*; he was interested in Jules—who probably didn't have glasses and hair skimmed back into a ponytail and dull clothes. Probably Jules amused herself with heli-skiing and exotic travel and dressed in either French couture or fascinating, clever, ironic clothing from Notting Hill boutiques.

As I opened the door, my iPhone pinged with a new message, and I glanced eagerly at it to see Rosie's response to my email.

> *Ames,*
>
> *Your Leo is quite the man of interest! He's French-Israeli* [I was half-right! I gloated] *and definitely a scholar of Tudor England. Grew up all over the place. Went to college at Harvard and then PhD at Oxford. What did he want?*
>
> *Lucky you. The last interesting man I met was my grandfather's roommate at the nursing home.*
>
> *But, on second thought, be careful.*
>
> *Love and kisses.*

I went to bed dreaming of long-dead English queens and jam-covered bean sprouts.

Chapter 3

On Saturday night, there was a party in Bloomsbury for some of my friends from my pre–Atlantic Bank job at an international development consultancy called IDC. We had all met right after college and bonded through a fierce training program and then bounced around from assignment to assignment but somehow maintained our bond. We were a tight group, the eight of us who were currently in London, and I trusted them as much as I trusted anyone. Which is to say, a little bit.

They greeted me with raucous cries of "Here comes the sellout!" and "How's your golden parachute?" They had never forgotten that I deserted IDC to earn a private banker's salary and move from my scruffy digs in Deptford to my miniature flat in Knightsbridge. That was two years ago, but these guys had long memories.

"You're just jealous," I said, hanging up my Burberry coat alongside their faux leather and woolen jackets.

"You betcha," Bob the Bear said, lumbering up to envelop me in a huge hug. An American like I was, Bob had leapfrogged over the rest of us to become head of the London office. His nickname said it all; his paunch hung comfortably over a generous belt, and his shoulders were easily as broad as any linebacker's.

When Bob liked your work, he roared in approval. When he wasn't happy, he roared even more loudly. At Atlantic Bank, Audrey *never* liked my work. She expressed her approval of the Kristens and Matts and Jakes with a small, almost imperceptible half smile. Her disapproval, with which I was very familiar, was a faint wrinkling of her eyebrows and a minute compression of her thin lips.

With an effort, I pushed her out of my mind and settled down to enjoy the evening.

After several margaritas (the theme of our get-together was "it's still summer vacation"), I found myself telling Dorcas and Stephen about my strange encounter that day. "Hmm," Stephen said, tugging on his beard. "Leo Schlumberger . . . that name sounds familiar."

"He pronounced it the French way. Schlum-bear-*zhay*," I volunteered. "Rosie says he's French-Israeli, whatever that means."

"It means he's interesting," Stephen said.

"I can look him up for you on Monday," Dorcas offered. "I know you say Rosie's good with computers, but I'm better."

Dorcas was in her early sixties, of a generation that had grown up without PCs and Macs and iPads, but she had fallen in love with the technology as soon as it was introduced. I admired her. Despite the graying hair, sensible shoes, and unending supply of twin sets that seemingly marked her as a dull suburban housewife, she was in fact a cutting-edge computer whiz.

"Sure," I said. Then, "No! I really don't care—never mind."

We played a party game, Have You Never, as different from my office fun facts and Freaky Fridays as possible. The idea was to catch out your fellow players in a lie—in which case the liar had to either swig a bottle of beer or scarf down an entire slice of pizza. With pepperoni, onions, and extra anchovies.

"Have you never . . . gone skinny-dipping?"

Dorcas claimed that she had never, at which Bob reminded her of a diplomatic incident involving a sweltering day and a seemingly deserted lake in Eritrea. To keep her company, he swigged a bottle of beer too.

I kept my mouth shut, a reminiscent smile on my face.

"Have you never"—he paused, looking straight at me—"run straight into danger?"

A ripple ran through the group. Momentarily sober, we all looked at each other. Our careers took us to some of the most desperate places on Earth, and avoiding danger was more a hope than a reality.

I kept silent.

"Ames?" he questioned.

Still silent, I gulped down the bottle of beer, and the room erupted in applause. Bob shook his head, more in sorrow than in anger, and the game moved on.

We all sang a drunken round of "God Save the Queen" and "God Bless America" to close out the night; I bestowed kisses all around and then clambered into my Uber at around two in the morning, happily blitzed and full of bonhomie.

"Have a good night, then?" the driver asked.

"Great!"

He turned on a soft-rock station, and we roared away. I gazed out the window at the bright lights and endless activity of a warm Saturday night in London for the short ride home.

But as I closed the car door behind me and started up the front stoop to my building's outer door, a tall shape materialized out of the darkness behind me.

"Hey, Jules," Leo said.

I jumped about ten feet into the air and let out a small screech. He moved in closer, so close that I could feel his warm breath on the back of my neck.

"Have a good night?" he asked. But his tone wasn't playful or amused like the Uber driver's.

"Yes," I said, reflexively shifting into a defensive stance. My father had insisted on self-defense training; we had spent too much time in dodgy countries for him to allow any vulnerability.

"Um . . . sorry to approach you like this," he said, backing up a step. I thought he sounded genuinely apologetic, and I relaxed a little. "I was just passing your place after a night out and thought I'd see if you were available to talk."

"I'm not," I said. "Sorry."

"I thought we agreed to stop apologizing," he said, with a slight smile in his voice.

"Okay, fine." I was happy to abandon British pseudopolitesse. "How about you just leave me alone, then?"

"I wish I could," he said feelingly. "But I need you to help me—"

Another voice broke the warm stillness of the night.

"Is this man bothering you, then?"

It was a London bobby. He loomed even larger than Leo, his hand on his nightstick and his eyes narrowed in suspicion.

"Sorry," Leo said. "I didn't mean to—"

"Thank you. Thank you so much," I babbled to the bobby as Leo eyed me in astonishment. "I don't know this man, and he—"

"Be on your way, then," he said crisply to Leo, who melted into the night without another word—but not before sending a reproachful look my way.

Perhaps smelling the alcohol on my breath, the bobby said sharply, "And you, young lady, should be safe inside by now. Good night, then."

"Thank you. Good night. Thank you."

Of course I dropped my keys on the sidewalk while the

policeman watched, frowning. But I didn't care about his disapproval. He had dispatched Leo much more swiftly than I seemed able to do, and for that I was grateful. I waved goodbye to my hero as I unlocked the door and slipped inside.

But now I knew I would have to do something about Leo.

Chapter 4

He left me alone for the rest of the weekend, but on Monday morning I spotted him immediately on the tube as it rumbled from station to station in a loop of endless stop-and-go, enlivened by the occasional power loss and abrupt squeal of brakes that knocked the portly fellow next to me smack into my ribs. Leo smiled tentatively at me and tried to squeeze through the sea of packed-in people toward me, but even his height and strength were unequal to the task. As soon as the doors opened, I dashed up the steps, taking them two at a time, and panted through the security desk at work.

The next day, he was waiting for me outside my gym when I emerged after a particularly boring session on the treadmill. He was holding two coffees and trying to look hopeful and harmless. I ignored him and entangled myself in a mass of Asian tourists; a selfie stick whacked him in the forehead, and I whipped away through the crowd.

I wondered if he could possibly be as harmless as he seemed.

By Thursday, I still hadn't figured out what to do about him; despite his ineptitude, he seemed to have uncanny luck at finding me. Still, I was surprised when I looked up from my computer to see Yvette, Audrey's personal assistant, standing in front of my desk. "Your ten o'clock is here," she said shortly.

"My ten o'clock?" I didn't have any appointments that morning, but Yvette had already turned on her heel and marched back to her own desk. Heaving a sigh, I smoothed my pants and stood up, confused.

Then I turned the corner to our little reception area, and my breath caught. There, standing by Yvette's desk, frowning over his cell phone and looking very, very tall, was Leo.

I should have known, I realized belatedly. He had popped up everywhere else: at my gym, on my commute, on my street. Of course he would show up eventually at my office. I drew a deep breath. "Mr. Schlumberger," I said coolly, determined not to show any emotion.

Still, maybe the best thing would be to simply let him tell me his tale; I could set him straight and send him on his way. Maybe I would even learn something from him.

"*Doctor* Schlumberger," Yvette corrected me. She smiled at Leo, and he smiled back while I seethed. If he wanted to flirt with empty-headed, stick-insect Yvette, then why didn't he annoy *her* and leave me alone?

And of course I hadn't washed my hair this morning, and I was wearing another dull gray pantsuit, and my glasses were slipping down the bridge of my nose. I wanted to look invulnerable and icily professional for this confrontation with him—not mousy and colorless.

But then, that was my banker persona—the eminently forgettable Amy.

Wordlessly, I gestured toward the glass-enclosed conference room, and he preceded me in, making a great show of pulling out a chair for me and standing until I was seated (for Yvette's benefit, I supposed).

"What are you doing here?" I hissed at him. "This is too much. I'm going to call the police."

He looked astonished. "What? What for? What have I done?"

I sighed. "Never mind."

"That woman—is she one of the sorority girls? The pseudo-French stick insect?"

I almost smiled at his echo of my thoughts. "Not really. Yvette's an assistant, not a banker."

"Ah," he said. "So, she's not mean to you?"

Everyone in this office is mean to me, I thought. *I'm the fish out of water.* Then I said, "Wait a minute. Do you mean Yvette's not really French?"

"With that accent? I'd say she's straight out of Manchester."

Now I really did smile. But I recovered myself quickly and asked, "What are you doing here?"

"Um . . . I'm in the market for a private banker."

"Do you have net investable assets of at least twenty million dollars?" I asked politely. "If so, we would be delighted to discuss your business."

"Well . . ."

I started to stand up to indicate that this meeting was over, but he grinned at me and I remembered myself, sinking back into my seat.

"I suppose you want to tell me about Jules," I said, crossing my legs primly. If I had to be mousy, by God, I would be the mousiest Amy ever.

"Why are you calling yourself Amy?" he asked.

"I . . ." I stopped and shook myself mentally. "Actually, because that's my name. And I thought I would be asking the questions, not you."

We eyed each other with mutual expressions of distrust.

"I thought professors love to talk," I said.

"Actually, I prefer the Socratic method: asking questions and letting the truth emerge."

I let myself slump farther into my chair and began fidgeting with my hair.

He looked disconcerted. "Sorry, I don't mean to make you uncomfortable," he said uncomfortably.

I smiled inwardly and took my advantage. "Why are you looking for a woman named Jules?"

"Why are you calling yourself Amy?" he countered. "At first I thought you must be running from an abusive boyfriend or ex-husband—"

I drew myself up, affronted.

"But once I got to know you, I realized that you didn't fit the profile."

I was my father's daughter. I was not a victim. Or a runner. But it troubled me that he had figured that out so quickly. "You don't know me at all," I said sharply.

He smiled at me. "Well . . . perhaps we could remedy that?"

I was insulted that he thought I would fall for his easy charm. Yvette might be fooled, but I wasn't.

"Get out," I said, forgetting all my good intentions.

To my surprise, he stood up. "Look, Jules, Amy, whatever you're calling yourself, I'm sorry if I . . ." He stuck there, clearly unsure what exactly he had done.

I opened the glass door and waited. After a moment, he shrugged and left.

Yvette glanced up at me. "That was quick," she commented.

"Unfortunately, he doesn't have enough money to fit our profile," I said loudly. Leo, waiting for the elevator just outside the open office doors, turned and winked at me.

❧

I spent the rest of the morning arguing with the Dubai Atlantis about the penthouse. They claimed it was being held for an American celebrity, and I argued that my sheikh was much more important. I won by offering a positively obscene amount of money, and we hung up on the best of terms.

Then my sheikh informed me that the girls had decided they wanted to go to New York instead and would like the presidential suite at the Four Seasons. Also, they wanted to bring their new puppies, so could I please arrange for quarantine to be waived for the dogs?

Oh, yes, and wire them $100,000 in cash for the trip.

Steaming, I filled out the currency transaction report that bankers are required to file for cash transactions of more than $10,000—we filed thousands of these every year—and started a round of negotiations with the Four Seasons. The other vice presidents in my office (the three Kristens, the two Matts, and the two Jakes) all had assistants, but I was deemed unworthy of the perk, so I did all my dirty work myself.

All the sheikh's dirty work, that is.

But the truth was that I had crashed and burned at the IDC job with my recklessness in Chechnya; for this reason alone, I had to make the Barclays job work. I couldn't flame out again. If that meant that I had to be meek, humble Amy with my coworkers for another year or two—or three, God forbid—well, so be it. I had to make this work.

So I was not in a good mood when Leo waylaid me outside my office at the end of the day.

"Jesus," I said. "You again?"

He looked tired. His beard was well beyond a five-o'clock shadow, and he definitely needed a haircut.

"Me again," he agreed. "Sorry. Fancy a drink?"

"Not with you." *The hell with it,* I thought. My coworkers could bully and intimidate me, but not a random man who couldn't even call me by the right name.

"How about some fish and chips, then? I know a smashing little pub just around the corner. . . ."

He was well in control of himself; his accent was pure British.

My mouth watered, but I said, "No, thank you."

"Um . . . all right, then. We can just walk and talk."

"No, we can't."

While he argued, I glanced down at my phone and tapped the Uber app. Moments later, a dark car glided up to the curb, and I hopped in.

"Bye," I called, leaving Leo staring after me. His face was a mask of anger now, and he seemed to be muttering to himself again. I smiled in satisfaction as I settled back into the seat.

Leo popped up all week. It was positively genial, so I couldn't feel much beyond annoyance and some amusement, but he wouldn't let up. When I took the tube to work on Monday, he was there, waving at me from across the crowded car. When I came out of my hairdresser on Wednesday morning, he was there, waving from across the street. And when I arrived at my office building on Friday morning, he was there too, holding the door open for me with a polite flourish.

Belatedly it occurred to me that I had been too hasty in throwing him out of my office. I should have had that "conversation" he wanted and figured out how to get him out of my life.

Besides, in the bustling financial district of the city of London, with Savile Row–clad bankers jostling kamikaze bicycle messengers for space, Leo, in his professor's tweeds (metaphorically speaking), was the least threatening thing around. Still, I tried. "I could get a restraining order, you know."

He laughed out loud. "For what?"

I bit my lip. "If you would just tell me what this is all about, maybe I could help. Or at least steer you in the right direction." *Away from me*, I thought.

"I did tell you!" he exclaimed.

"No, you didn't."

"Yes, I did." He thought for a minute. "Didn't I?"

"No."

He smiled at me—the first genuine smile I had seen on him. It transformed his face, but I was immune to easy charm, especially in a man who kept calling me Jules. "Fish and chips, then? At noon?"

"Noon," I agreed. Best to get it over with, in a public place.

"Hey, Jules," he said, his smile deepening.

I turned away.

"Okay, then. Amy."

I turned back.

"Love the trainers."

I looked down to see that in my rush to leave the office, I had put on one blue sneaker and one white one. Crap. I looked up to scowl at him, but he had already disappeared into the crowd.

Chapter 5

That morning, we had a meeting on mandatory volunteer work. I barely managed not to point out the oxymoron and listened with growing amusement as Audrey reminded us that everyone had to log forty "volunteer" hours per year. "We're doing a publicity campaign on our commitment to community service," she explained solemnly.

Kristen R. waved her hand in the air. "Kristen S. and I helped build a village in Costa Rica last summer!" she announced. "It was so inspiring!"

Kristen S. pulled out her cell phone, scrolled to some pictures, and then passed it around the table; when it came to me, I forced myself not to laugh out loud at the shots of the Kristens swinging through the jungle on zip lines and lying on golden-sand beaches.

I handed the phone back. I had never been to Costa Rica, since it was the most prosperous country in Latin America and really didn't need foreigners to do anything except spend tourist dollars there. "Looks great," I murmured.

"Did you go anyplace besides Costa Rica?" asked Jake. "My college roommate spent a week in Haiti, building a schoolhouse."

Kristen S. shuddered. "My parents would *never* let me go to Haiti!"

For a moment I felt wistful; when I was at IDC or with my father, I spent most of my time in blisteringly hot or freezing-cold (and always dangerous) places like that—the barrios of Central America, the high mountains of Tibet—and I loved it. Every hot/cold, nerve-jangling minute of it.

Matt S. said, "The Jakes and I spent last Saturday building houses with Habitat for Humanity." He proudly displayed a green-and-black thumbnail. "I swing a mean hammer!"

"You'll lose that nail for sure, bro," Jake S. predicted, and they high-fived each other.

"What an after-party!" Jake T. put in. "Those Habitat people are great drinkers!"

Audrey turned to me, and I pushed my glasses up on my nose. "What are you doing for your volunteer hours, Amy?"

I swallowed uncomfortably. "I work with a group of Syrian refugees every Sunday."

Incredulous stares.

"What?" Audrey asked.

"At-risk teenagers," I half whispered, feeling all eyes focused on me in disbelief.

"Why?" someone asked. Clearly, I had missed the point of "mandatory volunteer work." It was supposed to be full of camaraderie and fun, not dreary, dark-skinned teenagers.

"Well . . ." I couldn't tell them that I had once been something of an at-risk teenager myself—and that was without the heavy burden of being a Muslim refugee in a European country. "It's something to do," I said lamely.

More silence.

Eventually Audrey said, "Honestly, Amy, it's just community service. You don't have to get carried away. Just go to the

SPCA for a few hours and play with the puppies and kittens that are looking for homes, all right?"

I nodded obediently.

"Amy's so *peculiar*," Kristen R. whispered to Kristen S.

Leo hadn't specified a meeting place, but he was waiting for me in the lobby of my building when I came down at noon. He was leaning against the wall, his dark eyes intent on the elevator doors, watching for me.

I noticed several women sending covert glances his way. He was that kind of man: tall, black-haired, and black-stubbled; a little mysterious; a little moody; scruffy but still with an indefinable air of command.

It occurred to me that maybe I could have an affair with him. It had been more than two years since Scott.

"Let's go to the local on the next street," he suggested. "They'll do you some smashing fish and chips."

Once again, I noted his odd mixture of British and American idioms. Schooled at Harvard and Oxford, I recalled. I wondered what he considered his home. Perhaps he was homeless, like I was.

So when we sat down, I asked him, "Where are you from, anyway?"

"Um . . . well, that's a complicated question, my dear Jules." Then, as I half stood up to leave, he said, "My dear Amy, I mean."

I sat down again.

"Let's see. I was born in Paris. Moved to Tel Aviv when I was six. Back to Paris when I was twelve. Went to New England for prep school and college. Did my military service in Israel. Did my PhD at Oxford. I live in Oxford now."

Well, that explained the intriguing mix of accents.

"So, your native language is . . . French?"

"French, Hebrew, Arabic, English . . . Who knows?" That smile flashed again; I wondered when he would realize that I was immune. Unless I decided not to be, of course.

"Now it's your turn," he said.

"Let's see," I said, mimicking him. "I was born in Moscow, but my parents are American. My father was an international energy consultant, so we moved every few years. I lived in Washington for a while, then back to Moscow, Saudi Arabia, Jordan, and Ukraine. Went to UCLA."

He was staring. "So, what is *your* native language?"

"English, of course." I was embarrassed to admit that I had no flair for languages. I did speak Russian, but only because I had spent so many years in Russia, being raised by nannies there.

"You said your father was a consultant? What does he do now?"

"He's dead," I said flatly.

"Oh." He said something in Hebrew (at least, I think it was Hebrew) and bowed his head for a moment. "I'm sorry."

I couldn't bear his sympathy. Even fifteen years later, the wound was too raw. My father had been gunned down on the streets of Moscow, apparently the victim of mistaken identity. He lay on the sidewalk for hours, his blood draining away into the icy, slushy snow while pedestrians gave his body a wide berth and the police drank huge mugfuls of vodka to stay warm.

I had been thousands of miles away, drinking huge mugfuls of margaritas at a beach party in LA.

"And your mother?" Leo asked after a moment.

"Oh, she left when I was ten. Sick of traveling the world in my father's wake." And, as I had learned many years later, sick of his affairs too. "She lives in California with her second husband and his twin daughters." Both tall, slim California blondes whom she adored and I detested. We rarely spoke.

"How very . . . American," Leo said. He had never sounded more French.

Time to turn the questioning on him. "How about your family?" I asked. "Are they in Israel?"

He shrugged. "My parents and two of my sisters are there."

"How many sisters do you have?"

Again that smile. "Four. I'm the eldest, followed by four girls. For my sins."

"Wow."

"Quite."

The fish and chips arrived, dumped on the table by the sweating, red-faced pub owner whose stained apron bore witness to all the meals he had cooked that day. Leo thanked him with a nod, and we dug in.

Leo swallowed a huge bite and asked me if I was close to my mother now.

"Oh, no. My father was my best friend."

He cocked his eyebrow at me.

"He wanted a son," I explained. "Instead, he got me. So he decided I would be his buddy. We went on adventures together." I smiled at the memory.

"Adventures?"

"Oh, like, we went rock climbing in Morocco and heli-skiing in Canada and desert trekking in Jordan. You know—adventures."

"*Quel casse-cou*," Leo said.

I didn't speak a word of French, which was perhaps fortunate. I Googled it when I got home, and I think he said, "What a daredevil."

But now Leo was examining me closely; I thought that, perhaps for the first time, he was considering me as a person rather than as his pathway to Jules. As always, I had dressed to fade into the background at the bank, and I could see him trying to reconcile the woman in front of him with his mental image of an adventurer.

"Heli-skiing in Canada?" he asked.

"Yes," I said reluctantly. How had we gotten back to his questioning me?

"Anyway," I said, "the purpose of this lunch is for you to tell me about Jules—and why you think I'm her."

He took one last bite, patted his mouth with a paper napkin, and then took a long swallow from his beer.

"You—Jules Seymour, I mean to say—are the last living descendant of Queen Katherine Parr and possibly the heiress to a considerable tract of rural England."

My jaw dropped.

He grinned at me. "Now are you interested?"

Obviously, the man was a lunatic. But he was a very well-educated and interesting lunatic, so I sat back to listen to his fairy tale. After all, it was best to humor lunatics. Besides, this was much better than what I had been imagining.

"Katherine Parr was the last of Henry VIII's wives," Leo began. "She was one of the most interesting of his wives. Well, they were all interesting—except for poor little Catherine Howard, maybe. She was just a flighty girl, and then, of course, there's Anne of Cleves. . . ." His voice trailed away as he stared back into history, lost in his thoughts.

"Katherine Parr," I prompted gently.

"Oh! Yes. She was extremely well educated. A Reformist, of course. And practically a saint to put up with Henry."

"I thought Henry VIII was really good-looking!" I protested, thinking of the handsome, well-built Jonathan Rhys Meyers in TV's *The Tudors*. I had lusted after him when the series was on.

Leo smiled indulgently. "In his youth, yes, of course. But by the time he got to Katherine Parr, he was an old man, so obese that it took six stout grooms and a purpose-built crane to heave him onto his horse. He had a weeping, open wound on his leg that had to be drained very painfully every day, and it stank to high heaven. God only knows how he and Katherine . . . well . . ."

Disappointed, I said peevishly, "Then why did she marry him?"

"My dear girl, one didn't refuse the King of England."

"So, what does this have to do with me?"

"Katherine had a daughter, Lady Mary Seymour."

"Seymour?"

"Yes," Leo said. "You will be happy to know that Katherine married for love after Henry went toes up and left her a very wealthy, handsome widow. She married a reckless scoundrel named Tom Seymour with indecent haste after Henry died, and had a baby barely a year later, at the very advanced age of thirty-five."

A year older than I was. "Good for her," I said.

"But poor Katherine died when the baby was only a week old, of childbed fever."

"Oh."

"And her useless husband, Tom, was executed for treason when the little girl, Lady Mary, was only seven months old."

"Oh, dear." I found myself saddened by this long-ago tragedy and pushed away the rest of my uneaten meal. Leo reached out a long arm and helped himself to some chips.

"So, what happened to the baby? I assume she was your Jules's great-great-whatever-grandma?"

"Yes, exactly," Leo said. "She was lost to history after her father died. Until recently, it was assumed that she died in infancy. But . . ."

Here it came. "But what?" I asked, curious in spite of myself.

"I've found evidence suggesting that she survived her childhood, grew up to marry, and had a son, the many-greats-grandfather of Juliette Mary Seymour. You."

"Not me," I protested. "Though it would be nice."

My iPhone dinged, reminding me that it was time to get back to the office, so I couldn't question Leo more on his "evidence." I had to admit that my curiosity was piqued. I knew I would be diving into Google as soon as I got home from work.

But more than anything, I had learned that Leo was nothing more or less than an eccentric Oxford don after all. When I thought about my fears, I had to smile. A historian obsessed with a long-dead queen and her progeny. How much more harmless could you get?

Chapter 6

That morning, I had gotten an email from Audrey, whose desk was ten feet away from mine. It was a Google Calendar invitation to Kristen R. and me for a meeting at two o'clock that afternoon. *What the hell*, I thought apprehensively as I accepted the invite. Audrey was constantly meeting with the other vice presidents, who handled much more important members of the Saudi royal family. My minor clients, with their constant nagging demands, were well beneath her consideration.

Today, the two Jakes were wearing matching bow ties, having decreed that Fridays would be Bow Tie Day. And a new Kristen had just started—Kristen M., whom I had privately dubbed Kristen the Younger. She was only twenty-three, a recent graduate of Princeton, where she had been (of course) the president of her eating club. She would be assisting Kristen P. and Kristen R.

Glumly, I watched them bonding over "Do you know So-and-So?" and squeals of "Oh my gosh, I *love* your earrings!" Through some strange osmosis, Kristen the Younger had already sussed out my inferior status and had wasted no squeals on me; just a quick introduction and handshake were enough. I wasn't a member of the sorority.

My computer pinged to remind me that it was time for my

meeting with Audrey. I gathered up some random files and hurried to the conference room, speculating about how late Audrey would be this time. The average for a meeting with me was fifty-seven minutes, although I hadn't factored in the number that she just blew off. In the past year, I had met with her exactly twice. Which was fine with me.

Her assistant poked her head in the door to tell me Audrey was running late. What a surprise. I leafed through my files, trying to look busy, but my stomach was sour with anxiety. What had I done?

Forty-five minutes later, Audrey and Kristen R. hurried in together, talking in hushed tones about a derivatives investment for the Saudi minister of finance. My boring old sheikh never invested in anything sexier than US T-Bills, so I listened with some envy.

Audrey sat down and turned to me. "Amy," she said, "you have a problem."

Well, fuck me, I thought. I tried to look appropriately frightened.

"The FBI has launched an investigation into Sheikh Abdullah for tax evasion and money laundering."

I stared at her in disbelief. Sheikh Abdullah? *My* Sheikh Abdullah? Conservative old Dull Boy, as I had nicknamed him, whose idea of a daring investment scheme was buying a thousand shares of Microsoft?

I shook my head but then remembered to be deferential. "Sorry, but . . . I don't think he even knows what money laundering is."

"Well, the FBI is serious about this," Audrey said. "I trust that your documentation is in order?" Her tone conveyed her doubts.

I thought of the piles and piles of currency transaction reports and other routine forms that I filed on the sheikh's behalf. US authorities required bankers to submit these forms whenever a client initiated a transaction that seemed "suspicious"—whatever that meant.

"I think so," I said, with a good show of uncertainty. Already I was starting to question myself. Dull Boy liked to use cash because he didn't understand computers and didn't trust banks. Had I filed every form every time? What if I had slipped up?

Audrey said slowly and carefully, as if I were a toddler, "Amy, you are aware that banks are on the front lines of the battle against money laundering. Criminals and corrupt government officials need to access the banking system in order to conceal the source of their funds."

"I know that," I said, smarting inwardly. "I don't think I could have forgotten—"

She went on, ignoring me, "We have a very important responsibility to cooperate with the authorities in this valuable work."

With a huge effort, I swallowed my angry words. "I'm aware," I murmured.

Kristen R. said, "Audrey, I went to B-school with a guy who's with the FBI now, in their financial crimes unit. Let me ping him and tee up some ideas about how we can work together."

Audrey almost smiled at her. "Super idea, Kristen. Thanks." She turned back to me, her lips compressed again in a tight line. "Amy, I'm asking Kristen to second-chair you on this. She's going to go through all your records to see where you might have dropped the ball. Please run everything by her from now on."

Well, fuck me twice.

When I got back to my desk, I just stared blankly at my equally blank computer, my thoughts racing. There was absolutely nothing in my files to suggest that Dull Boy was a money launderer. I would stake my life on that. As for tax evasion, the old man had once asked me what the IRS was, so I had my doubts about his ability to conduct tax fraud as well.

But now I was saddled with Kristen R. as my "second chair." In her faux-sweet, solicitous way she was bound to (kindly) point out any number of ways in which I might have slipped up. Thousands of transactions, thousands of documents, thousands of filings . . . After all, you couldn't expect perfection from an elderly public-university graduate.

And then there was Dull Boy himself. I shuddered to think of his reaction to an investigation by US authorities. He was no jihadist, but he had the usual Saudi view of dissolute, godless Americans. *Those bumbling clods at the FBI are going to screw up all my hard work with Sheikh Abdullah and his family*, I thought bitterly. *I'll be lucky if he trusts me to arrange dog sitting for his poodles after this, let alone handle his money.*

Fuming, I was starting to shut down my computer for the day when a new email flashed on the screen. It was from my friend Rosie. Subject line: *Your historian.* Eager for a distraction, I clicked on it.

Did some more digging. Do you know about his military background? He served in a seriously elite unit with the IDF [Israeli Defense Forces, I interpreted] *but all very hush-hush, so I can't get a handle on what he did, exactly.*

Hmm.

Do you have any deep, dark secrets that he might be trying to uncover? Be careful, Ames.

I knew, of course, that Leo would have served in the IDF— all eighteen-year-old Israelis are supposed to do their service. But there is service, and there is *service*, from desk jobs to liaison jobs to the elite, hardcore military units. Despite his "sorrys" and stammering, I somehow wasn't surprised at all that Leo's service had been of the latter variety.

My mind flashed involuntarily to the FBI investigation, but I shook my head to dismiss it. Ridiculous. Leo might be many things, but he definitely was not an FBI agent; his tailing of me had been seriously inept.

Decisively, I shut down my computer and closed the lid.

On Sunday morning, I dressed in my nonbanker clothes—skinny jeans, leg-hugging boots, deep-blue blouse, swingy earrings—and set out for King's Cross station for the three-hour ride north to Bradford. I tucked my black cashmere sweater under my cheek and slept while the train bucked and swayed its way through the grimy London suburbs and up north to the even grimier Bradford suburbs. By eleven, I was in the refugee center, collecting my charges for the day: ten Syrian teenagers with sullen faces and slouchy attitudes. But the three girls' faces lit up when they saw me, and one even smiled. I smiled back.

An hour later, we were all splashing and shrieking in the YMCA's indoor community pool. The girls' burkinis didn't slow them down one bit. I taught everyone Marco Polo, and we played pool basketball until Amal, who had watched his entire family drown in the Aegean Sea on their desperate flight from the horrors of Aleppo, shouted with glee like the thirteen-year-old boy he really was and won the game with a perfect shot. "Swish!" he shouted, his favorite new English word. "Swish! Swish! Swish, Ah-mee!"

Osama, whose father had been tortured to death by Syrian soldiers, slapped him on the back, and they high-fived exultantly. Layla's sweet, round face was creased into an ear-to-ear smile—Layla, whose little brothers had been gunned down while foraging for food amid the devastation of Homs—and she said to me, "The boys are so silly." It was the first time I had ever heard her speak, after six months of our Sunday excursions, and I glowed inside. Then I realized that my fingers were wrinkled like prunes and that Layla was shivering under her black burkini.

"Out of the pool," I announced. "Time for ice cream."

The debate over ice cream flavors was loud and enthusiastic. The two most religious boys argued strenuously over whether chocolate was halal ("It looks so delicious," Osama said wistfully), while the girls hesitated between strawberry and coconut, finally agreeing to a half scoop of each. I had spent enough time in war-torn hellholes like Syria that as I watched these kids dither, so free of fear and grief, my heart warmed. Then a voice in my ear said, "Um . . . I think I'll have peach melba," and I turned with a start to see Leo standing behind me.

"Shit!" I said, all the small pleasures of the day giving way to annoyance. How on earth had he tracked me down?

"No peach melba?" he asked. "Perhaps lemon sorbet, then?"

"How the hell . . ." How on earth had he found me at this small ice cream shop on the gritty backstreets of Bradford?

"So, this is how you spend your Sundays?" he asked. "That's not what I would expect of a private banker."

I shrugged. This was the real me, not the private banker Amy.

"You're really enjoying yourself," he said thoughtfully. Once again, he examined me closely, and I wondered what he was seeing. I knew I was reasonably pretty—well, at least, I had thought I was pretty until I joined the PYTs at Atlantic Bank. But I wore no makeup, having been raised mostly by a father who had no patience for such female fripperies; I dressed in simple, casual, Gap-style clothes. In my banker's uniform, I was forgettable. But in my skinny jeans and silky blouse, I wondered if Leo thought I was pretty.

Well, that could be useful.

"Where are your glasses?" he asked unexpectedly.

"I only need them at work."

He looked politely skeptical. "Sorry—your eyesight is fine when you're not at work?" Put that way, it did sound absurd; I couldn't tell him that the glasses were part of my private-banker persona.

Leo exchanged some words in what sounded like fluent Arabic with a couple of the Syrian boys and then turned back to me.

"Why Syrian refugees?" he asked. "And why Bradford?"

I ran quickly through my options. The truth wouldn't do; perhaps a partial truth would suffice. "I've traveled a lot," I said. "Seen a lot. I wanted to help—and there aren't a lot of people lining up to work with Syrian refugees in Bradford."

"Hmm," Leo said. I could almost see his too-quick, too-inquisitive mind at work and wondered again how he'd tracked me down. But then Osama bounced over and asked Leo a question in Arabic, and soon all the males were chatting together. The girls were deferentially quiet behind them, licking their ice cream and listening closely. I couldn't understand a word.

I let Leo drive me back to London—how could I not, faced with the alternative of another three-hour train ride and a late-night arrival at King's Cross? His car turned out to be a surprisingly smart Audi with a luscious-smelling, buttery leather interior and seats that cushioned me like a featherbed. I briefly pondered how he could afford such a car on an Oxford don's salary, then shrugged.

Leo said, "So, tell me again why you spend your Sundays traveling six hours on a train to hang out with a bunch of Syrian teenagers."

"Why not?" I countered, absurdly defensive.

He paused. "I don't know," he admitted. "You're right—why not?"

I smiled.

"You don't speak Arabic," he said. "If you're going to work with refugees, why not Russians?"

"Jeez, Leo," I said. "You go where the need is, not where it's easiest to go."

"You are so right," he said warmly, and for just a moment there was a flash of camaraderie between us. Then the moment passed, and I could have kicked myself for, once again, revealing too much.

"Besides, I get to go to glamorous Bradford every week," I added lightly.

"It just doesn't fit with . . . It doesn't fit. *You* don't fit, somehow." He was clearly puzzled, and I was suddenly wary.

"We have to do mandatory volunteer work for the bank," I explained. "Forty hours a year."

"Mandatory volunteer work?" he repeated, grinning. "Has anyone noticed that that's an oxymoron?"

"My thoughts exactly," I said. Sometimes we seemed to be in perfect sync; it was worrisome.

Leo looked pensive. "Does anyone else work with refugees?"

I shifted uncomfortably. "No, they build villages in Costa Rica and houses for Habitat for Humanity. And play with puppies at the SPCA."

He laughed out loud, and I couldn't help but join in. "Costa Rica is a very prosperous country," he said, in a perfect echo of my own thoughts, "and I'll bet those spoiled kids with their manicured hands are remarkably ineffective at building houses."

"You should have seen Jake's thumb," I told him, and he laughed again.

A more comfortable silence fell between us. Then Leo said, "You surprise me."

Warning signs flashed in my mind, and I sat up straighter.

"I'm not surprising. I'm dull. I'm a private banker who arranges vacations and personal shoppers for my clients."

"Who also heli-skis and spends her weekends teaching refugee kids how to swim," he replied. "And wants to be Dora the Explorer."

I cursed myself for allowing him these glimpses into my inner life. "Mostly, I like to be alone," I said. "When I'm not working."

"And what do you do when you're alone?"

"I like to do crossword puzzles. In Russian."

"Impressive," he said.

"I like to read a lot too," I said, with perfect truth.

"What do you like to read?"

"Oh, spy novels; books about explorers or Everest expeditions; anything set in Russia—except for *Anna Karenina*. What a wimp!"

He was smiling again, and I throttled myself silent. "I rest my case," he said.

I decided to turn the tables. "How did you find me today, anyway?"

"Oh! Sheer coincidence."

"Coincidence?" I asked.

"Yes, I was on the northbound train, planning to visit with some old friends, when I saw you—so, naturally, I changed my plans."

"Naturally," I said dryly. We exchanged mutually suspicious glances—I didn't believe in coincidences, and he didn't expect me to believe in coincidences—but we appeared to be at a stalemate. I closed my eyes and pretended to sleep for the remainder of the drive into London.

Chapter 7

On Saturday night, I had dinner with my old pals. Two of them were going to Afghanistan for six months, so the plan was to help them consume enough alcohol to carry them through their entire assignment—make them into "alcohol camels," as Stephen put it. When I had worked at IDC with the gang, I too had traveled to exotic places, like Myanmar and Egypt and Yemen. As international development consultants, we went only to poor countries that were just this side of lawlessness. There were never any boring, safe destinations—no Paris or Taiwan on our airline tickets.

In fact, I admitted to myself, I was bitterly jealous of Dorcas and Will. I loved a good adventure. I loved the heady thrill of fear and excitement and sheer adrenaline when I walked the dusty streets of a foreign—very foreign—city and soaked in the otherworldly smells, the strange language, the openly curious and suspicious glances of passersby as I cast equally curious glances their way. Living in safe, boring London was like being exiled to a convent. Being with Dorcas and Will, now on the eve of their latest adventure, was like having my nose pressed up against the window of a fragrant French patisserie, never to be allowed inside.

Also, I hated that everyone teased me about selling out and leaving the international development world for a cushy, high-paying job in private banking. I was a solitary soul by nature—and by my father's upbringing—but I had rarely felt so isolated as I did in this job.

I was doing my first tequila shot with Dorcas when Bob the Bear sauntered in. I couldn't hide my dismay to see his hairy, meaty arm slung around Leo as if Leo were his prisoner rather than his soon-to-be drinking buddy. "Look what I found lurking outside," he announced. "Says he's yours, Ames."

I glared at Leo, who shrugged back at me. "Sorry for busting in," he said apologetically. "But once I told Bob I knew you, he insisted I come in."

The rest of the group glared too. We were a tight group, our little gang of eight, and outsiders were not welcome. Four of the gang were married couples: Dorcas and Will, Tom and Meryl. Bob had gone through two wives and was in no hurry to find a third. Stephen had left his wife at home with their new baby, and Lydia never brought a date, possibly so that she could flirt with all the men simultaneously. We never brought—what on earth was Leo to me, anyway? A casual acquaintance?—casual acquaintances to these gatherings. We even met in our homes rather than pubs, for privacy.

"Two-drink limit on everyone tonight," Bob boomed, looking sternly at Will and Stephen, our biggest drinkers. They groaned, but Bob insisted, "No spilling of Amy's embarrassing secrets. Let's give the poor girl some cover. Now, Leo"—he slapped Leo on the back so hard that his not-insignificant frame shuddered—"can drink all he wants." And he steered the bemused Leo over to the makeshift bar on Dorcas and Will's kitchen table.

Will winked at me. "So, we shouldn't admit that Ames really is—what's the name? Julia?—in deep disguise?"

"Jesus, Will," I said. "Don't encourage him."

"Do we know Leo?" Dorcas asked, peering over the top of her glass at me.

"Yes, actually, I mentioned him to you last week," I admitted.

Meryl, my closest confidante in the group, looked confused.

"The guy who thought I was his long-lost friend, Jules," I explained to her.

"Oh, yes."

"Monsieur le Docteur, n'est-ce pas?" Lydia asked coquettishly, sidling up to Leo.

Leo winced, even more than he had from Bob's hearty slap. "God, no. I mean, sorry, yes, but please don't call me that."

Bob put another tequila sunrise in his hand. "Drink up, Monsieur le Docteur," he commanded. "Zen ve vill learn all your secrets."

This was, I knew, exactly what Bob was planning; I wondered if Leo knew it too.

Leo, with an expressive glance at me, drank.

I sighed and took a big swallow of my own drink.

But soon Leo was sitting at the piano, pounding out old Beatles favorites while seven of the eight gathered around, singing lustily along to "I Saw Her Standing There." Bob shouted triumphantly, and Leo said, "Er . . . quite." With a pang, I realized that my friends liked him.

Then he looked at me, and our eyes met for a second. Quietly, Leo played the opening chords of "Hey Jude," and everyone began to sing. But after a moment I realized that Leo was singing "Hey, Jules" instead, and my face flamed. That bastard. Using my very favorite song against me.

Despite Bob's best efforts and his best tequila sunrises, we didn't really learn anything about Leo except that he could play piano and sing hits from the '60s. And, despite Lydia's best efforts, Leo insisted on seeing me home. Stephen, drunk as a skunk, hugged me goodbye and whispered, "You go, girl!" in my ear. But Meryl hugged me too and murmured, "Be careful" as I turned to go.

Meryl's judgment was generally much more sound than Stephen's.

As we slid into the Uber together, Leo said, "I like your friends."

"We've been through a lot together," I said.

"Yes we have, *motek*," Leo said.

"Not you and me! My friends and me." I paused. "What's *motek*?"

He grinned. "Look it up."

Well, two could play this game. "*Vyidiot*," I said, in my best Russian accent.

"No, I'm not."

"Yes, you are. And since when do you speak Russian?"

"There are *beaucoup de* Russian Jews in Israel, let alone Russian crooks in London. One picks up the odd phrase or two."

I thought "you are an idiot" was an extremely odd phrase to pick up.

"You," Leo said, "have a very interesting group of friends. And you are a very interesting woman."

I had to stop this. So I said, "Sorry, but we're just a bunch of boring people with boring jobs who drink to forget our boring lives."

Leo shook his head. "I beg to differ."

The Uber stopped in front of my building, and Leo got out to open the door for me—a surprisingly old-world gesture. I wondered if he was expecting me to invite him up. I was still pondering the idea of an affair with him, but I was leaning against; he saw too much to be a comfortable lover.

"Well," I said.

"Lunch Wednesday?"

I hesitated. "If you promise to leave me alone until then."

"Hand to heart."

"Well, then," I said ungraciously, "I guess so."

"I'll text you then. Good night."

And he hopped back into the Uber without giving me the opportunity to ask how he would obtain my cell phone number.

Of course I Googled *motek* as soon as I got in the door. It meant "sweetheart" in Hebrew.

Well, if Leo thought he could wheedle something out of me with a few sweet words and smoldering smiles, he didn't know me at all.

Chapter 8

Divorced, beheaded, died.
Divorced, beheaded, survived.

On Sunday morning, I settled in with my computer and a giant Mr. Goodbar to try to figure out why Leo was so obsessed with Katherine Parr and her long-lost great-great-whatever-granddaughter.

This little ditty summed up the fate of Henry VIII's six wives.

Divorced: That was Catherine of Aragon, who was married to Henry for nearly two decades but bore him only a daughter, the future Queen Mary. To Henry, who was a man of his times, plus an utter boor (to my disappointment), the lack of a son was obviously Catherine's fault, not his. So he broke from the Catholic Church, divorced the aging Catherine, and pensioned her off so that he could marry . . .

Beheaded: Anne Boleyn, of course. The high-spirited, high-stepping Anne had been raised at the French court, which gave her that Parisian je ne sais quoi, a superiority of taste, and sensuality and secretive knowledge. Henry fell head over heels, and Anne was smart enough to keep him out of her bed until she had reeled him in. But she too bore him only a girl, the future Queen Elizabeth I, and Henry accused her of sleeping with other men (including her own brother). Poor Anne lost her head over her inability to give the hateful Henry a healthy son, clearing the way so that he could marry . . .

Died: Jane Seymour. (*Aha! The Seymours enter the picture*, I thought). Jane was a prim, rather boring little missy—Anne's polar opposite—who had the great good fortune to bear Henry, at last, that all-important son, the future King Edward VI. But then Jane's luck ran out and she died of childbed fever, leaving Henry so grief-stricken that he made the terrible mistake of marrying . . .

Divorced: Anne of Cleves. This Anne was nothing like the first. She was a doughy-faced, unlovely, ungraceful foreign princess whose relations fooled Henry into marrying her by sending him a much-Photoshopped (or whatever the equivalent was in those days) portrait. Charmed by the woman in the image, Henry was appalled by the real-life version, whose lack of hygiene and good looks made it impossible for him to bed her. Fortunately for this Anne, Henry didn't care enough to behead her. He simply divorced her and sent her away so he could lose his head over . . .

Beheaded: Pretty little Catherine Howard (the one who Leo had said wasn't particularly interesting, I remembered). Flighty, giddy, silly, tragically young, Catherine forsook the gouty old king to gambol with various men of the court, almost certainly sleeping with several. Henry was humiliated and, for perhaps the first time, agonizingly aware of the loss of his youth and vitality. So he sent this Catherine to the executioner rather than the nunnery. The poor, empty-headed girl spent the night before her death practicing with a makeshift block in her cell so that she would look her best when she laid her head on the real thing. And this paved the way for Henry to take his final wife . . .

Survived: Katherine Parr. This Katherine, unlike her two namesakes, had very little interest in marrying Henry when his fancy turned her way. Already twice wedded and widowed, Katherine was in love, for probably the first time in her life, with the dashing, handsome Thomas Seymour. (*The plot thickens!* I thought.) Tom was the brother of Henry's favorite wife, Jane Seymour, so he was the King's brother-in-law and uncle to the little Prince Edward.

But Henry decided on Katherine, and his will was not to be denied. ("My dear girl, one didn't refuse the King," I remembered Leo saying.) Unlike the handsome, athletic monarch of the TV series, Henry by this time was a huge, bloated mass of illness and ill temper. I could only imagine Katherine's dismay at contemplating him, rather than the sexy Tom Seymour, as a bed partner. She was a woman of good sense, though, so she made the best of her marriage and tended Henry both carefully and conscientiously.

When Henry died, however, Katherine's good sense deserted her. She married her Tom in a secret ceremony just a few short months after the King's death, and without the permission of his council. Tom proved exactly the type of husband one might have expected, dallying with Princess Elizabeth—a nubile, lively girl of fourteen, compared with Katherine's nearly elderly thirty-five—and conspiring against his brother, Edward Seymour, the Lord Protector during the childhood of the boy King Edward.

Thus, Katherine's happiness was short-lived, and, as Leo had said, she died barely a week after giving birth to her daughter, Lady Mary Seymour. Then the fatally foolish Tom was executed for treason, and the baby girl was an orphan and an unwanted reminder of the Queen's folly and her little-mourned husband.

Seven-month-old Lady Mary was given over to her mother's closest friend, Catherine Willoughby, the Duchess of Suffolk.

Eager to learn her fate, I paged down swiftly but was disappointed to find that, just as Leo had told me, the baby had disappeared entirely from history. Quickly, I Googled "Lady Mary Seymour" and, after lots of digging, finally came across an obscure article on the forty-seventh page of references, titled "Fate of Lady Mary Seymour Discovered?"

Ha, Leo the historian! I exulted. *I'll show you!*

The answer to the long-lost child's fate, the author wrote, might lie in a Latin book of poems and epitaphs by John Parkhurst, Katherine Parr's chaplain, who also served the Duke and Duchess of Suffolk. Published in 1573, the book included the following poem, which the author was kind enough to translate for me:

> *I whom at the cost*
> *Of her own life*
> *My queenly mother*
> *Bore with the pangs of labour*
> *Sleep under this marble*
> *An unfit traveller.*
> *If Death had given me to live longer*
> *That virtue, that modesty, That obedience of my excellent*
> *Mother*
> *That Heavenly courageous nature*
> *Would have lived again in me.*
> *Now, whoever*
> *You are, fare thee well*
> *Because I cannot speak any more, this stone*
> *Is a memorial to my brief life*

Though no name was given, the researcher concluded, this must surely have been the epitaph that Parkhurst, who would have known Lady Mary Seymour (perhaps even baptized her?), wrote on her death.

I shut down the computer and sat with my head in my hands, too depressed to even open the Mr. Goodbar. I felt no exultancy after all; the story was too tragic. Imagine surviving the embraces of the gross old king to marry your one true love, only to find that he was a knave after all—and then to die a miserable, painful death.

And the baby, the poor little girl who was orphaned and dead before she even knew her parents . . . I was not a sentimental woman, but even I was moved and saddened by the demise of this little family.

Poor Leo. I would have to break the news to him gently.

The next day was Sunday, so I trekked up to Bradford again, half hoping, half fearing that Leo would follow me again. But I took my kids to play soccer with the YMCA team, and he never showed. Mariam told me she had read her first book in English, though (*The Cat in the Hat*), and Mohammed asked me to help him prepare for a job interview (bagging groceries at the local Waitrose). It was just as well that Leo was a no-show, of course; I had already let him see way too much of me. He was likable and seemed harmless, despite the whole Jules thing, but he was also much too curious and quick; I simply couldn't let him see any more.

Monday was boring and uneventful, except for an agonizingly uncomfortable phone call with Sheikh Abdullah, in which I tried to explain the concepts of tax evasion and money laundering to him. He interrupted me only once, to remind me that his granddaughters would like personal shoppers to guide them through the trendiest boutiques in New York's SoHo district.

But his assistant called me on Tuesday morning to pass on the ominous news that Abdullah's sons, Kareem and Nasir, would be in London the following week to meet with me. Ominous because I had never had any contact with either one. They seemed happy to do nothing but collect the massive dividend payments that financed life in their many homes (Courchevel and Vail for the skiing, London and Manhattan for the shopping, Antibes for the glamour, Mustique for the sun, and Riyadh for their conservative father). The Kristens and Matts and Jakes, in fact, were constantly jetting off to one of *their* sheikhs' fabulous homes for birthday parties and anniversary galas, but my relationship with Dull Boy was limited strictly to the phone.

His sons were well educated, though—at least in comparison to the barely literate Abdullah—and would surely understand the implications of an FBI investigation. Audrey decreed that Kristen R., my designated handler, would lead the meeting and I should take notes. I couldn't decide whether to be insulted or relieved, so I settled for both.

My stomach growling, I settled back in at my desk, relieved for once to anticipate another boring afternoon arranging for Tiffany bracelets to be purchased for the sheikh's granddaughters. Since he had only eight granddaughters and was demanding twelve bracelets, I amused myself by speculating about who the other recipients might be.

But then the other shoe dropped, in the unlikely form of an email from my mother.

Chapter 9

My mother and I exchanged polite emails a couple of times a year, so I was startled to see her name on the message. It had been only a month since our last exchange. But that was nothing compared to the content of the message.

Hello, dear,

Hope all is well with you. As you will see from the itinerary below, your sister Kali is landing at Heathrow this afternoon and will be expecting you to pick her up. I haven't wanted to burden you [Ha! I thought], *but I'm afraid that she has gotten herself into a great deal of trouble, and Warren and I are at a loss. We hope that some time away will do her good, and appreciate your stepping up to support the family.*

Best,

Mom

I read the note once, then read it again, still disbelieving. Scrolling down to the bottom, I saw that Kali was arriving on a Virgin Atlantic flight in—let's see—ninety minutes.

I read it one more time, a cold lump of horror settling into the pit of my stomach. This could not be happening. Had they all gone mad out there in California? Had the earth suddenly upended itself? I hadn't seen Kali or her twin, Kelley, in at least five years and wouldn't have known her if I'd fallen over her. My mother sent Christmas cards with pictures of two vapidly pretty blond girls that I consigned to the wastebasket after one brief glance. I didn't need to be reminded that my mother had left me without a moment's regret, apparently, but was a loving mom to these girls.

Reaching for my cell phone, I fled for the stairwell, where I could be assured at least a modicum of privacy. But neither my mother nor her husband, Warren, answered their phone. Probably, I thought angrily, they were screening to block out any call from me.

Holy fuck. *Holy shit.* What was I going to *do*?

My mother detested foreign travel, after those years trailing my father all around the globe. It was possible that Kali had never even been out of the country before. The girl must be around sixteen or seventeen.

What would happen if I just didn't show up at the airport?

But I couldn't forget when IDC forced me to see a psychiatrist after Chechnya, for the first of what were supposed to be weekly meetings. She told me, after all of eighteen minutes, that I had abandonment and trust issues. No shit, Sherlock. In the two years since then, I had never gone to another "weekly" session.

So I wasn't about to abandon this teenage girl at an airport in a strange country.

Disbelief had turned to rage by the time I threw myself into a seat on the Heathrow Express train. I stabbed viciously at the keys of my cell phone, but it was clear that no one in California had any intention of taking my calls. I emailed my mother one sentence—*I'm putting her on the first plane back to California*—but got no response.

I reread my mother's message for the tenth time. Kali wasn't my "sister"; she was my stepsister. No real relation. Just because my mother had been idiotic enough to take on her second husband's twin daughters didn't mean I had any responsibility to them.

I was definitely putting her on the first bloody flight back to America.

Tensely, obsessively, I twisted my hair around my fingers until the train arrived at Heathrow. Then I hurried through the crowds to Arrivals and watched for an anonymous blond surfer girl. I twisted my hair into tight coils and registered dimly the beginnings of a blinding headache.

I was punching the numbers on my cell phone one more time when I got my third unpleasant surprise of the day. A girl tapped me on the shoulder and said, "Hey, Sis! Remember me?" and I swung around to see someone quite different than the Barbie doll I recalled.

Kali—or so I supposed it must be—had transformed into a lank-haired, stoop-shouldered specimen of the worst in teenage American taste. Her hair hung in greasy, dull brown strands around a once bland face that was now pebbled with piercings. The one in her eyebrow appeared to be a little infected, I noted, but the one in her lip seemed the most painful. I winced just to look at it. Her eyes were still blue, of course, but she looked wary, like a cornered animal, not like the sunny child I so vaguely recalled.

What on earth had happened to this girl?

"Kali?" I said doubtfully, half hoping to be wrong.

When she nodded, her eyes shied away from mine. "Look, I didn't want to come here any more than you want to have me. Just put me on a plane. Anywhere."

I couldn't stop staring.

She indicated the ratty backpack at her feet. "This is all I brought. I'd really like to go to Thailand. They have amazing dope there. If you'll just whip out the plastic, I'll be on my way."

Words failed me. Kali still avoided my eyes and twisted her fingers in her already knotted hair, making the tangles even worse. I winced again, this time almost in sympathy. We had no genetic relationship whatsoever, but we shared the same nervous tic. It must be my mother's influence.

"Come on," I said shortly. "Let's get you something to eat and figure out what to do."

Kali blinked at me. "You don't want me here."

"I certainly don't," I agreed. Shock had made me blunt, and I regretted the words as soon as I said them. I was painfully familiar with the sensation of being a stranger in a strange land. It was the story of my life, from Chechnya to Atlantic Bank; perhaps it was even why I spent my Sundays with the Syrian teenagers. How could I be so unwelcoming to this broken girl?

And yet how could I let her into my life?

Unexpectedly, Kali's heavily made-up eyes glittered with tears. "Your mother—Evelyn—must have told you what a screw-up I am." She brushed impatiently at her face and grimaced as she accidentally touched the eyebrow ring.

The sense of almost sympathy was growing, but I fought it grimly.

"Well, not exactly . . ."

"She doesn't know the half of it," Kali said, defiant again. "I'm much worse than they even think I am."

I swallowed hard. Two things were becoming clear to me: I couldn't send this broken girl back to California, and I certainly couldn't set her loose on the world with her grimy backpack and taste for "amazing dope."

I might have to keep her. At least for a day or so.

I picked up her backpack, my decision made. "Kali," I said,

"if you're going to stay with me, there are some things we need to get straight."

We talked and negotiated and talked some more. She drove a hard deal, but in the end we reached a mutually satisfactory agreement. She would sleep on my couch and not bother me any more than was humanly possible, and I would pay her a hundred pounds per week to behave. If I saw any signs of drug use—and I assured her I knew all the signs—then she was on a plane back to California.

Still, I worried. I lay awake in my bed almost all night, listening as she tossed and turned, until she got up at about 3:00 a.m. to make herself some coffee. My thoughts raced. What could I do with her? Was it safe to leave her alone in my flat? Was it safe to give her cash? How serious was her taste for drugs?

I hated having someone in my space, and I hated even more the feeling of being responsible for another soul. An outsider at work, with no family ties, even an outsider from my old IDC gang, I had lived for the past fifteen years, since my father's death, essentially relationship-free. Freedom, as Janis Joplin had told us, was nothing left to lose.

And here I was, saddled with a sullen, defiant, lost teenager.

When I stumbled out of bed on Wednesday morning, I had settled nothing in my head. Kali was asleep, so I left her detailed instructions on taking the tube to my office and set off, welcoming the solitude as I hurried to the tube.

Of course, as soon as I turned on my computer, the lunch with Leo popped up. I sighed loudly. How much worse could this week get? But then I reconsidered. Maybe this would be an almost welcome distraction from my assorted worries. After a moment's thought, I texted Kali and invited/ordered her to join us for lunch, figuring that would keep her out of trouble, for an hour or so, anyway. Besides, Leo would have to behave in front of her, and it would be easier to hold him at arm's length with someone else there.

When I closed my computer and put on a light jacket just before noon, Matt B. said, "Going out to lunch *again*, Amy?"

The tiny and stick-thin Audrey said complacently, patting her flat abdomen, "I'm never hungry at lunchtime."

My stomach growled, startling us both.

Audrey half smiled kindly; a pathetic soul like me was to be pitied, not scolded.

Somewhat to my surprise, Kali was waiting exactly where I had told her to wait in the lobby of my building. The buttoned-down bankers cast curious and slightly hostile glances her way—she was an unwelcome interloper in their staid world—and her mouth had settled into a defiant twist.

Leo pushed himself off the wall across the lobby where he'd been leaning and sauntered over. "Who's this, then?" he asked.

"This is my stepsister from California, Kali. Kali, this is my . . . my acquaintance Leo."

Leo smiled at her. "What's your name, again?"

"Kali."

"And what's your sister's name?"

"Kelley."

Leo was momentarily taken aback, then rallied. "I mean this sister," he said.

Asshole, I thought. Did he still think I was his Juliette?

"Amy," she said, sounding surprised. "And she's not my sister. She's my stepsister. We're not really related."

Amen to that, I thought.

"Ah," he said. "Well, then. I get two lovely ladies for the price of one. *On y va, mes amies.*"

Kali looked at me with some confusion.

"Never mind," I said wearily.

But by the time our food arrived, my annoyance at Leo for the "What's your sister's name?" question had eased. He was pleasant in an avuncular way to poor Kali, and he was about to absorb a heavy blow. So I smiled at him when he came back with our second round of beers, and lifted my glass in a toast.

"To Lady Mary Seymour," I suggested.

"To Lady Mary Seymour," Leo echoed. As he had when I'd told him about my father, he bowed his head for a moment and murmured some words in Hebrew. The show of piety surprised me, and I cleared my throat.

"Who's Lady Mary Seymour?" Kali asked.

Leo, clearly delighted at the chance to introduce a neophyte to the wondrous world of Tudor queens, opened his mouth.

But I interrupted. "Leo, I have some bad news for you." As quickly as I could, I told him about the website and the epitaph and the baby's death. "I'm sorry," I added awkwardly at the end.

To my surprise, he burst out laughing, in such an infectious way that I felt my lips twitching upward as well, and even Kali almost smiled. "I don't understand. What's the joke?"

"You," he chortled. "You looked like you were going to tell me the Beatles were splitting up and Elvis was dead and Donald Trump was going to be president for life, all on the same day. My dear girl, Lady Mary Seymour is most certainly dead."

A little affronted—why had I bothered trying to spare his feelings?—I sniffed, "Well, I thought you would be upset to learn that she died in infancy and that there's no long-lost heir after all. Excuse me for caring."

He chuckled again and then put a comforting hand on mine. "Thank you, *motek*."

I stood abruptly, so abruptly that my chair scraped roughly against the stone floor. "Excuse me. I have to go to the loo."

Kali, whose eyes had been following our conversation like those of a spectator at a tennis match, stood up too. I could see that she was full of questions for me, and I braced myself.

"It's downstairs," he said.

I was still annoyed as we went down the narrow, winding stairwell into an even narrower, darker basement hallway. Typical of small pubs, the loo was a tiny, unventilated closet lit by one unenthusiastic thirty-watt bulb. I took the time to wash my hands and then opened the door again so that Kali could go in.

Suddenly the hallway light sputtered out, and in the same moment Kali let out a terrified shriek as she tumbled to the floor. Hard hands grasped me—the same hard hands that had flung Kali aside—and threw me back against the wall. A dark shape loomed huge as a man's body pressed against mine. I opened my mouth to shout, but his hand was across my mouth in an instant. I gasped for breath, my hand flying involuntarily to my waist, where my cell phone was clipped. Out of the corner of my eye, I saw Kali curled in a fetal position on the stone floor, her hands over her head in a desperate attempt to protect herself.

I braced myself for a blow, poised to take advantage of any opportunity to go on the offensive. But it never came. Instead, his tone low, whispery, and menacing, filled with sheer wrath, the man commanded, "You stay out of this, you hear? Stay out of it!" Furiously, my mind flitted through various options—kick, twist, strike—but I found myself stymied as much by Kali's presence as by the suddenness of the attack. I was consumed with anger and overwhelmed with rage but also an unaccustomed terror—terror for that panicked, helpless child on the floor. Pinned between the assailant's great bulk and the sweating wall, I struggled grimly in silence, but he had the advantage of size and weight and muscle.

Plus, there was Kali. Her presence and her vulnerability unmanned me, if that was the right word. My own vulnerability infuriated me. I heard my father's voice in my ear: *Fear is for cowards.* I gathered my strength for a vicious kick, not caring what Kali might think.

Chapter 10

And then, suddenly, the overhead light snapped back on, and I saw Leo's tall frame silhouetted against the dark stairwell, his eyes taking in the scene in one glance. His hand shot involuntarily to his waist too, and he moved forward slowly; I recalled his military training and unclenched my fists.

"What's all this, then?" he asked calmly.

The man threw me toward Leo. I staggered and would have fallen had Leo not reached out to steady me. I heard my attacker's footsteps receding into the blackness behind me and saw Leo's eyes narrow in calculation. I knew, without a word being spoken, that he wanted to abandon his burden—me—and go off in hot pursuit. Just as I wanted to abandon my burden—Kali—and join him. But common sense prevailed, and he drew me against him in a bear hug instead. I forced myself to go limp against him, trying hard to be a damsel in distress. Then he bent to lift Kali off the floor and held her in a tight embrace too. She started to cry.

"What the hell happened here?" he asked me.

I put an arm around Kali, pretending to swipe away tears on my own face. "He pushed her down and grabbed me," I said, angry at the shakiness of my voice. "He told me to 'stay out of this'—whatever that means—and then you . . ." At the mention of Leo's fortuitous appearance, I let my voice falter. Kali's sobs grew louder.

He sighed, and I remembered his four sisters. He must be a champion at dealing with sobbing women. Sure enough, he gathered us both into his arms. "There, there," he murmured. "It's all right, *motek*. It's okay now."

Forgetting my damsel-in-distress act, I drew away again and smacked him lightly on the arm. "I'm fine," I said.

Leo's face cleared, and he smiled at me. "And she's back," he said, sounding relieved.

Kali glared at me. "Don't be mean to him," she said.

As I spooned up my soup—nothing like a good scare to send the appetite surging—I eyed Leo thoughtfully. Keep out of what, exactly? Leo and his Queen Katherine Parr obsession? Preposterous. Sheikh Abdullah and his financial affairs? Hmm.

But then why had Leo automatically reached for a gun when he saw me struggling with the man?

Kali chattered nonstop—apparently, fear loosened her tongue, just as adrenaline quick-started my appetite—and treated us to an endless soliloquy on stupid college applications ("I'm too dumb to get into a good school, and who cares anyway?") and the stupid school that had kicked her out ("I was only selling weed to high school kids; it's not as if I was forcing heroin on kindergartners") and, of course, her new hero: Leo. "Wasn't he wonderful?" she asked me, suddenly looking like that sunny child again for one brief moment.

Leo grinned and encouraged her while I listened absently, too caught up in my own thoughts to pay much attention.

Once again, my father's voice echoed in my head. We had been preparing for a rock climb in the Haut Atlas region of Morocco; the climb was highly rated for difficulty, and I was frightened, looking up at the unyielding crags and terrifyingly steep ascent my father intended. "I don't think I want to try this," I said, starting to undo my roping.

"Fear is for cowards," my father said dismissively. "Now, do you want to go, and should I find myself a braver companion?"

I went.

I was twelve years old at the time.

So, in the end, I never found out why Leo had thought my story of Baby Mary's tragic death so amusing. He promised to put Kali in an Uber back to the flat, and I returned to my office in a daze of exhaustion. I knew this feeling from my years of adventuring with my father: A rush of adrenaline was always followed by an urgent desire for food and sustenance and then an equally urgent desire for sleep. I was in the sleep phase now.

I staggered through the remainder of the day and Ubered home, too tired for the tube and a little uneasy about the thought of being pressed up against all those strangers' bodies. Kali was there but had sunk back into a sullen silence, for which I could be only grateful. I fell into a deep sleep on my bed without even taking my shoes off, only to be awakened a few hours later by the chirp of my cell phone.

"Amy here," I said groggily.

"'Amy here'? Is that how you always answer the phone?" Leo.

"No, I . . ." I sat up and tried to brush some sleep from my eyes. "How did you get this number?"

He ignored that, of course. "Did he have an accent?"

"Did . . . what?"

"Your attacker. Did he have an accent?"

"Yes," I said slowly, thinking back. "Yes, he did."

"Middle Eastern? Mediterranean?"

"No. Russian, I think."

"Russian?" Leo sounded surprised. "Are you sure?"

"Of course I'm sure, Leo. I lived in the bloody country for five bloody years."

"Huh."

"Is that what you woke me up for?" I asked, annoyed now.

"No, of course not," he said.

Pause.

I said, with exaggerated politeness, "Then may I ask what the purpose of your call is?"

"Oh. Right." Now he sounded distracted. "I called to tell you why I . . . well, never mind that now. See you around, all right?"

And he hung up.

"Was that Leo?" Kali sounded animated again for the first time since lunch. "I wanted to talk to him and thank him again."

"Go to sleep," I said, and put the pillow over my head.

Chapter 11

"Catherine Willoughby, Duchess of Suffolk," I Googled.

It was the next day, and to quiet the butterflies in my stomach, I was killing time at work before our meeting with Sheikh Abdullah's sons. And I was curious. If the Duchess had been Katherine Parr's bestie, so much so that she took in the baby after Tom Seymour's death, then why had she let the poor infant die so quickly and, apparently, anonymously? Babies died all the time back then, of course, but still . . .

Catherine Willoughby, as Leo would say, was an interesting woman. I wondered if he had a crush on her as well; he seemed enamored of all the Tudor women. Perhaps he cried out the names of long-dead queens when he was making love.

With effort, I went back to Catherine Willoughby. She became one of the wealthiest heiresses of her generation at age seven, when her father died. Two years later, the King's brother-in-law Charles Brandon, Duke of Suffolk, purchased her wardship from the King and became her legal guardian. There were rumors that Brandon planned to marry her off to his ten-year-old son, but then Brandon's wife (the sister of Henry VIII) died, and Catherine's glittering fortune—and perhaps the witty, high-spirited Catherine as well—became an irresistible temptation to Brandon himself.

Just six weeks after his wife's death, the forty-nine-year-old Brandon married the fourteen-year-old Catherine. By all accounts, the marriage was successful. She bore him two sons, and the union made Suffolk one of the greatest magnates in all of England. Catherine, who was known for her sharp tongue and even sharper intelligence, was a youthful and stimulating companion for the clever Brandon in his later years.

She and Katherine Parr became very close friends, bonding in part over their shared dedication to religious reformation, and she was frequently at court. In fact, when Brandon died in August 1545, the fickle King was alleged to be considering Catherine—still in her midtwenties and quite attractive—for the dubious position of his seventh wife. (He was annoyed with Katherine Parr at the time.)

So it was not surprising that she was made guardian of Baby Mary upon Tom Seymour's death. What did surprise me, though, was her strong and very public resentment of the child—which seemed quite miserly for such a wealthy and cultured woman. As the Queen's daughter, Lady Mary required a household of her own, including a governess, rockers, a wet nurse, laundresses, and various other assorted servants. But no money accompanied the child to pay for these heavy expenses. The Crown had seized Tom's holdings upon his execution, and the Duchess complained bitterly to anyone who would listen.

The Lord Protector Edward Seymour, Mary's uncle and bitter enemy of her late but unlamented father, showed no interest whatsoever in funding his niece's upkeep. Eventually the Duchess appealed to William Cecil, then a prominent courtier, and he intervened on her behalf. Reading her letter to Cecil, I was struck by her cold references to "the Queen's child," as she called poor Mary, and by her obvious resentment of the little girl, which infused the entire missive.

Why, I wondered, had she been so bitter about the burden of one orphaned baby? As the mother of boys and the best friend of the child's mother, shouldn't she have felt some warmth toward the tiny girl? And she was one of the wealthiest women in the realm. Couldn't she have paid Lady Mary's expenses out of her petty cash if she wanted?

It all struck a discordant note, and I found myself eager to get Leo's take on the matter.

In fact, I was eager to see Leo again, period. And that struck a discordant note too. My last job review at IDC had described me as "hard, heedless, suspicious," and even though I had submerged that personality in Amy the banker, I had already recognized Leo for what he was: an easy, self-assured charmer hiding behind a mask of Hugh Grant–ish Britishism.

But still, I wondered about the lost baby.

"Amy," Kristen R. said, and I started, quickly closing my computer. "Kareem and Nasir are on their way up. Can you get everyone some coffee, please?"

Bitch, I thought automatically. But I nodded meekly as I gathered the coffee cups and made my way into the conference room.

The men stood when I entered the room, and I smiled at them.

"It's a pleasure to meet you," I said hopefully. "I've really enjoyed working with your father over the last two—"

"Amy, please put the coffee down so we can get started," Audrey interrupted.

The men remained standing until I seated myself, and I was pleased by this touch of courtesy. Maybe it wouldn't be so bad after all.

Kareem, the older brother, began with a long litany of pleasantries. They were so pleased to meet us. We had performed so many services for the family for so many years. We had shown our loyalty in so many ways. . . .

Accustomed to florid Arabic oratorical style from my time in Riyadh and Amman with my father, I listened patiently and waited for my turn. But when Kareem finished, Audrey quelled me with a warning look and began her own little speech.

Audrey was calculating and selective with her considerable personal charm, but when she turned it on, there was no escaping its brilliance. The al-Saud family were our most valued (and valuable, I thought cynically) clients. We held them in the highest esteem, blah blah blah. She failed to mention that this particular sheikh was a very minor family member, of course—which was why I had inherited him.

Nasir, the younger brother, said not a word. Both men wore conservative, Western-style business suits, beautifully cut and fitted, with Hermès ties and what I judged to be thousand-dollar shoes. Maybe multithousand-dollar shoes—I was no expert. As Kareem stretched out a hand to take the coffee, I noticed that his nails were perfectly buffed and manicured. I hid my own uneven, uncolored nails in my lap.

I turned my mind back to the conversation. Kareem appeared to be, at last, leading up to actually saying something. "These developments are, of course, trivial." He waved a hand dismissively. "We have nothing to hide."

"Of course not," Audrey murmured, and Kristen nodded in agreement. Nobody looked at me, so I didn't bother nodding.

"But we have enemies in the kingdom," he went on. "And in America too. The godless among you do not have the grace of Allah."

Audrey's smile froze momentarily, too fleeting for the men to notice.

Now we're getting to it, I thought.

"We appreciate your discretion," Kareem concluded. "Indeed, your value to us lies in your discretion." He sat back, as if some very important message had been delivered, and took an appreciative sip of coffee.

An uncomprehending glance flew between Audrey and Kristen.

I understood exactly what he meant, and was thinking furiously when Kareem turned to me. "Ms. Schumann, you of course have been my father's most trusted emissary. We are especially grateful for your discretion."

Uh-oh. We were in London, where Swiss-style banking secrecy laws did not apply. If the FBI wanted information, I was pretty sure we had to give it to them. Surely Kareem knew this.

"Yes, of course," I said, sounding shy even to my own ears. "I am afraid, though, Sheikh Kareem, that if the FBI issues subpoenas—"

Both Audrey and Kristen cut in simultaneously.

"You can count on us," Audrey said.

"You don't have to worry about anything," Kristen said.

His dark eyes rested on me for a moment. "We are tender among ourselves and our family," he said slowly. His very British English was flavored with an undercurrent of Middle Eastern intonation, like Leo's, but it had a very different effect on me. I had heard similar statements from Arab men before. They were usually followed by a chilling commentary on what happened to those who violated their circle of trust.

Now he fell silent, obviously calculating that I knew where he was going, and I nodded my head in submission. Message received.

But Audrey, cheerful and completely oblivious, said, "You're in good hands with us, sir. Kristen Rivers and I will be handling this matter personally, and she has a source at the FBI. Why don't you fill us in on that conversation, Kristen?"

Kristen's expression was the perfect combination of concern and reassurance. Today she had captured her shining blond hair, which she usually wore down, into a modest bun at the back of her head and had on a knee-length dress with Puritan-style collar and sleeves. She always knew exactly how to dress for the occasion.

"I went to school with one of the FBI folks, and he says the investigation is in its early days. He thinks that—"

"And he will make it all go away?" Kareem interrupted.

"Not exactly," Kristen said, exchanging glances with Audrey. "But he tells me—"

Kareem stood up. "Thank you for dealing with this matter. Those who serve the House of Saud—and those who do not—will always receive the appropriate recognition."

I felt a small shiver run down my spine. Again, I understood exactly what he meant. Audrey and Kristen beamed.

Glancing at his brother, who still had not said a word, Kareem added, "I am delighted that we are, as always, in perfect unity. My father will be most grateful for your service."

And most vengeful if we fail, I understood. As they stood over us, I realized that the silent Nasir was almost a head taller and several stones heavier than his older brother. He was built like a tank. *The muscle?* I wondered.

Audrey stood up too. "Sheikh Kareem," she said, "your family are honored and valued partners of Atlantic Bank."

"Indeed," he said. "You will do well to remember that."

And the two men walked out the door.

"Well!" Audrey said, falling back into her chair, all the charm turned off like a light switch. "What a mess you've gotten us into, Amy."

Me? I stared at her indignantly, too gobsmacked to defend myself.

"Kristen, I'd like to socialize some ideas with you and the senior team. Can you ping everyone for a pop-up meeting at five?"

"Sure," Kristen said.

I said cautiously, "I think we need to bring the lawyers in on this. And maybe hire some protection for the office."

"Why?" Kristen asked. "They couldn't have been more pleasant."

"I don't know," I said hesitantly, wishing that I could put aside my mask and shout at my oblivious colleagues: *They were threatening us! We should be afraid! Very afraid!*

"I don't know what meeting you were in," Audrey drawled. "But I didn't hear any threats. Did you, Kristen?"

"I've spent a lot of time in their corner of the world," I said, trying to sound reasonable, instead of infuriated at their blindness. "And I think that was language, coded language, that Arab men use to refer to—"

Audrey cut in, shaking her head. "Honestly, Amy, sometimes I really wonder about you. Kristen, please arrange that team meeting."

They both looked at me.

"It might be best if you didn't attend," Audrey said.

In case they decided to throw me under the bus. I understood that code too. In silence, I walked back to my desk and sat down. I couldn't think of a single thing to do, other than update my Stupid Jargon list with "socialize some ideas" and "pop-up meeting." My favorites so far were "tease that out" and "noodle on that," but "socialize some ideas" was pretty good.

I put my head in my hands. The sheikh, Leo . . . With a pang of special pain, I remembered Kali. How had so much gone wrong in so little time? I knew why I was letting Leo stay in my life, or at least part of the reason. I wanted to know why he was chasing after Jules and why he thought I had anything to do with her. And I knew why I had accepted (very temporarily) the unwanted burden of Kali. I was a screw-up at her age too, and it was only my father's penchant for laughing off my misdeeds as daring adventures that saved me from her fate.

But still, honestly, why me?

Chapter 12

For the next week or so, Kali and I settled into an uneasy truce in my shoebox flat. I assured and reassured the shaken girl that the pub incident was just a random attack, one of those things that happen in big cities, and I gave her a can of Mace, which produced the first smile I had ever seen on her.

Predictably, she slept till noon every day but then set off on self-guided walks around London, armed with nothing more than a map of the tube and the hundred pounds I doled out, per our agreement. She had an uncanny sense of direction, it seemed; one long glance at the complex web of tube lines on the map, and she had it mastered to a degree that I had failed to achieve in my three years in the city.

I wondered. She clearly had some kind of gift. Was she good at math, perhaps? Geometry? But when I asked her, she assured me that while she wasn't as bad at math as she was at English, she was still too dumb for the honors and AP classes that her twin sister flourished in.

Well, we had that in common.

Mercifully, she was even less inclined toward casual conversation than I. So we ate our dinners in near silence, and she spent the rest of the evening buried in her iPhone. I gave her a tube of bacitracin for the infected eyebrow, which she took without comment. There was no sign of drug use at all; I began to wonder if she had ever used drugs, or if that was just part of a persona she had adopted.

Perhaps we had more in common than anyone would have thought.

Although I had dozed through the required psychology class in college, even I recognized the symmetry between Catherine Willoughby's resentment of the orphaned baby who was forced upon her and mine at taking in Kali. But at least Lady Mary was, presumably, an adorable baby, while Kali was a greasy-haired, multipierced teenager with a sullen manner and an iPhone addiction.

I would have to do something with her eventually, but I had no idea what. My mother finally deigned to pick up the phone and told me in no uncertain terms that Kali was not welcome at home. She had been kicked out of her exclusive high school, and they had no intention of taking her back. Warren was on antidepressants, and Kelley could not be distracted from her all-important college applications. Kali was my responsibility now; it was about time I showed some family loyalty.

Leo disagreed, vehemently. He called me the day after the attack in the pub basement to order me to send Kali away to safety. "Aren't you afraid?" he asked when I refused. "Do you really think you should have a child come to stay when you've just been attacked?"

"Maybe it was a random attack," I offered. "It happens."

"It's not a 'random attack' when the attacker is telling you to 'stay out of it,'" he retorted. "And by the way, what exactly was he telling you to stay out of? What have you gotten yourself into?"

"I don't know!" I snapped, angry that it was the truth. If

I knew, then I would know how to keep myself—and, more importantly, Kali—safe.

It couldn't be Sheikh Dull Boy, but Leo was right: It wasn't random.

Was it possible that Leo himself had set me up? He was the only person in the world who knew in advance what pub we would be at, and when.

Unaware of my thoughts, he went on, "Don't you think you have quite enough to do just taking care of yourself right now?"

Absolutely. And that was all I ever had to do. Take care of myself. Being responsible for another, helpless human being was appalling.

So I answered, with some heat, "Jesus, don't you think I know that?"

"Well, then send her away, for God's sake."

But where? And how? Unable to formulate a response, I simply hung up.

At work, I vacillated between irritation and absolute fury. Kristen the Younger, who had a keen sense of status despite her tender age, refused to give me some documents on Sheikh Abdullah that I needed to write my monthly status report. "I'll have to check with Kristen R. on that," she said, giving me a slightly pitying smile. Kristen R., when applied to, explained very sweetly and kindly that those documents were on a need-to-know basis now.

Our Friday-morning meetings always started with an ice-breaker, devised by Audrey. Dimpling, she announced that this week's idea was to have everyone say what was most fun about working at Atlantic Bank.

"I'll start," she said. "The most fun thing for me is working with all my peeps here."

Everyone clapped. I flipped to my Stupid Jargon list at the end of my notebook and added "peeps." Good God, Audrey was even older than I was; did she really think that talking about "peeps" would make her twenty-five again?

Kristen R. thought it was Friday trivia nights at the pub. Matt B. liked Bow Tie Fridays.

Kristen T. loved visiting with her clients in Dubai and Antibes.

Jake M., Kristen P., and Matt S. voted for Field Day, and I flinched at the memory. Last year for Field Day, we had done hot yoga and a marathon barre class led by our own Kristen P. I, who had never taken a ballet or yoga class in my life, was the class clown. My legs tangled hopelessly, and Kristen P. had to rescue me from a too-grand plié that threatened to end in an ungainly tumble. My pirouettes were the stuff of comic legend. Then we feasted on quinoa, sprouts, and a special treat: carob brownies that tasted of nothing other than wallpaper paste. It took me days of fish and chips to erase the bitter flavor from my mouth.

Kristen P., also dimpling, loved Wednesday barre classes with "the girls." I could not imagine anything more boring and pointless than ballet.

When my turn came, the table quieted. Everyone knew I didn't have any fun at work. "Working with the team," I said woodenly.

Pause. I cringed to think how my father would view mousy Amy, how I wished I could be my fearless self again—but I needed to make this job work. And so I needed to be mousy Amy.

Then Audrey said, "Ohhhhkaaay. Let's move on to shout-outs and high fives. A big shout-out to Kristen R. for all her great work on the FBI mess."

More clapping.

Kristen R. smiled. "And a high five to Kristen S."—Kristen the Younger, I interpreted—"for all of her support on that. She's off to a great start here!"

Kristen S. smiled too. "Right back atcha! Big high five to Kristen R. for being such a great mentor!"

I added another check mark next to "mentor" on my Stupid Jargon list and took another sip of Diet Coke. So far, the list included:

- Let's tease that out
- How can we leverage that?
- I teed up the idea
- Do we have bandwidth?
- Let's take a deep dive
- Let's ideate on that
- Granular
- Mentor
- In the weeds
- Ping
- Let me noodle on that
- Do they have skin in the game?
- Let's socialize the idea
- Peeps

Every time I heard one of the phrases, I added another check mark to the list and had to take another sip of my Diet Coke. By the end of our Friday meetings, I was always desperate for the bathroom.

After what seemed like eons, we were finished, and the weekly exercise in self-congratulation came to an end. I took one last look around the table and marveled once again at the young, beautiful faces, slim bodies, and überarticulate self-confidence of my colleagues. How narcissistic was Audrey, exactly, that she hired only mini-mes?

Except for me, of course, and I knew that was all Bob the Bear's doing. Damn him, anyway.

Back at my desk, I composed an urgent email to my friend Rosie.

I know you and Bob said I had to leave IDC and settle down in London, but please, please, Rosie, say I can quit this job! They're killing me.

She wrote back almost immediately:

NO NO NO. We talked about this, remember? Bob said you were taking too many risks out in the field. After that incident in Chechnya, he said you were going to get yourself killed and he couldn't allow you to stay. It's for your own good. And the money's pretty good too, right? Be sensible, for once in your life.

I bit my lip, then typed:

But I survived Chechnya, didn't I? And I wound up doing a lot of really good work there. I'll be more careful, I promise. I'm begging you, Rosie . . .

Again, her response was immediate and unequivocal:

NO NO NO!

I was aching to get away. Being mousy Amy at Atlantic Bank was doing my head in, as the Brits would say. All my life, I had reveled in the freedom of hopping on a boat or a train or a plane to some new place, some new challenge, whenever the impulse struck. My father and I had once jetted off on an hour's notice to Hawaii, where he had heard that fifty-foot surfing waves were developing off the coast. Years later, after three weeks working in postearthquake Nepal, I disappeared myself to a mist-shrouded mountain resort in Bhutan, trekking alone higher and higher into the hills to lose my memories in a simple exercise for survival.

But I was trapped now. I didn't want to take Kali on what I wanted desperately to be a solo adventure, and I couldn't leave her behind.

Still, I couldn't send her on her way either. I too had been despaired of (at long distance, thankfully) by my mother. I too had been an indifferent student who mastered the art of doing just barely enough work to scrape out a B minus, which was perfectly fine with my father. I drank too much, partied too much, took too many risks, both with my father and without him. For my sixteenth birthday, when we were living in Amman, I went skydiving with my father in a rattletrap old DC-6 that should have been mothballed years before. It struggled so mightily to get airborne that my father suggested we stick our legs through the fuselage and pedal.

That night, he went out with his lady friend of the moment while I snuck into the hotel suite some friends had taken over so we could drink bootleg alcohol. Sunday afternoon was for my father again, when we nursed our hangovers and sampled Asian delicacies such as bat soup and fried tarantulas, washed down with snake and scorpion wine.

No wonder I slept through English Lit on Monday morning.

Then, of course, everything changed with my father's death, at the beginning of my sophomore year at UCLA. Overnight,

I transformed myself into the most conscientious student on campus. I changed my major to Russian studies and developed my casual knowledge of the language into near fluency; I stayed up all night studying rather than partying; and I shot straight into the high-stress, high-stakes career that I had chosen. While my former classmates were partying in Silicon Valley, I was getting dysentery in Myanmar; while they were minting money at Goldman Sachs, I was running from terrorists in Chechnya. My lighthearted college pals disappeared from my life as I formed the deepest bonds of my life (post-Dad) with my IDC workmates. We were making the world a better place.

So Kali stayed. I would have to do something with her eventually, but I had no idea what.

Chapter 13

At the Friday meeting two weeks after Kali's arrival, Audrey decreed that the icebreaker would be fun facts, and that we should each tell one about ourselves.

Kristen R.: "I'm an identical twin. I have a sister who looks *just like me!*" The other Kristens squealed. I thought, *Another Kristen in the world? God help us all.*

Jake S., who was the scion of a great New York Jewish dynasty that had built half the museums and synagogues in the city: "My grandfather speaks only Yiddish." Everyone shrieked with laughter.

Kristen the Younger, dimpling: "I absolutely *idolize* Kristen R. I want to be her when I grow up!" Big hugs all around.

Audrey, also dimpling: "I love you guys! I'd rather be with my peeps here than with my fam!" More hugs.

Matt B.: "I once ate a fried beetle." More shrieks. I thought of eating tuna eyeballs and bird's-nest soup with my father and smiled to myself.

Me, after much thought: "I really like London cabbies. They usually speak English."

Embarrassed silence for poor, boring old Amy.

I amused myself thinking about how they would react if I

told a real fun fact: I climbed to Everest Base Camp for my twelfth birthday. Or: I got buried by an avalanche when I was skiing off-piste with my father in Switzerland. Or perhaps: I was in Aleppo when Assad's forces bombed it to smithereens.

Again I thought about begging Bob to take me back but knew he wouldn't. Only he, Rosie, and I knew I hadn't left IDC willingly. I had left at Bob's insistence, and he had wangled me the job at Atlantic. And now I couldn't think what else to do. I wasn't independently wealthy, was notably lacking in a whole lot of marketable skills, and had an odd résumé. I couldn't screw up this job too.

That afternoon, as my colleagues bantered and squealed about their weekend plans, it occurred to me that there had been no Leo sightings since our lunch at the pub. Kali had asked after him several times, her hero worship obvious, and I found myself angry with him for inspiring such devotion and then abandoning poor Kali.

Besides, there was the whole Jules thing.

So I texted him.

Where have you been? Have you given up on finding Jules?

Paris, and no.

Kali misses you. I realized that he might take this as flirtatious, but it was too late—I had already pressed SEND.

I miss her too. You up for an outing Saturday? Sudeley Castle?

Why? What's there?

It's KP's home.

A spark of interest flared. It would be fun to see Katherine Parr's home, especially in Leo's company. It wasn't the getaway I yearned for, but it was certainly a diversion.

OK, I texted back.

Kali would be delighted, I told myself.

Kali whistled with admiration when Leo pulled up in his smart Audi.

"Why were you in Paris?" I asked him, realizing how little I knew about his life beyond his obsession with Tudor queens and a woman named Jules. And that he had seemed to be reaching for a gun in the pub basement.

I hadn't had a lover in two years, and this seemed possibly long enough for me to have gotten over my PTSD—or whatever it was that had gripped me since Chechnya. Maybe Leo would do. He seemed like a man who would know what he was doing—an absolute must in a lover—but not a threat in any way.

Or was he?

Then again, it wouldn't be a bad idea to get to know him a little better—and to figure out why he had connected me to the long-lost ancestress of a queen.

Now that I was considering him as a potential bed partner, I scrutinized him more closely as he, with an apology, rolled down the windows. He wore khakis that might have fit him well a thousand washings ago but now hung limp and creaseless on his tall frame. His button-down shirt was rolled up to the elbows, revealing surprisingly muscular forearms (plus), but the ancient shirt had also been washed out to a rather nauseating shade of brown (minus).

Still undecided, I waited with interest for his answer.

"I was there for business . . . and family."

"Oh, right, you have two sisters living in Paris."

Kali leaned forward. "You have two sisters?"

He half turned to smile at her. "Four, actually."

"No shit."

I sent Kali a warning glance, and, surprisingly, she closed her mouth.

"What kind of business?" I persisted.

He hesitated. "Um . . . family business."

His hesitations and stammers seemed to come and go, I reflected. Maybe it was all an act.

"What kind of family business?"

"Uh, why do you want to know?"

"Why don't you want to tell me?"

"*Sacrebleu*," he said. "This is a side of you I've never seen before."

I smiled sweetly at him, enjoying his discomfort. It wasn't easy to discomfit Leo.

"My stepmother—Evelyn, I mean—said Amy was always asking questions," Kali volunteered. "It drove her crazy."

This time, my look at Kali held pure poison, but she went on, undeterred. "Evelyn said Amy was her father's daughter, and he was a nut case."

"He was not!"

"Was too. Evelyn said he was constantly putting you in dangerous situations, and she could only pray you didn't take after him—"

"It would be an honor to take after him! My father was a . . ." I stuttered, my tongue twisted with anger at her sacrilege. "You didn't even know my father! He was a hero! He was the best father I could have had! He took me on adventures; he was my best friend; we . . ."

Leo cleared his throat. "My family is in the art business," he said.

I had almost forgotten he was there; it took a moment to compose myself. "So why is that such a deep, dark secret?" I asked him.

"It's not a deep, dark secret!"

"Then why are you being so dodgy about it?"

He heaved a great sigh. "I'm not being dodgy. I'm the only one who's not in the family business, and it's complicated."

I thought about that for a minute. I had followed my father, the international consultant, into the "family business," just as he would have wished. "What kind of art business?"

"We own galleries."

"Where?"

"Paris. Other places."

"Do I have to drag every detail out of you?" I demanded.

"Oh, for . . . Look. My family specializes in dealing nineteenth- and early twentieth-century European art. A lot of impressionists and postimpressionists."

"Wow," I said. This was not what I had expected. But then it was no more unexpected that he would love candy-pink Renoirs than that he would yearn for long-dead queens, I supposed.

"Ooh, could you take us to Paris?" Kali squealed, suddenly sounding like a very normal, unpierced teenage girl.

Her enthusiasm loosened Leo's tongue. He went on, almost loquacious now: "My great-grandparents were art dealers in Paris and Avignon before the war. Thanks to a fortuitous combination of paranoia and wealth, they managed to escape with most of their fortune intact before the Nazis arrived—first to Switzerland, then, underwhelmed by the dubious hospitality of the Swiss, to Israel. After the war, my grandfather moved back to reestablish the business in Paris, and his brother remained in Tel Aviv. My family became experts in helping to find and restore looted art to Holocaust survivors. We now have businesses in Paris, Tel Aviv, New York, and Antibes. Satisfied?"

Oh my God! Leo was rich! Seriously rich! How had I not realized that earlier? I don't know why I was so surprised, given the American prep school, the worldliness, his air of ease anywhere and everywhere.

But he was an Oxford don too, not just another trust-fund baby like the Kristens and the Matts.

My silence must have telegraphed something to Leo, for he slanted a look down at me and arched an eyebrow. "Disappointed, *motek*? See, this is why you shouldn't ask questions."

Still I said nothing, and he shrugged.

Kali seemed to share my surprise. "So, you're one of *them*," she said accusingly.

"Who?" Leo inquired.

She exchanged glances with me.

"Never mind," we said in unison, and Kali settled back to pout into her iPhone.

But the ride was interrupted almost immediately by the discreet ring of Leo's cell phone, which was hooked into the dashboard. "Léo *ici*," he said, with a glance at me. "Rachel, Rachel, *pas si vite. Plus lentement, je vous en prie.*"

Kali leaned forward, her ears almost twitching in her eagerness to hear, and I wondered if she had studied French in school.

Leo must have wondered the same thing; in an instant, he switched to Hebrew. Because the phone was on speaker, we could both hear the agitated woman's voice on the other end and Leo's calming, placating tones. Finally, they hung up. He scowled, pressing some numbers on his cell phone, and a male voice answered. Leo addressed him in Hebrew too. They spoke briefly; then Leo disconnected to answer another angry woman's call.

I raised my eyebrows. When he disconnected from the second woman, I said to him, "Romantic troubles? Angry husband calling?"

He looked annoyed. "I wish," he said. "My sisters are having an argument, and they expect me to mediate. As always."

I considered, realizing that it was easy to see him in the role of all-knowing big brother. Then his phone rang again, and Leo, looking exasperated, picked up the call. To me, he said, "God gave the plague to Pharaoh and sisters to me."

My first view of Sudeley Castle was an enchantment. The sprawling edifice of richly mellowed Cotswold stone, set in lush gardens of still-blooming flowers and greenery, was exactly what I would have designed for myself if I could have. As we drew closer, I was charmed to see fawns scattered about the grounds, cocking an inquisitive ear as our car drove by, and even a few peacocks strutting about, displaying full, glorious plumage. The sky was a particularly soft shade of pale blue, with just a few clouds scudding overhead.

I sighed to myself in sheer pleasure.

Leo smiled at me. "Can't you just see her?" he asked.

"Who?"

"Katherine, of course. She loved this place. She would walk with her ladies in the gardens for hours every day, discussing religion and politics and flowers and falconry, always dressed in her finest robes. . . ." His voice drifted off dreamily, and Kali rolled her eyes at me. But it was a friendly eye roll, and I grinned back at her, our argument forgotten in mutual amusement.

"Anyway," Leo said, clearing his throat, "I have a special treat in store for you: We have been granted permission to access the library here, so I hope you're prepared for some dusty research."

Kali's face fell, and I couldn't blame her. Why spend the day in a dusty library when we could wander the beautiful grounds, walk in Katherine's own footsteps among her beloved gardens?

But the library was magnificent too, every wall a masterpiece of floor-to-ceiling books, with a handsome rolling ladder to access the very highest shelves. A wide gallery ran along the top of the room, with more books and a collection of red velvet chairs for comfortable reading. Kali stared in wonder, her phone relegated to her jeans pocket, for once.

I wasn't one drawn to old books—unlike Leo, apparently, who seemed starstruck at the sight of a dusty, moldering volume under glass in the middle of the room. But even I fell under the spell of the great room's classic grandeur. Kali reached out a hesitant hand toward a brightly colored book, and Leo woke from his reverie to snap at her, "Don't touch anything! Wait till they bring us the museum gloves."

She shrank back, and I gave Leo an accusing glare.

"Sorry," he said. "These books are very fragile."

The curator scurried in with three pairs of museum gloves and a box of assorted equipment that looked like a medicine kit to me. Leo took it and nodded his thanks. We sat around a plebeian modern table in the corner, and the curator started bringing us boxes.

"These are the Katherine files," Leo deigned to explain.

Kali, having donned her gloves, pronounced the boxes boring and got up to explore. "What's in these cabinets?" she asked, opening one at random.

"Miscellaneous materials," Leo said briefly. "Odd donations that they've received but haven't bothered to file. Nothing of interest to us."

Kali, apparently, was drawn to the miscellaneous. She sat down cross-legged on the floor and began sifting through the (very dusty) papers.

I started reading through Katherine's correspondence with her husband, Tom, and was immediately charmed. In June 1548, she wrote to him:

I gave your little knave your blessing, who like an honest man stirred apace and before.

"Oh, Leo," I cried. "She's pregnant and can feel the baby move!"

For Mary Odell being abed with me had laid her hand upon my belly to feel it stir. It hath stirred these three days every morning and evening so that I trust when ye come it will make you some pastime.

I was not a woman to go googly-eyed over babies, but for just a moment, in her own library, in her own castle, I could picture the dignified queen dowager, married for love at the ancient age of thirty-five and pregnant with her beloved's child. The child that would become Lady Mary, I remembered. Poor little orphaned baby.

I bent my head to the letters again.

Here was Tom's reply:

I do desire your highness to keep the little knave so lean and gaunt with your good diet and walking, that he may be so small that he may creep out of a mousehole.

"They were worried about childbirth," I told Leo, looking up at him.

"With good reason," he responded. "About one in three women died during her childbearing years, and at her age . . ." He sighed.

I sighed too. Poor baby. Poor Katherine.

Leo opened another box and reached carefully inside to pull out a few very odd-looking objects sealed in some sort of plastic.

"These were found in her chest of personal belongings after her death," he told me. "These are cramp rings." He held up two small circlets of dull metal. "For use against the pains of childbirth—"

"Did that work?" Kali asked, her eyes round. I hadn't thought she was following our conversation.

"One would doubt it," Leo said. "And here are three pieces of unicorn horn, a remedy for stomach pains."

Both Kali and I looked at the three tiny shards of what looked like petrified wood.

"If you say so," she said, returning to her papers.

"Katherine spent her last three months at Sudeley, preparing for her confinement," Leo explained. "She and Tom were excited about the baby. The account books show that she decorated the nursery, which overlooked the gardens and chapel, with crimson and gold velvet and taffeta. She bought furniture and china, as if preparing for a royal birth rather than the child of a mere baron."

"How sweet," Kali said. I wasn't sure if she was being sarcastic or not.

"Then there's this," Leo said, holding up another, plastic-encased object: an old, heavy, ornate ring with a reddish gem encircled by tiny seed pearls.

Kali commented, "Yuck. I could buy that for fifty cents at a yard sale."

Leo laughed. "Not this ring, my girl. This is a ring that Tom gave to Katherine, and it's inscribed, 'What I have I hold.'"

Even Kali couldn't think of a thing to say. She took the ring from Tom and turned it over, wonderingly.

"And Tom spent one thousand pounds having the confinement rooms prepared for her," Leo added.

"Wasn't he playing around with Princess Elizabeth at the same time?" I asked, proud to show off my internet-gained knowledge.

"Oh, yes," Leo said. "Right in these rooms and gardens here. Right under Katherine's eye. After he was caught going to her room early in the morning and pretending to tickle her while she was still in bed, Katherine sent her away."

"What a perv," Kali said.

"No doubt," Leo agreed. "Elizabeth was younger than you at the time."

Kali scowled. Suddenly she said, "I thought you told me the baby—Lady Mary—died when she was an infant."

"She did," I said, and Leo looked pained.

"She may not have," he said.

"Well, then whose is this?" Kali asked, holding up what appeared to be a small psalm book.

Leo took it and opened it to its gaily decorated frontispiece, which was inscribed in a clear, childish hand: *Lady Mary, the Queen's Daughter*.

In the sudden silence that followed, Leo reached out and gripped my hand tightly.

Kali looked pleased. "Did I find something important?" she asked.

Chapter 14

Leo was muttering strange imprecations to himself in a mixture of languages. Delicately, he flicked past the frontispiece to the next page and gave a great shout. "Yes! Published in 1554!" Even more delicately, he put the book down on the table and looked at it for a moment, his head bowed as if in prayer.

Then he took the very surprised Kali in his arms and waltzed her around the polished floors, singing in some mad mishmash of French and Hebrew and English.

"What? What?" Kali demanded.

"Yes, what?" I asked, more calmly. "You already knew the baby didn't die in infancy. Or at least that's what you told me. So what's so exciting about this book?"

He dropped his arms and turned to me, grinning ruefully. "Well, I may have exaggerated a trifle about the extent of my knowledge. . . ."

"You told me . . . ," I started indignantly.

"There isn't—my God, there *wasn't*—any proof one way or the other. I thought *maybe* she survived, since there was no record of her death. And there were some—"

Even more indignant, I interrupted. "So you chased Jules—I mean, me—all around London just because you thought *maybe* the baby survived and *maybe* she had living descendants and *maybe* . . ."

"Forget that now!" Kali said. "Leo, what does all this mean?"

He picked up the book again and cradled it lovingly in his arms. "What it means, my dear girls, is that Baby Mary almost certainly did *not* die in infancy. She lived long enough to learn to read and write, which dramatically increases the chance that she lived to adulthood. Which means, in turn, that you—Jules, I mean—are in fact her direct descendant. Oh my God," he added. "What a find!"

Kali started to say something, but just then the library doors flew open, and the agitated curator bustled in. "Really, Dr. Schlumberger, what is going on in here?" His eyes fell on the little volume, which Leo still cradled. "What is that?"

In silence, Leo showed him the frontispiece. In respectful silence, the curator inspected it and then put on an eyepiece and examined it again. When the man looked up, his eyes were bright with tears.

"Lady Mary, the Queen's Daughter," he said quietly, almost reverentially. "In 1554. When she would have been . . . six years old."

"Quite," Leo said.

"We must . . ." The curator's voice trailed off.

"Quite," Leo said again.

After several urgent phone calls, the scholars agreed that the precious book had to go to the conservation lab at Oxford's Bodleian Library immediately and that Leo was the man to take it there. He signed receipts and daunting mounds of insurance papers before the curator's minions wrapped the book in even greater mounds of museum-quality paper and linen and boxing. I waited patiently, bemused by Leo's air of quiet triumph, while Kali tapped away furiously on her cell phone.

By the time we retired to the castle's tearoom late in the afternoon, it was obvious that the news had spread. Leo had to walk a gauntlet of men who wanted to slap him on the shoulder and women who wanted to shake (or kiss) his hand. Then a spontaneous round of "For He's a Jolly Good Fellow" broke out in the sun-splashed room. Leo kept trying to insist that it was Kali's discovery, really, but she absolutely refused to join him in the limelight.

Still, she was having a marvelous time. Caught up in the general spirit of bonhomie, I snapped a quick picture of her luminous face as she sang along lustily, and sent it to her parents.

Like an automaton, Leo put a spoonful of tomato bisque in his mouth and then looked at it in some surprise. "What is this?" he asked.

"Tomato soup."

"Did I buy this?"

"No, some American tourists brought over lunch for all of us."

"Oh."

"Eat some more," I said.

He was coming back to earth again.

"I'm hungry," he said with surprise.

I gestured at the table, laden with food that our newfound friends had bought us. "Well, you've come to the right place," I said.

Kali put a spoonful of soup in her mouth too, but the spoon clanked against the ring in her lip, and she winced. "Ow!" she said involuntarily.

Leo said, "Kali, I'm begging you, take those things out of your face. It hurts to look at you."

I smiled to myself.

"Well, thanks a lot," she said huffily.

"You know I didn't mean it that way. Just think how much

more comfortable you would be," Leo said coaxingly. Once again, we were allies.

"It's my statement."

"Of what? Bondage?"

She refused to answer.

Then a calculating look came into her eyes. "If you paid me," she said, "I might consider taking them out."

Leo paused. "How much?"

"Now, wait a minute," I said.

Intent on their negotiation, they both ignored me.

"One hundred pounds."

"Ten," Leo said.

"One hundred. Per piercing."

"Why, you little robber!"

I started to protest again, but within moments the deal was negotiated and Kali was tucking pound notes into her bag with a pleased look on her face. I noticed that she had switched to a small, cross-body bag like the one I carried.

I leaned forward. "Kali, I'll throw in fifty pounds more if you go to my hairdresser and get those lowlights taken out."

I had eventually figured out her lank, dirty brownish hair. She was the only natural blonde I had ever known who actually *darkened* her hair, apparently with some cheap drugstore goo.

"A hundred," she countered, fingering a greasy lock.

I sighed in defeat.

Exhausted by the eventful day, Kali fell asleep in the back seat of Leo's car as soon as we pulled out of the castle grounds. He drove with casual confidence, one arm draped over the top of the wheel and the other resting easily on the open window. I glanced over at him, taking in the hard muscles of his forearms and his broad, capable hands. He liked to roll his shirtsleeves up to the elbow, and I liked looking at his arms.

I had had men who were lovers and men who were friends—but never a man who was both. Leo intrigued me. Behind that Hugh Grant–ish stammer (which was very annoying; if I decided to sleep with him, I'd have to get him to lose that habit), he was smart and intuitive. He didn't seem to find me unapproachable or chilly or remote or intimidating—all of the things that other men had said about me (usually as I was bringing our affair to a close). Quite the contrary—he was alarmingly clued in to me.

Maybe I shouldn't sleep with him after all.

Clearing my throat, I asked him, "Aren't you tired?"

"No," he said, his eyebrows rising. "Are you?"

I knew I would be when I got home, but right now I was still warm with Leo's exhilaration.

To divert myself, I reminded him that he had never explained the importance of finding Katherine Parr's living descendant. Why did he care so much that he had stalked an innocent woman all over London, frightening her half to death?

"Right," Leo said. "I guess I never finished explaining it to you."

No, you had to "rescue" me from the man in the pub basement, I thought. Little did Leo know how easily I could have rescued myself, without the unwelcome encumbrance of Kali. My father had taught me well.

"It's quite simple. Baby Mary disappeared from the records before her second birthday."

"I know," I said impatiently. "But you don't think she died."

"I do not, and now I know she *didn't* die. Look, Amy, she was a very famous child—the baby of one of England's most powerful celebrity couples of the sixteenth century. Wouldn't the death of such a prominent child be mentioned? Somewhere?"

"Hmm," I said. "But the poem—"

"Makes no mention of the child's name and was published in 1573—twenty-five years after Mary's birth."

Huh. I hadn't realized that.

"And I found a letter. . . . It was in Catherine Willough-by's papers—you know, Katherine Parr's friend who took in the baby?"

I nodded.

"The letter was written to Catherine in France in the late 1550s, where she had fled with her second husband under Queen Mary's reign."

"And?"

"It said . . ." He glanced at me. "Well, it's in old English, but the gist of it is that the girl she was inquiring about 'was well and Godly, and mayhap would be promised to her cousin, a lad of the Seymour name.'" He glanced at me again. "Baby Mary would have been about ten years old at the time, ripe for a betrothal."

"Huh." It didn't seem like much to me. "And Jules?"

"Sudeley Castle itself recently passed into the hands of a twentysomething distant cousin of the Dent family."

"Okay," I said, wondering where he was taking this.

"The Dents were marvelous stewards of the castle and opened it to the public, as you just saw."

I nodded.

"But the Dents' only daughter died without leaving any heirs, so it passed to young Thomas Harwood. And young Thomas Harwood saw the pot of gold at the end of the rainbow."

"Speak English, would you please?" I asked.

"He plans to sell off the castle and its lands to a developer. They will close the castle to visitors, of course; distribute its artifacts to the highest bidders; and turn the building into a high-end condominium complex." His tone dripped outrage and something more—something close to grief, I thought.

"And the lands?"

"Multimillion-pound McMansions, a pool and tennis club to rival Wimbledon, and a resort hotel on the edge of an artificial lake. They plan to turn Katherine Parr's home into a tacky playland for the nouveaux riches!"

It *was* grief.

"I'm sorry," I said inadequately.

He dipped his head in acknowledgment.

"But aren't there regulations? Isn't the castle part of the historical trust or something?"

"Oh, yes, it's a listed building, but they can do whatever they want with the interior. And the lands, of course."

I thought back to the charming, lush grounds with their greenery and gardens, the tame and friendly deer, and the strutting peacocks and obscenely fat squirrels. "But what will happen to all the animals?" I asked foolishly.

"Oh, I forgot to mention. There's going to be a hunting preserve too."

I shuddered.

"The only person who can stop this atrocity," Leo continued, "is a living descendant of Queen Katherine Parr and Thomas Seymour. And, as it happens, I have found that living descendant: Juliette Mary Seymour." He stopped short of adding "you," but I caught his drift.

"I'm not Jules," I said wearily. He had never explained how or why he had connected me to her, and I was cautious about seeming too curious.

I heard Kali stir in the back seat. But she subsided, and I twisted my hair around my fingers. "I wish I could help you," I went on, quite sincerely. "But I can't."

Silence.

"I'm so sorry," I added.

More silence.

I twisted more hair. "Who's going to buy it?" I asked. "Who's the developer? Maybe you can scare them off somehow."

Leo laughed bitterly. "Oh, yes, that's likely."

"Why? I mean, why not?"

"My dear girl, the buyer is a Russian billionaire who has been buying up parcels of Cotswold land for years. God knows why," he added.

"Russian oligarchs love to invest in land," I told him.

"Really? Well, now they're planning to develop *this* land. And they're more likely to disappear me for interfering than to be 'scared off' by anything I can do."

"All right, well, I'm sure they need all sorts of permission and stuff. Surely the government won't let them—"

"The government *is* letting them," he interrupted. "For all its touristy facade, the Cotswolds is desperately in need of jobs. A massive housing-and-resort development is worth much more than a few moldy old artifacts and a minor tourist attraction."

"So, then . . . ?"

"So, then my only hope of stopping this development is to find Juliette Seymour."

"Jules."

"Yes. Jules."

"Well, why don't you just buy the land yourself?" I asked reasonably. "You're rich, aren't you?"

He gripped the gearshift so tightly that his knuckles turned white. "My family has money, but we're not the bloody mint! We're talking about hundreds of millions of pounds of parkland!"

"Oh," I said.

I wished I could help him. I really did. But I couldn't.

"I'm sorry," I said again.

In the back seat, Kali stirred once more, and I turned quickly to face her. "Still another hour to go," I told her. "Go back to sleep."

She subsided, and I looked at Leo again. "I really am sorry," I repeated, and he shrugged.

"Oh, I still have an ace or two up my sleeve. This isn't over yet, not by a long shot," he said.

I wondered what his next move would be.

Chapter 15

As it turned out, the next move wasn't Leo's at all. One minute we were driving along the narrow country road in the deepening twilight, shadows falling long across Leo's exasperated face as he negotiated with yet another high-pitched sister on the phone; the next there was a huge roar behind us, and Leo let out a bellow of shock and pain.

Kali screamed, and I whipped around to see a black van on our heels. Our car swerved wildly as Leo steered away from the van, and with another shock I saw that his right arm, which had been draped on the open window, was dripping blood. Through the growing darkness, I saw the dull gleam of a gun as the driver behind us withdrew his hand to steer his own car.

"What's happening?" Kali cried out, her eyes wild with fear.

"Get down!" I yelled at her. "Cover your head with your arms, and *get down!*"

Leo had regained control of the car and accelerated away from the van, but his face was white with pain. "You too," he said to me. "Get down!" He was trying to shout, but his voice came out a pale whisper.

"Do you have a gun?" I demanded.

"Of course I don't have a bloody gun! I live in Oxford, not the Bronx!"

Yet I could have sworn that his hand had shot reflexively toward his hip, just as it had in the pub basement.

"Pull over!" I shouted at him. "Stop the car so I can drive!"

His face was ashen. "What the fuck?"

"Pull over!" I screamed. "Just do it!"

In a daze, he brought the car to a screeching halt. Kali cried out again, and I practically levitated over poor Leo, shoving him into the passenger seat and taking the wheel myself. "Put on your seat belt!" I snapped at him. "And get the fuck down!"

As I had anticipated, the van had shot past us, taken by surprise by our sudden stop. I hunched over the wheel and waited until the van began to reverse, and then put my foot down, and we flew past it and into the night. Grimly, I drove as my father had taught me. Thank God for Leo's smart Audi and its supersonic engine.

The van driver recovered from his surprise and raced after us. I swerved hard to the right and then hard to the left as the gun hand appeared out the window again. Kali was crying in the back seat, but I forced myself to clear my mind and focus.

Two shots rang out. Fleetingly, I thought of the tires and how disastrous a blowout would be at this speed. Seeing a curve ahead, I slowed slightly and thought furiously. I could probably outrun the van—eventually—but how long could I keep up this speed on this road? Would "eventually" come too late? The burden of my two helpless passengers weighed on me heavily, clouding my thinking.

But then I remembered the Coke bottle, that old-fashioned glass bottle that they still sold in rural England and that Kali had insisted on keeping for a souvenir.

"Leo," I said. "Can you hear me?"

"Of course," he snapped. "I'm not bloody dead, am I?"

Out of the corner of my eye, I saw that he had torn up his left sleeve and wrapped it around his right upper arm to stanch the bleeding. With some relief, I realized that he wasn't helpless at all. We were in this together.

"The Coke bottle," I said.

"Right, then."

He straightened up and looked back. One of the bullets had smashed his side-view mirror to smithereens. With an effort, he picked up the Coke bottle with his good hand and weighed it.

I shut my mind to his pain. That was irrelevant to me right now.

A bullet smashed into the back windshield, and Kali sobbed. I couldn't think about her now either.

Leo said something, but I couldn't hear him between Kali's cries and the wind whipping through the open windshield.

"What?"

"Slow down and pull right on one!" he shouted at me. "Count it down!"

"Three!" I screamed. "Two! One!" And, infinitesimally, I lifted my foot off the accelerator and swung the car to the right so fast and hard that I felt its left wheels leave the ground for one terrifying moment.

Smash! Leo threw the Coke bottle right into the path of the oncoming van, and I heard a sickening crunch as its tires connected with the deadly shards, then the satisfying pop of one blowout, then another. The driver let off a volley of frustrated gunshots as we sped away, leaving the crippled van by the side of the road and slowing to a sedate pace as we approached the village of Westerly.

At a safe distance past the village, I pulled over to the side of the road and stopped the car. Delayed reaction was setting in. I brushed sweat off my face and for the first time allowed myself to look at Kali.

"Are you all right?"

She was crying so hard she couldn't speak.

"Shock," Leo said to me.

I nodded. "Kali!" I said sharply. "Take your hands from your face and look at me!"

She obeyed. Her eyes darted wildly, and her face was deadly pale.

Leo fumbled in the compartment under the seat and came up with a can of liquid. "Fizzy, sweet stuff," he said. "Full of sugar."

I opened the can and handed it to Kali. "Drink," I said.

Then I turned back to Leo. "How about you?" I asked him.

"A clean shot. The bullet went through." The color was returning to his face, though his lips were still white with pain.

I eyed him cautiously. "Do you want to go to—"

"Any hospital will recognize this immediately as a bullet wound and call the police." Just as cautiously, he eyed me. "Do you want that?"

"No," I admitted. "Do you?"

"No."

"Well, then. I've got some antibiotics at home. I can doctor myself up. How about Kali? Did the glass cut her?"

Glittering shards from the broken windshield were all over the back seat, but Kali, still huddled on the floor with her arms over her head, seemed to be unhurt.

Leo was still staring at me. "You're the one, aren't you?" he said. "It's you. *You're* the one they're shooting at. *You're* the one they attacked in the pub."

"Don't be crazy," I said.

"Then who the fuck are you? Time to put your cards on the table, Jules. Or Amy, or whatever you're calling yourself."

Kali had stopped crying and was listening to our low, heated words.

"*You're* the one," I said, just as sharply, my faint suspicions transformed into sudden realization. "You're Mossad, aren't you? Military intelligence . . . What bullshit. You're a fucking spy. You're the one they're after, not me."

Leo was speechless.

I started the engine again and put the car in gear. "Whatever you are, you're dangerous," I said to him. "Kali, I'm taking you home."

But of course, neither of us knew what "home" meant. Despite my anger and self-recriminations—how could I not have foreseen this?—I couldn't bring myself to just drop Leo off at home and leave him alone and injured. So we all went to Leo's.

"You have to send her back to her parents," Leo said in his kitchen. He was preparing to inject himself with a very business-like-looking syringe of antibiotics. I winced and looked away.

I didn't want to talk about Kali yet. I still felt too guilty. After a restorative dose of brandy, she was off exploring Leo's impressive house while I helped patch him up, and I couldn't blame her for her curiosity. A comfortable, family-size home in uppity Holland Park, where house prices started in the low seven figures, it was nothing like I might have expected for a bachelor. The kitchen took up the entire first floor, opening up to flow into a large sitting area with squishy-looking, pale lemony couches; a quiet, book-filled reading nook with more comfortable chairs and good lamps; and a conversation area around the massive, American-style TV. The kitchen itself was a cook's delight, centered on a huge, gleaming island and leading into what would be, in the daytime, a sun-splashed breakfast nook.

I was no domestic goddess, but I coveted that kitchen.

I turned my attention back to Leo. "I suppose you learned how to do this in the military," I said, indicating the syringe and bandages.

"*Mais bien sûr.* Basic field medical training. And you?"

Kali came back from her tour, saving me from an answer, and settled deep into one of the couches with a little sigh. Swathed in warm blankets and loaded up with so much sugar and brandy that she wouldn't sleep for weeks, she was watching us with bright, unblinking eyes.

I remembered one French phrase that my parents had used—first, jokingly; later, not so much.

"*Pas devant les enfants,*" I said. Not in front of the children.

"*Mais bien sûr,*" Leo said again.

Kali said to me, "Where'd you learn to drive like that?"

"My father taught me."

"And who the hell was your father, then?" Leo asked, possibly made waspish by the pain of arranging bandages over his ugly wound. "Evel Knievel?"

"Please don't fight," Kali begged from her couch, and I felt a pang, remembering how my parents had argued until my mother left.

"I spent a lot of time in war zones," I said briefly. "You learn things."

Leo grunted. Then he asked, "So, why is someone trying to kill you?"

"No one is trying to kill me. At least, if they were, they're pretty incompetent."

He nodded, conceding the point. "Then why is someone trying to scare you? I had almost decided that you changed your name to get away from an abusive boyfriend, but that just doesn't fit. What are you running away from?"

Once again, Kali opened her mouth. Once again, I quelled her with a sharp glance.

I scowled at Leo. "How do you know the attack wasn't about *you*?" I demanded. "Are you Mossad? What do you have to do with Sheikh Abdullah or his sons?"

He seemed genuinely taken aback. "Who?"

"My clients. Sheikh Abdullah bin Saud bin Arabiyya and his sons, Kareem and Nasir." Irrelevantly, I added, "He calls his eldest son Abu Bakr—father of Bakr—even though he has several daughters too, but of course it's only the son that matters." *Stop babbling*, I told myself. *Get a grip.*

He was silent, and we eyed each other warily, the instinctive teamwork of the car having given way to mutual suspicion. I said, "I don't know who you are, but you're dangerous and you're a bloody liar. Kali, let's go."

She protested, "I'm not going home to my parents. You can't make me."

"Oh, yes, I can."

"No, you can't. I'll just run away, and then you'll never find me."

I thought that might be true and exchanged glances with Leo. I could see that he thought so too.

Once again, the tide of resentment swelled up and threatened to engulf me. How could it be that at such a critical time, I had saddled myself with not one but two burdens?

Kali looked at Leo. "Can't I stay here with you?"

"No!" I snapped.

"This is the family's home," Leo said slowly. "We all use it when we're in London. In fact . . ." He looked as if a new and interesting thought had just occurred to him, and he gazed assessingly at Kali.

"How quickly can you get that hardware out of your face? By tomorrow night?"

"Why?" she asked.

He looked back at me. "I have some calls to make, but I'll call you later. And, Amy . . ."

"What?"

"Please, please be careful."

Leo called the next night to explain that his sister Élodie would be arriving in London the next day with her four children. Would Kali like to come stay at his house while they were there and help care for the children?

Would she?

"Four children?" Kali screeched at me. "*Four*?"

"It'll be fun," I said briskly.

"But I've never done any babysitting," she protested. "Kids are just squirmy little snot factories." She was dabbing bacitracin on the empty holes where her piercings had been and flinching with every dab.

"Take it or leave it," I advised. "You can't stay with me anymore."

"You can't trust me with children," she said. "I told you, I'm a screw-up. I wouldn't know how to keep them from drowning or choking. Or whatever."

"It's hard to drown in Holland Park," I said dryly. "And Leo tells me there's a nanny. You'd just be helping her." I paused and then added, "Don't be so hard on yourself."

She sniffled a little. "You don't know the half of what I've done. I stole someone's homework and tried to pass it off as my own. I drank so much they had to pump my stomach. I sold pot to my friends, and now I'll never go to college—not that I wanted to go anyway. I hate school."

I regarded her thoughtfully. "What *do* you want to do, then?"

"I want to do what you do: live in London and travel a lot and have cool friends, like Leo."

No one had ever wanted to be me before.

But I steeled myself. "Kali, you have no choice. You're going to Holland Park tomorrow, and you're going to help take care of Élodie's children, and that's that."

Tears glittered in her eyes, but I turned away and busied myself putting the kettle on. She would be fine, I told myself. We would all be fine.

Kali had recovered enough the next morning to flounce out of the apartment without a backward glance at me, and she climbed into the waiting Uber with an air of injured martyrdom. *Well, that's that*, I thought, mentally washing my hands of her. For the moment, anyway.

Now it was time to proceed with my plans. Leo would be busy introducing Kali and getting her settled, I figured. Perfect timing for my escape. I had pretty much thrown a dart at the map and decided to go to Berlin, where my grandfather had been stationed after the war. So I bought a Chunnel ticket to Paris and took an Uber to Paddington Station. Then I took the metro to St. Pancras and an anonymous express train to Heathrow, paying for the last two maneuvers in cash. Expensive and annoying, but it should throw Leo off my trail—if, that is, he was still interested in pursuing me after the nasty events and nastier exchanges of Saturday. As my plane lifted off, I gazed out the window in some satisfaction. So much for Leo Schlumberger, military intelligence or Mossad or whatever the fuck he was!

But I felt a small pang as I watched London become tinier and tinier in the distance. After my wandering life, it had become almost a home to me. I really liked its busy, narrow streets, where I could find a cabdriver with a doctorate in physics; its confused tourists looking the wrong way as they stumbled into the cab's path; and its mini-neighborhoods clustered around lush private parks and bustling high streets. And then the clouds came together, and London was lost entirely. I closed my window shade and closed my eyes for the rest of the short flight.

When we landed in Berlin, I took another anonymous cab to the Ritz-Carlton, where my grandfather had been billeted, proffering my company credit card with some satisfaction. It was one of the very, very few perks of my job. I wouldn't even have to take any vacation time; I could just say that I was scouting out the hotel for the sheikh.

Posh and quiet, the Ritz faced Potsdamer Bahnhof station. I was amused to see that a mini–ski slope was under construction in the center of Potsdamer Platz. Someone was hoping to relieve the gray monotony of central Berlin, but I was dubious. Even a big, garishly yellow sign for *Die Peanuts Movie* didn't help. I wondered if anyone had realized what *Die Peanuts* meant in English.

But my spirits rose as I walked briskly down Stresemannnstrasse, past a series of blank, emotionless German government buildings—stark reminders of the Soviet era—and cut over past the Brandenburg Gate. Then I crossed the street and nodded at the serious young marines who stood at attention, their eyes constantly in motion and their hands hovering near their automatic weapons. Guarding a US embassy these days was serious business.

They let me by, though, and I walked through the heavily barred gates into a reception area guarded by still more marines, through the security queue, and, after being frisked and searched, into the embassy itself. As I entered the lobby, a tall, graying man hurried toward me, holding out his hands.

"My dear girl! Such a pleasure to see you again! Welcome to Berlin."

He kissed me on both cheeks, European-style, then held

me off at arm's length to see me better. "You look just like your father," he pronounced. "God rest his soul."

I had forgotten that Henry Baynor, one of my father's oldest friends, was a devout Catholic. My father had always treated Henry's faith with a mixture of amusement and respect.

"It's great to see you too, Henry," I said. "Thanks for meeting with me on such short notice."

"For Ned's daughter? Anything! But come, my dear, let's not stand here in this cold lobby. There's an excellent beer cellar around the corner."

Exiting the embassy was much easier than entering it. This time I smiled at the younger, cuter marine, and he almost smiled back. Then he saw Henry by my side and stiffened to attention. Henry nodded at him. "At ease, son," he said.

The proprietor of the beer cellar clapped Henry on the back when we walked in and seated us in the back corner, where we could talk privately. Courtly and kind, Henry had friends everywhere, in every corner of the world, from the yurts of Mongolia to the rough sailors' bars of Marseille, my father used to say. Beers and nuts appeared magically in front of us, and I sipped appreciatively. "Delicious," I said as the cold liquid slipped smoothly down my throat.

"Hans brews his own," Henry said. "It's the best."

I took another long sip.

"Now, my dear, delightful as it is to see you," Henry said, "I suspect you have more on your mind than looking up old friends. No?"

"No," I agreed. "I mean, yes."

"Well, then," he said, "I am all ears."

So I plunged in, telling him about the investigation into Sheikh Abdullah and his sons, their veiled threats, and my fear that the FBI would destroy everything I had been working for.

He listened in silence, his piercing blue eyes never leaving my face. I finished with a description of Leo.

"He can't have anything to do with the investigation," I said. "Can he?"

Henry shrugged and held up his hands—who knows?

"But . . . why? What on earth is his interest—or Mossad's interest—in all of this? But what else could it be?"

Henry looked grave. "And how on earth did he find out about Jules?"

Chapter 16

How indeed? We had buried Jules so deeply that it seemed impossible that she had been resurrected. Leo couldn't possibly know. So I said, "Maybe he's just fishing."

"Maybe," Henry said.

Neither of us believed it.

"He's a historian, a researcher," I said. "He's probably a very good researcher."

"You have to lose him, my dear," Henry said. "Get him to lose interest in you. Do whatever you must."

I knew he was right. "But still . . . if I lose him, I'll never find out what he knows, or how he dug it up."

"Get rid of him," Henry said. "If you don't, you could lose everything that you've worked so hard for."

We talked for a while longer, and he promised to see if anyone at the embassy knew about Sheikh Abdullah or Leo.

"Be careful," I warned, suddenly anxious. "I don't want anyone to know I'm looking into this."

He smiled at me. "But of course."

I knew I could rely on his discretion. My father had once told me that before he retired to a desk position at the State Department, Henry had spent years as an NOC, a nonofficial cover officer, in the CIA. Most CIA officers, he had explained, worked overseas under "light cover," such as the State Department or USAID; if exposed, they would face nothing worse than an ignominious PNG (persona non grata) ticket out of the country. But NOCs were the most deeply hidden spies, working for nongovernmental organizations and known only to the very highest echelons of the agency. If an NOC were exposed, he might face torture, death, or a future as an anonymous star on the wall of the CIA's lobby. An avid devotee of spy novels and spy movies, I thrilled to the idea of knowing someone so glamorous.

So if anyone knew how to ferret out secrets without leaving a trace, it was Henry.

"Now," he continued, "you should go out and enjoy this beautiful fall day in Berlin. Be a tourist. Visit our museums. See that Berlin isn't all Soviet-era gray and dull. Relax, and I will be in touch as soon as I learn anything."

Be a tourist! Visit museums! I had traveled the world with my father, but our travels meant trekking and skiing and rafting and *doing*—not passively strolling through museums to view other people's past glories.

Henry was listing the tourist sites of Berlin for me, and my mind was wandering when I heard him say, "And then, of course, you must visit our Holocaust memorial and museum."

My mind snapped back to Leo—his family specialized in recovering the art of Holocaust survivors, he had said—and I leaned forward with sudden interest. "Where is the memorial?" I asked.

The Holocaust memorial, it turned out, was a square city block of tall, dark gray granite slabs that grew higher and higher as the ground sloped toward the middle, while the spaces between them grew smaller and smaller to increase the claustrophobia and the urge to escape. At first I wandered, dodging through the slabs, supposing that they were meant to evoke gravestones, traps, ghettoes, but I found myself surprisingly unmoved. Maybe it was the children cheerfully playing hide-and-seek among the towering slabs. Maybe it was the coldness and lack of humanity. Or maybe it was all just too abstract for me; I like the concrete and the actual, not the abstract and intangible.

And then I saw Leo.

He was moving slowly but purposefully among the concrete chunks, his eyes roving unceasingly, just like those of the marine guards at the embassy. I was frozen, the proverbial deer in headlights, when he caught sight of me and his face relaxed into a smile. "Hey," he called. "Wait up!"

I turned and darted away, thinking I could lose him in this travesty of a maze. Perhaps he would be affected by the symbolism of the grim place and would lose his concentration long enough for me to slip away. How on earth—how in the name of God—had he tracked me down?

Leo was no longer a mild mystery and a potential bed partner, I realized belatedly; he was an impending disaster. I flashed back to my sudden certainty that he was Mossad when we were in the car chase; in the cold light of day, my certainty had eased back into suspicion only, and I had relaxed my guard once more. I was tired of seesawing on Leo—nice guy, nuisance; man of mystery, Oxford don; Mossad spy, obsessed historian—but I knew this: Whatever or whoever he was, he was a danger to me and my mission.

Perhaps I could lose him in the small museum underneath the memorial. Surely that would distract him from his pursuit of me? I bought my ticket and raced down the stairs to the underground bunker that housed the museum, noting with satisfaction that he was nowhere in sight.

But once in the small, dark museum, I was the one who lost my concentration. The Germans were unsparing of themselves, and I found myself admiring them for that. There was no whitewashing of the horrific things they had done. No excuses. No revisionist theory. I paused before an exhibit showing a photograph of one family—squirmy toddler, self-conscious adolescent, worn parents, and stooped grandfather—who had been completely obliterated in Treblinka. All of them dead, murdered in the gas chambers.

Helpless victims were my worst nightmare. I could take whatever happened to me and my colleagues—it was what we signed up for—but the plight of the helpless seared my soul. Uncomprehending children and grief-stricken mothers; little boys grown old before their time; fathers driven to madness by their inability to protect their families: This was what I saw in Chechnya and Syria and so many other hellholes. My mission, inherited from my father, was to make the world safer for the helpless—otherwise, their plight would drive *me* mad.

That was why my responsibility for Kali was so horrifying. I thought that Leo could take care of himself, like me, but I *knew* that Kali couldn't. I couldn't erase the image of her curled in a fetal ball on the floor of the pub basement, or sobbing and terrified in the back seat of the car, and I knew myself to be responsible for her—the ultimate helpless victim. It was too much for me. That was why she had had to go.

Somehow I was not surprised when Leo came up beside me and put his arm around my shoulders. "Don't cry, *motek*," he said gently.

I relaxed for a moment against his shoulder. But just a moment; then I stiffened and pulled away, scowling at him. "I never cry," I snapped. "Just leave me alone, will you?"

"I wish I could," he said.

Loath to disturb the funereal silence of the museum, I pressed my lips together and marched off. He was only a few feet behind me when we ascended into the sunshine above.

"Dinner?" Leo suggested. "I know a charming little rathskeller not far from your hotel. . . ."

Oh my God. "I would not have dinner with you," I said clearly, "if you were the last man on Earth." Or at least not until he explained how he had found me again. I could dismiss his presence on the Sunday in Bradford as that of an obsessed historian who thought I had something he needed, or even, possibly, as coincidence. But this was over the edge; for the first time, I saw him as a real danger. *Get him to lose interest in you*, Henry had said.

He shrugged and spread his hands in a charming Gallic gesture. "Drinks, then?"

I turned my back on him and stalked away, but of course he stayed right by my side.

"Why are you so angry at me?" Leo asked reasonably. "You must have known I would follow you."

But I didn't think you would find me, I thought.

Why *was* I so angry, though? Suddenly it occurred to me that I wasn't angry so much at him as at myself—for the thrill that had raced through me when I first spotted him at the memorial. We had understood each other so completely in the car when he was shot. It was almost as if our bodies and brains were in perfect rhythm with each other, acting on the same instincts.

I had to face the truth: There was a small part of me that didn't *want* to get rid of Leo.

But I couldn't trust him either.

More seesawing.

So I said to him, "If you're not going to leave me alone, then how would you like to visit the Spy Museum? You should be right at home there."

Leo, either a great actor or a nonspy, looked honestly bewildered, and then his eyes narrowed in suspicion. "And why are *you* interested in the Spy Museum?"

"Why not?" I retorted childishly. I had been reading a John le Carré novel when Leo first found me, so I thought he had already divined my secret, half-ashamed passion for spies. *Argo* was my favorite movie ever (the brief glimpse of Ben Affleck's naked torso alone was worth the price of admission); *Three Days of the Condor* wasn't far behind it. When Henry was reeling off his list of tourist attractions, the Spy Museum had jumped out at me.

We exchanged glares of mutual distrust.

Leo shrugged. "*On y va*," he said. "Let's go, then."

The small museum was located, incongruously enough, in a small shopping plaza across Potsdamer Platz, underneath Toys "R" Us and next door to H&M. I especially loved spy gadgets and was immediately drawn to an exhibition of cameras and guns that could be hidden inside anything from a mitten to a ballpoint pen.

"These look like movie props," Leo said dismissively, coming up beside me. "I doubt they were ever used. I thought spies mainly spend their time bribing dodgy informers with stacks of American dollars."

I knew that was true and gave him points for admitting that he knew something about the field, though I resented him for piercing my spy novel-fueled fantasies. "They used this stuff during the Cold War," I said. "Didn't the CIA try to blow up Fidel Castro with an exploding cigar?"

"Yes, and that worked out so well," Leo said dryly. "How do you know, anyway?"

"Everyone knows about the cigar," I retorted as we moved past the lipstick telephones and gun purses.

"Yes, but do you seriously think spies went around garroting each other with piano wire and shooting knives out of desk pens?"

I did, actually, but I certainly had no answer for him. So I closed my mouth firmly, annoyed with him for ruining this fascinating exhibit.

It was getting cooler and darker when we stepped back into the shopping plaza. Defiantly, I headed for the Checkpoint Charlie Museum, even though my feet were killing me by then, and made him trail me through the exhibits about all the people who tried to flee East Germany and the tragic results that usually ensued. Leo rebelled when I started reading, word for word, every exhibit about human-rights abuses in the world today.

"Come on," he said. "I know you're not that interested in this stuff. You're a spy buff. Let's go get a nice Sacher torte and discuss our mutual interests."

"We have no mutual interests."

"All evidence to the contrary," he countered.

I considered. We had tried talking before, of course, and it hadn't worked. On the other hand—I felt another flip-flop approaching—I needed to know how he had found me in Berlin. And how he had connected me to Jules. "If I must," I said ungraciously. "But you're paying."

"With the greatest of pleasure," he said.

Chapter 17

"How did you find me?" I demanded as we sat down, before even putting my napkin in my lap or reaching for my water.

An approaching waiter, hearing my tone, shied away.

"And don't give me coincidence," I added. "I'm not an idiot."

"I'm aware," he said. "All right, cards on the table, then. I told you I was in military intelligence; well, I still have lots of friends there. I called in some contacts, and they found your flight and hotel reservations. From there, it was easy to follow you to the memorial."

I digested that, thinking hard. It might even have been true. "But why? Why go to all this trouble? You know I'm not Jules."

Now he paused to consider his words. "I know you're *connected* to Jules," he said finally. "I know you know *something*."

Again, I had to give him points for honesty—and insight. "But I'm not," I said, a little helplessly. "I don't."

"So you say," he said. "So you say."

The waiter, encouraged by our calmer tones, descended again, and we chatted our way through a delicious dinner, comparing our most and least favorite world leaders (he had a grudging respect for Vladimir Putin; I felt the same about Xi Jinping). He told me more about his sisters and nieces and nephews, and

I told him more about my father and our adventures. It was the most I had talked about my father in years, and I found it almost pleasurable to recount our times together. Leo listened without comment, toying with his cutlery as the waiter removed our plates.

"You certainly lived an interesting life together," he said neutrally. "You don't think that was perhaps too much adventure for a child?"

I flared up instantly. "Of course not! I loved it!"

"You were never afraid?"

I swallowed: *If you're scared, I'll find a braver companion.* "Fear is for cowards," I said.

"*Vraiment?* I was terrified more times than I can imagine when I was in the military."

I gazed at him, startled. Leo was certainly not a coward—I remembered him in the car chase. "Were you afraid in the car? When you were shot?" I asked.

"But of course! Weren't you?"

I thought back to his calm even as blood poured down his arm, his quick thinking, and his ability to turn a Coke bottle into a deadly weapon. I too was calm under fire, but was I afraid? "I don't know," I said.

"Well, I'll say it for both of us: I was scared out of my skin."

"I was scared for Kali," I said tentatively.

"Yes, she's helpless. Helpless victims terrify me more than anything."

A spark of oneness, of complete connection, flared between us, and I had to turn away from the understanding on his face. We waited in silence for the dessert.

But I relaxed again when the Sacher torte, overflowing with chocolate sauce and whipped cream, was placed in front of me. The cup of hot chocolate, topped with even more whipped cream, completed my capitulation. "All right," I said, spooning torte into my mouth and feeling the delicious warmth of pure chocolate fill my senses, "tell me why you're so obsessed with Katherine Parr."

"I am not the first man," Leo said, "to be obsessed with Katherine Parr."

I smiled at him. His defensive tone and the lock of black hair falling into his eyes made him seem around Kali's age. He must have been irresistible as a teenage boy; he certainly knew himself to be charming as a man and was not above using that magnetism to get what he wanted. All of my doubts returned.

"Henry VIII was determined to marry her, even though she had been widowed twice by then and was generally supposed to be barren."

"But clearly, she wasn't," I put in.

"No. Husbands one and three were old men, and husband number two was rumored to be impotent."

I smiled again at the thought of gossip lingering for almost five centuries.

"Maybe he was gay," I suggested.

"Quite possibly. And Tom Seymour probably married her for advancement and riches as much as for her winsome self. By all accounts he was quite fond of her."

I shrugged. Tom Seymour had dallied with the teenage Elizabeth under the eyes of his pregnant wife. I thought he was an ass. "I'm not too interested in Tom's opinions," I said. "When he died, Elizabeth commented that he had been a man of 'much wit but very little wisdom.'"

"Quite," Leo said. "At any rate, after a year or so of marriage to the King, Katherine was denounced by some of her political enemies for being too involved with the religious reformists and for trying to sway Henry to her opinions. She was in grave danger. Remember the fate of her predecessors Anne Boleyn and Katherine Howard. Anne was beheaded for sins much less grave than those of which Katherine Parr was accused."

I felt a shiver run down my spine. For all the pomp and glitter, how terrifying it must have been to be the wife of Henry VIII.

"And that was when he was younger and less evil-tempered than when he married our Katherine," Leo added. "But Katherine was smart. Today she would probably be prime minister. She knelt at Henry's feet and told him she talked politics only to distract him from the great pains he suffered from his infected leg. The old king raised her up and kissed her and sent the courtiers who had denounced her to the Tower."

"Wow," I said inadequately.

"And she was a marvelous stepmother to the King's children, Mary, Elizabeth, and Edward. Even Mary, a crabby spinster almost the same age as her stepmother and of a completely different religious bent, had nothing but good to say about her."

"Hmm," I said, as unimpressed with Mary—who, as queen, was dubbed Bloody Mary for the rampant murders of those who dared to disagree with her fanatical Catholicism—as I was with Tom Seymour.

"And as for Elizabeth," Leo went on, "she lived with Katherine and watched her stepmother govern the country when Henry took off to fight in France and designated the Queen as regent. What an experience for Elizabeth to see a 'mere woman' ruling men and country! Who knows what effect that had on Elizabeth when she became queen?"

"So . . . Sudeley?"

He sighed. "Ah, yes, Sudeley. *Motek*, it would be a tragedy to let that memorial to Katherine Parr be turned into second homes for Russian oligarchs and Saudi sheikhs."

Involuntarily, I thought of my own Saudi sheikh. Would he be interested in buying a McMansion in the Cotswolds? Quite possibly. And suddenly I too was sickened by the idea, positively nauseated at the vision of his granddaughters flaunting Tiffany bracelets and tiny bikinis at a garish swimming pool; beer-soaked parties (Saudis tended to let loose when released from the strictures of their homeland); and hunting rifles and dead deer in the grassy green parklands where Katherine Parr had once strolled, awaiting the birth of a long-awaited baby and discussing politics with her ladies.

I pushed away the remains of my Sacher torte. "What can I do to help?" I asked.

Leo grinned. "Well, if you could lead me to Jules Seymour, then she could present herself to the authorities and—"

I interrupted him. "Seriously."

"Seriously. Well, seriously . . . I don't know." He sighed and shook his head. "I just don't know."

We parted amicably, with an alarmingly amicable hug in the lobby of the Ritz.

Leo, I thought, was very good at this. But I was better.

So I set my alarm for 5:00 a.m. and an hour later was on a train speeding through the German countryside toward Prague. I had some old contacts there, from my IDC consulting days. They might be able to help me figure out if Leo had any ulterior motives and what had prompted the attacks on us in England. I stared out the streaked window, wondering if I had lost him for good. Maybe I would never see him again. Or maybe he would use those "contacts" of his to track me down wherever I went.

I put on my iPod, and the strains of an old Beatles tune filtered through my ears. I thought of Leo singing, "Hey, Jules . . ."

If I let myself be close to Leo, if I dared to let him in, then *would* it be better? My mother had deserted me, apparently uncaring that she was leaving me to the father who she thought would endanger me. In the end, my father was snatched from me too.

It had been thirteen years since my father died. (I still dated everything in my life by Before He Died and After He Died.) After he died and my party-girl life died along with him, I lost interest in men—well, to be fair, in all relationships—for a while. Eventually I realized that I missed sex, so I had a few affairs (five, to be exact). My last lover was Scott, a lanky, laid-back aid worker with sandy hair, wire-rimmed glasses, and a taste for quality weed. I liked Scott; he was good in bed and not much of a conversationalist outside the bedroom.

So he lasted longer than the others, until I watched him dissolve into a red mist when he was blown up by a stray land mine in Chechnya. I don't remember anything about what happened next; Bob said I ran straight into the choking cloud of blood and gunfire and filth, but I don't remember. I don't remember anything except waking up in a sweat-soaked field-hospital cot with a pair of twisted, smoking, wire-rimmed glasses clutched in my hand and hot, helpless tears rolling down my cheeks.

There had been no one in my bed since Scott.

As the train rocketed eastward, the countryside deteriorated rapidly. I gazed with some surprise at the communist-era machinery and decaying factories that littered the East German landscape—rusting, depressing hulks that were apparently still in operation somehow, spewing filthy fumes into the air and spitting out the kind of gray, worn workers whom I associated with the Soviet Union and not modern, unified Germany. We crossed the Czech border, and things only got worse. Now the hunks of ruined machinery appeared to be no longer functional, just collapsing into themselves to pollute the landscape for miles around.

My mood darkened, and for a moment I experienced a fleeting sensation of . . . well, I suppose it was homesickness. Absurd, for a woman who had lived her life in all corners of the world and didn't have anything that could be called a home, or even a hometown. My tiny flat in London hardly qualified. My father was gone, and my mother lived as far as she could get from my nomadic career in Europe and beyond.

So what on earth was I homesick for?

The train conductor made an announcement in Czech, a language of which I understood not a single word. Blessedly, he began to repeat it in English: "Ladies and gentlemen, we are now approaching . . . *Czlctxlkd prhsysfksk spslkhyys.*" Or something like that. Outraged, I stared at the blameless loudspeaker. Why get my hopes up when he was just going to lapse into Czech again? And how was it possible for a language to contain no vowels?

Determinedly, I stared unseeingly out the windows and watched for the lights of Prague.

The Prague train station was no more or less revolting than train stations everywhere else in the world (except for Switzerland, where you could eat off the pristine floors). I had traveled enough to be ruthless, though, and shoved my way to the front of the platform, only to discover a flight of at least fifty steep steps up to the main concourse. Shit fuck shit fuckity. I glared at the stairs and at my sixty-pound suitcase. There was no way. So, grimly, I fought my way back to the other end of the platform to find an out-of-service escalator and a long ramp tucked into a tiny, dark corner where trains apparently hibernated for the winter. I glanced around uneasily. This was a perfect spot for a mugging, and I was absolutely alone and vulnerable, burdened by my heavy bag.

Suddenly, I wouldn't have minded Leo's annoying but reassuring presence, just to escort me through this nasty tunnel.

But I made it safely and emerged into the harsh lights of the station, only to discover that my driver was not waiting by the Burger King, as we had planned. My phone had no bars, so no Uber. With another spate of mumbled curses, I made my way to the three-block-long cab line and was stabbing furiously at my unresponsive phone when a dark Mercedes glided up to the curb beside me. Somehow I wasn't surprised when the driver reached across to open the passenger door and smiled up at me.

"Need a ride?" Leo inquired.

I wanted to throw myself on the filthy sidewalk and pound my fists and legs with fury, as I had when I was a toddler. "I never saw anyone have such tantrums as you," my father had told me admiringly. My mother had just rolled her eyes.

But I was thirty-four, not four—and Leo's contacts within Israeli military intelligence were apparently quite efficient. So I heaved a great sigh and climbed into the car, leaving my bags on the sidewalk for Leo to deal with. He tossed them into the boot with admirable ease and climbed in beside me. "The Interconti-nental, I presume?" he asked.

I shrugged.

But I couldn't maintain my huffy silence for too long. I asked, "How the hell do you keep finding me? Military intel-ligence again?"

"I'm a researcher—that's what I do. I research. And I have great contacts." He glanced unsmilingly at me. "You'd be sur-prised what I can learn about people."

My stomach clenched with anxiety.

Leo glanced at me again. "Stop twisting your hair," he said.

Chapter 18

As I got off the elevator the next morning, Leo stood up from a chintzy, fussily flowered armchair and folded the newspaper he had been reading. It was in French, I noticed. Once again, I observed other women watching him covertly and felt a frisson of pleasure that I was the one he was waiting for.

It's only business, I reminded myself.

Also, Leo puzzled me; sometimes he acted like Hugh Grant's nerdier little brother, and sometimes he seemed almost alpha male. I didn't want a man whom I couldn't understand; it didn't feel safe to me.

I decided not to sleep with him after all.

Leo put his arm around my shoulders. "Breakfast?" he asked.

We chatted about innocuous things over our meal: which cities we liked best (Tel Aviv and Avignon for him, London and Moscow for me), which cities we liked least (we agreed on New Orleans and, surprisingly, Istanbul), and what countries felt most like home.

"I have a love-hate relationship with France," Leo admitted.

"That's how I feel about Russia," I confided. "But I don't really have a home."

Disliking the flash of connectedness between us, I pushed

my chair back from the table with a nasty scrape and stood up. "Shall we walk?" I suggested.

I hadn't been to Prague in a while, so Leo led me down Parizska (Paris) Street, past Gucci and Louis Vuitton and Tiffany, to Old Town Square, which struck me as slightly less Disney-esque than the one in Warsaw (which was actually built in the 1950s). I loved the filigree and decorations on the old buildings and the way they seemed to lean against each other for support.

"Fortunately," Leo said when I expressed my thoughts, "Prague isn't in an earthquake zone."

We strolled past some shops, and I thought that if I actually had a home, I would have liked to buy some of the pretty hand-painted pottery and etched crystal that the store windows displayed. Perhaps one day I would, and I would fill my home with pottery and objets d'art from all of the many, many countries I had visited. I could tell visitors, *Look, this vase came from Poland and this shawl from Turkey and this painted pitcher from Prague . . .*

I shook my head to dismiss these silly musings and walked on. Leo wove a path through the old Jewish Quarter. Thanks to the very efficient Nazis, there was not much left to see except an old cemetery, so old that people had been buried two, three, four, five on top of each other to make room for the newest generation. In some places, five or more thin gray gravestones leaned precariously against each other, almost touching the next set of gravestones to the right or left and testifying to the presence of multiple layers of dead just below.

Leo vaulted over the crumbling cemetery wall with infuriating effortlessness, so I had to do the same, although my thin Keds were hardly the ideal shoes for such a move. I skidded a little on landing but ignored Leo's outstretched hand. We dodged the silent gravestones in the growing gloom as the first rain-drops began to fall. Sometimes all I could hear was the sound of my own quick breathing and Leo's slower, calmer breaths.

"This is depressing," I pronounced.

"Let's go up to Prague Castle," Leo suggested. "If you're up to it."

I snorted in a very unladylike manner.

"I'll have you know," I said as my sneakers skittered sideways once more on the loose gravel, "I'm an expert mountain climber. I've climbed Denali and Pike's Peak and—"

I broke off as my ankle twisted on the slippery path, and Leo caught me with the ease of long practice.

"If only I had some pitons!" I snapped. "Or at least cleats."

Surprisingly, he ignored the opportunity to tease me. "I know, the footing is terrible" was all he said.

So I took his hand and let him help me out of the graveyard.

And then we started the ascent to Prague Castle. When Leo had said "up to the castle," he really meant *up*. We had climbed about a thousand steps and were still climbing when I paused to take a breath and admire the view. Leo said nothing, waiting patiently, as I watched a class of grade-school children scamper past me, skipping easily up the stairs.

Well! I pushed myself off the rock and resumed climbing in grim silence. At the top, I paused again, enjoying the welcome feel of burning thigh muscles. How I missed those climbs with my father! "If only I had better shoes," I said again, and I saw Leo smile to himself.

We watched as one young couple carried their sleeping baby's stroller between them all the way up the steep steps and staggered onto the pavement at the top, collapsing with groans of exhaustion. But they high-fived each other with the grins of true comrades, and I felt a twist of envy.

Leo hadn't even noticed. "A high defensive point and good fresh water source," he muttered to himself.

"What?"

"It's a solid defensive position," he explained. "Good site for a medieval castle."

"If an army managed to climb up here and still had the strength to attack," I said, "then they deserve to win."

He grinned. "Tell that to the Czechs."

He heaved me to my feet, and I groaned as fifteen blisters burned at the same time. "Are you okay?" he asked.

"Of course I'm okay," I snapped.

"I know, Denali and Pike's Peak and all that," he said. "Only to be defeated by a pair of worn sneakers and blistered toes."

With a martyred sigh, he reached into his wallet and pulled out—blessing of all blessings—a handful of crumpled Band-Aids. "Here," he said, tossing them to me. "Bandage up those blisters."

I stared at him. "Why on earth do you carry Band-Aids in your wallet?"

He grinned again. "Instead of condoms, like a real man, you mean?"

Infuriatingly, I blushed.

"Because I have a dozen nieces and nephews, that's why," he said as I finished applying the bandages and stood up, blissfully pain-free.

"Thanks," I said.

"*B'vakasha*," he replied. "Shall we explore the castle?"

Leo headed straight to the museum, and I sighed to myself. Spy and Cold War museums were fun, but history museums, not so much. In all of our travels, my father had never bothered taking me to museums. They were full of dead people's stuff, when we were so gloriously alive—alive and free and outside in the bright, blinding sun or frozen mountains. History was meaningless when we were alive and outdoors and together. For a moment, I remembered Kali's accusation—*he always took you into danger*—and felt chilled. But I loved the danger and the reckless abandon with which he courted it; the more I dared, the prouder he was. Playing it safe was for boring people, my father had said. Not us. I felt a sudden stab as I thought of where my life had taken me—to mousy Amy the banker—and wondered what he would have thought of it. But I didn't have to wonder; I knew.

Suddenly feeling low, I followed Leo obediently and wandered aimlessly through the dead exhibits, while he stopped short in front of a grubby brown stone fragment. Prayerfully, he said to me, "Do you realize this is five thousand years old? Look, *motek*."

I looked. Grubby stone—that was all I saw.

Most of the exhibits had come from graves. "Thank God for funerals," Leo commented, and my nose wrinkled with distaste.

I realized that this was my real chance to escape from Leo. His utter inability to bypass a single historical artifact was my greatest advantage. If I could just shake him for a few hours, I could get away, and maybe he wouldn't bother to track me down again; he would have to tire of this game eventually. He moved among the ancient grave goods like a man in a trance, occasionally shaking his head in disapproval at something that didn't meet his standards or in disbelief at the wondrous treasures he was viewing.

"Jules," he said in a low voice, "*voyez-vous*, these jewels were buried with the corpse of a six-month-old boy in the ninth century. Just imagine, those parents welcoming a healthy boy into the world. God be praised, a boy! And then having him sicken and die after he survived childbirth and those first dangerous months. They must have thought he was safe. They presented him with gold and jewels, and then . . ." His voice trailed off.

The "jewels" just looked like more dingy brown stone to me. I commented, "At that time, parents must have expected to lose their children young."

He swung around to stare at me. "That's a myth, you know. Parents grieved deeply when they lost their children. Why, the inscriptions on the graves of—"

"Yes, yes," I interrupted, losing interest. But as I looked more closely at the grubby lumps, their shapes began to emerge: tiny child-size gold bracelets and rings, brooches and pendants. Suddenly I too could feel the parents' grief at the loss of a beloved child.

I, who had always considered myself the most unsentimental of women, felt my eyes moisten. Horrified, I moved away from the case and reminded myself that this was the moment to escape. Leo would never be able to tear himself away from his grimy treasures in time to follow me.

But it seemed unsporting, somehow.

Instead, I took his arm and steered him over to a child-size suit of armor. "Tell me about this," I said.

He told me, at great length. At last we moved on, and Leo was momentarily rendered speechless by Vladislav Hall, the largest secular room in medieval Prague, which stretched for multiple football fields under great vaulted ceilings. His lips moved silently in some sort of intense internal colloquy, until I prodded him quite painfully in the ribs and he woke with a start.

Next on Leo's agenda was the monastery library, yet another huge chamber. Great stones formed the walls and pillars, and the coffered ceilings seemed at least a mile high. Yards of bookcases and cabinets, dotted by a few enormous portraits, were the room's only decoration, and the dim lighting only emphasized the massiveness of this temple of books.

Intimidated by the size and grandeur, I envied Leo his easy entry into the sacrosanct rooms. He showed his ID to the uniformed guard, who immediately pulled out his walkie-talkie. Within moments we were surrounded by a group of admiring academics. "This is Dr. Leo Schlumberger of Oxford," one exclaimed to another.

"*The* Dr. Schlumberger? The one who wrote *Dialectic, Dissent, and Discourse in Medieval* . . ."

Leo's fan club dispersed eventually, and tourists watched admiringly and enviously as he donned plastic gloves and strode over to a shelf of manuscripts. He pulled down a dusty volume and paged cautiously through it. I tried without success to peer over his shoulder.

His eyebrows rose, and he grinned. "Well, well," he said. "Who would have thought it?"

I couldn't contain myself any longer. "What? What?"

Maddeningly, he closed the huge ledger and returned it carefully to its place. "Just a spot of philandering among the churchmen," he said.

I shrugged and moved on to gaze up at a portrait of a *very* grand lady. Her dress was dripping with lace and pearls and finery, her jewels shone with gold, and her face was set in the haughty stare of a person who knows herself to be of great consequence.

"I wonder who she was," I mused in spite of myself. "I wish they would label these things."

Leo glanced up. "Oh, that's one of Maria Theresa's daughters," he said absently. "They all looked alike. See the Hapsburg chin?"

Impressed in spite of myself, I looked more closely.

"One of Marie Antoinette's sisters," he added.

Was there anything he didn't know?

"Actually," Leo said, taking my hand and guiding me over to the opposite side of the room so we could sit, "there's a funny story about Marie Antoinette and her brother, the Austrian emperor Joseph II. Her family was worried that after five years of marriage to Louis XVI of France, she still hadn't conceived a child. Marie's mother wrote to her every month asking if she'd gotten her period, and if so, was she having sex on the right day, and was she trying to entice her husband into bed?"

"Well, was she?" I asked.

"Probably. But poor Louis was just a boy when they married—fifteen and young for his age. He probably had no idea what to do with a pretty girl like Marie. They probably didn't consummate their marriage for seven years."

I suspected that Leo had known what to do at fifteen.

"Anyway," he went on, "Maria Theresa sent her son, Emperor Joseph, to Versailles so he could try to figure out what was going on. He and Louis talked for hours. No one will ever know exactly what the two men discussed, but within months Marie Antoinette was pregnant."

"So, what do you think . . ." I trailed off.

He shrugged. "All of France was gossiping in quite astonishing detail about the King's impotence. One courtier wrote in a letter that poor Louis had a tiny penis; others speculated that he had some genital malformation that required surgery."

I winced, and Leo nodded. "Quite," he said. "Joseph wrote to the Grand Duke of Tuscany that 'it's not a weakness of the body or spirit. . . . In his marriage bed, he has strong erections, he inserts his member, remains there for perhaps two minutes without moving, withdraws without ejaculating, and, while still erect, bids good night. It's incomprehensible.'"

"I'll say," I murmured.

"Joseph added, 'Ah, if only I could have been present once, I would have set him straight! He should be whipped until he discharges in anger like a donkey. My sister does not have the temperament for this, and together they make an utterly inept couple.'"

"So the Emperor of Austria was Marie Antoinette's Dr. Ruth," I said, smiling.

"Quite," Leo said again. "You see how much fun history can be? It's all about the people." He stood up. "Shall we continue our tour?"

I stood up too, and he took my hand. "Come," he invited. "*On y va.*"

We strolled out of the library into a darker afternoon. Storm clouds were threatening, and the day had turned from bright sunlight into a lowering gloom. I glanced around uneasily, noting that most of the tourists had disappeared and we seemed to be alone on the huge stone plaza. "Maybe we should head back to the hotel," I suggested.

"But we haven't seen the—" Leo began to protest.

And then a shot exploded.

Chapter 19

Well, not "exploded," precisely, because the shooter had used a silencer. But the bullet whizzed past Leo's ear with a nasty whine and struck the stone wall behind him with such force that small fragments of rock flew out in a lethal spray. I jumped back involuntarily, and Leo swore.

"This way," he snapped, grabbing my arm, and we broke into a run. Singularly handicapped by the uneven stone underneath our feet and the treacherous, dark shadows cast by the dying sun, I tripped several times in my useless shoes and was held upright only by the sheer force of Leo's grip. We raced around the corner of the monastery, dodged in and out of dark alcoves, and ran up and down staircases that led nowhere. The castle grounds were a maze, perfect for a game of hide-and-seek. Deadly serious hide-and-seek.

Leo dragged me into an anonymous outbuilding, and we slipped behind some ancient, musty curtains as I pressed my hand to my mouth to hold back the sneezes. "Where do you think he is?" I whispered, proud of the steadiness of my voice.

"I don't know." Leo's voice was tight and clipped. I glanced at him and saw blood running down his cheek. One of the flying stone fragments must have cut him, I thought. Again. Again, Leo was bleeding, and someone was chasing us.

He must have read my thoughts. "Being with you is very bad for my health," he said dryly.

"Being with you is very bad for mine," I retorted. We exchanged suspicious glares.

"We can't stay here," Leo muttered, and he twitched the curtain aside for a cautious look.

Following his nod, I eased out from behind the curtains and stood looking about. We were in a weapons armory, and I recognized the irony. Leo was probably itching for a gun at his waist. I knew I was. None of these ancient, rusted, dull weapons would serve us now, however.

"Come on," he whispered, and we began to edge our way out of the building.

A dark figure appeared around a corner, and another whipped out from behind a stone pillar. The two men were advancing slowly, their weapons drawn, and Leo was poised on the balls of his feet, ready for action. What kind of action, I couldn't even begin to imagine. We were pretty badly outgunned.

Gun. That gave me an idea.

"Bloody hell," Leo said clearly. "Stay back, Amy."

He didn't have to tell me twice. I edged back into the armory and looked around frantically. Then I saw the old blunderbuss.

Without taking the time to be scared, I flung off my sweater and wrapped it around my hand and then smashed the glass of the exhibit case and grabbed the blunderbuss.

Alarms rang out. *Good*, I thought.

Staggering under the weight of the heavy weapon, I ran back to the half-open door and threw it to Leo.

I prayed that I was right about the blunderbuss.

Leo seized the weapon in his hands and fired.

Or misfired, I should say. As I had hoped, there was enough gunpowder in the ancient barrel to produce one hell of a ball of gray, choking smoke. The two attackers retreated in haste, and more alarms rang out. In the distance, I heard cars revving up and police sirens beginning to blare.

Leo dropped the blunderbuss and grabbed my arm once more. "We have to get out of here," he said.

So we ran again. Down and up the staircases, in and out of blind alcoves, back and forth among the winding alleyways, until, at last, we found ourselves at the top of the Golden Lane, a charming little shopping street built into the ancient stone of the castle grounds. Leo ducked into a public WC to wash the smoke and grit from his eyes and the blood from his face, while I, seized by an inexplicable desire, plunged enthusiastically into the tiny shops.

Leo found me drooling over a gorgeous porcelain doll wearing a hand-sewn Czech traditional costume and had to drag me away.

"Are you crazy?" he snapped. "Shopping for souvenirs when we're running for our lives?"

"We're not running now," I said. Couldn't he understand that just for a moment, I wanted to be an innocent tourist?

"This game isn't fun anymore," Leo said.

"It never was," I retorted.

Our eyes met, and suddenly I was brimming with fury again. "You bloody idiot!" I threw at him. "You got us shot at again!"

"Me?" he retorted. "You're the one hiding behind a fake name! It's you they're shooting at!"

"Don't be ridiculous," I snapped.

"I thought maybe it was an abusive boyfriend, but spurned boyfriends don't shoot at strangers in the darkness! Who the fuck are you, anyway?"

"Who the fuck am I?" I hissed back. "Who the fuck are *you?*"

We glared at each other, practically panting in our mutual

rage and suspicion. Then the fight went out of me, and I almost sagged, drained of energy and anger.

"Let's have something to eat," Leo suggested, more pacifically.

As the adrenaline burst subsided, I was suddenly hungry. Again. So I agreed and let him lead me into a very chintzy, flowery teashop that reminded me of the porcelain doll he had made me abandon.

After we'd ordered, Leo leaned back in his chair and studied me again. "Tell me more about your sheikh," he said.

"Why?"

"Because. Maybe he's the one behind these attacks."

My chubby, grandfatherly Sheikh Abdullah? "No," I said firmly. "Besides, I have to maintain client confidentiality."

"Well, that's helpful," Leo said sarcastically. "It's just that when people try to kill me, I tend to take it personally. I'd like to know who and why."

"Tell *me* about your work with Mossad," I returned sharply. We scowled at each other.

Leo sighed. "I do not work for Mossad. Never have and never will. After my time in the military, I don't want anything to do with war or politics again. I want to study long-dead queens and live a long, peaceful life." He studied me for a moment. "Can you say the same?"

A long, peaceful life? No, I was my father's daughter. I demanded, "Aren't you still in the reserves? Don't you have to serve when Israel goes to war?"

"Well, of course. That's true for all Israeli men."

"And don't you carry a weapon?"

"Again, most Israeli men who are in the reserves carry weapons when in Israel. *Motek*, this all means nothing. I am an academic, plain and simple."

For a moment, I pictured a world in which aging, stooped professors dueled with swords and pistols in wild conflict. One graying academic would parry a blow from another, proclaiming, "Never will I agree to a textual discourse on the Devonshire Papers! Never, I say!"

Ridiculous.

I studied Leo closely until he squirmed with discomfort. Tall. Strong build. Quick as a cat. Probably comfortable with any manner of weapons. Multilingual. Cool under pressure. Of course he was a spy. A Perfect Spy, as my favorite author, John le Carré, would say.

We sat in silence as the waitress brought us a massive tea service of scones, clotted cream, jams, cookies, and tiny finger sandwiches. I dug in hungrily, and Leo followed suit.

"I have an idea," he said.

"What?"

"Let's do some more sightseeing tomorrow. Let's see if they follow us. Maybe we can trap them and figure out what they're after."

"Are you crazy?" I demanded. "We're not armed, and they are. How do you think you can take on—"

"I don't *think* I can," the gentle and peaceable university professor said. "I *know* I can."

Chapter 20

Well, I knew I could too.

So the next morning, ostentatiously armed with a guidebook and map, we set out to do more sightseeing. Our first stop, chosen by me, was the KGB Museum. I was amused to realize that it was just a few doors down from the US embassy—conveniently located for clandestine meetings, I thought.

Leo, who had wanted to visit the ancient-history museum, was sulking. "Why are you obsessed with spies, anyway?" he asked me as we waited by the entrance.

"I love spy books," I told him. "And spy movies."

"But why?"

I shrugged. "Who knows? My father turned me on to them when I was little."

Leo said, "Tell me again what your father did?"

"He was an international energy consultant," I recited.

"For whom?"

"The same company I worked for when I first moved to London. International Development Consultants, IDC."

"But what exactly did he *do*?" Leo persisted.

Honestly, I had no idea. My father's work at IDC was the least interesting thing about him. I knew he was trying to make the world a safer place; that was what he always told me when I asked about his work.

I shrugged, and Leo would have pressed me further had the doors not opened. It was a strange, strange place—a small, dark series of rooms filled with glass cases and indeterminable objects. The guide and owner, who spoke in a thick Russian accent and never gave his name, struck me as an intriguing character at the beginning. But very soon I was shying away from him whenever he passed too close to me, and I was glad of Leo's solid bulk behind me.

As with the Spy Museum in Berlin, there were more gadgets and more of Leo's disparaging comments; he actually laughed out loud when the owner pointed to a Maxwell Smart–style shoe phone. I wasn't finding any of it funny, though. The owner—I had nicknamed him Vladimir in my head—certainly knew how to handle a firearm, as he brandished machine guns and Glocks with equal relish. In his thick accent, in the dark, gloomy room, he told hair-raising stories about interrogations gone wrong and assassinations gone right.

Then we got to the swords and knives. I hid behind Leo and absolutely refused to touch any of the lethally sharp weapons our guide passed around so casually. I cringed when Vladimir demonstrated martial arts moves that ended in garroting or stabbing or both.

When we emerged into the fresh, sunny outdoors, I shook myself as if awakening from a bad dream. "That was creepy," I said to Leo.

"You see? I told you we should have gone to the ancient-history museum."

I tucked my hand into his arm, enjoying the feel of hard muscle under my fingers. Leo smiled down at me. "Where to next, *motek*?"

"Someplace not creepy and not tragic."

"Well . . . I was going to take you around the old Jewish Quarter."

That would be, I suspected, both creepy and tragic. "Why don't you go on your own?" I suggested. "I'd like to walk around and do some shopping."

He looked at me dubiously.

"Really," I said. But I liked that he knew me well enough to be suspicious of my sudden desire for retail therapy.

"Well," he said, "what about our plan to entrap our followers?"

"I never agreed to it," I said firmly. "I just want to go shopping."

"All right," Leo said reluctantly. "You should be safe enough as long as you stick to Parizska Street and go straight back to the hotel."

I assured him I would, and he hesitated. "Please be careful," he said, frowning at me.

"I'll be safe," I assured him, with complete sincerity.

"Well, then . . ." With a swift movement, he pulled me into his arms and just stood for one long moment. "Bye for now," he said, turning and tossing the goodbye over his shoulder. "See you at the hotel."

Like a besotted fool, I was momentarily frozen to the spot. I watched Leo's disappearing back with a curious mixture of desire and outrage. If he thought he could use that charm to break me down, then he didn't know me at all.

In something of a daze, I got myself turned around and headed back down the street to the US embassy. We went through the same rigmarole of passports and fingerprints and cameras until I was inside the safe haven of the embassy's inner sanctum, guarded by a dozen heavily armed marines and the power of the US government. *See, Leo,* I thought, *I told you I'd be safe!*

JANE ELIZABETH HUGHES

This time, my father's old friend was bearded, not clean-shaven, and tall, not stooped. But he had the same wary eyes and air of command that Henry in Berlin had had—and Leo too, come to think of it.

"Thank you for meeting with me, Angus."

"The pleasure is all mine," he said. "I'm so sorry about your father. I knew him well."

"Yes," I said. "Thank you." I hated when people said that. No one knew my father as well as I did.

He led me into a large, comfortable office with barred windows and gestured to a big captain's chair in front of his desk. "Please," he said. "Sit."

I sat. I imagined that most people did what Angus Moore told them to do. Again I thought of Leo.

"Did Henry get in touch with you?" I began. "We met in Berlin?" I didn't know why I was speaking in questions, except that this tall, keen-eyed man was looking down at me from his perch on the desk with such an assessing stare.

"Yes," he said. "Henry and I spoke at length. We are both concerned about your safety, and in our capacity as, shall we say, in loco parentis . . ."

No, we shall not, I thought, with some heat. No one could ever stand in for my father. And no one needed to.

"We think you should return to London immediately and break off all ties with this man. We're not sure who he is, exactly. . . ."

Well, join the crowd.

"But since you've been attacked only when you're with him and there are some questions about his intentions . . ."

I smiled involuntarily, and Angus broke off, in some confusion. He waited, and I said weakly, "'His intentions' sounds like such an old-fashioned phrase."

Angus said, with a half smile, "I wasn't suggesting he would be asking for your hand. . . ."

"Of course I didn't mean . . . ," I said at the same time.

An embarrassed silence.

Angus cleared his throat. "At any rate, you should get away from your young man and go home and back to work."

I knew his advice was well meant and eminently sensible, but I resented him all the same—not least for his assumption that Leo could not possibly be interested in my own humble self. Angus knew that too.

Gently, he said, "My dear young lady, I am sure your father would tell you just what I'm telling you: At best, this man brings you bad luck. At worst, well . . ."

I nodded and stood up. "Thank you for your time," I told him.

He kissed me on both cheeks and stood back as I walked out the heavy doors, tripping over the floor jamb in my haste to escape. I knew he was right: It was time to end whatever this was with Leo and get on with my job.

When I returned to my hotel room, even worse news awaited me. My friend Rosie had emailed me from Washington:

Your man of mystery looks like trouble. Heard back from a friend about his military service. He was definitely military intelligence and apparently disappeared for months at a time, probably deep undercover. God knows what he's mixed up in now.

You'd better shake him.

Chapter 21

Originally I had thought that if I let Leo hang around long enough, I would figure out what he was really after and how he had found out about Jules. But after weeks of his shadow hovering over me, I was still not a jot wiser. He had revealed nothing, and I knew nothing more—except that he was dangerously attractive and not above using this allure to get what he wanted. All of my advisors—Angus, Henry, Rosie—were right: He was a nuisance at the very least and a danger at the most. It was time to cut him loose.

And I had begun to think he was telling the truth. I had even begun to think he was genuinely sweet on me, but no. It was all business.

Anyway, I was a loner. I didn't travel in pairs. The only traveling companion I had ever wanted was my father.

Grimly, I started throwing things into my bags. I didn't know why I had packed so much. Maybe I hadn't been sure I was returning to London.

But I was—back to boring London and prissy, narcissistic Audrey at Atlantic Bank and her flock of mini-mes. No more Leo, no more jaunts through the winding, medieval streets of Eastern Europe, no more strangers on the attack, no more wild flights, no more museums and guns.

No more Leo.

Briefly, I regretted the porcelain doll outside Prague Castle.

Three hours later I was airborne, thanks to a half-empty EasyJet flight and the wonders of my corporate American Express card. And eight hours after that, I was back at my desk at the bank, sorting through emails and phone messages.

Leo knew where I was, of course. He knew where I lived and worked. Hell, my stepsister lived with his sister! So I would never "escape" him, but I was done with him. How could I even think about sleeping with a man who lied to me, consistently and thoroughly? He could follow me around for the rest of my life if he wanted, but we were done.

Not that there ever had been a "we," of course. And not that I wanted to sleep with him—or anyone.

Kristen R. dimpled at me. "How was Berlin?" she asked politely.

Audrey glanced up with a brief frown. "Kristen," she said, "do you have time for a pop-up meeting? I'd like to really dig into those numbers on Sheikh Osama before our ten o'clock."

For the first time, it occurred to me that Audrey actively disliked me. It wasn't just my differentness: my lackluster pedigree and advanced age and general mousiness. She actually disliked me. I wondered, did she resent having been strong-armed by some of Bob the Bear's friends into hiring me? Or did she just dislike everyone who didn't slavishly copy her every tic?

And I realized I actively disliked her too.

I masked my expression with a blank smile and went back to my emails again.

Sheikh Abdullah was pleased with the Tiffany bracelets and wanted three more. Once again, I pondered the recipients' identity and made a note to myself to do some discreet digging. You never knew what nuggets of information would turn out to be useful.

He also wanted me to track down a case of rare Château d'If wine (the 1992 vintage, he specified) and to book tickets for his favorite wife, Nouri, to a spa in Switzerland. Hmm. I amused myself by speculating about which part of her body was going to be lifted or lipo'ed this time. But then I realized the spa (i.e., plastic surgery clinic) was just outside Zurich, the private banking capital of the world, and made another note to myself. Nouri wasn't going to meet with other bankers, was she?

I could just imagine Audrey's reaction if my only client left the bank.

The last email was from Jake S., with the subject line *Field Day Madness!* Groaning inwardly, I clicked on it. Jake S.'s excitement was palpable. This year's Field Day promised more "fun and thrills" than ever. Jake advised everyone to wear clothes "you don't mind getting wet and muddy" and exhorted us all to "come with a spring in your step and a smile on your face!"

Ugh.

Ugh and fuck. I looked at the calendar and realized Field Day was this Saturday.

I glanced at the email again and recalled that Jake's last name was Segal. I remembered his fun fact about his grandfather's speaking only Yiddish. Gripped by a sudden need to know, I asked him what Jews say when they refer to a dead person.

He looked blank.

"Something *shalom*?" I persisted.

"Oh, yeah. *Alav ha-shalom*. It means 'peace be upon him.'" Jake glanced around, embarrassed at knowing something so utterly uncool.

I knew lots of Jews and could not recall ever having heard anyone use that phrase before. "Do all Jews say that?"

Jake looked appalled. "Christ, no! Only religious people. Or really old people." His tone suggested the two groups were equally repugnant. "My grandfather used to say it about my grandma." He paused. "Why do you want to know?"

"Oh," I said evasively, "I heard someone say it on TV, and I wondered what it meant. Thanks, Jake."

He had already forgotten the conversation.

But Leo was neither religious nor old. Was he?

Pushing aside the paperwork on my desk—Sheikh Abdullah had requested another $40,000 in cash for his wife's upcoming trip, and I had the usual boring documents to fill out—I decided to use one of our threat risk assessment matrix (TRAM) forms to analyze how much of a threat Leo could be.

Threat Risk Assessment Matrix

Potential Threat

Dr. Leo Schlumberger

Personality Profile

Intelligent, speaks multiple languages, highly trained ex-IDF [that sounded ominous, I realized]. Puts on stammering, apologetic British act but really quite personable. Wealthy, worldly, head of large family of art dealers. Motives unclear.

Scenarios

1. Journalist/scam artist. [I couldn't quite figure out his angle or what the scam could possibly be, but Nigerian princes don't hold a monopoly on scams, and this might be a devious way of gaining access to Atlantic Bank. Journalist seemed more possible, though still unlikely; what scandal was he hoping to expose? Dull Boy? Surely not.]

2. Villain/spy. [But why? Why? Why? Again, maybe the bank was a target of some bad guy(s); maybe there was a

blackmail scheme afoot. But what did this have to do with a woman named Jules?]

3.   Obsessed historian. [Leo could be just what he said he was. I had been certain after the car attack that he was in Category 2, but had reconsidered since then. The one certainty in this whole web of uncertainties was that he was obsessed with dead Tudor queens. And that just didn't seem to fit with Category 1 or 2.]

Probabilities

Scenario 1: 5 percent, I decided. Okay, 10 percent.
Scenario 2: Ditto.
Scenario 3: 80 percent, then? Was that right?

Policy Recommendations

1.   Scenario 1: Lose him. Whatever he wanted, it wasn't in the best interests of me or the bank.

2.   Scenario 2: See above. Avoid him at all costs. Continued contact was not worth the small benefit of untangling the Jules mystery.

3.   Scenario 3: ????? Was he as harmless as he appeared? Then again, there was the whole Jules thing and the 20 percent high-risk scenarios.

I reread my matrix and frowned; Audrey would instantly reject it and demand definitive statements, instead of the question marks. As in, "My assessment is that Dr. Schlumberger is highly likely to be benign; nonetheless, continued contact is discouraged because, while the probability of malign intentions is low, the potential damage arising from them could be high."

I frowned again. That wasn't right either. If I cut off all contact with Leo, I would never learn why he was convinced that I knew something about the elusive Jules. And also, I liked the guy. He was smart and intuitive and had been very kind to Kali—in fact, he was pretty good company when he wasn't trying to charm information out of me. I had no friends aside from my ex-colleagues from IDC, who were always globe-trotting while I sat and moldered in London. And the Katherine Parr and Baby Mary story had captivated me too; I wanted badly for them to have a happy ending.

Putting it down on paper seemed to magnify the ambiguities rather than resolve them, as I had hoped. Perhaps the TRAM wasn't a good assessment tool after all. All I had were more question marks. More flip-flopping.

So, then what should I do?

I had no idea.

I put the report into the shredder at the side of my desk, pulled out my cell phone, and dialed Kali.

"I only have a few minutes" was her greeting.

That was how she had answered her phone every time I'd called since she'd gone to France with Leo's sister. I hadn't realized how much I enjoyed her hero worship of me until it was gone.

"Why? What are you doing?" I asked. "And how are you?"

"Fine. The twins are getting ready to jump into the pool, and Benji"—she pronounced it the French way, Bahn-*zhee*—"just woke up from his nap."

"Where's Élodie?" I asked, worried that Kali was taking on too much.

"She took Amélie to her piano lesson."

I digested that. I had had only a few brief conversations with Kali since she had become assistant nanny to Élodie's four children—nine-year-old Amélie, six-year-old twins Leah and Sara, and nine-month-old Bahn-zhee—and, annoyingly, I still felt responsible for her.

"Are you okay?" I asked. "Are they working you too hard?"

"Oh, no, it's just very busy around here. Leah! Don't go outside without me!" In execrably bad French, she roared, "Leah, *faites attention! On y va!*" And to me, "Gotta go. Byeee!"

Spirits lifted by Kali's obvious contentment, I pressed the off button and scrolled again through the pictures of her and the children that she had texted me that morning. I wondered when Oncle Léo would go to visit his sister.

I had my "regular quarterly check-in" with Audrey scheduled for four o'clock that afternoon (everyone else had weekly check-ins) but got a text from her assistant at five thirty to say that Audrey was running late and would reschedule.

Yeah, I thought. *And I'm the Queen of Sheba.*

Thoroughly disgruntled, I walked back to my quiet, empty apartment.

And then it was Field Day. As instructed, I wore an old T-shirt and jeans to the posh Bellwood Club, just outside London, only to discover that my workmates were all, to a man (or woman), clad in lululemon from head to toe: tight-fitting capri yoga pants, even tighter tank tops, and sporty headbands.

Wrong-footed again.

Jake S., beaming and bustling about with importance as the organizer of Field Day, divided us into teams for the first activity, toilet papering. Each team was to wrap one unlucky person in toilet paper until not a speck of skin or clothing was visible. The first team to thoroughly mummify its colleague won.

Needless to say, my team selected me to be the mummy.

I stood as still as possible while shrieking, laughing sorority girls raced around me with rolls of toilet paper; I breathed in soggy tissue through my nose until they tut-tutted and told me, "Stop breathing! We can see your mouth!"

Was this supposed to be fun?

Audrey's daughter Pia's team won. Pia, at thirteen, was a mini-Audrey, only more openly competitive. She would learn to mask that in charm as she grew older, I thought. My team abandoned me to unwrap the toilet paper as best I could. It clung to my sweating T-shirt, and I peeled off soggy, disgusting lumps while my teammates high-fived each other for their great effort.

Next was the water-balloon toss. Kristen R., who had been captain of her lacrosse team at Princeton, flung the balloon at me with such enthusiasm that it crashed open against my chest and chin, soaking me in cold water and clingy, rubbery strands of broken balloon. Grimly, I brushed off the water as the Kristens giggled together at the sight of my wet T-shirt, and Kristen the Younger whispered something to Kristen T. about my bra.

Pia's team won again. I was beginning to discern a pattern.

Then came the all-time favorite: musical chairs. Pasting a manic grin on my face, I ran around the chairs with everyone else and was pleased to discover that I was almost good at this one. Everyone else was more concerned with dimpling and socializing, while I was laser-focused on getting a chair. Eventually it was down to just Pia and me. I rolled my shoulders and concentrated as Audrey started the music again.

The music stopped, and there was a chair behind me! Triumphant at my imminent victory, I plopped myself down into it, only to feel the whoosh of air as it was pulled out from under me. I fell, hard, to the floor instead. The jolt reverberated all the way up my spine to the base of my neck.

Chortling, Jake S. helped me to my feet as everyone else crowded around to congratulate Pia on her win. "You should have seen the look on your face," he said, still grinning.

I limped away.

The "barbecue" was vegan, and with some dismay I contemplated the platters of quinoa, tofurkey, and bean sprouts on the table. I had a headache from my head to my toes, I shivered when the cool wind hit my wet T-shirt, and my knees were bruised from being bowled over by the team of Pia and Kristen the Younger during the sack race.

In short, I was hungry. So I loaded up my plate with nuts, olives, and bread—the highest-calorie items I could find—and threw in a carob brownie for dessert. Everyone else nibbled daintily, commenting on the crispness of the sprouts and the nuances of the curry naan. I would have killed for a slab of meat and a baked potato dripping with butter and salt.

Then I bit into the carob brownie and promptly spat the mouthful back onto my plate. Kristen T. looked at me with raised eyebrows and then shrugged and turned back to Matt B. The "brownie" was worse than Vietnamese bat's-nest soup, and I started planning what I would eat if I ever got home. A box of chocolate biscuits, an extra-butter bag of microwave popcorn, a huge bottle of Fanta . . .

Audrey stood up. "I want to offer a toast," she said, dimpling, "to the most amazing team *ever!* Do you know when I'm on vacation with my family, I can't wait to get back to my peeps at the office? I really miss you guys!"

I glanced over at the suddenly expressionless Pia and thought, *It could be worse; I could be Audrey's daughter, instead of her employee.*

"The Truth Game!" Jake S. cried, pounding the table. "Let's end with a round of the Truth Game!"

Squeals of excitement. I shrugged to myself. I was an accomplished liar.

Apparently, the team members were supposed to tell a truth about themselves that they'd never told before. If anyone else already knew the "truth," then the "truth teller" had to chug a handful of sprouts.

I shuddered—anything to avoid that.

Audrey was the first truth teller. "Well"—she smiled, pushing her jet-black hair behind her ears and smiling her adorable gap-toothed smile—"I really feel like I'm not a day older than you guys."

At forty-five, the tiny Audrey was built like a thirteen-year-old boy, with nonexistent hips or boobs. In her lululemon capris and tank top, I had to admit, she barely looked any older than the twentysomethings around the table.

Whoops of delight greeted her statement. I thought she should be forced to gobble down the sprouts because we all already knew that, but her "peeps" thought it perfect. Surprise, surprise: There were no challenges.

Jake S. went next. "I have a crush on Kristen S.," he confessed with an equally adorable, almost shy smile.

Kristen the Younger, I interpreted. She blushed sweetly, and the Matts high-fived each other. "I knew it!" Matt B. cried.

Kristen the Younger said, "I think Matt S. is really cool," and Jake S. looked deflated.

Kristen R. said, "I want to be Audrey when I grow up" and was immediately challenged.

"We *all* want to be Audrey when we grow up!" Kristen T. shouted. "Everyone knows that!" So Kristen R. had to eat her sprouts.

Matt S., who had drunk too much elderberry wine and clearly misunderstood the game, said, "I hate hot yoga. And I hate vinyasa yoga even more."

Horrified silence. I wondered when Matt would be forgiven for actually telling a truth.

Pia said, with a glance at Audrey, "I want to be just like my mother when I grow up."

No one challenged Audrey's daughter. Ever.

My turn. I said, "I hate working out at the gym."

Pause. Clearly, no one knew how to respond to something so unimaginable.

Kristen T. said, with some confusion, "I don't understand."

Kristen the Younger said sweetly, "Oh, Amy, you're so funny! I always thought California girls were supposed to be real balls of fire, but you're just . . ."

"Mousy" was the word she was searching for, but I wasn't about to supply it. "Quiet," she said.

Ha! I thought. *She should see me with Leo, dodging bullets and spitting fire.*

Somebody chortled, and I berated myself for having come up with such a stupid lie. Next time, I would just say I wanted to be Audrey when I grew up.

Blessedly, Field Day was over. I endured a round of kissing and hugging and damp promises of eternal love and fidelity. I was just changing from my sopping-wet sneakers into street shoes when Kristen R. and Audrey came over to me.

"A word, Amy?" Audrey said.

"Yes?" I felt at a disadvantage, sitting on a chair while they stood over me, so I stood up on my one shod foot.

No dimples were in sight. Audrey said to Kristen, "Tell her what you told me."

"My source at the FBI tells me they're planning to freeze Sheikh Abdullah's accounts until the investigation is over."

"Jesus," I said involuntarily, and Audrey frowned. Nouri's trip to Zurich flashed into my mind, and I said, again, "Jesus. No."

"Of course," Audrey said expressionlessly, "if you don't have the sheikh's accounts to manage, then there's no place for you at Atlantic Bank."

And, leaving me hopping on one foot, they walked away.

Chapter 22

All thoughts of biscuits and popcorn fled my mind as I dazedly put on my other shoe and made my way outside to the waiting Uber. Everyone else was chattering excitedly about the "after-party" they were planning at a Covent Garden pub, and no one even noticed my silent escape.

I turned on my phone but sat staring at it, ignoring the Uber driver's attempt at polite conversation. Usually I chatted away to Uber drivers because I wanted my rating to stay high. Tonight I couldn't manage it. Instead I clutched my phone, wondering who to call.

Absurdly, Leo flashed into my mind.

I shook my head. If those accounts were frozen, two long years of work would go down the drain. Those bloody, blasted FBI clods! Two years of putting up with Audrey and the Pretty Young Things. Two years of filling out forms and kowtowing to the sheikh and submitting to petty humiliations. Two years for *nothing!* And I was getting so close.

Bob, I thought. *I should call Bob. He'll be able to help me.* But then I remembered he was in Afghanistan with Dorcas and Will. There had been an emergency of some sort, and he had rushed out to help them. Fervently, I wished I still worked for IDC and could have gone to Afghanistan too, to help my colleagues.

So, no Bob.

Rosie, my computer-whiz friend in DC, might have some information. Quickly, I tapped out an urgent text asking her if she could find out anything about the FBI probe but then deleted it. This was an Atlantic Bank iPhone, and I didn't want someone accessing my messages in an investigation. It would have to wait until I got home.

Leo, I thought again.

Ridiculous.

But somehow I wasn't surprised when the Uber pulled up in front of my house and there he was, patiently leaning against the lamppost as if I had conjured him up. He straightened and strolled over to me as I got out of the car.

"Rough day at the office?" he inquired, taking in my bedraggled look and reaching out to pluck a strand of wet tissue paper from my chest. He glanced at it quizzically before flicking it to the ground.

"Field Day," I said.

"Ah. Team bonding and all that?"

Unwillingly, I smiled. "Audrey and her peeps bonded."

"The Pretty Young Things."

I nodded.

He reached into his jacket pocket and pulled out a letter-size envelope. "May I come up?" he asked, gesturing toward the stoop.

It had been an awful day. Just minutes before, I had been yearning for my silent apartment and a bowlful of junk food. But now, weary and defeated and flip-flopping again, I couldn't stop myself from nodding and handing him the key. He unlocked the door, and we proceeded up the stairs in silence.

Once inside the apartment, Leo headed immediately for the kitchen. "Get yourself into a nice warm shower and some comfortable clothes," he threw over his shoulder. "I'll make some tea."

Just tea? I wondered.

"With brandy," he added, as if he could read my thoughts.

Well, thank God for that.

Warmed by the brandy and a cuddly, fleecy sweatshirt, I sat next to Leo on the couch and stared into the fire he had built. "Everything is about to be ruined," I said to him.

He stared at me. "How did you find out?"

"Well, Audrey told me, of course."

"How in God's name does Audrey know about Nemtsov?"

"What? I was talking about the sheikh and the FBI."

"What?"

We stared at each other in mutual incomprehension.

Leo laughed. "Let's start all over again. You first. What's about to be ruined?"

"My work," I said. "The FBI is going to freeze my sheikh's accounts, and I'll be out of a job. I worked so hard on this, and it's all about to be trashed by those stupid, bumbling oafs!"

"I'm sorry to hear that," Leo said politely. "But don't you hate that job anyway?"

"Yes, but . . ." I trailed off and shrugged. "You'd never understand."

Leo rolled his eyes.

"What were you talking about, anyway?" I asked.

He pulled out the letter again. "This is a work permit for Sudeley Castle. Nemtsov is on the brink of receiving permission to close the castle to visitors and begin interior demolition."

I stared at the letter in confusion. After Rosie's information, I had determined that the whole Sudeley affair was just a pretext—but why? Good God, why?—for Leo to approach me, but he seemed utterly sincere.

"Look, for the love of God," Leo said, "I need your help. I'm begging you. I'm pleading with you—for the sake of history and all that's good and true in the world—please, please, tell me about Jules."

I wished I could help him. Truly, I did.

But, "I'm so sorry," I said. "I just can't help you."

He looked at me in silence. "I think you can," he said at last.

"I'm sorry," I repeated.

Leo dropped his head back against the sofa and threw an arm over his eyes. I twitched uncomfortably, twisting my hair around my fingers.

"Don't fidget," he said, eyes still closed.

I gulped down more tea and brandy.

"Leo," I began.

"Quiet. I'm thinking."

I shrugged and drank some more.

At last, he said. "Fine. I understand. Will you at least go on another field trip with me?"

Another field trip? "Every time I travel with you, people chase us and shoot us," I said. "I don't think you're a great traveling companion."

Amazingly, he grinned. "We're just going to Grimsthorpe Castle," he said. "I think we'll be safe there."

"You think?" I repeated, unconvinced.

He sat up straight and lifted his shirttail to show me some olive skin and . . . the dull gleam of a gun, tucked into a discreet holster on his jeans.

I gulped. "You can't carry concealed in the UK!"

"And yet I am," Leo said.

"Jesus," I said, for the third time that day.

"So, Grimsthorpe?" he persisted.

Why not?

"Okay," I said.

"Okay, then." He reached out a long arm to pull me hard against him and dropped a light kiss on my hair before getting up to go.

"Lock the door behind me," he said, and was gone.

Grimsthorpe Castle! My internet research that night revealed little. It was tucked into a remote corner of Lincolnshire, open to the public on Sundays. But because the web page had not been updated for several years, I suspected it was not much of a tourist attraction. On the bright side, it did have a lovely tearoom.

"So, why Grimsthorpe?" I asked as I settled into the welcoming leather of his Audi.

"Grimsthorpe," Leo pronounced solemnly, "was owned by Catherine Willoughby, the Duchess of Suffolk. She was Queen Katherine Parr's best friend and guardian of the baby Lady Mary Seymour when she was orphaned."

Oh, yes, the one who had so resented having to pay for the baby's upkeep.

"Presumably," Leo added, "Baby Mary was sent to Grimsthorpe when she passed into the Duchess of Suffolk's care, following the execution of Tom Seymour. The baby was about seven months old then."

I nodded. "So, she lived at Grimsthorpe?"

"Yes. There are no surviving artifacts from that time. They've all disappeared or been dispersed to other sites, but it occurs to me that there may be records of where some of those artifacts are."

"There won't be any exciting discoveries today, then?" I asked, remembering Kali's momentous find at Sudeley. I still felt a chill down my spine when I recalled her light, curious voice saying, "Lady Mary, the Queen's Daughter," and the rapt look on Leo's face. I was a little disappointed to learn that Grimsthorpe would not yield any such moments.

"Afraid not," Leo said. "But there is always that teashop."

Grimsthorpe lived up to its name; heavier and gloomier than Sudeley, it had stones stained black with age and was deeply shadowed by the huge, hulking trees that loomed over it. I shivered as we walked through the heavy gates and into the great hall, whose dark, low ceilings threatened to enclose us.

"Ugh," I said decisively. "Did I ever tell you I'm claustrophobic?"

Leo glanced down at me. "No, you're not."

"Yes, I am."

"No, you're not. Didn't you go spelunking with your father?"

Dimly, I remembered telling him about our caving expeditions in Morocco. "That's different," I said.

"I don't like it here either," he admitted.

We wandered through the rooms, their stone walls weeping with moisture and the massive, gloomy furniture increasing our sense of depression. Leo took my hand as we proceeded into the Willoughby Room, the only room in the castle with furniture supposedly dating from Catherine Willoughby's era. Remembering how many trustworthy people had warned me away from him, I gently eased my hand out of his grip.

"Here's an account book of the Duchess's," I said, wandering over to the lady's desk that stood in a dimly lit corner.

Leo peered closely at the small, faint writing. "This is from 1540," he said. "Too early for us."

"Oh well," I said. "Are you ready for some tea?"

He was still looking at the account book. "I wonder where the others are," he mused. "There must be references to expenditures for the baby in later account books."

"You said there's nothing here . . . ," I began.

"No. But where did her papers go?" he murmured.

I shrugged. "Tea?" I suggested again.

Lost in thought, he didn't answer, so I took his arm and shook it gently. "Tea," I said more loudly.

He shook himself, like a man coming out of a trance.

"Tea," he repeated obediently.

"Tell me," I said over a mouthful of clotted cream and strawberry jam, "how you traced the baby's descendants to this modern-day person." I couldn't bring myself to say "Jules."

"Research," he said absently, still brooding on the missing account books.

"Leo!" I snapped. "Pay attention!"

He blinked. "Sorry. Yes. Well, I found references to a man called Edward Seymour—Ned, that is—who was born in Lincolnshire around 1570 and whose grandsire was said to be 'that knave and rascal Tom Seymour, brother to our late and sorely lamented Queen Jane.'"

"Ohhkaay," I said dubiously.

"So I thought his father might have been the Seymour cousin mentioned in the letter I told you about—the lad that Lady Mary may have been betrothed to. Then there's another letter from the 1580s, referring to 'Ned Seymour, son of the Queen's Daughter.'"

"Hmm," I said.

"That was the hard part," Leo said, clearly indignant that I wasn't more impressed. Probably his girl students swooned regularly at his feet. "Finding the original descendants, I mean. After that, it was pretty easy to trace this Ned's family down through the years. They were prominent landowners and fortunate enough to keep producing sons to carry on the name."

"Until now," I said unguardedly.

This time, his glance at me was more intent. "Yes," Leo said. "Until Jules."

I didn't say anything.

"So my theory is," Leo continued, "that Baby Mary married a cousin of some sort, thus keeping the Seymour name, and they had at least one surviving son, Ned. This Ned was a swashbuckling sort too, excessively handsome and auburn-haired, like his grandfather. I think Ned was our Baby Mary's son."

"Maybe. But wasn't Seymour a fairly common name? Weren't there lots of Seymours around?"

Leo ignored me. "This Ned was something of an adventurer too," he went on. "Traveled to Araby and the Indios and brought back lots of exotic Orientalia for his family, including a monkey and a little brown-skinned girl, whom they exhibited for guests before she died of the plague. Poor thing," he added.

"So, what about Mary? Are you sure she was this Ned's mother?"

"Not clear," he admitted. "I just can't figure out why there's no record of Mary herself. It's as if she dropped off the face of the earth sometime around her first birthday and never appeared again. Nothing at all, until the reference to Ned, Tom Seymour's grandson."

"What sort of reference are you looking for?"

"The usual: account books, letters, parish registers, diaries . . . something! *Someone* must have spent money on her. Someone must have seen her or talked to her. Someone must have married her. But there's nothing. Absolutely nothing."

He sighed, and a lock of curly black hair fell across his forehead.

An odd thought crossed my mind, but it seemed too random to say aloud. Instead I said, "Mary was a very famous baby, right? That's what you said—the Queen's daughter, the orphaned child of a celebrity couple."

"Right. That's why I don't think she could have died so anonymously that no one, ever, in all of England, mentioned it. The death of a child that famous would have been talked about countrywide."

"Maybe," I said, voicing my thoughts aloud, "maybe someone disappeared her."

Chapter 23

This time, his glance at me held nothing but respect.

"Yes," he said. "I thought of that. But why? Whom could she possibly have threatened? She was the Queen's daughter, yes, but not the King's. She had no claim to the throne. . . ."

His voice trailed off in frustration, and once again a thought flitted through my mind. This time, I caught hold of it and held it.

"Let's try to find those other account books," I suggested.

Leo smiled at me, and our eyes met. "Quite," he said.

On the outskirts of Winchcombe, Leo pulled into the gravel parking lot of a small gastropub. It was called the Queen's Fancy and had walls of mellow Cotswold stone, as well as a real thatched roof. "Tea?" he suggested. "Again?"

Suddenly, I was starved. Fortunately, "tea" in England could mean anything from an actual cup of tea to a five-course supper. I hoped he meant the latter. "Sure," I said.

Leo had to duck his head as we passed under the low stone doorway and entered a dimly lit chamber filled with rickety wooden tables and chairs, and a long bar at the end of the room. Firelight flickered from the ancient stone fireplace, and instinctively I gravitated toward it. "I'm cold," I said in surprise.

"Don't worry," Leo said. "They'll have a fire going in our room." His voice was low and inviting.

I shivered. "Okay," I said, a little unsteadily.

I sat at the table closest to the fire, and Leo went up to the bar to order. His black hair curled at the nape of his neck, and I wondered what it would be like to entangle my fingers in the curls and pull his head down to mine.

I also wondered how many women had done just that.

"Here you go," Leo said, putting a steaming drink on the table in front of me and breaking into my thoughts.

The drink was some sort of hot toddy, foaming with whipped cream and heady as champagne. I drank thirstily and ate every morsel of the steaming, rich cottage pie Leo also brought me.

As I leaned back, replete and warm, Leo said abruptly, "It had to have been money."

I looked at him, admiring the arch of his dark brows and the slight flush on his cheeks. "What?" I asked distractedly.

"Why someone might have disappeared Baby Mary. It had to have been money."

"Uh-huh."

"Her mother was one of the richest women in all Christendom," Leo went on.

Clearly, his thoughts were not heading in the same direction as mine. I sighed. "But I thought Katherine Parr's money went to Tom Seymour and he forfeited everything to the Crown when he was executed for treason," I said.

"Yes, but Katherine Parr was smart and wily. What if she arranged for her money and estates to go directly to her baby? She had reason to mistrust Tom, after all."

"But she adored him," I protested. "Or at least she was in lust with him."

"You can be in lust with someone and mistrust them at the same time."

My cheeks flamed, and I took a long gulp of my hot toddy.

Unheeding, Leo went on: "She had watched Tom dallying with Elizabeth in her own garden when she was pregnant with his baby, for heaven's sake! Would it be so surprising if she made sure the baby inherited, instead of Tom?"

I shrugged. Leo eyed me for a moment and then got up to fetch more drinks from the bar. Once again, I watched him.

Uncharacteristically, he matched me drink for drink. "I don't think I should drive," he said, surprised, after the third—or fourth?—toddy.

"Uh . . . should we get an Uber?"

"And leave my car here? Not a chance."

My heart started to pound. "So, then . . ."

He looked almost saturnine, the reddish hue of the firelight giving him a high color. Now he was watching me closely. "So, then . . . ," he repeated.

Why not? I asked myself. He certainly had the air of a man who knew what he was doing, and it had been so long. . . . And I was certainly attracted to him, as any red-blooded woman would have been.

And maybe it would clear the air between us. Maybe, once our barriers were down, I would finally be able to figure out who he was and what he was after.

Why not?

Leo saw the decision in my eyes. "Check," he called.

At the front desk, I stood behind Leo and pretended to look at the rack of brochures while he talked to the clerk. "Double room, please," he said.

Double room. I tried to remember which underwear I had on.

The clerk said, "No reservation?"

"No," Leo said, a little impatiently.

"Well, then, I dunno."

"My good man," Leo said, "I feel confident that you can find a corner to stick us in."

The clerk, a pimply boy who clearly resented being torn away from his iPod and headphones, shrugged.

For a moment, Leo seemed to be at a loss. With an inner smile, I realized that while he may have worn his wealth lightly, he was much more at home in a Ritz or Four Seasons than in this village inn. He said, "I'm Leo Schlumberger, from Oxford." With a sidelong glance at me, he amended, "*Doctor* Leo Schlumberger."

Pimply Boy couldn't have cared less. "Rooms aren't made up, mate," he said, putting his earphones back in and raising the volume. "Maids come in the morning, y'know."

Tinny strains of some band screaming about death and annihilation came from his ears. I thought he would probably lose his hearing before he was thirty.

Leo, clearly accustomed to deference from hotel clerks, shifted his feet in frustration. I could almost hear him thinking. Then he reached over and took the earphones from Pimply Boy's ears. "My father is a close friend of Lord Jonathan Rothschild," he said.

Pimply Boy and I both stared at him.

"And Lord Rothschild is the main sponsor of the Glastonbury Music Festival," Leo went on.

Ah. Light dawned. For the first time, I noticed Pimply Boy's shirt, emblazoned with the music festival's insignia.

"Would you like pavilion tickets this year?" Leo asked.

In record time, we were in our room, with another fire blazing and clean, crisp sheets on the bed. Pimply Boy, now our devoted servant, even supplied a bottle of wine, a bowl of strawberries, and two (relatively clean) wineglasses.

"Well, then," Leo said, "would you like some berries? I'm afraid there isn't any champagne, but . . ."

I grinned at him. "Listen," I said, "you don't have to put on a great seduction scene. I've already decided to sleep with you."

He looked a little taken aback.

"I thought I planned this quite cleverly," he said.

"Well, think again."

His eyes sparkled in the firelight. Alone with him in the small, close room, I was more aware than ever of him as a man: his tall frame, his dark eyes intent on mine, his hard and knowing hands. Suddenly twitchy, I moved away.

I hadn't had a relationship since Scott, and he had been more of a sleepy stoner than a man of the world. I hoped everything still worked; I hoped Leo wasn't too much of a connoisseur.

Buying time, I took a glass of wine and sipped it, then wrinkled my nose.

"Local stuff," he explained. "It takes some getting used to."

"Like you," I said.

"Like me," he agreed solemnly. "But once you know me . . ."

I wondered if I would ever know him; sometimes he seemed almost as sealed off as I was. We were well matched, then.

"Okay, then," I said, putting down my glass. "I'm ready."

So was he.

Chapter 24

I couldn't get enough of him. The first time was fast and furious and blazing with need; the second time, longer and gentler and sweeter. When he was inside me, my body felt full and complete. My hands tangled in his black curls, and my lips sought his, over and over and over again. The third time was magical, and at last we fell asleep tangled together, his rough-haired legs entwined with mine and my head on his shoulder.

Just before I drifted off, mindlessly content, I thought, *This might be so much more, frighteningly more, than I expected.*

Naturally, I was furious with him when we woke up.

"This can't happen again," I said. It was supposed to have been just sex—the scratching of an itch. But now it felt dangerous.

"Well, now, that would be a crime. We were perfect together. In fact, we *are* perfect together."

I looked at him. My face felt raw from his black-stubbled cheeks, and my body felt replete and languid. I couldn't help smiling. I felt as if I were smiling all over. I just couldn't help myself. I drifted over toward him and put my hand on his arm.

"Now, that's better," Leo said. He dropped a casual kiss on the top of my head. "Where do you suppose my boxers went to?"

I shrugged. "Probably the same place as my bra."

"I'm hungry," he said, hunting under the covers for our missing undergarments. "Can you call down for some breakfast?"

"Seriously? Do you expect room service here? We were lucky to get clean sheets."

Leo looked put out, and I wondered if this was his first time ever in a hotel without room service. *It must be fun being rich*, I thought.

Suddenly his phone pinged, and he picked it up, triumphantly flourishing the boxers that he had unearthed from under the chair. Unconcernedly, he dropped the towel that had encircled his lean waist and began pulling on the shorts with one hand, putting the phone to his ear with the other.

"*Allô? Léo ici.*" He pronounced it the French way—*Lay*-oh—and I glanced at him curiously. The black hair on his chest tapered into a V below his navel, and I looked away, embarrassed by my interest, as he talked into the phone.

Then his tone sharpened, and he switched into Hebrew. I couldn't understand a word, of course, but I knew he was angry. With a "*Merde, alors!*" he threw the phone on the rumpled bed and rapidly collected the rest of his clothes.

No morning sex, then.

"What's the matter?" I asked.

He didn't look at me. "Family business," he said shortly. "My bloody *beau-frère*—uh, my brother-in-law—got himself into some bloody stupid mess, and of course I have to go rescue him."

I picked up my bra from the floor. I was wearing a light camisole and could have just slipped the bra on under the camisole, but instead, I wriggled out of the lacy slip and slowly, slowly began the business of putting on my bra.

But Leo didn't even look at me. All his attention had gone back to his phone. He was frowning at a text message and muttering under his breath. I finished dressing in silence.

Leo threw the phone back on the bed and turned back to me. "Sorry, *motek*," he said. "This isn't what I planned for today at all. But I have to go to Paris immediately. How about if you drop me at St. Pancras in London, and then you can keep the Audi until I get back?"

"You're taking the Eurostar train?" I asked. I willed him to ask me to join him, thinking of days along the Seine and nights at the beautiful old Paris Ritz, with its two-thousand-thread-count sheets and fluffy, buttery duvets. Croissants in the morning, strawberries and champagne in the evening. I had never stayed at the Ritz, of course, but a girl could dream.

"Yes."

"Oh. Okay."

"Come on," he said, a little impatiently. "If we hurry, I can catch the"—he checked the gold Rolex on his wrist—"the eleven o'clock."

All business, Leo kissed me lightly on the cheek when we pulled up outside the old train station. "Don't forget, the Audi takes only supreme unleaded. Don't park it on the street; put it in the garage. And be careful when you—"

"I'm going to drown your stupid car in the Thames," I said clearly. "Get out. You'll miss your train."

With another glance at his watch, Leo jumped out of the driver's seat and stood watching until I moved over the central console and settled myself in. The seat was still warm from his body, and I resented him even more for making me want him so desperately when he had, so obviously and so thoroughly, moved on. *Asshole*, I thought.

Leo leaned in through the open window. "To be continued, *motek*," he said, suddenly remembering that I was something more than a chauffeur.

"Over my dead body."

He smiled. "I don't think so," he said, and walked away.

Infuriatingly, it took a few moments for me to gather my wits enough to put the car in gear and drive away. I wondered what trouble his brother-in-law was in and whose husband he was. Hopefully not Élodie's. I had bundled Kali off to Leo's sister to get her out of trouble, not into it. I wondered if it had anything to do with me. In this day and age, spies weren't supposed to sleep with their targets—assuming that's what I was to him. If the phone call hadn't come, would Leo have been asking me questions about Jules? Would I have been stupid enough to answer, in the hazy afterglow of perfect sex?

Was that what last night had been all about?

Feeling sick, I drove home and crept into my own silent, empty bed for a nap. I hadn't gotten much sleep the night before.

But once I was lying down, I stared sightlessly at the ceiling. Did I really believe that Leo had seduced me to get information from me? He couldn't have faked that warmth and passion and tenderness and mindless, hot desire.

Or could he have?

Chapter 25

Ruthlessly, I called Kali the next morning at six o'clock. After all, France was an hour ahead of London. Surprisingly, she didn't sound sleepy when she answered with a French *âllo*.

"Kali? How are you? It's Amy."

"Oh, hi! I'm fine. But little Benji has an ear infection, so poor Élodie was up half the night with him. So I got up early to take him to bed with me while she gets a little sleep. The twins' school is closed today, and each of them has a friend coming over. . . ." She chattered on about the family. I was relieved at her obvious happiness but impatient at the same time.

Eventually she wound down, after telling me in excruciating detail about Amélie's football (i.e., soccer) match. I asked casually, "Is everything all right with Élodie and Gabriel? Leo had to rush to Paris for some crisis with the family business."

"Oh! That's right—they were furious when they found out about it."

Pause.

"Found out about what, exactly?"

"Well, we're not supposed to talk about it. . . ."

"We." Already, she seemed to have a new family.

"I'm sure Leo will tell me when he gets back," I said mendaciously. "He wouldn't mind if you told me."

"Well . . . okay, I guess. So, Jacob—he's married to Maya, the youngest sister—did something really stupid, and now the Sûreté is investigating."

"What did he do?" I asked.

"Actually, it's just like your sheikh," Kali said innocently. "Jacob sold a painting—or maybe he bought a painting; I don't understand it all. And he thought it was a fabulous deal, but the price was too high. And now the Sûreté is investigating the business for money laundering."

Suddenly, my heart was pounding so hard I couldn't breathe.

Kali went on, oblivious: "It's funny, isn't it? I had never even heard of money laundering a month ago, and now I can't stop hearing about it. You know how that happens? You hear about a new thing one day, and then it pops up everywhere."

Money laundering. Oh my God, Leo's family firm was involved in money laundering. Like my sheikh. And I was the stupidest, silliest woman in history. I had actually believed he was interested in *me*.

I wet my lips. "But, Kali, I thought Leo wasn't involved in the family business. Why did he have to rush back?"

Kali laughed. "Leo's the big brother. Whenever anyone has a problem, any kind of problem, they call on Leo to solve it. He's like a superhero to them."

I could understand that. His air of easy competence was one of the most attractive things about him.

I hated him.

Kali said, "I don't want to sound dumb, but what exactly is money laundering?"

I wet my lips again. "Crooks and criminals and corrupt politicians make a lot of money. But it's no good to them if they can't use it, and to do that, they need to deposit it in a bank."

"So?"

"So, banks are required to report all cash deposits of more than ten thousand dollars, and any other type of deposit that seems suspicious." I thought of the hundreds and hundreds of reports I had filed in relation to the sheikh's transactions.

"Okay," Kali said.

"The crooks and criminals need to get their money into the banking system without anyone getting suspicious. That's where money laundering comes in. It's a way to 'wash' dirty money through a series of transactions so that it finds its way into the banking system without raising any suspicions."

Kali said, "I'm still not sure I understand."

"Okay, here's an example. Say . . ." I thought for a minute. "Well. Say that an auction house sells a painting for ten million dollars. The painting's only worth one million, really, but the seller gets ten million. That's a way to launder nine million dollars, by getting it into the banking system as part of a legit transaction."

"And that's illegal?" Kali asked.

"Very. If bankers—or art gallery owners—help the crooks launder money, the bankers and gallery owners can go to jail too."

Not that that was much of a deterrent, though, I thought. Practically every major bank in the world had been hit with fines for money laundering in the past decade. Also casinos, property developers, offshore trusts, shell companies . . . and art and auction houses.

I felt sick.

After I said goodbye to Kali, my mind raced, but my body was slow and clumsy. I couldn't get the clasp on my bra to close, I broke a nail on the coffeemaker, and I stubbed my toe on the coffee table. The stubbed toe helped. I hopped around, cursing for quite a while, and that made me feel a little bit better. Then, defiantly, I drove Leo's precious Audi to work and lodged it in the dodgiest parking lot I could find. Take that, asshole!

When I sat down at my desk and logged on to my email, I saw that Audrey had just sent me a message: *Amy, I've asked Yvette to schedule a one-on-one for us this week to discuss your issues with teamwork.*

Surprising myself, I burst out laughing. Sometimes all you could do was laugh.

Another message appeared on my screen, with the subject line *Saudi connection.* The sender was unfamiliar to me: Arturo@art.co.ca, a Canadian address. This one gave me an Atlantic Bank account number to look into.

Huh?

I read it again. Then I hit REPLY and typed in *Who is this?* But the message pinged back immediately: *Undeliverable.*

Well, that was no surprise.

I forwarded the email to my friend Rosie and waited impatiently for her response, before realizing that it wasn't even 4:00 a.m. in Washington. Frustrated, I tapped my foot and stared at the message. Then I logged on to the Atlantic Bank server and typed in the account number from the email.

Access denied, the computer retorted.

I stared at the screen some more. As an officer of the bank, I had access to all account information. What in God's name . . . ?

I typed in the account number again.

The computer emitted some kind of loud alarm that made my coworkers pick up their heads and stare at me. *Access denied,* it insisted.

Another email appeared in my inbox, and I clicked on it

eagerly. This time, the sender was an admin address from Atlantic Bank.

You are trying to access restricted information. Internal Security officers will contact you shortly. You are blocked from the Atlantic Bank server until further notice.

And then my screen went dead.

Chapter 26

I sat back in my chair and closed my eyes. Had someone set me up? Or were there accounts so dark and hidden that you got cut off for just trying to access them? Who was Arturo?

And how the *hell* was I going to get any work done today without a computer?

That last question was answered quickly enough. Yvette walked over to me with an air of great importance and said, a little smugly, "You are suspended from the computer system while a breach is being investigated. Audrey says you should go home. We'll call you when the investigation is complete."

I gaped at her. "But . . ."

"Audrey says you should go home," Yvette repeated. "I don't want to call security, but—"

I stood up. "I'm going, I'm going."

"And you can't take anything but your pocketbook," Yvette added. "Leave your cell phone here."

That was okay. I had a second, private cell phone in my bag. I ran my fingers through my hair, picked up my purse, and walked out of the office, followed by the stares and intense whispers of my teammates. Nothing this interesting had happened at the office since Yvette's false eyelashes had fallen into her coffee cup.

Outside on the sidewalk, my legs suddenly felt weak, and I sank down onto the low wall in front of the building. What in the name of holy hell had just happened? Who in the name of God had sent that email, knowing I would be suspended or even fired as a result? My mind started to clear, and I listed the possible suspects in my mind.

Leo? I couldn't bring myself to believe it.

One of my "teammates"? Possibly. They would love to see me get into trouble.

Audrey? I didn't think so. This wouldn't look good for her either.

The sheikh? Maybe. But he didn't even know how to send an email.

The sheikh's sons? Hmmm.

But why? Why!

Maybe it wasn't someone bent on getting me into trouble. Maybe it was someone who thought he was being helpful in directing me to that mysterious account. Again, who?

Leo?

One of my former IDC colleagues?

One of my father's old friends?

I was out of ideas.

I fished my personal cell phone from my bag and walked a block away, in case someone was watching me. I couldn't even think of whom to call, but finally I dialed the US embassy in Berlin and waded through several layers of bureaucracy before Henry came on the line.

"Is this line secure?" was his first question.

I peered at my little Nokia cell phone. "I don't know. I think so."

"What happened?"

I told him.

"It wasn't me," he said immediately. "A Canadian email address, you think?"

"Yes, it was 'dot CA.'"

"Could be anyone, of course," he said. "Probably routed through dozens of servers around the world."

I nodded. I had already thought of that.

There was a silence. I could almost hear Henry thinking hard. Presently he said, "Fancy a trip to Avignon?"

I stared at the phone again. "Avignon, France?"

"Yes, it's lovely there this time of year. Very few tourists."

"I don't know," I said.

"An old friend of your father's is retired there. He can show you all around."

Oh. Okay.

I said, "Where can I find him?"

"No worries, he'll contact you. Safe travels, now." And he hung up.

By the time I got off the Heathrow Express at the airport, I had decided the most likely suspects were my Saudi clients— the sheikh's sons, in particular. They might be afraid I knew something about their father's dealings that could hurt him, and thought they needed to get me out of the way. Maybe they had even been behind the attacks on Leo and me. At the time I had thought the notion preposterous, but now I wondered.

On the other hand, if the sheikh really wanted me out of the way, his operatives had been pretty clumsy. The only wounds had been to Leo. I was untouched.

Pondering that, I started searching the airport for a pay phone—few and far between in this age of terrorism. I hunted one down in the EasyJet baggage claim area and dialed Kali's number. I wanted someone to know where I was.

"I'm taking a little time off," I told her.

"Again?"

It was a fair point.

"I lost my computer access at work, so I can't do anything there anyway until they fix it."

Kali sounded puzzled. "What do you mean, you lost your computer access?"

"Something got messed up in the system."

Kali said slowly, "Are you all right?" I knew she was remembering the attack on us on the road from Sudeley, and cursed myself for rousing her fears.

"Of course! I'm going to Avignon. The weather's perfect this time of year, and there aren't any tourists."

"Avignon? That's not so far from us in Antibes. Maybe I'll come and meet—"

"No!" I interrupted. "Didn't you tell me you were heading to Tel Aviv at the end of the week?"

"Well, yes, but—"

"You can't desert Élodie," I said firmly. "Didn't you tell me one of the kids has an ear infection?"

"That's true," she admitted. "It's a madhouse around here. Benji's trying to crawl, the twins are whining and fighting, and Amélie just discovered boys. Élodie's pulling her hair out."

"Better you than me," I said, with an inward shudder. "Anyway, keep up the good work, and I'll call you from Avignon."

"Wait!" she said. "Do you have a new cell phone number?"

"Sorry," I said quickly. "I'm losing the connection." And I hung up.

Still, I was glad Kali knew where I was going. Just in case.

Several hours later, I collected my bag at baggage claim—once again, I didn't know how long I would be away, so I packed heavily—and headed wearily for the rental car counter. I was feeling prickly. I wanted a means of fast escape, if necessary.

"No cars," the clerk said blandly. He was very French. I suspected he enjoyed my discomfort.

"I reserved one."

"We do not have the reservation."

"Oh, for . . ."

"Madame, we have no cars."

I looked at him in despair.

"Perhaps you try Econocar?" he suggested, with only a hint of a smirk.

When I got to the front of the Econocar line, the perky girl seemed unaccountably cheerful. "Oh, yes, madame, we have the perfect car."

"I just need a compact. Manual transmission is fine."

"Oh, no, the Americans always want the bigger cars, with automatic transmission," she said. She seemed to be smirking too. "We have the perfect car for you."

The car was a monster, as big as a Cadillac SUV, with huge wheels and a bumper as large as a barn door. As soon as I got into the driver's seat, I realized I couldn't see over the massive dashboard and hiked the seat to its highest position. Then I realized the windshield was so big that some clueless engineer had put two wide chrome bands in either side to support it, perfectly placed to maximize the blind spots.

I got out of the car again and looked at it disbelievingly, trying to decide whether or not to get back into the long Econocar line inside. Then a voice behind me made me jump.

"Why, it doth bestride the narrow world / Like a Colossus / and we petty men / Walk under its huge legs and peep about."

It was Leo, slightly misquoting Shakespeare.

Chapter 27

I swung around to look at him, my heart leaping. "Leo! What the hell—"

"Kali told me something was wrong and said you were headed for Avignon."

"Leo, I'm not one of your sisters. You don't have to rush to my rescue."

He looked at me with some surprise. "Bloody hell, I should hope you're not one of my sisters! Otherwise, God would have to smite me for my thoughts."

For the first time in two days, I smiled.

He said, "What is this thing? Is it a car or an ocean liner?"

"It's my rental car."

"But why?"

"They lost my reservation and . . ."

He laughed and pulled out his cell phone. "Don't worry, *ma chérie*, I can get us a car."

But I didn't want Leo to "rescue" me. I didn't want to be another of his protectees.

"This will be fine," I said. I looked at him challengingly. "Do you want to drive?"

"God, no!" he said, and I thought of his smart little Audi, still warehoused in the dingy London garage.

I held out the keys to him. "But you know the way," I said.

He sighed deeply and climbed into the driver's seat. "Damn and blast," he said. "What are those two things in the windshield? They block half my view."

"I think the windshield was so big that they had to put those supports in," I said.

"Damn and blast," he said again.

His mouth set, Leo muscled the car out of the airport. It was so big that he had to back up and maneuver twice to get around the corner in the car park. Then he had to retract the side mirrors to inch his way through the tollbooth.

"I think we used a quarter of a tank of petrol getting out of the car park," he said to me.

"Oh, for heaven's sake, stop complaining about the car. I thought men were supposed to like big cars."

"Not this man," he said. "I'm begging you, please let me trade this in for a foxy little Audi. Or at least a Saab."

"No," I said firmly. I didn't need his charity.

He fetched up a great sigh.

"Why are we in Avignon, anyway?" he asked me.

"I know why *I'm* in Avignon," I countered. "The question is, why are *you* in Avignon?"

He glanced at me. "Because you're here," he said.

My stomach fluttered again, but I tamped it down firmly. *Remember the way he left you in London?* I reminded myself. And the money-laundering connection.

Somehow, though, I couldn't believe he had made love to me in the line of duty. The magic of that night was real. I was sure of it. I watched him for a moment, his eyes hidden behind his dark sunglasses and his big, capable hands firmly in control of the massive steering wheel. I remembered those hands on my body and shivered.

"Are you cold?" he asked.

"No," I said. "Not at all."

This time, his glance at me held mischief and speculation. "Me neither," he said.

I couldn't stop watching him.

"So, what are we doing in Avignon?" he asked again.

Every nerve, every inch of my body was telling me to trust him. I took a deep breath and told him everything: the mysterious email message, my suspension, even my call to my father's old friend.

He listened in silence.

"I think I may know who you're meant to meet with," he said at the end.

Suspicion flared again. "Who? How would you know?"

"There's an ex-Sûreté man, Gilles Messur, who specialized in financial crime. He retired to Avignon a few years ago. My family consulted him a few times when they were unsure of provenance. He helped them authenticate some art that the Nazis had stolen. A good man," Leo added.

I remembered Kali remarking that she'd never heard of money laundering a month ago, and now it cropped up everywhere. It was a lot of coincidence to swallow. But then I looked at Leo again and felt a lifetime of distrust beginning to crack. *Coincidences do happen*, I told myself.

"Speaking of which," I said, trying to sound casual. "Kali tells me your family is being investigated for something?"

"Hang on," Leo said. He was trying to force the car through a narrow gap and onto an exit ramp. He leaned forward in concentration as he passed within a millimeter of the cars on either side of him. "Sorry," he said. "What was that, again?"

"What are you being investigated for?"

"Oh, my sister Maya has a cretin for a husband. Jacob brokered a sale last year. He found a buyer for a dubious Matisse at some exorbitant price. Élodie's husband, Gabriel, really didn't think it was authentic, but Jacob found a buyer even dumber than he is. So the sale went through at seven point eight million euros."

"And then?" I suspected I knew what was coming.

"Well, it turned out that the seller and buyer were linked in a drug-trafficking ring, and it was just a way to get the money into the banking system. Money laundering, with my idiot brother-in-law as the mediator."

"Money laundering," I repeated. It was the common denominator in everything that had happened to me recently. The sheikh, Atlantic Bank, now Leo and his family. "Did Jacob know he was assisting in a money-laundering scheme?"

"Are you kidding? He practically broke his arms patting himself on the back for his wonderful deal. He wouldn't recognize money laundering if it stood up and slapped him in the face. Cretin," Leo said.

I hesitated. "*Should* he have known?" That was the legal standard, I knew. If someone was "willfully blind" to a transaction that was obviously shady to a reasonable person, then that someone was legally culpable.

Leo shrugged, concentrating on the road ahead. "*Sacrebleu*, these lanes are narrow! I don't know. Should he have known? Probably no, from a strict legal perspective. Probably yes, from my perspective. But he can claim sheer stupidity; there's plenty of evidence of that."

I wondered if I could claim "sheer stupidity" too if the sheikh turned out to have actually engaged in illegal activity. It was a tough choice: Either you were guilty of helping crooks hide their money or you were too stupid to know they were using you to hide their money.

I supposed I preferred the stupidity defense.

Leo turned off the highway and into a narrow lane, cursing under his breath as the car crept up a steep hill.

"It's like trying to steer a bus into a one-car garage," he said to me, a little snappishly.

"If you're nervous," I said sweetly, "I'd be happy to take over the driving."

He grunted and muscled the car around another tight corner.

The hotel was lovely. Pots of flowers hung over the entrance, and flower-bedecked Juliet balconies adorned the mellow stone walls. Inside the lobby, Leo steered me over to a discreet antique desk. I stood back, admiring the eighteenth-century furniture and cozy fireplace in the corner.

I could never look at a fireplace the same again. I moved a little closer to Leo.

The clerk greeted us in a pure Oxbridge accent, so Leo addressed him in English as well.

"Hello, I'm Leo Schlumberger. I believe my family's contact at Banque de Paris made a reservation?" he said, with a slightly embarrassed glance at me.

So, Leo's family also used their private banker for all the scut work! I glared at him, wondering if his family treated their bankers as dismissively as the sheikh treated me. But Banque de Paris had done its work. The manager of the hotel himself hurried into the lobby and bowed and scraped us all the way up to our room, a lovely double suite with a Jacuzzi bathtub and shimmering views of the city lights. "This will do very well," Leo said. "Thank you."

The manager left, and Leo turned to me. "Shall I light the fire?" he suggested.

Chapter 28

Money laundering, I reminded myself. *Remember money laundering and the chain of coincidences and Jules.* But then Leo smiled at me and reached out a long arm to pull me against him. I went unresisting.

"Actually," he murmured, his voice husky, "I think the fire's already been lit, *motek.*"

I put my arms around his neck and kissed him.

"I have an ulterior motive for this little jaunt," Leo told me as I nestled in his arms under the divine duvet.

"Oh?" I thought Leo probably had motives hidden under motives hidden under motives. The problem was that I didn't know what they were. But I was too full of mindless pleasure at that moment to worry about it.

"Beyond bringing you to this hotel, I mean," he said, kissing my neck.

"Mmm."

"After we meet with your friend in Avignon, I'd like to drive to Cadaqués, in Spain. It's only a few hours."

Even I, who had European geography implanted in my brain, had never heard of Cadaqués.

"Why?" I asked sleepily.

"I found a reference to a Father Ramon Moscardo in some of Catherine Willoughby's papers. He was her steward for the time that Baby Mary was with her, and moved back to Barcelona some years later."

Catherine Willoughby . . . My fuzzy brain searched for a moment, then remembered: She was the Duchess of Suffolk, who had taken but resented the orphaned baby. It was under her care that the child disappeared.

"So? What is Cadaqués?"

"It's a fishing and artists' village in northeast Spain. You'll like it," he predicted, brushing some loose strands of hair from my face. I loved the touch of his fingers on my skin.

"But . . . Father Ramon?" I asked, forcing myself to concentrate.

"I think I may have traced his descendants to a villa in Cadaqués. Maybe they have some of his papers, and maybe he mentioned Lady Mary somewhere."

"That's a lot of maybes," I said.

"Yes," he said. "But I thought it was worth the trip—especially if I can make it with you."

I smiled to myself, and he kissed my mouth.

"Of course," he added, "that was before I saw the car you rented."

Leo was right: Gilles Messur left a message for me at the front desk that night. I was to meet him at a café in the Place de l'Horloge.

"I know that café," Leo said. "It has a small parking lot. Let's take the *Queen Mary* and dock her there so that we can leave for Spain directly after we meet with Gilles."

"Okay," I said, a little dubiously. A "small" parking lot didn't seem quite right for the *Queen Mary*, but we got into the car, and it took Leo only six maneuvers to get out of the parking space. I sat back and watched him drive.

"*Merde alors,*" he said distinctly. He had been muttering under his breath in an impressive array of languages. I couldn't understand a word but assumed they were all curses. *Merde* I understood, though.

"Leo," I said, "I really don't think you can make it around this corner." Sudden claustrophobia gripped me as I looked at the dark stone walls of the buildings on either side of us, so close I could reach out and touch them. Allegedly it was a two-way street, but the *Queen Mary* took up the entire roadway.

Leo swore again as a car approached from the other direction. The driver leaned out his window and grinned at the sight of our behemoth.

Leo reversed the car and tried to edge it around the corner for a right turn but had to stop, back up, and maneuver again. His lips tight, he said to me, "Am I going to make it this time?"

I peered out. "I don't think so. . . ."

"Well, open the bloody window and stick your head out if you can't see!"

"Leo, I couldn't see over the hood of this car if I were on stilts."

"Try!" he snapped.

The other driver, now laughing out loud, had gotten out of his car and was standing across the street, a respectful distance away from the *Queen Mary*. He had been joined by more grinning observers, highly entertained by the spectacle. No one offered to help.

Leo brushed some sweat out of his eyes and backed up again. "Can I make it now?" he ground out.

I closed my eyes and prayed. "Maybe."

The car edged around the corner with a millimeter to spare on either side, and the watching crowd erupted in whoops and catcalls. We nosed up another two blocks, and then Leo stopped short, staring in disbelief at the GPS.

"Is this a joke?" he said sharply. "Is this a bloody joke?"

The GPS called for another right turn, this time into a street that was no more than an alleyway. I broke out in nervous giggles.

"Next time, I say let's get another car," he bit out.

The "small" parking lot, of course, was impossible. With a shrug, Leo pulled the *Queen Mary* onto the sidewalk and killed the engine. "Maybe they'll tow it," he said hopefully.

I doubted anyone would be fool enough to try to tow an oil rig–size vehicle through the lanes of medieval Avignon. Unfortunately.

Leo got out of the car and shook himself, aiming a vicious kick at the car's bumper as we headed for the square. It was a charming spot, bordered by the ancient stone buildings of old Avignon and filled with gaily colored café tables and umbrellas. The cafés were overflowing with chattering, animated tourists and townies, comfortably sharing the pleasantly cool fall day and Provençal sun. I wondered if there was a souvenir shop nearby.

Leo took my arm and steered me toward a man sitting alone at a table, reading *Le Monde* and sipping a café au lait. The man was small and dark. Sunglasses covered his eyes, and his hair was light brown, thinning at the top. I had never seen a more nondescript person in my life. I doubted that I could pick him out of a lineup.

"Gilles, it's good to see you again! This is my friend . . ." Leo hesitated, and I realized he almost never used my name.

"Amy Schumann," I said, shaking his hand. "Thank you for meeting with us."

"It is my pleasure," the man said, his French accent making the rote words seem meaningful. "And a double pleasure to see you again, Leo!" He addressed Leo briefly in French, and Leo responded in kind. The two men laughed, and Gilles slapped him on the back. I wondered what they had said.

"But we are being impolite," Gilles said, turning to me. "Sit, sit. Let us order some *café* and some *pain au chocolat* and talk."

I wasn't sure if I should trust this man, especially now that I knew he was a connection of Leo's. So I hesitated, but Leo broke the slightly awkward silence and told him all about my sheikh and the FBI, much more succinctly than I could have. At the end I put in, "And I think he's sent his people after me. To scare me out of cooperating with the FBI. As if I would anyway!"

"Of course not," Gilles said, shaking his head. "They would ruin everything." He mused for a while. I watched him hopefully. At last he said, "I still have some contacts. Perhaps I may be able to discuss this with a few people. Let me see."

I beamed at him.

Leo said briskly, "Well, that's sorted, then. Shall we . . ."

Surprised, I realized he was trying to keep the conversation away from his family's business. I said tentatively to Gilles, "Another thing. Leo's family business, Schlumberger, is also under investigation for money laundering."

Leo frowned at me, but Gilles chuckled. "I know all about that. I've discussed it with Leo and his uncle Schmuli."

Leo had talked to him that recently? I glared at him.

Gilles went on, oblivious: "*Ça ne fait rien!* That is to say, there is nothing there. Leo's brother-in-law Jacob . . ." He paused and looked at Leo. "Forgive me. . . ."

Leo said, with feeling, "Believe me, there's nothing to forgive."

"Well, then Jacob is our modern version of the village idiot. Believe me, young lady, Jacob Sephardi is not capable of masterminding his way out of a paper bag, let alone a money-laundering scheme. Now, if it were *you*, Leo . . ."

And we all laughed merrily at the very idea.

Chapter 29

Motoring out of the old city was even worse than driving in. By the time we got out of the ancient town and onto the highway, Leo was white around the mouth, and I had developed a headache from giggling. After a while he said mildly, "I can't imagine what you found so amusing about that."

"I've never seen you so flummoxed," I told him. "Not even when gunmen were chasing us and you got shot."

"Well, I'm glad I entertained you," he said, but without heat.

"And you really shouldn't blame yourself for the bicycle," I assured him. "After all, who would leave a bike lying in a traffic circle like that?"

"I suppose it was pretty funny," he admitted. "After all, what kind of idiot would take this vehicle into the backstreets of medieval Avignon?"

The same kind of idiot who would insist on leaving a note of apology and two hundred euros in the basket of a rusted bicycle that probably dated back to World War II.

I laid my hand on his thigh and enjoyed his slight movement of surprise and pleasure. *My idiot,* I thought. But I didn't say it aloud.

Leo found a classical music station and began humming along.

I fell asleep, exhausted from my fit of giggles. When I woke up, he was conducting the orchestra with one hand, the other draped over the steering wheel. "Good morning," he said with a smile.

I yawned. "Where are we? Are we almost there?" I glanced around, surprised to see that the road signs were still in French. Surely we should have crossed the border into Spain by now.

"We're taking a slight detour," Leo said blandly.

I eyed him suspiciously. "Where?"

"Relax, *motek*, this is not an abduction. It is a delight."

"Where?" I asked again.

"To Carcassonne."

"What?" In all my travels, I had never heard of Carcassonne, any more than Cadaqués. "Why?"

"My dear girl, I have no ulterior motive. Carcassonne is one of the most beautiful places on Earth, and I have it in mind to take you there."

"Take you there" could have two possible meanings.

But wait a minute. "I thought you were on fire to get to Cadaqués and see those papers. Why are you suddenly willing to take a detour?"

"I'm on fire for other things as well," Leo said.

This time, there was no mistaking the double entendre, and I swallowed hard.

"But why Carcassonne?" I persisted.

"*Mon amie*," he said, "why not? It is romantic and lovely, and it is on our way. More or less," he added, in a burst of honesty.

Why not? That had been my mantra for my first night with Leo—and look where that had gotten me. I gave up and sat back in my seat to Google Carcassonne, curious to see what Leo, who had traveled almost as much as I, would consider the most beautiful place on Earth.

Carcassonne, it turned out, was a walled medieval town not

far from the Spanish border. I shrugged. Medieval was Leo's thing, not mine.

We exited the highway and made our way through a series of successively narrower, winding roads lined with flowering bushes and stone walls. Leo had the feel of the car by now, though, and swore only once, when we fetched up behind a farm vehicle that was chugging along at approximately five miles per hour. I closed my eyes as he swung into the wrong lane to pass.

Leo caught a glimpse of my face and said, as he smoothly steered the car into the proper lane, "Relax, *motek*. You can trust me."

But that was just the problem: I *couldn't* trust him.

Eventually, Leo pulled into a prosaic, graveled parking lot and shut off the engine. I looked around at the sea of cars and said, "*This* is Carcassonne?"

He shouldered our bags and held out his hand to me. "Wait for it," he said.

We walked through the parking lot and turned right into a narrow stone passageway. Leo pointed up. "*That* is Carcassonne."

Following his gaze, I looked up at the massive, mellowed stone walls of the ancient city. Just beyond the walls, I could see rooftops—thatched and stone—and the graceful spires of an old church. "Hmm," I said, reserving judgment.

Our passageway took us to the base of the walls themselves, and a stone staircase cut into the timeworn stonework. We began climbing. There was no one else around. It was nearing dusk, and the staircase was silent and dark. Leo said, "Imagine the line of medieval monks and pilgrims passing through these walls, huddled behind them for protection from the Saracen invaders."

My imagination caught, and I could see it too. We climbed some more stairs, and then still more. Leo pointed at some slits in the stone wall. "Arrow slits," he said.

"Did they pour boiling oil on the invaders?" I asked, some dimly remembered history class surfacing.

Leo laughed. "Oil was much too expensive. Mostly, they threw rocks."

I shifted my mental image.

We continued climbing. For Leo's sake, I did some heavy breathing and paused once to rub my (perfectly nimble) thighs. He climbed easily, with no noticeable effort.

When we emerged from the walls, it was to find a small square bordered by the medieval church and monastery on one side, the ancient town hall on another, and a lovely old building on another. Carved into its stone lintel was the discreet HÔTEL DE LA CITÉ DE CARCASSONNE, 1635.

"Wow," I said, admiring the hotel's flower-draped windows and beautiful old stone facings.

"*Voyez-vous*," Leo said, turning me around to look back over the walls we had just climbed through. "The valley."

The view was spectacular. Lights were blinking on in the valley, and the rough, rambling Pyrenees loomed in the background. "Wow," I said again.

Leo said complacently, "I thought you'd like it."

Our room, once again, was actually a suite, this time with two fireplaces—one in the sitting room, one in the bedroom. Leo suggested "le room service," and while he was on the phone, discussing what sounded like a very complicated menu, I sank into the deep, welcoming sofa and held out my hands to the crackling fire, trying not to think.

Leo called out, "Do you like *les tartes aux fraises*?"

"Huh?"

"Never mind." He went back to the phone.

I went back to trying not to think. But I couldn't. I was remembering all the omissions and half truths I had gotten from

Leo. He had told me he had nothing to do with his family's business, but obviously he *was* involved. His sister had called on him when there was a problem, and he had dropped everything (me, in particular) to perform a rescue. He had not said a word about his family's troubles with money laundering when I poured out my troubles to him. He had never mentioned Gilles, a money-laundering expert whom he apparently knew quite well.

He had been in military intelligence, so deeply undercover that his service record was impenetrable.

And then there was Jules. She should have been even more opaque; no ordinary mortal could dig her up. And Leo's tracking skills—the only way he could keep finding me was by hacking into multiple computers. What ordinary mortal could do that?

I couldn't doubt his passion for saving Sudeley Castle and Katherine Parr. But could I doubt his passion for me?

On that note, Leo hung up the phone and came to sit next to me. He reached for my hand, which had been fiddling with my hair, and curled his own fingers around mine. "Stop fidgeting," he said. "What are you so nervous about?"

"Leo, really," I said. "Why are we here? What's this all about?"

"Didn't I tell you before to stop thinking?"

Yes, that was what he had told me on our first night together. With some effort, I pulled my hand from his and turned to face him. "Why didn't you tell me about Gilles? And about the investigation of your family's business? Don't you think it's a funny coincidence, both of us being accused of money laundering?" There. It was out. I held my breath, waiting for his response.

He was silent, studying my face. "Wait a minute," he said. "Are you thinking that my family's money-laundering problems are somehow related to your sheikh?"

"Well . . ."

"Are you nuts?"

I shrugged. "I don't think so," I said. I watched him.

He seemed more surprised than angry. "First of all," he said. He cleared his throat and started again. "First of all . . . *Sacrebleu*, I don't even know where to start! This is madness."

He had never sounded more French.

"Is it?" I asked evenly.

"Oh, for . . . All right. First of all, every art and antiques house worldwide has to be on constant guard for money launderers. It's a perfect vehicle for bad guys to get their money into the banking system. All of us have been investigated at one time or another."

I supposed that was true. But still . . .

"Second," he went on, "my family's mission has always been to find art that was stolen by the worst people on Earth and restore it to its rightful owners. Do you seriously think we would knowingly collaborate with terrorists and human traffickers to wash their money clean?"

"Most of the organizations in need of money laundering are drug traffickers," I said.

He stared at me. "And do you think I am someone who would help drug traffickers?"

I bit my lip.

"*Et enfin*," he said, forgetting his English for a moment. "So. Is your sheikh an art collector?"

"No. At least, not that I know of."

"And you would know because you would have to transfer the funds."

"Yes."

"Is your sheikh Muslim? Saudi?"

"Yes, of course."

"Do you really think he and his family would do business

with an Israeli firm? Are you familiar with the Arab boycott of Israeli businesses?"

That was a good point too.

"We don't have any Arab Muslim clients," he said, a little stiffly.

I digested that in silence. "But still," I said lamely, "it's quite a coincidence."

He snorted in disgust and got up. "If that is how you feel," he said, "then I have nothing more to say to you."

I called after him, "But what about Jules?"

He turned back, lifting a dark eyebrow at me. "What about Jules?" he countered.

"How did you . . ." I stopped short, not sure how to finish the question.

"How did I find her? I am a historian, my girl, a researcher. That's what I do. I research. And I have very useful contacts—as I've told you before."

I shook my head, disbelieving.

"And I don't believe you either," he said. "Now. I think our lovely meal has arrived, and I plan to enjoy it. You can do as you will."

Stiffly at first, I sat down across from him after the waiter had left, eyeing him across the expanse of snowy white linen and savory, bubbling dishes.

"First," Leo said, "we have *le cassoulet.*" He lifted the lid, and a warm, herbed aroma drifted out.

"What's in it?" I asked as he ladled some into my bowl.

"*Ça ne fait rien,*" he said. "I'm not trying to poison you."

I sniffed and took a small bite. "It's delicious," I said.

"*Mais bien sûr.*"

He tended to speak French when he was angry, I realized. Tight, clipped Oxbridge English was for more formal discussions, and American English was for casual. Hebrew was for warm affection. I wished he would switch to Hebrew. I was beginning to wonder if my suspicions were overblown.

But then what about Jules?

Still, we both relaxed as we ate the meal, lulled by the superb wines and subtle, perfectly seasoned food. By the time we got to the *tartes aux fraises*—luscious strawberry tarts filled with sweet whipped cream on a pastry as light as springtime air—I was feeling positively mellow.

"Sorry about earlier," I said to him.

"Okay," he said, expressionless.

"It's just that . . ." But I couldn't summon up any more anger, not when I looked at his strong, lean body lounging back in the chair, or his supple hands looking absurdly large around a tiny, fragile, rose-covered teacup.

"We will forget it, *motek*," he said. With relief, I realized we were back to Hebrew.

Chapter 30

We made love—first on the deep rug in front of the flickering firelight and then in the huge king bed, Leo tossing small tasseled pillows onto the floor with abandon while I tried to brush aside the rose petals—and talked all night.

At one point I said to him, "Tell me about your family."

"My father was a survivor—"

I interrupted, "A survivor? How old was he when you were born?" I started calculating backward, but math was never my strong suit.

"Forty-five. He spent the last two years of the war in Dachau, digging graves for the dead. He was ten when the war ended."

Dachau. An eight-year-old boy. I shuddered, and Leo pulled me closer.

"He and his older brother were the only two survivors of our family. They spent the next twenty years trying to pry their art and antiques from the German and Swiss bastards who had stolen it; then they turned it into a business."

Quite a successful business, as I knew now.

"But my father had his first heart attack when I was only thirteen. That one wasn't so bad, but the next one, a couple of years later—that was bad. After that he was basically bedridden, and he died when I was nineteen."

Almost the same age that I was when my father died, I thought. Yet another coincidence.

"My uncle and cousins took over the business, thank God, but still, I felt so guilty for wanting to go into academia. . . ." His voice softened. "My father would say to me, 'Why you not sell art, like your cousins? It's good, honest work. Why you spend your time with your head in books about dead people? If you're going to study books all the time, at least you should study the Torah.'

"I still feel guilty," Leo said, almost inaudibly.

This time, it was my turn to hug him tighter, and we clung together for a moment.

"So that's why your sisters . . ."

"Yes. My father married late, and after me, my mother just kept popping out those girls . . . and then he got sick. They thought his time in Dachau might have weakened his heart. . . ."

I pulled his head down to mine and kissed his lips.

"So that left me," he finished.

Yes, of course. I had no difficulty imagining the teenage boy with a grieving mother and four little sisters, struggling to fill his responsibilities as head of the household. I thought he would be the head of any household he was in. His Hugh Grant mask had never been very good; he was much more alpha male than stammering nerd.

Then I remembered. "Wait a minute!" I exclaimed. "You told me that your grandparents escaped before the Holocaust, to Switzerland and then Israel. You said—"

"I know what I said. That's the story for public consumption."

I looked up at him, trying to read his face in the dim light.

"My father and uncle were ashamed of what they did.

Ashamed that they dug graves for the Nazis. So they made up that story and told it enough that I think they came to believe it."

"Oh." I couldn't think of anything more to say.

"It's not a sad story, *motek*," he said. "My father died in peace. And when he died, my sisters couldn't be down for long, and the youngest ones—the twins—barely even knew Abba. My biggest responsibilities were keeping them from boys as long as humanly possible. You're the one I feel sorry for, growing up as an only child."

"Oh, I loved being my father's only child!" I could never have shared him.

"The irony is," he commented, "that my father survived the worst dangers the world can throw at a man and then died peacefully in his bed, while your father lived a sane, peaceful life and then died a violent death."

I said unthinkingly, "My father didn't live such a peaceful life."

"Oh, yes—the adventuring," Leo said. "What was the most dangerous thing you did together?"

I closed my eyes and thought hard.

"Jeez," he said. "I didn't realize it was such a tough question."

"I think the most dangerous was . . . yes. It was Everest."

"Everest?" Leo said, blinking. "You climbed Everest?"

I couldn't blame him for sounding dubious, as I remembered my carefully heavy breathing on the climb up to Carcassonne.

"No, of course not. We planned only to go up to Base Camp. But my father was getting twitchy, the weather was beautiful, and I think he was a little envious of the climbers who were going up to the top. So we decided to go up to Camp Two."

"We?"

"Well, he decided. And of course I was dying to go along."

Leo looked at me skeptically.

I paused.

In fact, the only personal item in my London flat was a small photo of my father and me at Base Camp. My face was scorched a painful red from cold and windburn; my father was grinning and holding a brimming champagne glass in his hand.

Now I thought of that picture and could remember only how frozen I was, and how I wished my legs would stop quivering, and how I worried that my father would notice my trembling lips.

Really, was it so awful to admit fear? My father thought so, of course, but . . .

For the first time in my life, I confessed, "Actually, I was terrified."

"Well, I should think so," Leo said.

"Anyway, we got only a few hundred feet higher than Base Camp before the guides made us turn around."

"Well, thank God for that. I wouldn't have liked you as much with a black nose and toes," Leo said.

"Oh, you should have seen the frostbite on the climbers who came back from the summit," I told him, recoiling still from the memory. "It was horrible—black noses and cheeks, and toes practically falling off. Even my father was a little taken aback."

"I should think so," Leo said again.

And for the first time, the very first time in my entire life, it flitted through my mind that perhaps, just possibly, just maybe, my father wasn't perfect. He protected me, sometimes, but maybe I was also a little afraid when I was with him too.

Was it possible that he had been—just a little bit—a bully?

"Am I the first girl you've brought to Carcassonne?" I asked.

He hesitated, and I sat up sharply, pulling the covers away from him and around my suddenly colder body.

He pulled me back against him again, and I snuggled into his warmth.

"*Motek*, I hate to break this to you, but I wasn't a virgin when we met."

"Thank God," I said, and he laughed. But still . . . Carcassonne? Already I thought of it as our place, the place where we talked and made love all night.

"Who was your first, anyway?" he asked.

"Oh—I thought we weren't going to talk about that."

"Why not? I want to know every little thing about you."

You already know too much about me, I thought. Aloud I said, "A guy in college. I was never much of a player, though. Too involved with my father and then . . . after . . . with my job."

"It sounds very lonely," he said.

Again, my London apartment came to my mind. The sitting room–kitchen was neat and shining, with nary a thing on the plain white counters. It was decorated in what I liked to call early IKEA—a few white bookcases filled with paperback spy novels, a few white cabinets filled with plain white dishes and cheap glasses (four of each), with two generic blue pillows that my friend Dorcas had insisted upon, and a light blue throw rug left by the previous tenant. Everything was clean, sterile, and anonymous—just as I liked it. If someone broke into my apartment, they would find no clues to my life, my personality, my being.

Only now did it occur to me that my impersonal flat was not so much neat as empty, not so much cool as frozen. Seeing Leo's squashy, comfortable family house had brought that home to me with a bang . . . and for the first time, I wondered if I was lonely.

I shook off these thoughts and asked, "What was your first time?"

"I was fourteen, maybe thirteen. A girl at school." He kissed the top of my head. "I was a clumsy oaf."

I doubted that. But I said, "Well, then I'm glad you've learned some lessons along the way." Then I thought about what he had said. "You were only fourteen? Seriously?"

"Boys grow up fast in Israel."

I had been to Israel many times and knew it to be a sophisticated, very twenty-first-century country. "You were in Tel Aviv," I pointed out, with some asperity. "Not the killing fields of Sudan."

"Ah, well." He stretched briefly and pulled me closer again. "Then I was just a horny teenage boy."

That sounded more likely.

As dawn approached over the ramparts of the medieval town, we fell asleep in each other's arms. When I woke up, it was close to noon, and Leo was sitting on the sun-splashed balcony, drinking coffee and reading the newspaper. "Good morning," he greeted me. "What a lazy girl you are."

I smiled at him. "Good morning to you too."

He smiled back. "Get up already, would you? We're supposed to meet Kali in Cadaqués at three o'clock."

I snapped to attention. "Kali? Kali's going to meet us?" Involuntarily I thought of the gunmen in England. I had sworn to myself that I would not put her in danger again.

"It'll be fine," he said, reading my thoughts. "Anyway, she's due for a few days off. Those kids of Élodie's are driving her mad."

"But how . . . ?"

"I bought her a plane ticket to Barcelona and arranged for a car to drive her to Cadaqués."

I could just imagine the "car" his Banque de Paris private banker had arranged—probably a Mercedes sedan with a powerful, purring engine and a wine cooler in the back seat. Kali would be thrilled.

We had time to scramble up the medieval ramparts in Carcassonne for one daylit view of the valley before we left. I had to focus all my attention on my feet because the walkways and stairs were a thousand years old and completely unreconstructed. I appreciated the authenticity and charm but worried about twisting an ankle or knee on the worn, uneven, and slippery gravel.

In the end, though, it was an older woman climbing ahead of us who twisted her ankle and fell to the ground. Leo, who, I had already realized, had some medical training—presumably from his years in the military—dropped my hand and was at the woman's side in a flash. He glanced at the ankle, already the size of a baseball and swelling rapidly, and said to her husband, "Let's help her sit up on this rock."

Easily, Leo helped to lift the not slender woman to a sitting position and bent again to look at the ankle. He said to her, "This is just going to keep swelling until you get down and put some ice on it. Do you think you can make it down the stairs?"

The woman bit her lip and looked at the long, narrow stone staircase we had just climbed, but nodded. I thought she was trying not to cry.

Leo glanced at her husband. "I could carry her—"

"No," the woman said firmly. "I can do it." And she stood up on what had to be a very painful joint, put her hand on the rocky wall for guidance, and, limping heavily, started the long way down.

Leo told her admiringly, "You are tough. I've seen hardened soldiers cry and refuse to walk at all with ankles less badly sprained than that."

The woman straightened her shoulders and continued with a little more spirit in her halting steps.

As they passed, I said to Leo, "When I was on Denali with my father, I twisted my ankle and walked-slash-slid all the way down on my own."

"Ah," he said. "Well done, you."

And suddenly it occurred to me that my father—my own father!—had shown me less respect and compassion than Leo had just shown this stranger.

Chapter 31

Having mastered the car, Leo confidently maneuvered the *Queen Mary* around the tiny, winding streets of Cadaqués, a white-washed fishing village that perched precariously on the rugged seaside cliffs. Gaily colored boats dotted the harbor, while farther out the blue waters sparkled and glittered in the afternoon sunlight.

In the center of the town, in a little traffic circle with a statue of Salvador Dalí in the middle, a girl with long blond hair was just getting out of . . . yes! A midnight-blue Mercedes sedan. I would barely have recognized Kali had it not been for the car. Her face was fresh and lightly tanned, with a slight sprinkling of freckles that made her look five years younger than when she had stepped off the plane at Heathrow two months earlier. But the biggest difference was her expression. She looked happy and confident, chattering to the driver in what even I recognized as awful French.

Leo reached her first and swept her into a great bear hug. "Kali! You look *magnifique!*" he told her.

Kali blushed.

"And your French sounds amazing," he said mendaciously.

"Well, you know," she said seriously, "it's important to speak to the children in their own language. Though I am trying to teach them English too."

"Élodie says you're wonderful with them," he added, and her face turned up to his in pleasure.

"Really?"

"*Absolument*," he said.

Leo took her backpack and turned, pointing to one of the steep hills leading out of town. "Salvador Moscardo lives up there," he said. "It's only a ten-minute walk."

Thirty minutes later, Kali was huffing and puffing, and even I felt my cheeks warm with exertion. I stood beside Leo as he rang the doorbell. He glanced down at me. "God," he said fervently, "I hope he has the household account books."

He couldn't be faking this passion either, I thought. I pressed his hand tightly, and Kali's gaze sharpened. "Are you two . . . ," she began. But fortunately the door swung open, and she closed her mouth again.

"Señor Moscardo?" Leo asked. And he was off in a flood of Spanish. The man answered and then nodded, and Leo talked some more.

I watched the men's faces, praying Leo would find what he wanted here. Both nodded and shook hands, and the door closed again.

"What?" I asked. "What did he say? What happened?"

"We have an appointment to meet him at his studio tomorrow morning," Leo explained.

"But does he . . ." I trailed off, unable to finish my question. It was so important to Leo. I couldn't bear it if he were disappointed again. I felt guilty enough about my inability to help him.

Then Leo took off his sunglasses and looked down at me, and I realized his eyes were shining. "I think he has them," he said.

We had dinner at a café on the harbor that evening, watching the sun set over the blue, blue ocean and the white sails bobbing in the distance. "This is beautiful," Kali said.

"I have to say," I told Leo, "you do take me to the best places."

"That reminds me," Kali said. "Are you two—"

"Why do you think Father Ramon Moscardo may have written about Baby Mary in his papers?" I asked Leo, cutting her off. I wasn't ready to discuss Leo and me yet.

"Because of this letter, which he sent in 1549 to his brother," he said. Pulling out his cell phone, he clicked open a document and read aloud, "'The babe is unlov'd and unwanted; such wee ones often pass into a better place ere long.'" Leo looked up. "Now, why would he write this? Baby Mary was still alive and presumably well when he sent this letter. The following month, Catherine Willoughby sent another of her infuriated letters to the Lord Protector, demanding money for the baby's upkeep."

"Maybe he was issuing a warning—or a prediction," I suggested.

"But to whom? Who cared about the poor little thing?"

Kali asked, "Where did you find that letter?"

"He wrote the letter to his brother, who was steward of another house in England," Leo said. He seemed distracted, his thoughts turned inward.

Kali said stubbornly, "I can't believe that Catherine Willoughby didn't care about the baby. She was such a delicious age when the father wrote that letter. Nine months old, right?" At Leo's nod, she went on, "That's the same age as Élodie's baby, Benji, and he's absolutely"—she paused, searching for the right word—"enchanting. Besides, she was the baby of Catherine's best friend."

"Remember, people couldn't afford to be too sentimental

about children then," Leo reminded her. "As many as one-third would die before they reached their teens—"

I cut in, "But that's not what you said at Prague Castle!"

Two sets of eyes focused on me. "What?" Kali asked.

He glanced at me blankly.

"Leo, when we were at Prague Castle and we saw the funerary goods for that little boy, you said his parents were clearly heartbroken. Look what they put into the grave for him. Remember?"

"Yes, but—"

"But what? Are you telling me that Mother Nature upended herself in the sixteenth century and mothers didn't care about their babies?" I badly wanted Baby Mary to have grown up and lived a long, happy life.

"Catherine Willoughby wasn't Mary's mother," Leo said quietly.

"So what?" Kali snapped. "I'm not Benji's mother either."

We both looked at the girl, her cheeks flushed with indignation and her eyes bright with passion. She had told me Élodie had taken her to have her hair stripped of the gooey brown dye so she was blond again. She was fresh-faced as well because Élodie somehow hadn't managed to find the time to take her to buy makeup after the twins threw her vials and potions into the laundry.

I wondered if Kali had transferred her hero worship from me to Élodie and, absurdly, felt a sharp twang of jealousy.

Leo and Kali were still talking. "Maybe she was just pretending to resent the baby," Kali suggested. "Maybe she wanted people to think she didn't like her and wouldn't take care of her. Babies need lots of snuggling and attention, you know," our resident childcare expert said.

"But why on earth?" I asked.

Silence.

"*Someone* must have cared about her," Leo said. "She was the first cousin of the King."

Kali frowned. She still didn't have a firm grasp on the Tudor family tree.

"Her father, Tom Seymour," I explained, "was the brother of Jane Seymour, King Edward VI's mother. She was the one who died in childbirth."

"Oh, right. Well, maybe someone was afraid she might try to take the throne from him?"

Leo glanced at me. "We thought of that. But she had no Tudor blood at all, no claim to the throne."

"Well, then . . ." Kali's voice trailed off as she tried to think of a reason why Catherine Willoughby would have feigned disinterest in and dislike for an "enchanting" little girl, her BFF's daughter.

I was hardly sentimental or maternal, but even I—I looked at Kali, so precious and so fresh, almost reborn—even I would take care of such a child. I looked away.

Leo had reserved a suite for us at the Casa Dalí, a whitewashed villa perched on the rocky cliffs above town, with a ground-floor tearoom decorated with what Leo said were original Dalí prints. The suite was two bedrooms and a living room, a corner unit (of course) with a wraparound balcony that offered panoramic views of the town, harbor, and dark blue, glittering sea beyond. With a glance at Leo, I picked up my bag and started to follow Kali into the second bedroom.

"Oh, no, you don't," he said.

"But Kali—"

He turned to the girl, who was trying not to smile. "Kali," he said gravely, "will it traumatize you if I share a room with your sister tonight?"

Neither of us corrected the "sister."

Just as gravely, she said, "You have my blessing."

He turned back to me. "You see? Now, get over here, my girl."

So I followed him into the master bedroom.

The next morning, we ate breakfast overlooking the harbor and then discussed our plans for the day. We would descend on Señor Moscardo en masse, hoping that whatever papers he had would be in English, not Spanish. "Elizabethan English is hard enough to read," said Kali, whose education had been magnified by our fits of historical research. "Elizabethan Spanish would be impossible."

"I can read Elizabethan Spanish," Leo said absently.

"Of course you can," I said, a little sourly.

Kali said to me, loyally, "You can read Russian. That's a really hard language."

Not medieval Russian, though, I thought. I remembered Leo's telling me that his Spanish was "fair" and scowled at him. I hated being bested at so many things by a man.

Seeing my face, he grinned at me with the sparkle of the night before still in his eyes, and I reddened.

Kali grinned too. "Ah, young love," she teased, and Leo laughed out loud.

It wasn't love, I thought. But it was *something*.

Señor Moscardo's studio was above the town too, but up a different hill. So we had to walk down the steep, narrow streets into the village, replete with the aromas of baking bread and fish, and back up more steep, narrow streets that wound their way up into the foothills of the massive Pyrenees. The sights were magnificent: dark, looming mountains on one side and the long stretch of heaving gray sea on the other. I could imagine why artists loved this place so much.

Leo had to stoop in order to get through the low stone door-way of the studio, but once inside we were dazzled by the richly detailed seascapes that lined the walls. Murmuring in Hebrew, Leo studied the paintings closely, and I realized that despite his professed disinterest in his family's business, he surely knew and appreciated fine art. "Hmm," he said to me. "Some of these are quite good."

I suspected that was very high praise. For Señor Moscardo's sake, I hoped so. And maybe if Leo bought some of his works, he would be more kindly disposed toward us.

The man himself appeared, shuffling out of a back office that was crammed with half-finished canvases, scrolled-up work, and all manner of brushes and paints. Leo said to him, in English, for our sake, "I represent Schlumberger's, and I like your work."

Moscardo's eyes widened.

Leo pointed at one massive seascape. "I would like to buy that piece and"—he swiveled, indicating three small oils that together formed a jewellike triptych of Cadaqués harbor—"those pieces and . . . that one."

The third was a landscape depicting the Pyrenees enveloped in a misty, romantic cloud. I didn't know why, but it sent chills down my spine. I had never wanted any object so much in my life as I wanted that painting. There were tiny figures climbing up the craggy mountains into the mist and looking up at a hint of shimmering rainbow through the clouds, feathery-soft plants at their feet. It made me think of my days in the outdoors with my father, always looking up, always feeling light and free and, somehow, above the mortal plane.

Kali said to Leo, "Is your family going to resell those paint-ings? I thought they sold, you know, like, Renoirs and Picassos."

"Which one do you like?" he asked her.

She pointed at the triptych. "I love that one."

"It's yours," Leo said. "The seascape is mine, and your sister gets the mountain landscape that she's looking at so lustfully."

We both turned to him, faces aglow, and he waved it off.

The now beaming Señor Moscardo held out a very plebeian cardboard box to Leo. "The papers of Father Ramon Moscardo," he said in heavily accented English, and shrugged. "I don't know why you want them. They have sat in my attic forever, and my father's attic before that. . . ."

With visible effort, Leo took the box politely rather than grabbing it out of the graying artist's hands. "*Gracias*," he said. "*Muchas gracias*."

The little man bowed politely. "*De nada*."

I had the feeling that he really thought it was nothing, and prayed, as fervently as I ever had in my life, that he was wrong.

Chapter 32

We decamped to the café next door, where Leo ordered pots of coffee and trays of pastries, enough to make the proprietor almost as happy as Señor Moscardo, and we commandeered an empty table in the back. I thought briefly about how easily money paved a path for Leo and his ilk. When Señor Moscardo asked diffidently about payment for the paintings, Leo handed him a card and scribbled a name on it. "Schlumberger's bursar," he said briefly. As easy as all that.

Then Leo handed out museum gloves to us again, and my thoughts returned to the papers. Kali whined, "But whyyyy? They've been sitting in a moldy attic for years and years and . . ."

"Around five hundred years," Leo said briefly, and her eyes widened. "Put them on."

He handed around papers—keeping the best for himself, no doubt—and we all started reading. Or tried to; most were in English, but the old script was much too faded and stylized for me to understand much. Next to me, Kali kept sighing in disappointment as here and there she deciphered lines that turned out to be a recipe for butter bread or a bill for linen hangings.

Leo, engrossed in his papers, noticed nothing.

"Here it is," he said. "*Voyez-vous.*"

We crowded around to peer over his shoulders, but I still couldn't make out the crabbed handwriting.

"I can't read it," Kali said, sounding even more like a disappointed toddler.

"*Ici*," Leo said, too taut to remember his English. "'Twenty shillings for a mantua for the Lady Mary. Two shillings sixpence for laundress to the Lady Mary.'" Carefully, he turned another page of the half-crumbling vellum scroll. "'Three shillings tuppence for linens'—diapers to you, young ladies—'for the Lady Mary.'"

Impressed in spite of myself, I looked more closely at the unfamiliar script. It barely resembled English to my untrained eyes. But still, how remarkable, how touching, to see the long-ago minutiae of a long-gone life. For the first time, I really understood Leo's passion.

"And then," he said, with a very Gallic shrug, "there's nothing. No reference to Mary ever again. Except for that book that you found at Sudeley, Kali, the one inscribed 'Lady Mary, the Queen's Daughter.'"

"I don't understand," Kali said, a little petulantly. "I get why you were so excited about that book, but if there's no mention of her here, after the . . . linens, then why are you so excited? Doesn't that mean she did die as a baby after all?'"

I didn't understand either, but she was right. Leo was beyond excited; he was rapt.

Cautiously, I reached out and flicked through the next pages to the end of the book. Leo was right: There were no more references to Lady Mary. She had disappeared, as all the historians said.

I opened up the next book while Leo watched me indulgently. "It's addictive, isn't it, *motek*?"

Like Kali, I wondered why he was smiling.

But I wasn't addicted. I was looking for something.

Then, unbelievably, I found it.

"Leo," I said. "Look at this. Linens for the Lady *Amanda.*"

"Yes," he said.

I paged forward. "Three shillings for laundress for Lady Amanda. Eight shillings tuppence for . . . oh my God. Eight shillings tuppence for nursemaid for Lady Amanda." I looked at Leo. "What the hell? Who was Lady Amanda?"

"According to Father Ramon, she was a ward of Catherine Willoughby's," he said. "A distant cousin who had been orphaned, so she came into Catherine's household, coincidentally, right around the time Lady Mary 'disappeared.'"

Another "coincidence."

I almost had it. It was so close . . . but I wasn't quite there yet. Kali sat watching us interestedly but uncomprehendingly.

"If," I began, "if Catherine had other wards—"

"As did most noble households," Leo interrupted me.

"Yes. Okay. If Catherine had other wards, if she was in the habit of taking in other children, then why did she resent little Mary so much?"

Leo looked as if he couldn't believe he had to spell it out for me.

"Remember when I thought you had changed your name? When we first met?"

"Yes," I said cautiously, and Kali stirred with surprise.

"I thought you were in some danger," he said. "Maybe from an abusive boyfriend?"

"Yes . . . ," I said again. Then the lightbulb went on, with a crashing, blinding burst of brilliance.

"Leo," I said, almost breathlessly, "you think Lady Amanda *is* Baby Mary, don't you?"

"You said it yourself," he said. "Lady Amanda appeared

right after Lady Mary disappeared, in late 1549." He pulled out another volume and started leafing through it, almost reverent in his treatment of the fragile pages. Then he looked up at me. "'Governess for Lady Amanda,'" he said quietly. "In 1554. So she must have been about five years old in 1554, about a year older than Mary would have been."

Kali had gotten it too. "But how could they have pulled it off? Wouldn't people notice it was the same baby?"

"Not if they kept little Mary out of sight for a month or two and then introduced Amanda. All babies look alike, after all—"

"No, they don't!" Kali protested.

He ignored her. "And at that age, in those times, she would have been so swaddled up that no one outside the nursery would really have seen her face anyway." He turned to me. "It could have been done. You see how it could have been done."

All babies looked alike to me too. "I see," I said slowly. "But why? Why on earth would Catherine have done that?"

Leo looked deflated, but only momentarily. "Good question," he admitted. "But I'll bet we can find answers."

Kali looked dubious.

Leo tried to give the box of papers back to Señor Moscardo, but the artist waved dismissively. A flood of Spanish followed. Leo smiled and nodded at the old man, and we turned to go. I gathered that Schlumberger's "bursar" had been more than generous and the paintings were already being packed for their flight to London. Kali and I smiled at Señor Moscardo as well, and he almost smiled back.

Leo insisted that we go straight back to our hotel rather than stopping for food, or at least a celebratory drink. So, once again, we slogged down one hill and up another. Then it began to rain. As the rain grew steadier, the roads became narrow, rutted streams, and Kali and I held on to each other for support.

Leo strode on ahead with his jacket draped over his precious box of papers, oblivious.

As we settled back into the warmth of our suite with some relief, Leo, a man with a mission, went straight to his computer. "Call the desk," he tossed over his shoulder. "Ask for coffee. Lots of coffee. And whatever . . . else." Unable to tear himself away any longer, he turned back to his computer.

I looked at Kali and shrugged. Together we managed to order hot soup, hot coffee, and hot tartes from "the desk," and then I made her change into dry clothes before we perched over Leo's shoulder. He was paging through long lists of names and dates, muttering under his breath.

I asked, "What exactly are you looking for?"

"A record of Amanda Willoughby's marriage. A lot of careful digging should eventually turn up some letters or diary entries mentioning the wedding of a ward of Catherine Willoughby. Anyone being married from that house would merit some comment. But if we're lucky, we might be able to find it in the parish register." He grinned. "Which happens to be online. God bless the British Historical Trust."

"What if she didn't get married in Catherine Willoughby's parish?" Kali asked.

He shrugged. "Then we'll start the really tedious digging."

But we *were* lucky. Only a few moments later, Leo shouted triumphantly, "That's it! Bloody hell and *sacrebleu*! That's it!" He pointed to a line on the screen and read it aloud: "Lady Amanda Willoughby of Grimsthorpe Hall, spinster, wed to Lord Edward Seymour, August 15, 1564."

We stared.

"That's it," Leo said again. "That's it." Suddenly subdued, he had the air of a man whose dreams had come true and who didn't know what to do next.

Kali said it for him. "So, what do we do now?"

Leo closed the computer and looked straight at me. Our eyes met, until I looked away.

"That," he said, "depends on your sister."

Chapter 33

I refused to respond to Leo's statement to Kali, and he worked furiously on his notes for the rest of the day while Kali and I shopped our way through the little village. Dinner was a mostly silent affair. Leo ate in abstracted silence, I was shell-shocked that it had come to this, and Kali created an uncomfortable barrier between us.

Back in our beautiful bedroom, Leo helped me pull back the thick white comforter, and I took my hair down from its messy bun, very messy, after the day's rain and humidity.

He said, "We have to discuss this sooner or later. Now that I've traced a clear path from Lady Mary Seymour in 1548 to Juliette Mary Seymour in 2017, all I need is Jules to stop the property deal."

"But you haven't traced a 'clear' path," I said. "It's all conjecture."

"I'm confident I can persuade enough fellow historians," he said calmly. "That's as 'clear' as a five-hundred-year-old path ever gets. The weight of the evidence is on my side. But . . ." He crossed the room and stood in front of me. "But . . ."

"You need Jules," I said flatly.

"Yes. I need Jules."

He watched me closely as I stepped back from the intensity of his gaze. "I'm sorry," I said, turning away. "I can't help you."

"Please," he said. "I'm asking you. In the name of all that's good in the world."

It was extraordinary to hear a man as confident and competent as Leo reduced to begging insignificant little Amy Schumann. I felt sick. "I'm sorry," I said with finality, and a door slammed shut between us.

We went to bed in utter silence.

The next morning, Kali begged to return to one more store, where she wanted to buy a piece of pottery that she thought Élodie would like, so Leo and I sat awkwardly together at the harbor café while we waited for her. In silence, I watched fishermen bringing in their nets from an ancient trawler and throwing fish into barrels on the beach.

Clearly groping for a safe topic of conversation, Leo said, "Élodie says the kids are fascinated by Kali. Élodie made her get a whole new wardrobe, though."

"I noticed," I said.

More silence. Leo tried again: "I know Kali says she's dumb, but I think she has some sort of learning disability."

"Why? Don't you think her parents—my mother and her father, I mean—would have noticed?"

"From what she says, I think her twin sister, Kelley, helped her through school for a long time."

I thought about that.

"I'm sure Kelley thought she was doing a good deed," he added, "but really it would've been better to let Kali fail so that she could have gotten the help she needed."

"How do you know so much about this?" I asked.

"Amy, I have a dozen nieces and nephews, not to mention

sisters. I know how sisters operate. And I'm a professor. I know something about different learning styles."

"But then why did Kali fall apart in high school?"

"Because Kali and Kelley were in different classes. Kelley was in honors and AP sections, and Kali wasn't. So, for the first time in her life, she was doing her own schoolwork. And when she started to screw up, her parents just thought it was part of general teenage idiocy rather than a genuine problem." He sighed. "Too bad for Kali."

I couldn't believe Kali had confided in Leo about all this—and that he had seen her so much more clearly than I had.

"She's certainly not dumb," I said slowly, thinking of her skill in negotiating with Leo and me.

"No," he agreed. "Anyone who can blackmail you and extort money from me is quite . . . clever."

I was oddly pleased to discover our minds working along the same lines.

And suddenly, just like that, my decision was made. It was time. I needed to know for sure.

So I made an excuse to Leo about buying some pottery for myself and slipped away from the café before he could voice his surprise. From a street vendor, I bought one of those burner phones that feature prominently on *Homeland* and *Covert Affairs* and every other spy show on TV. There's a reason why they're so popular; they're quite effective at avoiding detection.

Then I walked up a few blocks from the seafront and bought a SIM card at another store. I slipped into the rank alleyway behind the store, careful not to breathe in too deeply, and delicately used tweezers to extract the SIM card from my new phone. I crushed the fragile card under my boot, as I had been taught, and then inserted the new SIM card. Glancing around one more time and seeing nothing but mice and spiders all around, I punched in the number, a code, and then another number.

"Line zero seven seven two," a brisk voice said.

I swallowed and metaphorically squared my shoulders. "Rivka?" I said. "This is Jules Seymour. From CIA."

Chapter 34

"Yes?" she said cautiously.

"You remember me? We worked together on the Chechnya operation in—"

"Yes, of course I remember you." Her Hebrew accent was much heavier than Leo's, and much less delightful.

Forgetting my milieu, I drew in a deep breath and coughed as the filthy odor hit my lungs. "I'm sorry for this, Rivka, but I have to ask you about one of your agents. At least, I think he's one of yours. Leo Schlumberger."

There was a long pause. She said, "And what exactly are you asking me?"

I hesitated too. I had hoped she would make this easier, but Rivka Rivlin (God knows what her real name was), the deputy chief of overseas operations for Mossad, never made anything easy.

I said simply, "*Is* he one of yours?"

There was an even longer silence while Rivka deliberated. I held my breath. At last she said, "No, he is not."

I felt as if I'd been punched in the stomach. "What? Are you sure?"

She laughed; Rivka Rivlin actually knew how to laugh. "Of course I'm sure, Jules."

"Well, then whose is he? Don't tell me he works for the Jords. MI6?" It wouldn't be so bad if he were a Jordanian agent. They were terrifically cooperative, but everyone hated MI6.

"No and no," Rivka said. "You misunderstand me. Leo Schlumberger is not associated with any of our colleagues."

It was worse than I had thought. "So . . . he's freelance, then? A gun for hire?"

"You children, you see mysteries in everything," Rivka said. "No and no again. He did very valuable, very secret undercover work during his military years, and of course we approached him multiple times after that. But he has no interest. None whatsoever."

I was silent, dumbfounded. That was what Leo had said too, that he had just wanted to bury himself in historical research after his scarring military years. So Leo was just who he said he was? I couldn't believe it.

"Actually," Rivka said, suddenly loquacious, "it's probably for the best. He's too much of a free agent for us."

Maybe it was even true; I didn't think that Rivka would lie to me. It seemed that Leo *was* just who he said he was: a historian who was obsessed with Tudor queens and saving Sudeley Castle.

Still shocked, I thanked Rivka and said goodbye and then automatically crushed the burner phone under my boot and scattered its bits among trash cans in several different alleys. I began a slow, meandering path back to the café, thinking furiously. I had been so certain that Leo was Mossad. He fit the part perfectly. Rivka herself had said they'd "approached" him multiple times. I could only imagine what form those approaches had taken.

Me, I had rushed into the arms of the CIA as soon as I had recovered from the seismic blow of my father's death. I wanted nothing more than to race into the profession my father and grandfather had embraced, to return to our nomadic, sometimes dangerous, often heart-pounding lives in the service of the agency. I was an agency princess, daughter and granddaughter of agency legends, and got every assignment I wanted. But I had run straight into the red mist in Chechnya, and the powers that be (i.e., Bob the Bear and his cronies) had put me out to pasture at a desk in London. My cover job at Atlantic Bank, they insisted, put me in the ideal position to trace terrorist money back to its sources.

And I had been sure—absolutely, positively sure!—that Leo Schlumberger fit into this puzzle in some way. Mossad was deeply suspicious of other intelligence groups, including the CIA, so it often "forgot" to identify its undercover agents to us. By the same token, only a few people outside the CIA knew me. Rivka was a rare exception because of our joint operation in Chechnya. And Rivka *never* talked.

My spirits plummeted, and my steps began to drag. But that was the problem: If I allowed Leo to identify me publicly as Jules Seymour, my cover would be forever lost. I would have to work as an "overt" CIA employee, which meant at a desk in Washington, not even London. I would spend the rest of my career sitting at a computer, watching the adrenaline-soaked exploits of field agents from a safe distance. I would never be Amy Schumann or Marina Ostrova or Anna Petrova again. Just Jules.

It struck me then that I was actually disappointed that Leo was just a civilian, someone who would never understand my life. I thought again of the shattered marriages between agency nonofficial cover officers like me—NOCs—and nonagency spouses, and of the impossibility of making something work with a civilian.

But I could never abandon this life for a man. Deep down, where I rarely ventured, I knew that at first it had been all about following in my father's footsteps; it was the family business, after all. But now it was about more than my father, even; it was about protecting all of the innocents of the world—Kali, Élodie, the children, even Audrey and the PYTs—from the very worst that humanity had to offer. I had never chosen this life; it had chosen me, and, I thought wryly, I was stuck with it now.

I could never share it with Leo.

It didn't bear thinking about. In a silent funk, I rejoined Leo and Kali, and we got into the car and drove away from the serene beauty of Cadaqués.

Leo dropped off the *Queen Mary* at the Barcelona airport, where he planned to catch a flight to Paris. I was heading to London, and Kali was taking a puddle jumper back to Antibes and Élodie and the children. I envied her. I was returning to a silent apartment in London, and I didn't know when—or if—I would see Leo again. He hadn't said anything about his reasons for going to Paris rather than London, and I was afraid it was because he didn't want to be trapped in the seat next to me for the entire flight.

As we walked into the terminal, I told myself that when my Señor Moscardo mountain landscape arrived, it would warm up my flat slightly. I hugged Kali goodbye, and she whispered in my ear, "Don't let Leo go! Whatever the problem is, you can fix it!"

"I don't think so," I said.

Her pretty mouth set grimly. Turning to Leo, she said sharply, "Please take care of Jules. She's my sister, after all."

Leo's face, for once, was easy to read. Shock and pleasure and then rage washed across it in fleeting waves. I said, "Kali!" but she was already running toward her gate.

Slowly, Leo turned to face me. "Hey, Jules," he said.

Chapter 35

"So, when were you going to tell me?" he asked. We were sitting on a concrete barrier outside the airport, where I could be sure that no one would overhear us. The air between us was fraught with tension and betrayal and anger.

"Never, hopefully," I said. "The only people who know, outside my family and a few higher-ups at the agency, are my 'IDC' friends." I used finger quotes around the name.

"I wondered about that," he said. "A CIA front company?"

I nodded. "And a couple of others, because of a joint operation in Chechnya. That's it."

"Then why on earth does Kali know?"

"The agency's changed; now they insist that your immediate family know, so that you're less isolated and less likely to crack up. Also so that if you're killed in action, it's less shocking. I told my mother, and she told Kali and Kelley two years ago, when I joined Atlantic Bank. Anyway, I had to explain my name change."

Leo was dumbfounded. "I thought no one was ever supposed to know about undercover agents."

That was how Mossad worked. Again I wondered if Rivka had told me the truth.

"We never knew about my father until he died, and my mother didn't want history to repeat."

"It's remarkable that Kali didn't slip earlier," he said, clearly thinking back.

"I paid her a hundred pounds a week not to."

"Ah," he said. "That would explain it. She should have asked for two hundred."

"She did. We settled on one hundred."

"Ah," he said again. "Do go on."

I shrugged. "What else is there to say?"

He started to speak but then closed his mouth and looked at his watch instead. "Delightful as this has been," he said coolly, "I'm afraid I have to go catch my plane."

I stared at him. "You're leaving? Just like that?"

"I do have a life that doesn't include you, you know."

That stung. Looking at him more closely, I realized he was angry. His mouth was tightly compressed, and his eyes were black with fury. I hugged myself and shivered, as the day had turned gloomy and gray.

"What . . . why are you going back to Paris?" I asked, hating myself for sounding clingy.

"I have to catch a flight to Dubai."

That caught me by surprise. "Why?"

"My dear little spy, I am speaking at a conference of medieval and Renaissance scholars at the Dubai Atlantis. Nothing to interest you."

I swallowed, and he stood up, shouldering his bag. "To be continued," he said. "I suppose."

I shrugged, just beginning to understand how deeply he felt betrayed. What was there to continue? I couldn't break my cover and be chained to a desk for the rest of my life. Sudeley Castle would become a high-end condo project, and I would always be the woman who had lied to Leo and refused to help him when I could have saved Sudeley.

He nodded briskly at me and strode off.

I rarely cried. But if I had been so inclined, this certainly would have been the moment for a tear or two. Instead, I threw my bag over my shoulder with much less ease and grace than Leo and headed back into the teeming terminal. I couldn't believe he had actually left. Didn't he have a lot more questions for me? Wasn't he curious about my life in the CIA? Couldn't he understand, just a little bit, the depth of my commitment to that life and the impossibility of destroying it for a heap of stone walls?

Staring out the window as the plane lifted off, I swore to myself I would never get entangled in such an intense relationship again. This was why I had remained single and fancy-free for all these years; I had held all of my other lovers at a very careful arm's length, even Scott. The only CIA marriages that had a chance were those between two officers, who understood each other's work and were comfortable with secrets.

I was actually disappointed that Leo wasn't one of us. Then, I thought, he would have gotten it; then we might have had a chance. But an undercover officer and a civilian? Never.

After all, look at my parents.

The moment the wheels touched the tarmac in London, I eagerly switched my phone back on and waited while it loaded a few messages. Kali, apologizing for outing me at the airport; Dorcas, reporting that she was back in London and suggesting lunch . . .

No Leo.

Then another message appeared, from Yvette at Atlantic Bank. It was brief, almost grudging:

Amy,

You have been reinstated and may return to work on Monday. Please remember that Tuesday is Christmas Team Day, so we will be at the office in the morning and the climbing walls in Westway in the afternoon.

Y

Game on, I thought, silently blessing Bob or Henry or whoever had engineered my return. But couldn't they have waited until after Christmas Team Day?

Monday was mostly silent at the office. I got polite nods and smiles from my coworkers, while Audrey glanced at me as if she couldn't quite remember who I was. I wondered what leverage had been used on her. I got all warm and fuzzy inside just thinking about how annoyed she must have been at being strong-armed into taking me back.

In the afternoon, though, the PYTs all started chattering about the following day's Christmas Team Day. (I noted that no one even bothered with the American, PC "holiday" fig leaf here. Jake S. and Matt S., who were Jewish, didn't seem to mind.) Kristen R. confessed she'd been practicing her climbing at Westway for the last month, Kristen the Younger proclaimed her barre classes were strengthening her core, and Kristen T. trumped that with her strength-training classes.

I couldn't help smiling to myself. I had zero interest in organized sports or aerobics classes. They produced about as much of an adrenaline rush as safe, boring London. But give me a sheer cliff face to climb with the right shoes, with the right equipment, or some rapids to raft, and I was brilliant.

I reminded myself that I would have to hide my skills, however frustrating that would be, and appear as inexperienced and incompetent as they all expected me to be. If necessary, I could fall off the wall.

Chapter 36

Christmas Team Day started at the office, though, and we all gathered around the big conference table promptly at nine with our skinny lattes and no-whip, no-cream soy drinks. I was the only one with a scone, and Kristen the Younger eyed me with a slight smile. "Carbo-loading for this afternoon?" she asked.

"Yup," I said, forcing myself to look embarrassed. "I'll need something to keep up with all of you guys." I longed to whip out a picture of me at the top of Denali or at Everest Base Camp in a howling white blaze of wind and cold, but my cover was rock solid. Kristen the Younger exchanged amused glances with Kristen R., and one of them murmured, "Oh, I'm sure you'll be fine."

You bet your ass I will, I thought.

Audrey tripped in and cooed, "So wonderful to be with all my peeps today! Pia will be joining us at Westway this afternoon . . ."

A chorus of delight arose from her peeps, and I winced, remembering how Audrey's daughter, Pia, had somehow managed to "win" every competition at Field Day. When I wasn't feeling sorry for her, I found her intensely annoying.

"But this morning I have a special surprise for you! I've

brought in a consultant to conduct a Myers-Briggs assessment of the team, and I'm sure it will be a very special time of bonding for all of us!"

The PYTs applauded enthusiastically, burbling about how much fun this would be. I scowled slightly, trying to dig up what I knew about Myers-Briggs. It was a method of determining personality type, I thought.

"I've always wanted to do Myers-Briggs," Matt B. enthused.

Matt S. said, "Audrey, you always have the best ideas!"

Audrey dimpled. "And this," she said, "is our ringmaster for the morning."

A tall, gaunt woman came into the room, and everyone applauded again. I joined in, a little dubiously. The woman looked as if she hadn't enjoyed a meal in forty years. She wore free-spirit clothes, draped in various organic linen and cotton fabrics and tunics and scarves, but the tight set to her mouth belied the warm and fuzzy impression that her clothing was intended to make. I disliked her on sight.

She was named Nola, and I immediately set myself to speculating on what her mother had actually named her at birth. Shirley? Maude? Ludmilla?

Nola handed out the personality tests, and I amused myself by filling in everything as the bland, boring Amy would while tabulating in my head what Jules Seymour would say.

"After a stressful day, I need some time alone to relax." Amy fervently agreed; Jules, I thought, would rather have a raucous night at the pub with her mates (but then go home alone).

"It takes people a while to get to know me." Well, that was something Amy and Jules could actually agree on. *Strongly agree,* I wrote, thinking of Leo.

"I would rather be called practical than inventive." Amy agreed; Jules disagreed.

"I prefer to go with my gut." *A thousand times yes!* Jules cried. *No*, Amy inscribed dutifully.

"I find it difficult to meet new people." *Yes*, shy Amy murmured. *Not at all*, Jules said.

"Sometimes I feel very vulnerable." *God, yes*, Amy whispered. *God, no*, Jules roared.

"I enjoy being spontaneous." *Absolutely*, Jules said. *In fact, why don't we ditch this whole stupid thing and go out for a drink?*; *No*, Amy said.

"I don't let my emotions cloud my judgment." Amy strongly agreed. *Hmm*, Jules said, thinking once more of Leo.

"I avoid confrontation because I don't like hurting others' feelings." *Oh, yes*, Amy said earnestly. Jules laughed.

"I like to be engaged in an active and fast-paced job." *Not really*, Amy said. *Yes and yes and yes!* Jules shouted.

"I feel that the world is founded on compassion." *I hope so*, Amy wrote. *Ha!* Jules said.

"I find it difficult to speak loudly." *Yes*, Amy murmured. *Are we almost done with this ridiculous questionnaire?* Jules barked.

"I value justice rather than mercy." I paused—something else we could agree on. *Yes*, I wrote firmly and handed in the form.

While Nola "scored" our questionnaires (*I thought this was a no-judgment zone*, I thought sourly), everyone chattered about their responses. The Kristens squealed over how similar their answers were—what a surprise!—while the Matts seriously discussed the benefits of sensing over intuition. Because I couldn't figure out the difference between the two, I drank my Diet Coke in silence.

"Well!" Nola said. "I see that the fit within this team is remarkably good, on the whole."

Gosh, I thought, widening my eyes and looking interested. *What a surprise.*

"It's no wonder you work so well together," she went on. "This is a team of strong extroverts . . ."

Well, fancy that, I thought.

"And very similar personality types. This is a group that prefers sensing over intuition . . ."

Matt S. smiled triumphantly at Matt M.

"Thinking over feeling . . ."

Well, of course; feelings have no value in the marketplace.

"And judging over perceiving."

That, at least, is true.

Audrey said complacently, "As I told you, Nola, this is a terrific team. I love my peeps." She beamed at the group, who all beamed back at her. I fashioned my face into a big grin.

"Amy," Nola continued, "is the exception, of course. Amy is an introvert who prefers intuition over sensing and perceiving over judging."

There was an embarrassed pause as everyone contemplated poor old me.

"Well," Matt S. said kindly, "introverts are people too."

"Of course!" Nola said heartily.

I ducked my head and murmured my thanks to everyone for their tolerance and inclusiveness. Someday, I decided, I would get them. I sat back, plotting my revenge.

But the fun wasn't over yet. We filed out of the office in a giggling, chattering mass and onto the minibus Yvette had hired, which snaked its way through the never-ending London traffic to the climbing wall at Westway. I had never been there because (a) I hated indoor climbing walls—they were all so artificial and *safe*—and (b) I didn't want to advertise my skills so close to home, where I might run into someone I knew.

So I walked in slowly, trailing behind the crowd, and was careful to awkwardly fumble with the equipment when the patient instructor showed us how to use it. Kristen T. and the Matts, having put in some practice time over the past few weeks, appointed themselves as the class gurus and were kind enough to help the rest of us newbies. Kristen R., a born athlete who had not bothered to do any practice, easily adapted to the gear and started first up the beginners' wall. Reluctantly, I admired her natural form and prowess.

I was at the end of the line and watched my teammates with appropriate and admiring oohs and aahs. I had myself perfectly in hand and was preparing to make a thorough mess of my own climb when a disaster occurred: Pia arrived and pushed herself in front of me. "You don't mind, do you?" she said perkily. "I'll be much faster than you, so it makes sense for me to go on ahead."

You little brat, I thought, striving for equanimity. *You rotten little tweeny twerp.* I remembered how she had preened after "winning" every game at Field Day, and my blood started to boil.

"Just copy what I do," Pia counseled.

At that, I snapped. I gave Pia a hearty shove and said, "Just watch me and try to learn something." And I was off.

I scaled the beginner wall in under a minute, without a belay line to the instructor and without glancing down once; I ignored the angry shouting of the staff and glares of those below me. I passed the Kristens and the Matts, slid down so fast they didn't even have time to blink, and then ran over to the most advanced wall, where the Jakes were struggling at the bottom holds. I skimmed past them and saw, with satisfaction, that Jake M. lost his tenuous grip when he saw me taking the lead and avoided a giant splat on the mat thanks only to his instructor's firm hold on the belay line. This wall required some concentration, including a tricky layback maneuver to navigate a crack, and I forgot everything in the sheer pleasure of feeling for holds, relying on pure muscle power and hard-won skill. It finished with a tricky overhang, but before my mind could process the challenge, I had brought my left foot up nearly to my shoulder and used the leverage to pull myself up—my first heel hook in years—to achieve the summit. I was the only person there.

I hung for a moment at the top of the wall, enjoying the applause of the other climbers and instructors. I hadn't even broken a sweat.

But then I realized what I had done. Belatedly, I saw the gaping faces of my officemates below and saw Pia whispering furiously to Audrey. *Oh, shit*, I thought. Was it too late to fall off the wall? Probably—better to brazen it out.

I rappelled down quickly and took off the gear, handing it to an admiring instructor. "Are you on a climbing team?" he asked me. "Because we'd love you to join. . . ."

I let him press his card into my hand and turned to face the music.

Kristen the Younger said, "Amy! We had no idea! Where did you learn to do that?"

"Oh, here and there," I said, trying to look abashed.

Matt B. asked suspiciously, "Were you taking lessons? For today, I mean?"

Kristen R. said to him, "Don't be silly. That takes years of training, not a few lessons." She studied me. "Where *did* you learn to do that?"

I gathered my wits. Really, this wasn't a disaster, just a slight hiccup. Even nerds could have one small skill. So I said shyly, "My father taught me. He was a big mountain climber."

There was a small silence while everyone digested the news and tried to match it with their knowledge of Loser Amy. Matt S. asked, "What have you climbed?"

I tried to think of the easier, beginner peaks we had climbed when I was Pia's age, relying on my coworkers' inability to understand the difference between mountaineering and technical rock climbing. "Oh, just Mount Washington, Denali . . . um . . . Mount Rainier, El Capitan."

"Huh," Jake S. said, eyeing me. "Have you ever been on Everest?"

I laughed. "Are you kidding me?"

"I have," he said proudly. "I hiked to one thousand feet below Base Camp a few years ago."

That elicited a chorus of conversation, and I eased my way out of the circle to get a drink. *A lucky escape*, I thought. Then I caught a glimpse of Audrey's furious face.

Oh, crap.

Chapter 37

Having spent the rest of the day and night berating myself, I was not at all surprised to get an email from Audrey the next afternoon at work. *Let's meet at 9:00 a.m. tomorrow, Amy*, she wrote. *Uh-oh*, I thought.

When Audrey finally found time for me—at 5:57 p.m., just as I had given up and was putting my jacket on—she motioned me into her office and closed the door. "The FBI has closed its investigation on Sheikh Abdullah," she said, with no preamble.

I had expected this, but not so soon. "That's great," I said, reminding myself to send a crate of bourbon to Bob the Bear.

Audrey ignored me, of course. "I don't know why they backed off," she said, "but I expect it's due to some of my friends' influence in Washington."

Audrey had *no* friends; in fact, she had a "network." She didn't seem to understand that there was a difference between friendship and a prominent place in her mental Rolodex; all of her "friends" were business contacts. I almost could have felt sorry for her.

At any rate, I knew it was not her "friends" who had stopped the FBI. I nodded obediently and thanked her.

"However," she said, "your review is long overdue . . ."

This was said in a reproachful tone, as if it were my fault.

"And I'm afraid there are multiple issues with your performance, even aside from the FBI investigation."

Which was my fault too, I gathered.

"I have long feared you were not a good fit for this organization . . ."

Uh-oh. This was *really* not good. I couldn't afford to lose this job, not when we were so close to nailing the sheikh. Bob could probably salvage the job, once again, but that would mean letting Audrey in on my real identity—which was unthinkable. So far, we had managed to keep her unwitting. Bob had deemed her unreliable, so I wasn't sure if he would blow my cover in order to keep me at the bank.

"And your behavior at Christmas Team Day only confirmed that belief."

I started to speak, but once again she ignored me.

"So I'm afraid, I'm very sorry to say"—she paused, and I held my breath—"that as of today, you are officially on a thirty-day probation period."

I let out my breath in a whoosh of relief.

"You must demonstrate a real dedication to our mission, Amy," she instructed.

What mission? Making money? My mission was to, you know, prevent terrorists from blowing up half of London—unimportant, really, compared with the bank's mission.

"If you cannot show me you are capable of being a real team player over that period, then your career at Atlantic Bank will come to an end." Her eyes bored into mine. There was not a speck of feeling in hers. "Are we clear?"

I assured her that we were and that I would most earnestly and sincerely strive to become a valuable member of her team. She nodded curtly and dismissed me. We both understood that this was a thirty-day postponement of the inevitable, as advised by HR in order to prevent me from suing.

Well, if I couldn't wrap up this business in thirty days, then I didn't deserve to be my father's daughter. *If only you knew, Audrey,* I thought. *If only you knew.*

That Sunday, I took my Syrian teenagers rock climbing in Bradford, which was a huge hit. A few days later, I received official notification from the FBI that the investigation into Sheikh Abdullah had been closed, and emailed the sheikh with the news. No reply. I diverted myself by devising a plan to move his assets from negative-interest-rate Swiss bonds and US bonds with a 0.15 percent interest rate into something that might actually earn him some money, although I knew he would never consider it. That was one of the things that had attracted our attention to him in the first place—only crooks and criminals have no interest in making profitable, productive investments.

Still no word from Leo.

The following week, on Wednesday evening, I left work and went to the Four Seasons for a quick drink at the bar. I chatted with the bartender, left through the kitchen, and took a cab to the London Eye, where I picked up another cab, for the Park Lane Hilton. There, I had another drink, chatted with another bartender, and accepted a key to room 1037. Thank goodness for big-city hotels and cab stands; they were custom-made for the cautious spy evading detection.

And then I walked up ten flights of stairs to the tenth floor, exited cautiously, with my hand poised at my hip, and used the key to get into room 1015. The CIA security contractor behind the door looked me over quickly and let me pass into the very bland hotel room, where four more men were clustered. It was a good-size space, but the big, broad-shouldered alpha males with their piles of gear made it seem small and fussy. Two of them had heavy beards. All four wore dark wraparound sunglasses, despite the dim lighting in the room, and spoke in deep bass voices.

"The London takedown is Friday," the team leader, who gave his name as Shea, told me. "We've got enough info to make it happen."

My info! I exulted.

"Who are you taking down?"

He grunted. "The evil spawn." The sheikh's sons, I interpreted.

"Where?"

"I'm told you don't need to know that."

"Okay," I said. "What about the father?"

"Another team is on him. It's more difficult. He's in the sandbox." The Middle East, probably Saudi Arabia.

Only the leader was talking to me. The others conversed among themselves in the low voices of men accustomed to quiet, shorthand communication.

"The sons are coming in to meet with you. To tell you they're pulling their business."

Amy would be horrified; I grinned. It was a good way to lure them to London. They would have to sign signature cards in person to close their accounts and transfer money out of Atlantic. "Okay," I said again. Then, with sudden apprehension, I added, "You're not doing the takedown at the bank, are you?"

Shea shrugged. I didn't need to know that.

"What do you need me to do?"

"Keep your head down."

I could do that.

"And make sure you have copies of all the documentation," he added.

I nodded. That documentation was why I had spent two years of my life as a toady to Audrey and her peeps. "It's secure," I said.

He nodded. "Do you need help getting out?"

"No."

I slipped out, ran down the ten flights, and caught a cab at the entrance. Another tiresome round of taxicab tag to ensure that I hadn't been picked up at the hotel, and I was back in my own bed. As I fell asleep, I remembered Audrey's telling me I had to be more of a team player, and smiled to myself. When it was *my* team, I could play with the best of them.

The next day, I forced myself to do something I had been putting off for days: I had to fill out a "witting" form on Leo. All covert agency employees have to keep an official list of those who know about their agency status—the shorter the better. My father's list, until he died, had consisted of only one person: his own father. Mine, up until now, had also been admirably short: my mother, Kali, and Kelley, following the agency's strong admonition that I not keep immediate family in the dark.

But now I had to add Leo, and I knew this would be a big black mark on my previously unsullied career. To have a foreign national on one's witting list was bad enough; a foreign national with an intelligence background was even worse. And in the best of times, the CIA and the Israeli military had a tricky relationship.

Still, it had to be done. The alternative was that someone might discover it by accident one day, and that would be a firing offense. So, reluctantly, I filled out the form and filed it with Internal Security. Maybe I would be lucky and no one would notice it. I couldn't help thinking about my father's minuscule witting list and how he—my best friend—had lied to me for his entire life, leaving it to strangers to tell me the truth after he was dead.

I had always wondered why he didn't just leave me in ignorance forever. It would have been much easier. But he had left explicit instructions that I be told everything when he was gone, and, for the first time, I understood. The truth is better. Even if it's belated, the truth is better. So I was glad Leo knew the truth, even though he would never speak to me again. I would not out myself for the sake of Sudeley. I just couldn't.

There was no word from Leo himself.

On Friday, Takedown Day, I was jumpy inside but bland as ever on the outside. Amy dutifully worked on a five-year plan for the sheikh's investments that Jules knew would never see the light of day, while Jules tried not to fidget and slipped out every hour or so to check her agency cell phone.

Just after lunch, I got an unexpected email instead.

Hi Ames,
Lord Featherstone wants you at his house ASAP. Don't bring any guests.
Rosalie

"Rosalie." An official, urgent summons. Game on.

Chapter 38

Lord Featherstone was the bank's British director—Audrey's boss, I supposed, though he was very much an absentee director, and I had met him only once. I made my way to his Knightsbridge mansion, being ultracareful not to bring any "guests"—three taxis and two tube rides—and arrived slightly breathless. Was this the takedown, then? Or was it over?

Shea, my agency contact, met me at the door and ushered me into a high-ceilinged, dark-paneled reception room with no furniture except a mile-long polished table and chairs on a jewellike Oriental rug. The great man Lord Featherstone himself was there and nodded to me. "We need you for the takedown after all," Shea said.

"Why?"

"The sons think they're moving their funds to another bank. They need you to approve their signatures."

"Okay. But why here?"

"Their new 'bankers' advised them not to go to Atlantic, in case Audrey tried to prevent them from making the withdrawal."

I nodded briskly and got into character, stooping my shoulders and scooping my hair into a messy bun. I put on my glasses and squinted a little. "Let's do this," I said.

The doorbell rang.

Lord Featherstone slipped out of the room, and I heard male voices in the foyer. One of Shea's men, dressed as the quintessential British butler, opened the door; announced, "Their Excellencies Kareem and Nasir bin Saud"; and bowed his way out. Shea, looking every bit the high-level American banker in an Armani suit and wingtips, strode over and shook their hands. I said nervously, "Mr. al-Saud—Sheikh, I mean—what are we doing here? Can I call my colleagues and ask them to join us? Please?" I put a tremor in my voice and avoided eye contact.

"No. All we need is your signature," Kareem said. His brother, the muscle, remained silent and glared at everyone impartially.

The "butler" knocked again and crept in, trying to look unobtrusive. He carried a wide silver tray with shaking hands; I only hoped that under one of those silver domes was a very powerful gun. Nasir had never been known to travel with anything less than a Glock.

"Tea, sirs?" the butler inquired timorously.

"No!" Kareem barked. "This is not a social occasion!"

I visibly shrank into myself and watched as the tray tilted precariously. Quickly, Shea reached out to steady it after only three cups of tea had fallen onto the priceless Oriental rug, and the butler, murmuring in distress, knelt to wipe up the mess. Kareem, who had been splashed with some hot tea, wiped angrily at his bespoke gray suit.

Shea said calmly, "Gentlemen, here are the papers authorizing the transfer of your funds from Atlantic Bank to Bank Caribbean International."

"What?" I squeaked. "You're transferring your funds? Oh, no. Please reconsider, Sheikh—I mean, sir! Audrey will—"

"Mrs. Chiu has not protected our money," Kareem snapped. "BCI will take much better care of this."

Shea nodded and handed him a sheaf of papers with a gold-tipped pen.

I whimpered, "Please don't do this, sirs! What can I do to make you change your mind? Audrey will be so angry! What will I tell her? Oh, please, don't sign. . . ."

I let my voice trail off into a miserable silence as Kareem snatched the papers and signed, with a great flourish. "And here," Shea said, pointing to another page. "And here, and here . . ."

The pen scratched. Without even condescending to look at poor little me, Shea held the papers out to me and said, "Ms. Schumann, do you recognize this signature?"

"Yes," I said in a tiny voice.

"Do you recognize the signer?"

"Yes," I whispered.

"Then please sign here to authorize the withdrawal."

With an audible gulp, I dashed at my (perfectly dry) eyes and signed the papers.

"Congratulations, sirs," Shea said. "You have just joined the federal penal system and are headed for supermax."

It took a moment for his words to land. In the same instant, the butler stood up and bumped into Nasir, splashing his once immaculate front with hot tea and a bowlful of cream. Shea leaped at Kareem, who grabbed me from the back and pressed his gun to my neck. I made myself go limp.

The butler backed off Nasir, but the doors flew open and the rest of Shea's team spilled into the room. Seeing me in Kareem's grasp, they lowered their guns and watched Shea, their faces hard and intent.

"Give me those papers!" Kareem shouted. "Give me those papers, or I'll—"

"Oh, I don't think so," I said. With a deft twist, I swung around and kicked him so hard in the groin that he doubled up, sobbing, and the gun fell from his suddenly lifeless hand to the floor. Nasir turned on me, but Shea's men were on him in less than an instant, and he too crashed to the floor in a moaning heap.

I turned back to Kareem. "Those papers prove that you and your brother are the proprietary owners of that account, and will send you to supermax for the rest of your lives," I said coolly.

"My father . . . ," Kareem moaned.

"Is already on his way to his prison cell," Shea snapped.

"Let's get them ready for transport," the butler said, lifting the silver domes from the tray to reveal wire handcuffs and a long syringe. Sedatives for the journey, I supposed. Good idea.

"Well done," Shea said to me briefly.

"Right back atcha," I said, channeling the PYTs.

Shea almost grinned.

Now, *that* was teamwork.

I was back in my office by five and started cleaning up my desk immediately. At a few minutes before six, the summons came. "Amy! In my office at once!" Audrey roared. Audrey never spoke much above a murmur, forcing her listeners to stoop respectfully over her diminutive frame in an effort to hear everything. She never, never shouted.

This was it, I knew. Thank God.

All activity ceased. The PYTs had been planning an evening of hot yoga and trivia night at the pub, but now everyone settled back into their desk chairs, determined to learn the outcome of this epic occasion.

Steady as a rock, I strolled into her office. I didn't sit down.

"The sheikh's family have withdrawn all their money from our accounts!" she screamed at me. "Do you know how much money that is?"

"Seven hundred—"

"Seven hundred fifty-seven million dollars!" she shouted. "Three-quarters of a billion dollars! Gone! All gone in one afternoon!"

For form's sake, I tried to look abashed.

"How could you have let this happen?"

"How did they get the money," I countered, "without coming in here to do the signature cards?"

"They called Lord Featherstone at home and met him there! You mean to tell me you *knew* about this?"

"Of course I didn't know," I said quickly. "I just wondered—"

"How could you have let this happen?" she shrieked, so far gone as to repeat herself. "Do you know what this will do to our bottom line? Do you have any idea what you've done?"

I smiled slightly, envisioning all of the sheikh's ill-gotten money snug and safe in a nice, untraceable CIA account. The smile was a mistake.

"You're smiling? You think this is funny?"

Actually, I found tiny Audrey in a rage quite funny. I pressed my lips together to avoid laughing out loud.

"You're fired!" she shouted. "Get your bag and go! Get out of this bank! Get out of my life! I'll see to it that you never get another job in this industry again!"

God, please let it be true, I thought.

"With pleasure," I said, and walked out the door.

Of course, it wasn't that simple. Bob called me that night and told me I would get a call on Monday reinstating me at the bank. I almost burst into tears. "Why?" I pleaded. "You promised me, Bob. You promised me that if I nailed the sheikh, I could go back into the field again. I handed the bastard to you on a silver platter with enough documentation to put him away for three lifetimes, and this is what I get?"

"Sorry, old girl," he said cheerfully. "Sheikh Abdullah and his sons will spend the rest of their lives as guests of the US penal system, but there's a little old sheikh in Bahrain whose accounts you're going to get. He was in the Paris train bombing up to his nasty little eyeballs, and you're going to bring the bugger down."

"I'm begging you, Bob. Please, please, please get me out of Atlantic Bank. I'll go back to Chechnya. I'll go to Yemen. I'll even go to Afghanistan again if I have to, and wear a burka all the livelong day."

"Atlantic Bank," he said. "But don't worry; I put you in for war zone pay this time."

I paused, war zone pay being nothing to joke about. CIA officers got war zone pay for going solo into places like Fallujah and Tripoli, not London. It almost tripled my take-home pay.

"Really? War zone pay?"

"Yup."

"Well, then . . . is the Bahraini sheikh a big fish?"

"Close your eyes and think of the money," he suggested, and hung up.

So, on Monday morning, I didn't close my eyes as I slipped quietly into my old desk. But I carefully averted them from Audrey, and she just as carefully avoided seeing me. I wondered which "friend" Bob had enlisted to talk her down. Lord Featherstone, probably. I suspected he was the one who had gotten me the job in the first place. Dorcas had once mentioned he was in OSS during the war. I really didn't think that Bob would have outed me to Audrey; Lord Featherstone must be quite the great persuader.

The rest of the team eyed me cautiously, but no one spoke to me. I worried that the scene had called too much attention to me and that someone might start wondering just how I had gotten reinstated so quickly; my cover depended on being so spineless that no one in their wildest dreams could imagine me as a spy. I would have to be doubly Amy-ish to stem speculation.

And there was still no word from Leo.

But the week before Christmas, Kali texted me that she would be in London for the holidays with "the family" (Élodie's, I interpreted, not ours) and that Élodie absolutely insisted I join the Schlumbergers for the first night of Hanukkah. I refused, of course, but first Kali, and then Élodie herself, called me. Embarrassed by all the importuning, I gave in.

Naturally, all I could think about was whether Leo would be there. I hadn't seen or heard from him since his abrupt departure at the Barcelona airport, and I could only imagine how great his sense of betrayal still was. Even while lying in his arms, I had lied to him, over and over. And then for him to have learned I had the power to save his beloved Sudeley Castle with one public statement but refused to do it . . . I couldn't blame him for his silent fury.

So, very uncharacteristically for either Jules or Amy, I tried on a dozen outfits before settling on the first one I had set out: a black pencil skirt and dark blue blouse that complemented my blue eyes and fair skin. At least I hoped it did. I added the tiny diamond earrings my father had given me when I left for college—take that, Schlumbergers!—and skintight black boots that made my legs longer (hopefully), and set out for Holland Park.

As my Uber dropped me off and I walked up the brick path, I could hear children's shrieks all the way out to the street. So much for the "quiet family evening" Élodie had promised me. I rang the doorbell and waited apprehensively, smoothing down my skirt and brushing flakes of snow off my jacket. The door swung open, and there stood Leo, impossibly tall and dark against the candlelit background.

"Hey, Jules," he said.

"Please," I said. "Don't call me that."

He inclined his head slightly. "Of course. Won't you come in?"

He held the door open just enough that I had to brush against him to walk inside, and every nerve ending in my body tightened at the feel of his body against mine. "May I take your jacket?" he asked politely, for all the world like a well-trained butler rather than an ex-lover.

Awkwardly, I slipped out of the jacket and handed it to him. He draped it over the banister and held out his hand to me. "Come," he said. "Let's introduce you to the clan."

Chapter 39

"Amy!" Kali squealed, and raced over to give me a big hug. For a moment, I contrasted this meeting with our strained reunion when she first arrived in London just a few months ago, and I held her close. She looked wonderful, her fair skin tanned to a lovely glow from the Antibes sun, and she was wearing a designer dress that must have cost more than my entire wardrobe. I raised an eyebrow at it, and she said happily, "Élodie took me shopping for Hanukkah! Isn't it beautiful?"

The sapphire-blue wrap dress clung to her slim young body in all the right places but ended discreetly just above her knees. "Will Élodie take me shopping too?" I asked, and she laughed.

Children ran over and surrounded Kali like a wave of rolling surf. They jabbered at her in French and Hebrew, and she jabbered back in English and some terribly accented French. Proudly, she said to me, "This is Amélie and Leah and Sara and Ari and Sasha . . ." She pronounced all the names the French way, with the emphasis on the last syllable, and I had to smile at her enthusiasm.

The children were trying to drag her away for a game, and she gestured at me helplessly. "Go," I said, and they all ran off together.

I saw Leo across the room, and he started toward me. But a woman's voice called, "Léo!" and he turned away. The large, lovely room was alight with candles and some dim lamps. By the window, I saw a beautifully carved menorah with two unlit candles. The menorah was surrounded by little gold-wrapped chocolate coins that the internet had told me were called gelt, traditional gifts for children at Hanukkah. In the corner, Kali and the children were playing dreidel, which the internet had also explained to me: a traditional toy for the holiday, which spun like an oddly balanced top amid shrieks of high-pitched laughter.

The rest of the room was like a scene from a Broadway play about perfectly dressed, perfectly groomed women and their escorts. The women were all tall and dark-haired, like Leo, and dark-eyed. Two of the men were blond, one brown-haired, and one so dark-skinned he almost looked African. All had sparkling glasses in their hands and, surprisingly, munched on little doughnuts still hot and steaming from the oven. My mouth watered.

One of the women came up to me and kissed me on both cheeks, Gallic-style. "It is such a pleasure to meet you at last," she said, her English only slightly accented. "I am Élodie, and I must thank you for lending us your sister. She is delightful!"

Ah, Kali's fairy godmother. I thanked her in turn, and we chatted for a while, her keen dark eyes examining me intently. I wondered if she knew anything about Leo and me. Other sisters came up and were introduced, and the conversation turned to art. "Neoexpressionism is passé," one of them said.

"Not at all!" another objected, and they were off in what even I recognized as a sisterly quarrel. Polite and low-key, perhaps, but still the bickering of sisters. Élodie called out, "Léo! Come here and settle this. Your sisters are at it again."

He strolled over and draped a brotherly arm across Élodie's shoulders. "What's all this, then?" he inquired.

"She said that—"

"She's totally wrong about—"

"Enough!" he said firmly, with a glance at me. "We have company, remember?"

A little abashed, the women murmured apologies, and I assured them it was nothing. Then the youngest sister, Maya, said to Leo, "But still, Léo, we need you to decide about the Yad Vashem donation. Jacob thinks that—"

"Who cares what Jacob thinks?" Élodie interrupted.

"Leo, could you please tell her—"

"Leo, it's really important that—"

"*Dayenu!*" he cut in sharply. "*Dayenu!* Enough. I will think about the Yad Vashem donation and let you know when I've made a decision. Now, it's time to light the candles."

Everyone quieted immediately and gathered the children to stand around the menorah while Élodie, the oldest sister, chanted the prayers. Even the littlest children were still and solemn. The twins lisped the ancient words along with their parents, and Baby Benji's eyes were wide with wonder as the flames sprang up.

I watched Leo closely, thinking about his sisters and their complete reliance on him. No wonder he had such an air of command. He had probably been commanding since he was fifteen, when his father became so sick.

Three nannies took the children to the playroom for their own dinner, and we adults sat together at an endless table in the Versailles-size dining room. There were several cousins as well, so we made sixteen at table. The women's jewels sparkled in the flickering candlelight, and the discreet hum of conversation was warm and intimate.

Embarrassingly, I was placed between Kali and Leo at the table, and I was agonizingly conscious of his nearness as I took a nervous sip of champagne. Kali said, "Amy! Leo! I have great news. I've decided to spend a year as Élodie's au pair and then take it from there. Isn't that wonderful?"

"Great," I said, exchanging glances with Leo.

"Élodie's delighted," he said. "The children love Kali."

"But do you need a work permit?" I asked. "I don't want you to be working illegally."

Kali explained, "There's some kind of special permit for non-EU au pairs. Élodie's lawyers are working on it."

Leo said, "It'll be fine." Translation: Attila the Hun could become an au pair in Europe if he had enough influence and well-paid lawyers.

I asked, "How do the children go to school when they're bouncing from country to country?"

Leo stirred, uncomfortable as always when the topic of his family's wealth came up. "They have private tutors who travel with them."

"Ah," I said.

"But they're going to settle down in Tel Aviv next year and send the kids to the American school there," Kali put in.

I studied Leo for a moment. He wore his wealth and privilege so lightly. Sometimes it seemed to embarrass him, and sometimes he took full advantage of it (e.g., the Audi). Not for the first time, I wondered what it would be like to grow up knowing that anything was possible to you, that all paths were open. Was it liberating or pressurizing? From the moment my father died, only one path had been open to me—the CIA—and I had embraced it. But still . . .

Kali interrupted my thoughts. "Isn't that great, Amy?"

"Well," I said, only half-jokingly, "I guess my little girl is all grown up."

"You're not actually related—is that right?" Maya asked, glancing between us and failing to discern any resemblance.

"No, Kali's father is my mother's second husband. So we're stepsisters."

"Ah."

I wondered how they felt about divorce; was there a slight tinge of disapproval in Maya's tone?

"Amy's parents got divorced, and then her dad died later," Kali explained.

"I'm so sorry," Élodie said to me.

"My father was pretty amazing," I replied, lulled by her obvious sympathy. "I still miss him."

Kali sniffed.

"What does that mean?" I demanded.

"I just don't understand how you can hero-worship him like that. Don't you know why your mother left him?"

"Because she hated moving all the time. She had no sense of fun or adventure!" *And she left me too*, I thought.

I was dimly aware that Élodie had turned to her sisters and engaged them in conversation so that our little family spat could go unnoticed. Kali hissed at me, "No, she left because he slept with half the embassy!"

"That's her side of the story," I snapped, instantly defensive.

"No, Jules, that's fact."

I shot her a furious look at the "Jules," and she subsided, glancing around guiltily to make sure no one had overheard.

I quieted for a moment too, uncomfortably aware that my father probably had slept with half the embassy, and half of the other embassies as well. He had always had women dangling after him and rarely bothered to break up with one before moving on to another.

"So what?" I demanded.

"So what? He was an asshole—that's so what."

Leo, on my other side, leaned over. "Charming as I find these sisterly exchanges," he drawled, "if I want to hear siblings bickering, I can listen to my own sisters."

Sisterly! I glared at Kali, who glared back.

"She's not my sister." I didn't have any family.

"Could have fooled me," he shot back.

Struck by the realization, I closed my mouth. Maybe Kali *did* feel like my sister, and maybe my father *had* been an asshole. The world tilted, ever so slightly, on its axis.

Dessert was more of the little doughnuts, as well as bowls of sweet fruit and sherbet. I contemplated the fresh, luscious, out-of-season kiwis and strawberries, trying to total up the cost of this intimate family dinner. I was telling Leo about my Syrian teenager who had recently been admitted to university (to study English history, of all things!) when he leaned over and said to me, "Come outside for a minute."

I drew in my breath sharply, having resigned myself to the fact that the evening would pass without a single personal exchange with him. "Okay," I said unsteadily. "Just let me get my coat."

His sisters watched owlishly as we got up from the table together. There was a sudden silence, followed by a burst of low-voiced chatter as we left the room. "At least we've given them something to talk about," Leo said, smiling.

The back garden was cold and dark. I shivered slightly, and Leo put his arm around me. "I knew you were a spy all along," he said.

"No, you didn't."

"Well, I suspected."

I glared at him. "I'm very good at my job."

"Yes. You are. But I have four sisters; I know women."

I scowled even more fiercely, but my heart was pounding.

"Also," he went on, almost casually, "when I love someone, I really get to know her. I couldn't fall in love with someone who's a mystery to me."

My whole body felt suddenly alight with warmth. "You love me?" I breathed.

"Well, of course I do. Why else do you think I followed you halfway around Europe?"

"Because you thought I was Jules?"

"*Sacrebleu*, I could have gotten your DNA from a used Diet Coke can that very first day at Covent Garden," he said, "if that was all I wanted."

Remarkably, I had never even considered DNA. He had access to locks of Katherine Parr's hair, which were beautifully preserved at Sudeley Castle. He could prove, beyond any doubt, that I was her descendant. I thought about that and about the fact that he had never threatened to expose me without my acquiescence.

"I love you too," I said, and lifted my head for his kiss.

Chapter 40

When we walked back into the dining room, we were holding hands, and my cheeks were flushed bright with beard burn and happiness. Arch glances were exchanged around the table, though I observed that only Élodie was grinning widely. They didn't trust me with their precious brother, I realized. Well, that was all right; I had never trusted anyone either. Not Kali, not Leo, not anyone.

Seeing his family together, though, made me wonder if there was another path for me. I *had* entrusted Leo with not only my heart but my deepest-held secret. Could I be a part of this close-knit, deeply loving family, with all its bickering and shared history and delicious children? A few months ago, it would have seemed absurd; now, I realized with a jolt, it seemed almost possible.

And yet Leo and I had settled nothing. He hadn't explained his silence of the past few weeks, I still couldn't come forward and claim Sudeley, and he still couldn't save it without me. My mood darkened, and I sank back into my chair, suddenly exhausted.

Back at work on Monday, another shocker awaited. Audrey, unbelievably, had taken the day off, so the PYTs were running wild—perching on each other's desks and chattering about the weekend. The boys tossed a football around and played desk-chair soccer while the girls braided each other's hair in tight French plaits. I liked them much better like this, actually.

Then all of our emails pinged at the same time. A thrill of curiosity and slight apprehension went through the room, and everyone hurried back to their desks to open up the message.

Everyone,
Executive Vice President Audrey Chiu has taken an indefinite leave of absence.

Shocked gasps ran through the room.

Ms. Chiu is under investigation by the FBI, Interpol, and the British Conduct Authority in connection with the accounts of Sheikh Mahmud bin Sultan bin Ali, who has been arrested for financing terrorists through his Atlantic Bank accounts.

That was Audrey's sheikh, I realized, her personal client for more than a decade. Commissions and fees on his accounts were so high that she had received Atlantic's highest honor, the Banker of the Year award, three years in a row. I read on.

Ms. Chiu is not suspected of direct complicity in any crime, but she is being investigated under the doctrine of willful blindness, which I urge you to study carefully. Please consult Atlantic Bank's lawyers if you have any questions about this legal doctrine or your responsibilities with regard to it.
During this interim period, I will personally oversee the office, and look forward to meeting with all of you tomorrow.
Kind regards,
Lord Alfred Featherstone

Oh. My. God.

"What the fuck is willful blindness?" a confused and nervous Jake M. asked.

Kristen R., the smartest of the bunch, said, "The idea is that if a reasonable person should have suspected that something was wrong, then that person—Audrey—can be convicted of a crime for ignoring it. It's when you choose to be blind, despite all the signs of trouble."

Both Jakes gulped audibly.

I resolved to send Bob ten cases of the finest Scotch whiskey.

As if my cup weren't running over already, Leo called that night. "I've found something interesting about Lady Mary and her ancestors—your ancestors, that is," he said. "Nothing material to our problem, but still interesting. Care to have dinner tomorrow?"

"Sure," I said. And maybe a nightcap afterward? At my flat? My senses tingled with anticipation.

Lord Alfred Featherstone swept in the next morning to an unusually subdued office. Kristen R. was the first to stand up and offer her hand in greeting. "Alfred," she said, "it's so good to see you again. That was such a delightful weekend at Cliveden with you and your family."

"In the office," he said coolly, "I am Lord Featherstone, if you please."

A chastened Kristen sat down, and I found myself cheering inwardly. The other vice presidents attended board meetings and the occasional social event with our directors, but Lord Featherstone was very much an unknown. He had worked with OSS and MI6 as a young man, though, and I strongly suspected he was Bob's contact at Atlantic Bank.

"Let us proceed to the conference room," he said, and, without a glance to see if anyone was following, led the way.

Tall, gray-haired, stoop-shouldered, octogenarian men had never been my thing, but I was falling in love.

We sat around the conference table and introduced ourselves. After a while, Lord Featherstone snapped, "How many of you have the same name? Good lord, don't your parents have any imagination?"

I couldn't help it; I giggled. He looked at me with no trace of recognition; he was good, I thought. "And you must be Amy," he said. "A pleasure to meet you. I have heard excellent reports of you."

The room was utterly silent. "Now," he said, "we will go around the table again, and each of you will speak for three minutes—no more, and no less—on your current accounts. Jake T., you may begin." He set the timer on his Rolex watch and waited.

Jake began, "I've been doing a deep dive into the Sultan bin Saud accounts and believe they need some right-sizing. So I'm planning to model the bottom-line kicks; then I'll tease out the headlines and socialize some scenarios with the sheikh. I've been noodling on one—"

Lord Featherstone interrupted, "Young man, are you incapable of speaking the Queen's English? What on earth are you nattering on about? Amy, you appear to be a sensible person. Can you translate?"

I almost giggled again but managed to stifle the impulse. "He's analyzing different investments for the sultan's accounts."

"Well, then why didn't you say so?" Lord Featherstone demanded of Jake. Poor Jake's mouth quite literally hung open. Silent shock reverberated around the table.

Lord Featherstone harrumphed. "Cat got your tongue? Excellent. Kristen—any Kristen—it's your turn."

I had never enjoyed a meeting so much in my entire life.

So I was in a wonderful mood when Leo's Audi purred up to

the front of my building at six o'clock that night and I climbed in. Leo glanced at me. "Good day at the office?"

"Fantastic. Epic. Lord Featherstone is the love of my life."

"I rather hoped I was," Leo said.

I gulped and felt my stomach quiver. I could not think of a thing to say. I was afraid that he was too.

"At any rate," Leo went on, clearing his throat, "I booked a table for us in West Ken, a quiet little pub where we'll be able to hear each other talk."

Still incapable of speaking, I nodded dumbly.

We wound up at a quiet corner table; I wondered if Leo's private bankers had made the reservation for him.

"So," Leo said, after we had been supplied with frothy margaritas and bowls of pungent, fresh olives, "have you ever heard of Sir Francis Walsingham?"

I searched my memory and came up empty. "No."

"I'll give you a hint: He's been dead for more than four hundred years."

Oh, another one of Leo's historical obsessions. "No . . . oh, maybe," I said. "Didn't he have something to do with Queen Elizabeth?"

Leo beamed at me. "Gold star for the young lady. Yes, he was Elizabeth's spymaster. His staff included a cryptographer, a massive group of informants, and an expert at breaking and repairing seals without detection so he could intercept correspondence."

"Really," I said. I loved a good spy story.

"Yes. He uncovered numerous plots against Elizabeth and received regular dispatches about the Spanish military's plans so that England was able to defeat the Spanish armada in 1588. Quite a brilliant spy," Leo said, a little wistfully.

"That's cool," I said. "But what does it have to do with Lady Mary?"

"Oh, yes! Brace yourself, my little spy. It turns out that Lady Amanda Seymour was one of his informants. She regularly reported to him on the doings of Mary, Queen of Scots, who was aiming to overthrow Elizabeth and take the throne for herself."

"How on earth?" I asked.

"Lady Amanda's needlewoman had a sister who worked in Mary's household, so they helped to intercept Mary's letters and pass them on to Lady Amanda, who made copies and sent them on to Walsingham."

I was delighted. "And this was my ancestress?"

"Yes, indeed. Furthermore, it seems that you come from a long line of spies. Lady Amanda's grandson—the one whose trail led me to you—spied for King James, and *his* grandson was an agent for King Charles II in the Civil War. Another Seymour worked for Wellington to uncover intelligence against Napoleon. You have spying in your genes, my girl."

Thoughtfully, I remarked, "I'm agency royalty, you know." I took a huge bite of the hamburger the waitress had placed in front of me. It felt wonderful not to have to pretend anymore with Leo. There were so very few people in the world with whom I could truly be myself, Jules Seymour, with the big appetite and the thirst for adventure.

"What does that mean?" Suddenly alert, he asked, "Is this to do with your father? Even I couldn't find anything on him."

I shrugged and ate three french fries at once. There was no more need to hide things from Leo. He knew the most important secret. "My father, Ned Seymour, was under nonofficial cover—an NOC, like I am—for his entire career, and my grandfather was Wild Bill Donovan's right-hand man in the OSS. Supposedly, he led more missions into occupied France than any other American agent." I took another big bite of hamburger, and ketchup dribbled down my chin. Unconcern-edly, I swiped at it with a napkin.

"So, 'agency royalty' means you come from an agency family?"

"Not just any agency family, but an agency family with a whole display case in the CIA Museum at Langley. Of course, the name is disguised in the museum, but everyone knows it's us."

Leo grinned at me. "So, you come from a famous and pow-erful family too. We have something in common."

I realized he was right. "Children of CIA people are called princes and princesses at the agency. Everyone else resents us and thinks we swagger around, knowing everything and everyone."

"And did you swagger?" Leo asked.

"Well, maybe a little." I laughed, thinking of a new recruit in my training program who had called me an 'agency princess' for the very first time, and how much I had enjoyed my superior status.

"Jules Seymour, CIA royalty," Leo mused, and suddenly, for the first time, I realized that I didn't want to be an agency prin-cess anymore. I had fallen into the CIA after the shock of my father's death and the revelations that had followed it, but now it was my place, not his. It was *my* mission, *my* life's work, and I was doing it for myself, not for him, and certainly not in his shadow.

I wanted to be me, Jules Seymour—not the heir to my father's legacy.

"What are you thinking about?" Leo asked.

I shrugged, shaking the thoughts away.

"Why didn't you ever call me Amy?" I asked. "Don't tell me you knew from the very beginning. I'll never believe it."

"No," he acknowledged. "I thought you *knew* something about Jules, but after the first couple of conversations, I wasn't sure if you *were* Jules."

"So why . . . ?"

"You told me a lot about your dad," Leo said simply. "Not his real job, of course, but I just couldn't imagine him giving his daughter a mousy little name like Amy. You're Jules."

"It took me two years to create Amy's identity," I said indignantly. "That's why I couldn't tell you. What would be the point of being covert if I'm going to identify myself to every man who comes along?"

"I'm hardly 'any man,' am I?" Leo countered. "You sure know how to dent a guy's ego."

His ego seemed pretty healthy to me.

"I have to do such a bang-up job on the Atlantic Bank assignment that they'll send me out into the field again," I explained.

Leo reached across the table for a fistful of my french fries, and I slapped his hand. "No sharing," I said.

"Ah, yes," Leo said. "Isn't that your motto?"

We ate in silence for a few minutes.

I asked, "If you're just Leo, not Mossad, then why the gunmen?"

"I swear to you," Leo said, "on my nieces' souls. I do not know."

I believed him.

But then what was this all about? Sheikh Abdullah hadn't suspected me for a minute, according to his CIA interrogators, so that didn't explain it. Leo appeared to be clean, so that left, however unlikely, the last possibility: the Sudeley development. Did this all come back to Sudeley after all?

I simply couldn't imagine how.

But I could see that Leo, despite his admission of love for me, was still prickly. He couldn't quite forgive me for lying to him, and he definitely couldn't forgive me for refusing to help him save Sudeley. He might understand—in fact, I thought he did—but that didn't mean he could overlook it enough to be with me.

And sure enough, when he took me home after dinner, he simply leaned across me to open the door on my side. "Good night," he said. There was absolutely no inflection in his voice, and his face, in the hazy lighting of the dim streetlamp, was unreadable.

I hesitated. "Don't you want to . . ."

He sighed. "Good night, Jules," he said, and drove away.

Chapter 41

Alone again, I stumbled up to my flat in a haze of uncertainty and longing. Where was this going? Where could this go?

The answer was all too clear: nowhere. I turned on the radio for some noise in the too-silent room, and of course the familiar strains of "Hey Jude" filled the air. Our song.

That's me, I thought dully as John Lennon sang to me about a fool. Sadly, I turned off the music and climbed into my empty bed.

The next few weeks were uneventful as a slushy, gray London winter began to give way to a tenuous early spring. A new group of Syrian refugees arrived, doubling my band of teenagers, and I busied myself with them on the long, otherwise empty weekends. To my great pleasure, Lord Featherstone continued to ride roughshod over my terrified and chastened workmates. His insistence on "real English" flummoxed the PYTs. He outlawed virtually every phrase on my Stupid Jargon list and some others besides. On day three, he gave up on trying to tell one Kristen from another, so he began to call everyone in the office by their last name. "Rivers!" he would boom out, and Kristen R. would jump up as if shot from a cannon.

On day five, he got tired of the girls' attempts to charm him. They were accustomed to adoring old men swooning at the flirtations and flattery of pretty young women, and Lord Featherstone's stony reaction was impossible to comprehend. "Stop trying to flirt with me!" he snapped at Kristen the Younger, who froze mid-dimple. "I have three granddaughters, and if any of them tried to sweet-talk her boss like that, I'd have her thrown into a nunnery!" I was the only one he called by first name and the only one allowed to call him Alfred, which I did at every opportunity.

I met with my new Bahraini "clients" (i.e., targets) and gained access to all of their account information, so Bob was pleased with me as well.

But Leo had lapsed, once again, into radio silence.

And I dithered over whether it was time to file the dreaded "close and continuing" report on him with the agency. I could report our relationship now that I knew he wasn't working for a foreign government, but what was the point if our relationship—or whatever it was—was over? Maybe it had ended before it had really begun. My appetite plummeted, and I found it hard to get up in the morning. It felt almost like grief, and I tried to throw myself ever more passionately into my work.

One sleety evening that belied any promise of spring, I opened my encrypted home laptop and logged in to the agency records file. *Close and continuing relationship*, I typed in firmly. To hell with Leo and his moods. It was a close and continuing relationship for me, and perhaps always would be. *Leo Schlumberger*, I entered. With some relief, I answered no to those all-important questions: Is your contact associated with a foreign intelligence agency? Is your contact associated with any foreign government? No, no, and no. Before I could think, I pressed SEND and closed my computer.

I wondered what Internal Security would make of Leo.

The following week, I opened my Atlantic Bank emails to discover an invitation to my Bahraini sheikh's yacht for his eldest son's fortieth birthday. I drew in my breath sharply, feeling the sudden but welcome spurt of adrenaline in my veins. So, I had gained his trust enough to be invited on board his yacht. This was a golden opportunity to penetrate his inner circle, as I had never quite been able to do with Sheikh Abdullah—that was why the investigation had dragged on for so long.

Besides, early spring on the French riviera would be gorgeous.

I went through the tedious burner cell phone routine that evening so I could report the invitation to Bob. "Nice work," he said immediately. "I'll station an ops team on a navy vessel offshore, but I don't expect any trouble."

Neither did I. Even if the sheikh suspected me, I figured his own yacht was probably the safest place in the world for me. He would never expose himself to the inquiries and attention that any injury to me would bring.

"But be careful," Bob added, and I shrugged. Being careful was never much fun.

The next day at work, I announced my upcoming trip at the morning meeting. Kristen R. said immediately, "I'll go with you, Amy."

"Oh, no," I said involuntarily.

"Audrey said I should second-chair you on your accounts, and you've never been on one of these jaunts. I'm coming with you."

I looked at Lord Featherstone in mute appeal. He couldn't stand the Kristens. He deliberated a moment, apparently weighing the benefits of a one-Kristen-less office for a few days, and said, "No harm in having Rivers accompany you, Amy. Better to have two of you."

Despairingly, I realized no one had read him in on the Bahraini operation. He didn't have a need to know, so he didn't.

"Fine," I said shortly.

Kristen dimpled. "It will be so exciting to see the sheikh's yacht. I hear it's spectacular!"

You idiot, I thought sourly.

Two days later, we were on a plane to Marseille.

The yacht *was* spectacular. Tall and white and graceful, it dazzled the eyes in the pale, watery sun of early spring on the riviera. It was moored offshore, so we took the private tender from the small dock near Marseille, and the little boat cut through the waves with sharp-edged precision. The water was blue, blue, bluer than blue, and the sky a lighter shade of blue, with soft, scudding clouds above. Kristen said dreamily, "Isn't this beautiful?"

"Yes," I said, still sour. "Just wonderful." It had occurred to me that Kristen's presence would be extra insurance against any trouble, and I was sulking over the realization that this really would be the danger-free, idle holiday that she expected. What a bummer.

So I was perfectly relaxed the next morning when the yacht anchored off a small harbor in Juan-les-Pins, a beautiful and relatively unspoiled village just east of Marseille. The night before, I had managed to sneak into the sheikh's private study and copied his computer files onto my tiny flash drive, which was now hidden within a locket in my jewelry box. My mission accomplished, I was actually looking forward to diving off the ship's prow and snorkeling off the boat in the crystal-clear waters of the Mediterranean. The air temperature was a moderate sixty-eight and the water a cool seventy—perfect for snorkeling, despite Kristen's elaborate shivers. I braced myself to dive into the chilly waters and swim ashore.

But the sheikh came up to my elbow and said, "We will take the tender into the beach and then picnic there, yes? It will be warmer this afternoon."

I shrugged and pulled on my white linen shift dress over my bathing suit. "Sure," I said agreeably.

Kristen opted to stay on board, sunning herself under the greedy eyes of the sheikh's sons. She took off her slender wrap and lay down on one of the plush deck chairs, her pretty, delicate-boned face tilted up to the sun. I noticed the sheikh's son ogling her in her little white bikini and wished I could give her a burka. Today was her birthday, and at breakfast the sheikh had given her a Tiffany bracelet. Now she displayed it on her slim wrist, admiring the way it sparkled and dazzled in the sun.

The tender scraped up against a stone pier, and I found that I too was inclining my head toward the sun's welcome warmth. A few tourists were sitting on the rocky beach, applying sunscreen and chatting languidly, while some slicker-clad men fished off the pier. There were no other yachts anchored nearby. The scene could not have been more peaceful or idyllic.

The men who had brought us ashore set up an elaborate little encampment for us against the rocks of the steep cliff overlooking the harbor. I watched in astonishment as they produced remarkably comfortable lounge chairs, a small cocktail table, and thick, sheet-size towels. Next came an array of foods, from caviar on toast points (which I adored) to little strawberry tarts topped with real, fresh whipped cream (which I also adored) to frosty margaritas draped with oranges and lemons (my cup runneth over). Contentedly, I leaned back against my chair and sipped the luscious cocktail, lazily watching the sheikh stroll down to the waterfront to watch the fishermen.

I don't know what warned me. One minute I was sucking on a tequila-drenched orange, luxuriating in the sybaritic comfort of the soft lounge and sweet fruit. A split second later, I sensed, rather than heard, a sudden whoosh of air above me and leaped sideways, avoiding by barely an inch a massive rock that had hurtled down the cliff in a direct path toward my defenseless head.

Gasping, I didn't have to feign my trembles and fear as the sheikh came running back to me, brushing aside the worried calls of the innocent tourists. He was furious. "Are you all right, Amy?" he cried. "How did this happen? Come away from the cliff. Come away, quickly!"

He grabbed my arm, and I winced in sudden pain. Looking down, I realized the rock had scraped against my arm as it came rocketing down, leaving a network of scratches and blood in its wake. I pictured the weight of that rock crashing down on my head and, biting my lip, allowed the sheikh to guide me away from the cliff.

Then we both looked up to the top, and I saw, quite distinctly, the outline of a tiny figure running away from the edge of the stony drop. The sheikh saw it too and was purple-red with rage. "Criminal cretins," he hissed under his breath. "Criminal stupidity. Amy, are you all right?"

My training was kicking in, and I was thinking coolly again. I wondered if the sheikh was angry because his men had failed to kill me. I didn't believe in coincidences, and the odds that a giant rock would have picked just that moment to break loose and begin its lethal descent onto the head of Jules Seymour, CIA NOC officer, seemed poor to me.

I said tremulously, "I don't feel very well, Sheikh Sultan. I'm so sorry, but could we go back to the yacht now? I'd feel much safer there."

"Of course, of course. And we must clean your wounds as well," he added. "I will bandage them myself."

Over my dead body, I thought. But I nodded submissively

and drooped my way back to the tender, leaning heavily on the solicitous sheikh and wincing theatrically every time I moved my arm.

Still, I was shaken. I thanked every god in the pantheon for that mysterious sixth—or seventh, or eighth—sense that had alerted me to danger and impelled me to jump aside in the nick of time. I had been so sure that the sheikh was completely unsuspecting. It was disconcerting—and, yes, a little frightening—to learn I had been so wrong. My eyes darted around the beach as I considered, for just one moment, making a run for it while I was still on land.

But that would only confirm the sheikh's suspicions, and what about poor, dumb Kristen, oblivious and helpless on board the yacht? Besides, I didn't want to abandon that precious flash drive I had hidden in my locket.

My heart pounding, I climbed into the little white boat, and we raced toward the yacht at breakneck speed.

Chapter 42

Back on board, I shook off Kristen's exclamations and went immediately to my room, claiming an urgent need for a shower. I could see the sheikh's men hovering indecisively in my wake and tried to recapture my certainty that nothing would happen to me on the yacht. I was a little less sure now. Thankfully, the men stood back, and I made it to my room unharmed. I threw the lock and leaned against the door, breathing heavily.

Then I made a beeline for my jewelry box, thinking perhaps I should toss that fatally incriminating little flash drive overboard before they thought to search my cabin. But even as I hurried across the cool tile floor, inlaid with elaborate Arabic designs in brilliant shades of blue and green, I could see they had already searched—and hadn't even bothered to hide their tracks. The duvet was hanging over the mattress instead of being tucked in; my Kindle lay open on the bedside table instead of closed, as I had left it; and drops of liquid from my ever-present water bottle were spilled carelessly on the polished wood of the dresser.

Grimly apprehensive, I opened the jewelry box, but, as I had already known, the locket was gone.

Well, that at least explained the clumsy attempt at murder or maiming on the beach. The sheikh had probably acted on an outraged impulse upon hearing of my treachery. Until then, he likely had been as unsuspecting as I had thought; he probably searched every passenger's cabin daily. I cursed myself for my stupidity and carelessness. Bob would have my head for this.

But then I cooled down and realized that my initial calculation still held: As long as I (and Kristen, a very inconvenient witness, from the sheikh's perspective) was known to be aboard his yacht, I should be safe. Now that he had retrieved the drive, I was not a danger to him. Ergo, he was not a danger to me either.

And yet there was that rock. . . .

When I emerged on deck in a fresh blue sundress, my scratched-up arm discreetly hidden under a light shawl, Kristen was holding her cell phone in the air and scowling at it. "I'm trying to send pictures to the team," she complained, "but the internet is down. Mahmud"—she appealed to the sheikh's eldest son—"when do you think they'll fix it?"

He shrugged and spread his hands. "Tomorrow, maybe. Inshallah."

Kristen and I exchanged glances. Even she knew what the fatalistic "inshallah" meant. My brain was on high alert, registering the sinister implications of this development. I was completely alone, cut off from the ops team just a few miles out to sea. My certainty that I would not need them was fading, and I resolved to stick to Kristen like glue for the rest of the weekend. How ironic to be dependent on her for my safety. How humiliating. And how very precarious.

I was running through possible escape plans in my head when we all heard the noisy sounds of drunken revelry aboard a ship nearby. Fast approaching from the starboard side came a tatty rust bucket of a yacht filled with loud partygoers on deck, each one equipped with a cell phone camera and selfie stick.

"What the hell?" Kristen said, staring.

I wanted to cheer and wave an American flag. However much I had assured myself that I was safe on the yacht, I hadn't entirely believed it. "It's the cavalry," I said.

"What?"

The sheikh's son came up and grabbed me by the elbow. "Come below," he said. "Come now."

Something was sticking into my ribs, but I ignored it and made an agile leap to the side. He couldn't possibly shoot me in front of fifty cell phone cameras. "No," I said clearly. I waved and called out to the partiers, "Come join us! We have booze for everyone!"

"Get below!" the sheikh commanded, and his men advanced on me, shouting. A dozen cell phones clicked, and someone called, "This is great! It's live-streaming on Facebook!"

I shoved the men aside, roughly, but they kept on coming. I waved at the cameras again. I turned to Kristen. "Jump!" I commanded.

"What? I don't even have my bathing suit on."

The sheikh's men had hesitated, conferring. "Jump!" I said, more urgently.

"Amy, your behavior is thoroughly irrational. Don't think I'm not going to discuss the situation with Audrey when she returns—"

"Oh, for God's sake!" I shouted. I pushed her overboard, and she surfaced below with a small shriek as I threw myself into the cold water beside her. For once, she didn't look perfect. Her long blond hair was dark with water and clung in wet strands to her cheeks. "Swim," I said grimly.

The partygoers, crowing with laughter, were already chugging toward us in a small motorized tender. They hauled us aboard and waved at the sheikh, whose face was mottled with rage.

Kristen clung to the sides of the boat, panting. "I can't believe you did that," she said, shivering with cold and fury. "Are you crazy?"

Small thanks for saving her life, I thought. So I said, "You're welcome."

"What?"

Until I felt the gun in my ribs, I hadn't been sure that this was real danger. As welcoming hands pulled me up onto the rusted yacht, though, a delayed reaction set in, and I found that, to my annoyance, I too was trembling. Perhaps I had needed rescuing after all. I wasn't sure. Uniformed ship's officers wrapped Kristen up in warm blankets and hustled her away, but I stood up on the splintery deck, looking around for the CIA team leader, Shea.

Instead, I saw Leo.

He shouldered his way through the excited crowd and put his arm around me. For just a moment, I allowed myself to lean against him and feel the warm pulse of his heart against my soaked skin. Maybe there was something of Amy in me after all; sometimes it wasn't so terrible to let someone protect me. When I was sure my voice would be steady, I said, "I might have been in trouble there. I don't know how to thank you."

Leo's eyes traveled down my body, lingering at the sopping-wet sundress that clung lovingly to it, outlining every detail of my breasts and hardened nipples. "Oh," he said as he pulled off his jacket and draped it around my shoulders, "I can think of a way."

"But how . . . ," I began.

"Shh," he said. "The real cavalry is coming." I recognized, again, how closely our minds seemed to work together and then heard what his keener ears had already detected: the *putt-putt* of another small tender, crossing the waves toward us. The sheikh and his men were tiny specks aboard the now-unmoving *Ayesha*, roped securely to a white cutter. Dimly, I heard shouts and commands coming across the water. This small tender, apparently, was from the cutter.

A dark, closely shaven head appeared at the top of the ladder, and Shea climbed aboard, followed by six other heavily bearded, burly men with rippling muscles and hard faces. At last, my CIA team. The drunken crowd backed off quickly, and Shea surveyed the scene in grim silence.

He said to me, "What the fuck?"

"They tried to kill me on the beach at—"

"I know," he said impatiently. "But what the fuck?"

Leo shouldered in between them. "At last, the CIA," he said dryly. "Better late than never, I guess."

Shea inclined his head toward Leo. "And who the fuck is this?"

"Civilian male," I said briefly.

"Name? Nationality?" His sharp ears had caught the slight accent, and he was tense, poised for action.

"Name is L—" I started.

"Lowenstein," Leo said, cutting me off. "I'm Mossad."

Chapter 43

I was rooted to the spot. If the earth had opened up a gigantic chasm under my feet, I would have been less shaken.

"Oh, fuck," Shea said.

"Oh, fuck," I said, startling all of us equally.

"That your real name?" Shea demanded.

"Of course not," Leo said, sounding surprised.

"You have ID?"

"Of course not," Leo said again.

"Well, fuck me," Shea said. He turned on me. "You're collaborating with Mossad on this? Who signed off on that?"

Leo said to me, "Don't tell him anything."

I couldn't have spoken if I'd wanted to; my mouth was still gaping open. I closed it into a firm line.

Shea, scowling, glanced around the crowded deck. "What about the others?"

"All civilians," Leo said immediately. "Picked up at the Jewish Community Center of Marseille. They got free booze as long as they kept their cameras trained on that yacht."

Shea grunted. "I'm going to be filling out paperwork for the next month and apologizing to the fucking French for the next year."

"Or," Leo suggested, "you could just let us sail on back to Marseille while you take your prisoners out to the US Navy ship you've got waiting a couple of nautical miles farther out."

The two men, both alpha males of deeply competitive intelligence organizations, sized each other up. Shea stuck out his hand, and Leo shook it; each man's grip was like iron. To me, Shea said, "What were you thinking? Mossad!"

"They're supposed to be on our side," I said.

He shook his head. "What a clusterfuck." Then he and his team clambered back down the ladder and off our ship. My drunken shipmates broke out into loud cheers, and we set our course for Marseille.

Kristen was wearing one man's jacket and another man's scarf. Friendly Frenchmen were plying her with brandy from the ship's bar, and she seemed to be almost enjoying herself. Pushing Leo aside, I made my unsteady way toward the bar. I couldn't think. I couldn't even feel anything except the cold of my wet clothes and the even colder knowledge of my stupidity.

Leo. Was. Mossad.

Of course he was Mossad. I thought of his hard muscles, his keen eyes and sharp mind, his languages, his ability to master any situation, anytime, anywhere in the world. How he kept finding me.

Of course he was Mossad. Shea was right: What had I been thinking?

I took a brandy from the bartender, chugged it down, and held my hand out for another. Leo elbowed through the crowd to stand next to me, but I refused to look at him. And he had dared to be angry at *me* for lying to *him*! It infuriated me that I still couldn't figure out what he had been after, and whether he had achieved his goal.

Even more horribly, it occurred to me that maybe he had

pursued me because of my ties to the sheikhs. Perhaps I had
been his Mossad assignment. Maybe his passion for Sudeley—
and me—was faked after all.

Maybe when he seduced me, he was on the job.

Suddenly, I felt violently ill and ran to the ship's side just in
time to be sick over the rail. Leo followed me and tried to hold
my shoulders, but I shook him off violently and vomited again.
His touch nauseated me. "Get away," I said.

"But, *motek*—"

I lifted my head. "Get away from me," I said clearly, "or every
one of these cell phones will live-stream me shouting that Leo
Schlumberger is Mossad, at the top of my lungs."

He backed off, his eyes on me.

I turned to the rail again and held on tight, waiting for a
glimpse of shore so that I could get off this benighted ship and
never see Leo Schlumberger again.

Our new friends helped us down the gangplank and onto
the pier and offered us rooms in their homes and hostels. But
Kristen, suddenly belligerent again, turned on me and snapped
that I had gotten us into this mess; now I could bloody well
figure out how to get us into a good hotel with no money, no
credit cards, and no ID. I told her that was what the American
embassy was for, begged the loan of a cell phone from one of our
friends, and called my emergency contact.

"Seven oh eight one five oh Brahms reporting in," I said
briefly, walking away from the crowd so no one would hear me.
The number would show up on the cell phone's recent-calls list,
in case anyone looked, as US Embassy, Paris.

"Yes, Brahms, what do you need?"

"Money, ID, credit cards at the desk of the"—I eyed Kristen
thoughtfully for a moment—"Sofitel Old Port, Marseille. Reservations for two rooms."

"Roger that," the man on the other end said, and disconnected. Agency handlers weren't big talkers.

Kristen and I did a little shopping in the elegant hotel store—I purchased the first, and last, $60 underpants of my life—and then retired to our rooms for an exhausted night's sleep. Or at least that's what I assumed she meant to do. I slipped out to buy a cell phone and SIM card so that I could brief Bob and then, after a short conversation, dropped the card into the toilet and lay on my bed, staring up at the ceiling.

Leo had lied to me. Of all people in the world, I should have been able to spot a liar. Lying was my own specialty, my stock in trade, my life. My father lied to me for twenty years, and then I lied for a living. And then the man I thought I loved lied to me. It was, I thought, like the circle of life for lying. Everything always came back to lies.

I thought again of how he kept finding me, no matter where I was. *I'm a great researcher*, he had said. Was that a lie too? Furiously, I ferreted through the pocketbook that the agency team had returned to me; even more furiously, I extracted the tiny, dot-size locator chip that had been inserted under its lining, and flushed that down the toilet too, then lay back again to castigate myself some more.

How could I, a highly trained and experienced operative, have failed to consider the possibility of a locator chip? My friend Rosie had informed me that a smart civilian with high-priced software could hack into the lightly guarded reservations files of European train and hotel companies. . . .

But still, the answer was probably that I didn't *want* to consider it. I wanted Leo to be interested in me for myself—not in Jules the CIA officer, or even Jules the descendant of royalty.

Well. That hadn't turned out so well.

But then, astonishingly, I started to chuckle. At first I

thought it was hysterical, nervous giggles, but then I realized that, in fact, the absurdity of the whole situation was really quite amusing. Leo had lied to me, I lied to him, both of us lied to everyone else. I giggled again, thinking of Kristen, wet and furious in the cold water, swimming for her life—if only she had known it. Then I thought of Shea's face when Leo identified himself, and burst out laughing.

And then I was crying. I really couldn't blame Leo for lying to me—though I still couldn't figure out what his operation was—but he didn't have to make love to me so sweetly, so languorously, so thoroughly. The days of setting "honey traps" to ferret out information were long gone; now we used money rather than sex.

So what was his game?

Chapter 44

The next morning, I sat next to Kristen on the flight to London. She was barely speaking to me, which was just as well; I had nothing to say to her. I had already sketched out a story in which the sheikh's son made a pass at me on board the yacht and I panicked and jumped overboard rather than deal with the situation. It seemed plausible, something Amy might be clueless enough to do. Kristen thought so little of me that she would probably buy it.

My new cell phone pinged the instant we set down at Heathrow: Leo.

"How did you get this number?" I demanded.

He ignored this.

"Are you home?" he asked.

"I just landed."

"Good. I'll be in the air in ten minutes and in London about ninety minutes later."

I took the phone away from my ear and stared at it.

"Where the hell are you? The next flight from Marseille to London isn't until tomorrow morning."

"Private jet," he said shortly.

I should have known.

"Meet me at my flat at three," he said. "Don't bring any tails."

"As if I would!" I said indignantly. How dare he suggest that my tradecraft wasn't as good as his?

"Come in the back way," he said. "Code is three six seven two." And he disconnected.

I told Kristen I was going to the doctor because I needed some Xanax after my traumatic experience. Then I actually did go to a doctor. Some of the scratches on my arm were deep and slightly infected from the stone fragments I hadn't been able to dig out. The embassy doctor met me in a suite at the Park Lane and worked in silence while I squirmed and complained. He shook his head at the end and straightened up to put his instruments back into his large rolling case of Princess Catherine tea towels. He was wearing a shabby gray traveling salesman's suit that even I acknowledged was a decent disguise. Then I slipped out the employees' entrance and started on the multiple-taxicab-and-underground routine to ensure that no one was following me. It took almost three hours to get to Leo's, but I was most definitely tail-free.

He met me at the back door and eyed me warily as I shrugged out of my coat. "Did you see a doctor?" was his first question. "Those scratches could get infected. I think you need to see a—"

In silence, I showed him my professionally bandaged arm. "Okay," he said.

I sat down at the rustic kitchen table. "All right," I said. "All cards on the table."

He grinned at me. "I show you mine, and you show me yours?"

Momentarily diverted, I said, "I've already seen it. And it's not that impressive," I added, lying through my teeth.

"And perhaps you could return my locator chip?" he suggested. "Those little buggers are quite pricey."

"I flushed it down the toilet," I said indignantly. "I can't believe you put a chip on me!"

He looked surprised. "Didn't you have one on me?"

I hung my head. "I believed Rivka," I said.

He shook his head, despairing of such naiveté.

Furious again, I demanded, "When were you going to tell me?"

"Well, when were *you* going to tell *me*? If Kali hadn't opened her mouth . . ."

"If you hadn't had to identify yourself to Shea . . ."

We glared at each other in mutual distrust. Then his face cleared and he laughed. "What's so funny?" I asked sharply, although I already knew.

"You and me, of course. Both of us sneaking around, spying on each other, when we should have been working together all the time."

"Mossad doesn't play well with others," I retorted.

"Neither does CIA," he shot back.

I was quiet for a moment. "How did you know I was in trouble? On the yacht, I mean."

"As soon as Kali told me where you were going, I set up the operation. We knew your Bahraini sheikh was bad news."

"You knew? Why didn't you tell me?" It would have saved a lot of trouble, I thought.

"Are you kidding?"

I bit my lip. "So, then—"

"I couldn't warn you off, so I just set up a loose surveillance op in Marseille. One of our guys was on the beach at Juan-les-Pins and saw the rock fall"—*Of course, the fishermen*, I thought—"so when you went back to the yacht, I decided to bring in the party boat to check things out myself."

"Were the other people on the boat really civilians?" I asked.

"Yup. Just went to the Jewish Community Center in Marseille and told them I was Sam Lowenstein from Mossad and needed some help. I had three hundred volunteers." He grinned at the memory.

I smiled too but then sobered quickly. "What was real, Leo?" I asked. "Was anything real? Or was it all a lie? Great cover, by the way."

"*Merci*," he said. "Thank you. But it wasn't a cover. My primary job is not Mossad."

As if that made a difference.

He went on, "Yes, *motek*, sometimes I do missions for them if it fits with my profile. Historians and scholars travel a lot, you know. We can do collaborative research, attend conferences, speak on panels, mingle with scholars from all over . . . We have a freedom that other professions usually don't."

"Like private bankers," I said.

"But this mission was different. This mission I brought to Mossad, not the other way around. I found you purely in my capacity as an Oxford professor. I needed Jules to help me keep Sudeley and its historical artifacts intact. That part was absolutely true."

"And then?" I asked.

"And then you started telling me about the FBI investigation into your sheikh, and I recognized his son's name. Not when you said it at first, but then you called him by his full family name, Abu Bakr el Arabiyya."

"Recognized it as what?"

"A man with the nom de guerre Abu Bakr provided the funding for several terrorist attacks on Israeli tourists abroad, including the one at Sharm El Sheikh that killed seven women and children. We've been tracking him for years. But we knew him only as Abu Bakr. It was only when you mentioned his full name and linked his nom de guerre to a real name that the penny dropped. So I contacted Rivka, and we started an operation."

"On me," I said, feeling sad and defeated.

"Well, yes." In a sudden burst of candor, he said, "I can't believe you didn't make me! You, a top CIA case officer, actually believed I was just a garden-variety Oxford don." He was almost insulted.

"But Rivka said—"

"And I can't believe you believed anything Rivka said! The woman hasn't told the truth in so long, she doesn't even know what it is."

I realized he was right. Maybe I had just wanted to believe her because . . . well, because I wanted to believe her.

I had to defend myself. "I suspected you from the very beginning," I argued. "I knew the gunmen were after you, not me, and I thought you were Mossad. Remember how many times I said that?"

He shrugged, half acknowledging, half dismissing.

"But then . . . I got confused," I said.

By my feelings for him, we both knew.

Then I remembered Arturo, the mysterious sender whose email suggesting that I check out a certain account number had gotten me suspended from the bank. I had never seriously entertained the notion that Leo had sent the message, because I couldn't imagine any connection between him and my sheikh. But now that I knew there was a connection . . .

"Leo!" I burst out. I could feel my cheeks flushing red with anger. "Did you send that email that almost got me fired? Arturo from Canada?"

He didn't even have the grace to look embarrassed. "*Bien entendu*," he said. "But of course."

"You bastard! You almost ruined two years of work for me!" I was practically spitting at him in my indignation.

He spread his hands in that infuriating, charming French way. "But, *ma chérie*, how was I to suspect that the FBI had already tagged that account? I was as surprised as you were. Who knew they were that efficient?"

I simmered in silence.

He held out his hand to me, palm up. "Now what, *motek*? Can you begin to trust me a little? I've told you the truth."

Not all of it, I knew. He would never tell me "the whole truth and nothing but the truth," just as I would never tell him. We were both professional liars, working for rival organizations.

"I trust you," I said, deliberately slowly and hurtfully, "just as much as you trusted me."

He flinched.

"You see how that works?" And I picked up my new tote bag and walked out of his life.

Chapter 45

This time, I knew it was grief. After so many flip-flops on Leo, so many starts and stops, I should have been accustomed to yet another break. But this time was different—it was real, and permanent. I was sad when I woke up in the morning, sad when I went to work, and sad when I went home at the end of the day. Kali was worried about me; she called frequently and told me funny stories about the children to make me smile. But she never mentioned Leo, although I knew she saw him occasionally, and I never asked about him.

Now that my Bahraini sheikh and his son were behind bars for money laundering, mail fraud, and a few dozen other assorted charges, I was kept busy sorting out their accounts for the ongoing investigation. Alfred took me out to lunch and told me I could take on new clients if I wanted. He had hired two new vice presidents—one a heavyset, doughy-faced woman with a wicked sense of humor and a genius for investing, and the other a thin, young Pakistani man whose parents owned a tiny grocery store in Liverpool and who had worked his way through Edinburgh University. Rumor had it that Audrey would be returning as Alfred's second-in-command. I couldn't wait to see her reaction to the new hires. Probably, she would congratulate herself on the diversity of her peeps.

But nothing was fun anymore. I couldn't even laugh when Alfred had ten pizzas delivered to the office at lunchtime and Kristen R., her eyes round with wonder, tried a bite of the everything pizza. "Oh my God," she breathed. "I've never tasted anything so delicious in my life."

A couple of weeks after what I thought of as my Last Conversation with Leo, Lord Featherstone breezed in and ordered us all into the conference room. Matt B. started to protest: "But I'm just teeing up an idea with—"

"Spare me," Alfred snapped. "Conference room. Now."

Once again, we gathered around the long table, and I gazed around at the lovely young faces, plus our two newbies, Muriel and Kassim. I had to stifle a sigh. Most likely the purpose of this meeting was to announce Audrey's imminent return. Someone up there must really hate me, to take Leo out of my life and put Audrey back in.

As I expected, Alfred began with a brief announcement that Audrey would be returning "but in a different capacity." I'd barely had time to wonder what that meant when he cleared his throat and harrumphed loudly. "The real news, however, is that this branch of Atlantic Bank has been sold."

Gasps ran around the table. Even I sat up straighter.

"This branch—you—has underperformed badly over the past year under Audrey's leadership," he pronounced.

The PYTs, who had never been accused of underperforming in their entire lives, looked stunned.

"We have lost three major clients, all of whom are under investigation for money laundering and terrorist connections. As a result, Atlantic Bank has decided to follow my advice and divest itself of this unit. The sale is effective tomorrow morning."

Silence. Kristen R. asked, in the smallest voice I had ever heard her use, "Lord Featherstone, who are the new owners?"

"Banque de Monaco et l'Espagne. BME."

"Oh my God," Jake M murmured.

BME was a multinational bank, known to be tough, aggressive, and hard-driving. It was making a major move into European private banking and was especially successful in developing rocket-science mathematical algorithms to maximize its clients' investments.

"Outstanding," Muriel said. She had never met an algorithm she didn't love.

Kristens R. and P., as well as Kristen the Younger and the two Matts, looked sick. They had the weakest quantitative skills in the room.

"Brilliant," I said. Muriel and I exchanged smiles.

The next morning, the BME team strode in like conquering heroes, each one bearing a Starbucks cup overflowing with cream, as well as a rich, buttery scone or muffin. The aroma was intoxicating. Once again, we gathered in the conference room, but this time the PYTs had to stand awkwardly against the walls as the BME people, Muriel, and I snagged the chairs around the table. Just as the muted chatter settled down and I thought the meeting was about to start, the door opened again and Audrey walked in.

At the sight of her, the PYTs' faces lit up with joy and relief. I thought I saw tears in Kristen the Younger's blue eyes. "Thank God you're here!" she exclaimed, rushing to hug Audrey.

That was a mistake, as I could have told her. Even with her "peeps," Audrey disdained physical affection. She shied back from Kristen, whose arms dropped to her sides in embarrassment.

"Ah, Ms. Chiu," the woman who appeared to be leading the BME room said. "You're late."

Audrey's mouth opened and closed.

"Now," the woman said, "let us begin."

The BME leader, in her midfifties, was massive. Not fat, precisely, but taller than tall—probably more than six feet tall—with the shoulders of a swimming champion, meaty hands, and forearms as large and muscled as Leo's. Audrey, standing next to her, looked like a tiny child. The woman's name was, I kid you not, Brunnhilde.

Brunnhilde ran the meeting like a drill sergeant—or the Latvian prison matron she had probably been in a former life. Under the new order, each of the original Atlantic Bank officers would be teamed with a BME officer, and she doled out the assignments briskly and then sent us out just as briskly. Muriel, Kassim, and I were the only ones who did not need BME supervision, she decreed. To me, she said gruffly, "Ms. Schumann, you come highly recommended by one of our most valued clients."

The PYTs were owl-eyed with astonishment.

I played along. "Oh, that would be—"

"Schlumberger, of course."

"Yes, of course," I murmured. Audrey just stared at me, her eyes narrowed.

I delighted in watching the PYTs with their new partners. The BME team was truly multinational. Kristen the Younger's minder was a large, overly made-up, overly talkative Russian woman with bright-red dyed hair who boomed instructions in Kristen's ear while expressing her loud astonishment at Kristen's lack of quantitative skills. Matt S. drew an African American giant with bulging biceps and hard eyes who could only have been former Special Forces; Matt shrank in terror every time the man gave him a curt order. Jake S. was teamed with a small

Asian woman who spoke almost no English but manipulated multiple, massive spreadsheets at warp speed on the computer while poor Jake watched uncomprehendingly. And Kristen R.'s partner was a thirtysomething Frenchwoman who exuded ennui and chic with every breath; next to Clarice's soignée sophistication, our sorority girl looked almost dowdy.

As for Audrey, she was evicted from her office and given a plebeian desk on the floor, with Brunnhilde herself as her minder. I thought that if Brunnhilde had tried to give every PYT their worst nightmare, she had succeeded with flying colors. It was almost enough to take my mind off Leo and my other troubles. Almost.

As I had expected, the agency's Internal Security division was deeply distressed over my "close and continuing" with Leo, especially after I had revised it to disclose his Mossad affiliation. They recalled me to Washington for a long, tedious week of questioning that involved two polygraph tests and a thorough dissection of our relationship. When I admitted I hadn't seen him in more than a month, they strongly "suggested" I simply withdraw the "close and continuing" report, thus signaling an end to the relationship (and to Internal Security's angst over it). I told them I would think about it, but I just couldn't make myself close that final door.

Back in London, I had almost persuaded myself that I was starting to get over him when, one morning, I clicked on my Google feed to see the headline "Terror in Oxford! Bomb Explosion on Campus, ISIS Suspected." Suddenly, I wasn't breathing; I was only feeling. I grabbed my phone and tried to call Leo—or, at least, the last number I had for him. "This line is out of service," I was told.

I called Kali, my heart pounding and my mouth dry. "Have you heard from Leo?" I asked, without any preamble. "Did you see that there was an attack at Oxford? Is he there?"

Kali said slowly, "He's at Oxford. He's been working with some students on their dissertations. I just saw the news; it's so scary."

"Have you heard from him?" I asked again. Leo, the family protector, would surely call his sisters to let them know he was okay. If he was okay.

"No," Kali said. She coughed slightly, perhaps to cover tears. "I'm so worried, Ju—I mean, Amy."

She must have been really upset to use my real name. She knew better.

"Okay," I said. "Calm down. I'll drive up there right now and track him down. I'm sure he's fine."

"Thanks," Kali said fervently. "Thank you, Amy. I'll go and tell Élodie now; she'll be so relieved."

I hung up and looked at my phone for a moment. Was there anyone else I could call? But no, the agency didn't have assets in English university towns—at least, none that I knew about. I was on my own.

So I hopped into my car and drove at breakneck speed, tearing through roundabouts and recklessly passing slower cars to the right and left. It was a miracle that no police pulled me over, but then, I recalled, they had more pressing matters on their plate right now. And my heart sank again.

I pulled my car into the first garage I passed in the town center and threw the keys at the bemused attendant. Then I ran straight toward the plume of smoke that was still rising from a building on the outskirts of the university area. The sidewalks were packed with pedestrians, some wielding cameras and others running away. I shoved through them with equal recklessness.

Then I came to an abrupt stop, so abrupt that my sneakers skidded on the uneven pavement. The building, surprisingly gray and concrete and modern, was surrounded by a sea of police officers, firefighters, fire trucks, and ambulances. I had been at such scenes before, and I had to pause to catch my breath as grief and anger warred in my jumbled brain. *Goddamn those fuckers anyway*, I cursed silently. This—this was why I did what I did, why I masqueraded as mousy Amy and bribed scummy informers and spent thousands of tedious hours tracing dirty-money flows all around the globe. In my mind, I echoed the words of Harrison Ford in *Air Force One*: *Be afraid. Be very afraid. We're coming to get you.*

It was my mantra.

A small knot of reporters was standing to the side, chattering among themselves and into small recorders. I made my way toward them. And then I stopped short, for Leo was in the middle of the knot, reporter's notebook out and sunglasses on.

The flood of relief I felt was, of course, immediately followed by one of fury. He looked up and saw me. Our eyes met and clung for one electric moment, until he glanced away again. Grimly, I started toward him.

He preempted me, calling out as I approached the circle. "Amy! Are you covering this story too?"

I opened my mouth and closed it again.

"Don't you remember me?" he asked. "Sam Lowenstein, producer for France One. We met at—"

"Yes," I said. "I remember you."

"This isn't much of a story, though," he said, grinning at the other reporters.

"Can't believe I got out of bed for this," one of them complained.

"A ten-liner on page thirty," another groused.

I looked around at the sea of first responders, astonished at their casual air. Leo said, "So long, mates. Come on, Ames. I'll fill you in."

Still flabbergasted, I let him draw me away.

"So, *Sam*," I said, "what's the deal here?"

"Some eco-crazies," he said casually. "The scientists are working on genetically modified crops in this lab. Nothing to do with our line of work at all."

I stared at him suspiciously. "How do you know?"

"Why? Don't you believe me?"

"What do you think?"

"Interesting," he drawled. "Three questions in a row, and not a single answer. I know, my dear girl, because one of the idiots called in the threat at three o'clock this morning, describing exactly when and where the bomb would explode."

"Oh," I said.

"Doesn't sound much like ISIS, does it?"

"Any injuries?" I asked.

"One night watchman sprained his ankle running away after he heard about the phone call."

"Then why . . ." I gestured at the ocean of first responders, who were now beginning to pack up their equipment.

"Oh, you know," he said. "Poor old Brits are skittish. Can't blame them, can you?"

I gazed around at the scene, trying to decide if he was telling me the truth. Then I remembered. "But why didn't you call your family?" I demanded. "You must have known they would be frantic with worry when they heard about a bomb at Oxford."

"I did," he said, surprised.

"No, you didn't."

"Yes, I did."

We glared at each other. "I talked to Kali this morning," I said, annoyed that he would lie about something so simple. "She was really worried, said she hadn't heard from you."

"But I . . . oh," he said.

"Oh what?" I asked.

"I called Rachel, my second-youngest sister—she's our great communicator—and she contacts everyone else. She would have called Élodie."

I shook my head, still not understanding.

"Your Kali," he said, "is quite a minx."

And then I did understand. Technically, she had not heard from Leo. Not directly, anyway. "That little brat!" I exclaimed. "She got me running up here in a panic, when she knew all along you were perfectly fine."

"Our own little matchmaker," Leo said. "Now, *motek*, exactly how worried were you?"

"Not that worried," I snapped. I knew that I had failed to penetrate Kali's deception only because it was Leo—danger to Leo.

He put his arm around me. "But worried enough to drive up here at—I'm guessing—a hundred kilometers per hour?"

I scowled.

But my adrenaline rush had faded, leaving me, as always, a little shaky and vulnerable. I leaned against him, and he dropped a kiss on the top of my head. "I'm sorry you were worried," he said, in quite a different voice. "I should have called you."

I couldn't think of anything to say, and he put his other arm around me, holding me close and rubbing my back.

Then I remembered everything, and I drew away, furious at him, at Kali, and, most of all, at myself. "I'm glad you're not dead," I said. And I hurried away.

Chapter 46

I slogged through the next few weeks, grimly determined to wipe Leo from my mind and concentrate on my work. Work and my Syrian teenagers had been enough for me before I met him; it would be enough for me again.

So it seemed as if I was being rewarded for my efforts when I received a coded email from one of my Russian assets in early May, asking for a meeting. I had met Lyudmila Petrova years before, when I first started working, supposedly for IDC, in Moscow. She was a statuesque bottle blonde, towering over my five feet, three inches, a fast and loud talker who nattered incessantly in heavily accented English while playing with her clanking array of bracelets and necklaces.

I could never figure out what was real and what wasn't with Lyudmila. We weren't particularly friendly, but I enjoyed her bombast and chatter. It was a pleasant diversion from the rigors of everyday life in frozen Moscow.

We stayed sporadically in touch after I left Russia. Lyudmila eventually became a midlevel official at the Central Bank, responsible for handling the biggest international financial transactions. So I was surprised when she emailed me a few years later and suggested we meet for a weekend at a five-star beach resort in Portugal. As we lay side by side in our lounge chairs, it quickly became clear that Lyudmila was trying—clumsily, I thought—to recruit me (in my incarnation as an international development expert) as a Russian intelligence asset. We quickly came to an amicable arrangement; each of us would pass information to the other when it suited us.

Obviously, it suited Lyudmila right now to have an all-expenses-paid vacation in Portugal. It suited me pretty well too.

We carefully arranged our dates so that I would arrive on the day Lyudmila was leaving, so that there would be no record of us in the same place at the same time. I left London on a gray, drizzly day to land in the glittering sunshine of the Lisbon spring. Feeling almost cheerful, I rented a sporty little convertible, using my Marina Ostrova persona (London-based Russian émigré), and drove the three hours to the seacoast.

Once I had checked into my oceanfront room (what the hell—the agency was paying), I put on a demure one-piece bathing suit and topped it with an almost sheer, slinky cover-up. Then I filled a brightly colored beach bag with all the accoutrements of my disguise—sunglasses, sunscreen, face lotion, water bottle, Kindle, cell phone, and earphones—and wandered down to the pool. It was a lovely, undulating infinity pool with the unending horizon beyond it. The deep blue of the pool, sea, and sky was dazzling, and I paused for a moment to drink it all in.

Then I strolled around the pool, looking for just the right lounger. I selected one next to a tall, statuesque blonde who was wearing a teeny white bikini with an assortment of jangling bracelets and long necklaces; the jewelry covered more of her body than the bikini did. She was pretending to gaze out at the sun-drenched horizon, but behind the dark sunglasses her eyes were ceaselessly scanning the people at the pool. Lyudmila was not the world's most subtle spy.

"Is anyone sitting here?" I asked casually.

Lyudmila stared blankly at me, so I repeated it in Russian.

"*Nyet*," she said.

"*Spaseeba*." I settled myself next to her and began the annoying routine of applying sunscreen and lip cream. Lyudmila watched me in silence.

"Are you here for long?" I asked in Russian, making polite conversation.

"No, I'm leaving today," she said.

"Oh, too bad; I'm here for the weekend."

"Lucky you," she returned.

It was our scripted patter. If anyone had been watching, she would have veered from the script to warn me off. The coast was clear.

"Can I buy you a drink?" I inquired.

"Thank you. That would be lovely."

We chatted pleasantly while we waited for the drinks. If anyone understood Russian, all they would hear was two women of a similar age soaking up the sun and making idle conversation. Suddenly she said, "There's something different about you."

I started. "What do you mean?"

She studied me and then shrugged. "I don't know; I can't put my finger on it. But there's definitely something different about you."

I shrugged too. "My hair? It's a little bit shorter than—"

"*Nyet*," she said scornfully.

"Anyway," I said, suddenly uncomfortable, "what's up?"

She pursed her lips and stared at me some more. I waited.

"Well," she said, giving up for the moment, "I recently facilitated a foreign transfer by Vladimir Ossipsky. A very large foreign transfer."

Ossipsky! He had been on our radar screen forever; he

was a money man for the Russian Mafia who had stolen and plundered hundreds of millions, perhaps billions, with the full approval of Putin and his cronies. My skin prickled.

"What kind of transfer?" I asked.

"I think he's trying to transfer his money out of Russia," Lyudmila said.

He must have outlived his usefulness to Putin, I thought, *and is launching his exit plan.*

"Really?" I said, trying not to seem too eager. In this periodic game I played with Lyudmila, it was never a good idea to let her get an elevated idea of her own value.

"Yes. Sixty-five million euros. To Barclays Bank of London."

Wow. He was taking a big risk, moving some of his wealth to London, where scrutiny was so much tighter and bribery so much more difficult. If he was getting desperate, then we might just get lucky. I held my breath and said, without much hope, "I don't suppose you have a name or number for the account."

Lyudmila gave me a silky smile. "But that's the good part," she said. "I do! The account is in the name of VONE Limited. The Barclays folks are super paranoid after being indicted last year for the Iranian money-laundering scandal, and they insisted on an account name and number."

"The number?" I asked, no longer trying to hide my excitement.

She nodded and gave me the details. "You should be able to trace it from there," she said, with a trace of smugness.

I nodded, committing the name and number to memory. "Good intel," I said, stating the obvious. "Thanks, Lyudmila."

She waited a moment. "And what do you have for me? You know I take a big risk every time I leave the country to meet with you."

I glanced around at the beautiful pools and waterfalls, thinking that this wasn't exactly a hardship assignment. Lyudmila loved to pick posh resorts for our meetings. She insisted that nobody would notice us there. She persisted, "I really need something from you, Marina."

"Okay," I said, with a show of reluctance, having expected this and prepared a nugget. "We've learned that the Grosinski family in Crimea is agitating against Putin. You might want to take a look at them."

"Really," she said, a little skeptically. "And why would you pass this on to me? Is this a double cross, Marina?"

"Of course not," I said indignantly. The indignation was real; I would never be stupid enough to burn Lyudmila, who was a good source of intel. "The Grosinskis are also major-league cocaine traffickers. We'd be very happy to see them go away."

"Well, then," she said. "I know just the man for the job."

I tried not to think about what that "job" might be.

We clinked our glasses in a satisfied toast.

Suddenly she exclaimed, "I know what it is! You have a man! You're in love!"

"No," I protested.

"But yes," she said firmly. "It's a man, isn't it?"

"Not at all," I insisted.

She lifted a skeptical eyebrow, and I turned my face away. "Goodbye, Lyudmila," I said. "You don't want to miss your plane."

She laughed, for a moment an old friend and not a Russian agent. "You need a man," she advised.

"Goodbye, Lyudmila," I said again.

She laughed again and picked up her beach bag. "Ciao," she said, and was on her way.

Deeply unsettled, I leaned back on my chaise lounge and opened my Kindle. I had to spend at least two days here to keep up the show of an overworked single woman on a much-needed luxury vacation. But I couldn't help thinking about Lyudmila's observation. *It's a man*, she had said. *You're in love!*

What could she possibly have seen in my face?

Determinedly, I turned my attention back to the Kindle and decided to reread another John le Carré novel. But no sooner had I swiped my way to the first page than I saw someone else approach and stretch out on Lyudmila's old lounger.

"Hey, Jules," Leo said.

Oh, shit.

Chapter 47

"Is Lyudmila your asset too?" he asked casually.

"Oh, fuck. Did she set up a meet with you too?"

"Of course. Did you pay her expenses?"

"Yes," I admitted. "Did you?"

"Yes."

Our eyes met in mutual consternation, and even I had to smile. Imagine Lyudmila hitting both of us up for expense money. My estimation of her went up several notches.

We studied each other. "What did she give you?" I asked.

"Nothing too interesting," he said. "How about you?"

"Same."

Another pause.

"And what did you give her?" he asked

"Just a red herring. And you?"

"Same. Nothing important."

I had to hand it to him; he was every bit as good at this as I was. I wondered if Lyudmila had given him the same info about Ossipsky, though I wasn't sure why he would be a person of interest to Mossad. As far as I knew, Ossipsky's operations were in Western Europe and the UK, not Israel. But still, this could be a complication I didn't need. So I said, cautiously, "Are you tracking Russian Mafia now?"

"What? No. Terrorists, always terrorists. How about you?"

"Russians."

"Ah," he said. "Relax, *motek*. I don't think she gave us the same information."

He was *very* good at this.

My cell phone chirped just then, and I saw that it was a coded message. I needed to get to a secure phone. I eyed Leo uneasily and stood up. "Well," I said, "this has been lovely. But I need to go up to my room and pack. I'm leaving tonight."

"No, you're not," he shot back. "This is Friday, and you're leaving Sunday."

I glared at him. "How did you find . . . ?"

"Marina Ostrova? Come, now. It was child's play."

"Listen," I said uneasily. I had put a lot of time and effort into developing the Marina cover.

He stopped me with a look. "Jules," he said, "what's between us—whatever is between us—it's personal. Not business."

"Not for me," I replied.

He shrugged. "Dinner tonight?"

"No."

"Eight o'clock, then. In the bar."

"Don't wait too long," I said, and ran upstairs.

Once in the quiet of my room, I went into the bathroom and turned on the faucets—old-fashioned but effective. Then I went through the tedious process of unwrapping one of my burner phones, switching out the SIM card, crushing the old SIM card, and placing the call to the secure line. I would have to dispose of the phone and card as soon as this call was done—an annoying task when Leo might be watching me.

"Ostrova," I said briefly.

"Ostrova, I'm transferring you. Please hold."

I waited, impatient and annoyed at this delay. An unfamiliar yet familiar voice said, "Jules? David Harris here."

David Harris! He was director of the CIA, a legendary and much respected director whose own history as an NOC was one of the most remarkable in the organization's history. Talk about agency royalty! I had never had occasion to speak with him personally, and my stomach jumped with excitement. Either I was in a shitload of trouble or they wanted me to do something horrifically dangerous. Or both.

"Mr. Harris," I said. "Nice to meet you."

He laughed, a warm and deep laugh that put me a little bit more at ease. I remembered that Harris himself had been "outed" in a messy scandal that involved an ex-girlfriend, talk of a leak, and a massive Senate investigation. But he had come out smelling like roses—typical of David Harris, according to agency lore—and was a happily married man with several children.

"I'm sorry to do this over the phone," he said, "but it's much safer this way."

Do what over the phone? My palms were suddenly sweaty.

"I understand that you filed a C and C with Leo Schlumberger, a Mossad officer."

I was so edgy that I had to think for a second to remember what a C and C was. Oh, the "close and continuing" form.

"Well, yes," I said. "But he's not really full-time for Mossad, just does jobs for them once in a while."

"Is that what he told you?"

I gulped and told myself to stop talking.

"We don't really know Schlumberger's position in Mossad," Harris said coolly, "but we know he's up there."

This was bad news.

"Normally, we would have a big problem with this C and C," he went on. "A major, career-ending problem."

"I understand," I said, gripping the phone tightly.

"But in this case . . . well, all problems create opportunities, don't they?"

"I don't know, sir," I said cautiously.

"In this case, you have developed a major potential asset. Schlumberger could be our eyes and ears on Mossad. In fact, you are to be commended for your fine work in this vein."

"But I didn't . . . ," I began, horrified. They wanted me to spy on Leo!

"Your handler, Bob, will be in touch next week to discuss the mission," he said. "In the meantime, just continue what you've been doing. Try to gain his confidence, and don't do anything to make him suspicious."

"Mr. Harris," I said desperately.

"Yes?"

"Leo is *always* suspicious. And he doesn't let *anyone* into his confidence. This will never work."

"Oh," he said, "we disagree. You've turned a number of assets, and we are quite certain of your abilities. Don't worry, Jules. You can do it."

And he hung up.

In a half daze, I went through the motions, yanking the SIM card out of the phone, destroying it, and then soaking the phone itself in the toilet for long enough to fatally damage its mechanism. Then I slipped out of my room and tossed the remains of the card into the chambermaid's trash bag hanging off a cart in the hallway, and the dead phone in the plastic trash can in the hotel's exercise room. That done, I went back upstairs and lay on my bed, staring at the ceiling.

Then I got dressed and went down to meet Leo for dinner.

He whistled under his breath as I walked toward him in my cool, blue-and-white-striped sundress. It was tight around the bodice and then flared out slightly before ending just above the knee. I knew its shape flattered mine, while the light colors complemented my budding tan. "Wow," he said.

In khaki pants and a simple white shirt, tucked in, sleeves rolled up to the elbows to reveal his muscled, hair-roughened forearms, Leo looked every inch the tall, dark, and handsome man whom women hope for and romance writers dream of. Then I remembered my "mission," and my spirits plummeted.

"What?" he asked instantly.

"What what?"

"What just happened? Why do you look like that?"

"Look like what?"

"Oh, for God's sake," he snapped. "Just answer the question, would you?"

"Nothing happened."

"*Merde alors*," he said.

Both of us summoned up our best emotion-hiding skills, and we managed to chat about Kali and the children, Donald Trump's latest absurdity, and Brexit through dinner, pleasantly enough. He had two drinks, while I was careful to sip abstemiously at my Prosecco. But even one glass loosened me up, and by the time he was drinking his coffee, I was aware of my body yearning toward his. My mind didn't trust him, but my body and heart did. And now he had even more reason not to trust me. But still, his nearness, his slightly crooked smile, the athletic grace of his tall body . . . It was intoxicating.

Sensing my vulnerability, he asked me again, "So, what were you so upset about before dinner?"

God, he was persistent; I admired that. I would have to give him something. "It's the C and C," I admitted. Partial truth was better than no truth.

"You filed a close and continuing on me? Even after everything?"

He of all people knew what that meant, how serious—and risky—it was to declare a close and continuing relationship with an officer of a rival intelligence agency. "Well, yes, I . . ."

He got up and walked around the table to me, then pulled me, unresisting, to my feet, and our lips met in a long, lingering kiss. "I'm touched," he whispered, and then kissed me again.

"Get a room, mate!" someone yelled. But this was a romantic little seaside restaurant in southern Europe on a soft, balmy spring evening, and most of the faces were approving.

I leaned trustingly against him, feeling his heartbeat under the thin white shirt, and he tightened his arms around me. He put his hand on my bare arm, and I felt the heat from his body in rolling waves like the sea, rushing to engulf me and overwhelm me. I could scarcely breathe.

Leo cleared his throat and waved at the waiter. "*La cuenta. Rapido, por favor.*"

By the time we were in the elevator, I was almost panting and my cheeks were flushed. Leo put his arm around me and looked down at me, his eyes keen with speculation and heat. We fell into his room, Leo kicking the door behind us, and tumbled onto the bed like in a scene from the movies. He unzipped my dress with deft fingers, and I dragged his shirt back over his shoulders. "*Nom de bleu*," he said. "What did I do to deserve this?"

"Shut up," I said breathlessly.

So he did.

Afterward, I lay in mindless contentment in his arms, running my fingers through the black hairs on his chest.

"That was," Leo said, "lovely. Perfectly lovely."

Reluctantly, against every instinct in my body, I drew away.

"Hey now," he said lazily. "What's all this?"

But in the warm, intimate silence of the shadowy room, all I could think of was David Harris, his expectations of me, and the sheer awfulness of having to betray Leo, yet again.

I almost felt like crying.

But I never—well, rarely—cry. So I sat up, pulling the covers tightly against my body in the sudden chill. "Leo," I said, "they want me to turn you."

"Turn me into what?" I heard the smile in his voice as he rolled toward me and traced the outline of my breast with his long, deft fingers.

"An asset, you idiot." I pulled away again. "They want you to pass on info to me about Mossad ops."

"Ah," he said, drawing me back into his arms again. "Well, I suppose we should have expected that."

I supposed so too.

"Rivka wants me to turn you too," he said. "Just think: We could spend the rest of our lives spying on each other. Then we could write our memoirs and star in a blockbuster Hollywood film."

I said nothing, seized by a sudden paralysis at his casual mention of "the rest of our lives."

"Leo," I said at last, "this isn't funny. We work for intelligence agencies that are . . ." I hesitated, searching for the right word.

"Frenemies?" he suggested

It was as good a description as any.

"Well," he said lightly, "if you outed yourself as Jules Seymour—saving Sudeley in the process, by the way—then you would have to retire from fieldwork, and then the C and C wouldn't matter. If you're not an NOC anymore, nobody cares who you sleep with. We could be together."

This time, my withdrawal was sharp and appalled. "Is that what this is all about? The romance? The sex? It's all about Sudeley? You son of a bitch. You bastard. You . . ." I couldn't think of a word bad enough for him. The betrayal chilled me to my bones.

I jumped out of the bed and started throwing on my clothes, fumbling and clumsy in my haste.

"Hey," he said, sitting up and taking notice of my rage, "Jules, it was just a suggestion. It could be our happy ending."

"Not for me, you bastard," I hissed. "You of all people should understand that this is my *life*. I should give it all up to sit at a desk so that your precious Sudeley can be saved? Are you crazy?" I paused. "Would you do that for me?"

We both knew the answer to that.

I heard him swearing softly in the darkness. Then the bedclothes rustled and he stood up too, scrambling for his shorts. "Jules," he said, "I'm sorry. I didn't mean it that way." And he came toward me, his arms outstretched to pull me back again.

But it was too late. I was already out the door.

Chapter 48

It was always the same with Leo, I realized, as I sat in an uncomfortable middle seat on the flight back to London. Always the same. First I listened to the voice of reason and held him off, then I melted, and then something happened to make me see that he was, in the end, my betrayer. Not my lover.

How many times could I fall for the same song and dance? How long before I kicked the habit?

By the time the plane taxied to the Heathrow gate and people began stirring, collecting their bags and turning on cell phones, I was resolute. Back in London, back to work, back to my real life. I could be Amy, I could be Marina, I could be anyone—except Jules.

Fortunately, the following weekend I had already agreed to attend a party with the "IDC" gang to celebrate Dorcas and Will's short R and R break from Kabul. I was determined to seize the occasion for a face-to-face with Bob.

Dorcas took one look at me and hurried me over to the bar. "You look terrible," she said. "What have you been doing to yourself? Here—have a drink. Have two."

I knew it was true. Dorcas had a healthy tan, her eyes bright and clear, while I felt dull and pallid all over.

"How was Kabul?" I asked.

"Hell. You know."

I knew, and I envied her with every ounce of my soul.

"How did you get that?" I asked, pointing to the cast on her forearm.

"The spice-market bombing. I was meeting with an asset."

Insanely, I was jealous for a moment. *I must be losing my mind*, I thought.

"These days," I said bitterly, "my only scars are from Audrey."

"Oh, really? I thought the new bosses had her tamed." Dorcas always knew everything, often before I did.

"Well, now she's gone undercover. When her German handler couldn't hear her, Audrey whispered in my ear that Brunnhilde was a perfect example of why she never eats. She kindly warned me to watch my waistline."

Dorcas shuddered. "Dire." We each took a deep swig of our drink.

"But honestly, Jules, what is wrong with you? You look like death warmed over. No offense," she added.

I looked away, and my eyes caught Bob's. "Later," I said, downing my cocktail in one gulp and setting the glass down on the table. I was on a mission.

Hurrying across the room, I took Bob's arm and steered him away into the narrow hallway between the tiny living room and even smaller bedroom.

"Sorry about Audrey," he said. "We prolonged the investigation as long as we could, but there just wasn't enough there."

I shrugged; that wasn't my mission today. "Bob," I said, "haven't I been punished long enough? I'm begging you—*begging* you!—to let me go back to the field. I'd take Yemen, Afghanistan, Chechnya, even Iraq. Anywhere. I need to get out of here!"

He wasn't Bob the Friendly Bear anymore; he was my CIA

handler. His eyes, as he looked down at me from his great height, were cool and assessing. "Maybe," he said. "I'll tell you this, Jules: Your friend Leo can be a powerful asset to us, and to you. I don't think we've ever had anyone so highly placed in that organization."

"Bob," I began.

He ignored me. "They protect his cover very carefully, you know. After I met him, at that party in the fall, you remember"—I nodded; I remembered—"I was curious. So I had Rosie dig into it, but she couldn't find anything. So I dropped it. Jules, they haven't IDed him to *anyone*—not us, not the Jords, not the Brits."

I felt a small pang that my poor judgment on the yacht had forced Leo to identify himself. I hoped that I hadn't endangered him or any of his assets.

"Don't worry," Bob said, reading my mind. "He's as valuable to us now as he is to Mossad. This op is eyes-only clearance."

"This op"—my betrayal of Leo. It felt like a slap in the face.

"Bob," I said again, "as I told Mr. Harris, I don't think this will work. He doesn't trust anyone, and certainly not me. I'm never going to get anything out of him."

Bob smiled at me, the smile not quite reaching his eyes. "You get us some actionable intel from him on Mossad's thinking or ops, and it would probably go a long way toward getting you back out to the field. Where would you like to go? Yemen? Chechnya? Moscow? You can go to whatever hellhole you want if you give us Mossad."

"I can't," I said desperately, willing Bob to understand.

"I think you can. Remember, Langley would give you the moon if you developed him as an asset. Eyes and ears on Mossad! Jesus, it's the director's dream come true."

I was silent.

"And remember, you develop him as an asset, and you get out to the field again. No more Audrey and no more Pretty Young Things."

I had forgotten how good Bob was at this.

Dorcas spotted me as soon as Bob shambled back to the party, once again the big, friendly bear. "Jules," she hissed. "Talk to me. What were you and Bob huddling about over there? Why do you look like he just slapped you? What did he say to you? I'll kill him if—"

"He's just doing his job," I said wearily.

"Which is . . . ?"

"Nothing good." The Leo op was eyes only, Bob had said. I couldn't read Dorcas into it.

"Talk to me," she persisted. "You know how to do it. You can omit names, details, places . . . Broad outlines only is fine."

When I still hesitated, she said, "Come on, Jules. You look like you need a friend right now."

We were all very good at persuading people to talk to us. We were well trained. But I did need a friend. So I talked, telling her only that I had fallen hard for a man whom I couldn't trust—a man who had ties to a foreign intelligence service—and that the agency wanted me to turn him into my asset.

"Painful," Dorcas said thoughtfully. "But not impossible."

"How?" I asked.

"Well . . . you could say you turned him but just give useless intel," she suggested.

I had thought of that. But, I asked, "Do you really think Bob would fall for that?"

We both knew the answer.

She sighed. "At a certain point, Jules, you may have to decide what you want for the rest of your life."

I just looked at her.

"You knew what you were getting when you chose this life. Either marry another agency officer, like I did," she said clearly, spelling it out in case I was dumber than she thought, "or stay alone, like Lydia."

We both looked at the overly made-up Lydia, trying to work her wiles on every man in the room, even the very happily married Will.

"Fuck," I said.

"Yeah," Dorcas agreed.

Chapter 49

It had been several weeks since I had heard from Leo. My Google alerts yielded one brief notice about the pending sale of Sudeley Castle, but no details. I deleted it hastily. Not my problem.

And then one day after work, he was there again, leaning against the wall, waiting for me, as I got out of the elevator. My heart gave a great, almost painful thud and then plummeted. What now?

Without a word of greeting, he handed me a thick manila envelope.

"What is this?" I tried to give it back.

He stepped away. "Just thought you'd be interested," he said, and strode away. I couldn't help it. I watched him go until my eyes strained from watching and his tall head had disappeared into the teeming crowds of commuters. I held the envelope in suddenly trembling hands. Had Leo just betrayed his country for me? I hated the idea. I wouldn't do that for him, I knew. What would I do if there was intel on a Mossad op in the sinister, sealed envelope? Would I pass it on to Bob? Or would I destroy it?

In my apartment, I ripped open the envelope with sweaty hands. But the thick sheaf of papers inside had nothing to do with Mossad or the CIA. Instead, it was a genealogy of my family, from Queen Katherine Parr to Jules Seymour.

I got up to pour myself a tall glass of wine and then sat down again to go through the papers. Increasingly fascinated, I read about Katherine Parr's love marriage to Tom Seymour, the rakishly handsome scoundrel who dallied with then Princess Elizabeth before the eyes of his pregnant wife and then lost his head on Tower Green after an absurdly foolish attempt to kidnap the young king.

Next came the birth of little Lady Mary Seymour, her parents' initial joy so quickly followed by grief upon the death of her mother; Lady Mary's sojourn in the home of Catherine Willoughby, Duchess of Suffolk; the Duchess's increasingly sharp letters expressing her resentment at having the care and expense of the orphaned baby; and then Mary's transformation into Lady Amanda, her marriage to distant cousin Edward Seymour, and the birth of their son, Ned Seymour.

Leo, I realized, really was a brilliant researcher and scholar after all. The genealogy was exquisitely detailed and annotated.

He described Lady Amanda's success at spying on Mary, Queen of Scots; her discovery of the letters that, fatally, incriminated Mary in a plot against Queen Elizabeth; and her close association with Sir Francis Walsingham, Elizabeth's spymaster. Then came Amanda's grandson, another Ned Seymour, who helped expose various plots against the King; Ned's grandson's espionage work at the Romanov court in Russia; and *his* grandson's exploits defending the Crown against Bonnie Prince Charlie in the Forty-Five (the Jacobite rebellion of 1745).

And then the final pages: my grandfather Thomas Seymour, Wild Bill Donovan's right-hand man in the OSS, the notorious wartime predecessor of the CIA. My father, Ned Seymour, whose CIA work ended in his brutal assassination and an anonymous star on the wall at Langley. And me, Juliette Mary Seymour, agency princess. The end of the line.

Leafing through the pages, I wished with all my being that I could claim this family legacy as my own. I had been proud of my father and grandfather, of course, but this was remarkable. Inspiring. A family of schemers and spies, plotters, and king makers. A family who had helped to make history, all behind the scenes. And I, Jules Seymour, carried that family in my blood. The weight of my heritage, I thought with pride, was not heavy but as light and swift as the blood coursing through my veins.

But—my eyes fell on my encrypted agency cell phone, lying so innocently on the coffee table—if I outed myself, then I wouldn't be able to carry on my family's work. My destiny. I was born to this life, and to claim my family would be to betray it.

Still, I kept the genealogy by my bedside and looked through it every night before falling asleep, thinking and dreaming of the ancestors who had lived and died to serve their countries behind the scenes, in complete anonymity, unsung and unpraised. Truly, spying was in my blood.

A few weeks later, I saw a Google alert: "Sudeley Castle to be closed to the public," it read, and I clicked on the full article with a sinking heart.

Sudeley Castle, home of Queen Katherine Parr, is to be closed to the public next week following its sale to a syndicate of investors. The investors, led by Russian property magnate Boris Nemtsov, plan to sell the historical artifacts currently on display at the castle and turn it and its grounds into an upscale, gated community of multimillion-pound homes and vacation properties. Historians, including Dr. Leo Schlumberger of Oxford, have bitterly decried the move, but the development will provide hundreds of jobs for . . .

I stopped reading, sick at heart. It was all I could do not to call Leo and commiserate, apologize, soothe, give in. But what was the point of that? *He must hate me*, I thought. I couldn't blame him; I almost hated myself too.

And then, at last, Leo called me at work. "Is this line secure?" was his opening.

"No."

"Okay, then. I have some news for you. Can we meet tomorrow?"

"More news about Katherine Parr and her family?" I asked warily. Google Alerts had informed me that the groundbreaking ceremony for the new Queen's Castle development would be the day after tomorrow. I couldn't blame Leo for making one more attempt to persuade me. He must have been desperate. My heart was pounding, and, for the first time in weeks, I felt truly alive again. But what was the point of seeing him for just an hour or so to hear another tidbit about my ancestors? It would just leave me feeling more empty than ever. I clutched the phone in my suddenly damp hand.

"No. Nothing to do with that." He hesitated. "Listen, my girl, I promise you'll want to hear this."

I pressed my lips together tightly, but he took my silence for assent.

"The Dog and Lion at seven tomorrow night," he said. "It'll be worth your while." And he hung up.

It took me a moment to snap the cell phone closed. I was furious at him and at myself for my silly teenage-girl-with-a-crush reaction to the sound of his voice. At the same time, I was running through my wardrobe in my head, furiously considering and discarding options. *Is it too warm for the blue sweater? Maybe I should wear my black pencil skirt and white blouse? Or—I know!—how about skinny jeans and the cream cardigan?*

Then my mood crashed again. I was an idiot. I shouldn't even go to meet him. But, of course, I knew I would.

The next night, having chosen the skinny-jeans ensemble, I was careful to arrive at the gastropub a casual fifteen minutes late. It was a pretty cottage about thirty minutes south of London, surrounded by a small garden that was just beginning to flower in the cautious May sunshine. Leo was sitting outside in the gathering darkness at a rickety wooden table warmed by a space heater tucked discreetly behind it.

He stood as I approached. "Is this all right? I thought we could talk more easily out here."

"I don't think we have much to talk about," I returned, glad and sorry at the same time that he hadn't tried to hug or kiss me in greeting.

"Well, then prepare to be surprised," he said, and we sat down.

In the light of the flickering candles spread among the tables, I studied his face. His black stubble was more pronounced than ever; I wondered when he had last shaved. He needed a haircut; his hair curled against the nape of his neck, and I wanted desperately to tangle my fingers in it and pull his head down to mine. The dim light made him seem taller and more imposing than ever. I couldn't stop looking at him.

Leo cleared his throat, and I realized he had been gazing at me just as intently. I jumped. "So, what's this all about?" I asked briskly.

The waitress brought us margaritas, pretzels, and olives. I took a sip of my drink to distract myself from the power of his presence.

"The British police have located the man who shot at us in Sudeley. Remember? It was a routine traffic stop, but his fingerprints matched the ones on the rental car he used to chase us."

"Oh," I said, a little blankly. I had almost forgotten about that minor, unsolved mystery.

"I have his picture," Leo went on. He clicked on his cell phone and held out the photo to me. Bemused, I took a quick glance. I couldn't care too much about this detail when I was sitting across the table from Leo, our legs so close that they could almost be touching.

He snapped his fingers, grinning slightly. "*Faites attention*, Jules! Is this the man who assaulted you in the basement of that pub?"

I glanced again and shook my head. "I never saw his face. I couldn't identify him. But wait a minute. . . ." I seized the cell phone and looked at the picture more closely. "Holy fuck! Holy shit! I know this face!"

I dug into the concealed pocket of my bag and pulled out my secure cell phone. Then I logged on and started scanning my files furiously. "Aha!" I cried, and showed the picture to Leo.

"That's the same man!" he said. "Who the hell is this?"

"It's Vladimir Ossipsky, a Russian money launderer! I've been watching him for years. I've never been able to pin anything on him."

"Holy shit," Leo said. He held the two phones side by side, comparing the photographs. "It *is* the same man."

We stared at each other in growing comprehension, our minds working as one.

"Then the housing development at Sudeley . . . ," he said.

"Is a money-laundering scheme!" I finished, and we high-fived each other.

"Boris Nemtsov," he said slowly. "Boris Nemtsov is the developer. Yes, it fits. By God, it fits! They're using the Sudeley development project to launder money."

"Russian Mafia money," I added. "We have a file on Ossipsky that's about a mile thick."

His razor-sharp mind was already sifting through the implications, but I said it aloud first. "Now you can stop the development."

"Oh, yeah. You bet your sweet life I can stop it." He reached for his phone.

"Oh my God!" I exclaimed. "VONE! It's VONE!"

"I beg your pardon?"

"Someone—an asset—told me that one of my targets, Vladimir Ossipsky, had transferred sixty-five million into an account at Barclays. The account is in the name of VONE Limited—'VO' for 'Vladimir Ossipsky' and 'NE' for 'Nemtsov.'"

"I like it," he said.

"So I can save Sudeley *and* I don't have to give up my cover. I'll be a hero at the agency for nailing Ossipsky."

"But won't they still be after you to turn me?" he asked.

"Oh, I've got that all figured out," I told him.

Chapter 50

It had come to me in a flash, like the Ossipsky revelation. Leo and I were both very, very good; we could pull this off. In fact, I was surprised that I had worried so much about it. Love must have curdled my brain.

"How? What do you mean?"

"It'll be like my relationship with Lyudmila, my asset. We can pass each other real intel every now and then, enough to keep the bosses satisfied, but nothing that will actually do any harm. Eventually, they'll lose interest."

"Yes," he said slowly. "Yes, I think we can."

We smiled at each other in perfect understanding.

"Anyway," he said, his fingers tapping cell phone keys at warp speed and his face intent, almost as intent as when we were making love, "that's for later. For now, we have a groundbreaking ceremony to destroy."

Between Leo and me, our resources were formidable. We spent the night in his Holland Park house, not making love but making phone calls. We worked together seamlessly, exchanging ideas and responses almost as fast as our fingers flew over the cell phone keys.

"Do you think the hereditary constable . . ."

"Sure, why not? I've got a contact in the prime minister's office. What about you?"

"I think your contact is better than mine. Go for it."

"Don't forget the historical trust."

"On it."

By daybreak, it was all planned.

Even so, I was abuzz with nervous tension as we drove to Sudeley after a silent breakfast, and Leo's mouth was tight. As his Audi purred up the long, winding drive to the castle, I saw him looking at the great trees shadowing the graveled roadway and the deer grazing on fields in the distance.

"Don't worry," I said. "This is not the last time you'll see it this way."

He glanced at me but didn't even attempt a smile.

Then we rounded the last curve, but the ancient stone walls of the graceful castle were almost hidden by the mass of bright yellow construction vehicles blocking its drive. All manner of huge trucks and machinery littered the front, crushing delicate flower beds and dwarfing the lovely old castle. Beside me, I heard Leo curse.

In grim silence, we got out of the car and wove our way through the thicket of vehicles. Just in front of the castle was a makeshift dais on which Nemtsov himself stood, surrounded by his cronies and a few bodyguards (i.e., thugs) with earpieces and bulging jackets. Other assorted dignitaries surrounded the dais, and I looked them over, trying to figure out which ones we'd been able to turn in our phone marathon the previous night. A good-size crowd. Villagers and more dignitaries (but sprinkled, I hoped, with the recipients of our phone calls) milled about in front of the dais.

Nemtsov, his short and thick body squeezed into a designer suit that did him no favors, strutted up to the podium and adjusted the microphone. His small eyes were concealed by dark sunglasses, but I knew it was him. I had studied enough photos of the man to be able to spot him anywhere.

I felt Leo take a deep breath beside me.

Then, suddenly, a cavalcade of unmarked sedans and SUVs shot up the drive, sirens blaring, and stopped short just before the construction vehicles. The thugs immediately surrounded Nemtsov and began shouting commands, to which no one paid any attention. Car doors opened and slammed shut, and a phalanx of dark-suited men and women advanced on the scene. In the confusion, I saw several of Nemtsov's cronies leap off the dais and disappear into the crowd. I took a few discreet photos with my cell phone camera.

Leo was absolutely still.

A tall, imposing man with salt-and-pepper hair strode up to the dais and took Nemtsov's place at the podium. One of Nemtsov's thugs actually reached into his shoulder holster, but Nemtsov angrily shoved his arm down. The man at the podium didn't bother to introduce himself, apparently assuming everyone knew who he was.

I didn't. Leo whispered in my ear, "Interior minister."

"Before this goes any further," the man said, in a pure Oxbridge accent, "we will hear a statement from Dr. Leo Schlumberger. Dr. Schlumberger, will you please present your findings?"

"I must protest this interruption," Nemtsov said loudly.

Again nobody paid any attention. Leo, every inch the Oxford don, took out a sheaf of papers as he jumped up to the dais.

"I can prove," he said, "that the present-day Baroness Sudeley is the rightful owner of this property and that the 'sale' to Mr. Nemtsov is therefore null and void. Furthermore"—he had to raise his voice over the buzz of the crowd—"furthermore, the authorities have informed me that this 'sale' appears to be part of a broad-based money-laundering scheme instigated by the Russian Mafia."

Pandemonium broke out. Nemtsov's thugs again reached for their weapons. Nemtsov shouted at them, and an ocean of hard-eyed men suddenly surrounded them. In an instant, Nemtsov's men were disarmed and led—none too gently—off the podium, Nemtsov tight-lipped and his goons protesting loudly and vociferously.

"Shut up!" Nemtsov shouted. "Shut your stupid mouths!"

Keep talking, I thought. The Brits would get masses of intel from scared and talkative hired guns. I watched, smiling now, as the group was shoved into cars and driven away at high speed.

Leo and I had argued a little about whether to have the CIA or Mossad do the takedown, but we had eventually agreed to let the British have him. We didn't care whose bars Nemtsov was behind, as long as he was there for a very, very long time. Thanks to Lyudmila's tip on his Barclays bank account, I had managed to develop a very convincing paper trail on his transactions—convincing enough that he would not be seeing freedom for quite a while. The agency had turned the paper trail over to the British, who now owed us a big favor. Langley was thrilled with me.

Leo said calmly, "Shall I continue?" and the crowd roared again.

"I have here," he said, flourishing the papers we had prepared so carefully the night before, "a partial genealogy that traces the ownership of this property from Queen Katherine Parr to the current-day Baroness Sudeley."

We had doctored the genealogy to present enough information to prove that there was indeed a living descendant but omitted enough that it would be impossible for anyone else to find Jules Seymour. And, to be doubly sure, we'd had Rosie scrub clean the obscure records Leo had used in his original research to track me down.

"The baroness is shy and fears publicity," Leo continued, with just the slightest hint of a sparkle in his eyes.

Amy, I thought, with an inward smile. *Amy and Jules, united at last.*

"She cannot come forward in person at this time. But she is the nineteenth-generation ancestor of Queen Katherine Parr and Thomas Seymour, and thus the rightful owner of this property. She plans to keep Sudeley Castle open to the public and to create a museum on this site to showcase the lives of the Tudor queens. This museum and research center will create more permanent jobs than the housing development would have done."

Everyone shouted again, and Leo stepped away from the podium.

He was mobbed as soon as he jumped down into the crowd again, and I watched from a distance as he parried questions and accepted congratulations. At last the crowd dispersed, and Leo and I, holding hands, walked together through the massive stone archway into the great castle.

Sudeley, where it all began.

"Hey, Leo," I said.

"What?"

"I think they're going to let me escape from Atlantic Bank and go out into the field again."

He held me away from him, frowning slightly. "Where to?"

"I can't tell you that."

"But you know I'll figure it out."

I shrugged.

"Hey, Jules," he said.

"What?"

"We can go on adventures too, *motek*. We can ski and hike and go whitewater rafting. But we're not going to risk our lives doing it."

"What do you mean?"

"You were scared that day on the yacht. And I bet you were terrified in Chechnya too. And on Everest. And all those other 'adventures' your father took you on."

My father scorned nothing more than fear, and I had been ashamed of my fear when Kali and I were attacked in that London loo. But, like a healthy shoot poking through damp spring ground, I was starting to think new thoughts: What was wrong with being afraid? Was it possible that my father was a bully? Did I really need to take so many risks in my job? Why shouldn't a young girl be frightened at the thought of climbing Mount Everest, for God's sake? Would I let Kali do that?

No. In a million years, no.

"When we ski," he continued, "we will go up in safety-inspected lifts, we will not ski off-piste, and we will *never* drop from helicopters onto an ungroomed slope. Understood?"

I nodded. Maybe there was something of Amy in me after all.

"So, you really can't tell me where they'll send you?" he asked again.

"Nope."

"Hey, Jules," he said.

"What?"

"I'll always find you."

Acknowledgments

It takes a village! I would like to express my deep gratitude to the SparkPress team: Brooke Warner, Shannon Green, Crystal Patriarche, Tabitha Bailey, Paige Herbert, and Maggie Ruf. Your vision of an independent publisher that is by women and for women is truly inspirational. I am so fortunate to be part of the SparkPress family.

Another big shout-out goes to my long-suffering and ever-patient agent, Marcy Posner. You've always got my back! And more thanks to the world's best early reader team: Kim, Melissa, Laurie—you're really the midwives to my book, and I owe you lots and lots of Four Seas ice cream.

A big thanks as well to my patient and long-suffering family: Jerry, Alex, Anna, Zack, Cayla, Caroline, Benjamin, and Jilly— you put up with a lot, and I really appreciate it!

Best of all, thanks to Naomi, Liora, Maya, Gabe, Eden, Ellie, Cassie, and Lev for bringing me unbridled love and joy, forever and always.

About the Author

Courtesy of Benjamin Gruenbaum

Jane Elizabeth Hughes is an obsessive reader with two fully-loaded Kindles; she buys so many books that Amazon sends her a gift every year for the holidays. Unfortunately, reading novels all day is not an easy career path, so Jane has a day job as professor of international finance at Simmons College School of Business in Boston. She has also consulted with multinational corporations and governments for nearly three decades, including the Rockefeller Foundation, Inter-American Development Bank, and Asian Development Bank. An engaging and accomplished public speaker, Professor Hughes has written and lectured widely about international finance throughout the world. She published her first novel, *Nannyland*, with Simon & Schuster Pocket Star Books in 2016. A mother of four and granny of eight (the eldest is only seven, so she's a very busy granny), she is fortunate enough to live on beautiful Cape Cod, Massachusetts.

SELECTED TITLES FROM SPARKPRESS

SparkPress is an independent boutique publisher
delivering high-quality, entertaining, and engaging
content that enhances readers' lives,
with a special focus on female-driven work.
www.gosparkpress.com

Indelible: A Sean McPherson Novel, Book 1, Laurie Buchanan, $16.95,
9781684630714. Murder at a writing retreat in the Pacific Northwest,
but this one isn't imaginary. Authors only kill with words. Or do they?

Enemy Queen: A Novel, Robert Steven Goldstein, $16.95, 978-1-
68463-026-4. A woman initiates passionate sexual encounters with
two articulate but bumbling and crass middle-aged men, but what she
demands in return soon becomes untenable. A short time later she goes
missing, prompting the county sheriff to open a murder investigation.

Firewall: A Novel, Eugenia Lovett West. $16.95, 978-1-68463-010-3.
When Emma Streat's rich, socialite godmother is threatened with blackmail, Emma becomes immersed in the dark world of cybercrime—and
mounting dangers take her to exclusive places in Europe and contacts
with the elite in financial and art collecting circles. Through passion
and heartbreak, Emma must fight to save herself and bring a vicious
criminal to justice.

Peccadillo at the Palace: An Annie Oakley Mystery, Kari Bovée. $16.95,
978-1-943006-90-8. In this second book in the Annie Oakley Mystery
series, Annie and Buffalo Bill's Wild West Show are invited to Queen
Victoria's Jubilee celebration in England, but when a murder and a suspicious illness lead Annie to suspect an assassination attempt on the
queen, she sets out to discover the truth.

Pursuits Unknown: An Amy and Lars Novel, Ellen Clary. $16.95, 978-
1-943006-86-1. Search-and-rescue agent Amy and her telepathic dog,
Lars, locate a missing scientist who is reported to have an Alzhei-
mer's-like disease—only to discover that someone wants to steal his
research for potentially ominous purposes.

ABOUT SPARKPRESS

SparkPress is an independent, hybrid imprint focused on merging the best of the traditional publishing model with new and innovative strategies. We deliver high-quality, entertaining, and engaging content that enhances readers' lives. We are proud to bring to market a list of *New York Times* best-selling, award-winning, and debut authors who represent a wide array of genres, as well as our established, industry-wide reputation for creative, results-driven success in working with authors. SparkPress, a BookSparks imprint, is a division of SparkPoint Studio LLC.

Learn more at GoSparkPress.com